T0385140

Praise for *The Excitements*

'A sublime mix of comedy, drama and adventure ... one of the most enjoyable books I've ever read and genuinely one of my all-time favourites'
Jill Mansell

'Adorable. A brilliant combo of respect and affection and acute observation'
Alex Marwood

'Funny, heartwarming, wise and just so incredibly well researched'
Alexandra Potter

'Utterly charming and engrossing'
Jenny Colgan

'Not all heroes wear capes, some wear M&S cardigans! A triumph'
Mike Gayle

'A glorious, rip-roaring adventure, so funny and charming, yet laced with unexpected moments of real tenderness and reflection'
Lucy Dillon

'Funny, thrilling and brilliantly researched'
S.J. Bennett

'Intriguing and often thrilling. It's utterly wonderful'
Annie Lyons

CJ Wray is a pseudonym of bestselling author Chris Manby. Writing under several names, she is the author of more than forty books. She has written features (and obituaries) for several national papers and had a long-running column in the Independent. More recently, she has worked as a ghostwriter, helping a variety of people from Second World War veterans to soap stars tell their true stories.

Also by CJ Wray

The Excitements

AS CHRISSIE MANBY

Getting Over Mr Right
Kate's Wedding
What I Did On My Holidays
A Proper Family Holiday
A Proper Family Christmas
A Proper Family Adventure
A Wedding At Christmas
A Fairytale for Christmas
The Worst Case Scenario Cookery Club
Once In A Lifetime
Three Days In Florence
Saying Goodbye To Tuesday

BAD INFLUENCE

C J WRAY

ORION

First published in Great Britain in 2025 by Orion Fiction,
an imprint of The Orion Publishing Group Ltd.
Carmelite House, 50 Victoria Embankment
London EC4Y 0DZ

An Hachette UK Company

The authorised representative in the EEA is Hachette Ireland,
8 Castlecourt Centre, Dublin 15, D15 XTP3, Ireland (email: info@hbgi.ie)

1 3 5 7 9 10 8 6 4 2

A CIP catalogue record for this book
is available from the British Library.

ISBN (Hardback) 978 1 3987 1188 4
ISBN (Export Trade Paperback) 978 1 3987 1189 1
ISBN (Ebook) 978 1 3987 1191 4
ISBN (Audio) 978 1 3987 1192 1

Typeset by Deltatype Ltd, Birkenhead, Merseyside

Printed in Great Britain by Clays Ltd, Elcograf S.p.A.

www.orionbooks.co.uk

For Simon Robinson

Chapter One

Merevale, a village in the Cotswolds, May 2023

The postman always rang twice on a Friday, to check that his ladies weren't dead.

'It's like bleeding *tenko*,' Jinx's neighbour Val complained. But really most of the older women in the village rather liked their Friday morning reveille. It was comforting to know that someone was looking out for them; that they wouldn't lie dead on the floor for weeks on end, making a terrible smell, before anybody realised they were gone. The postie, Glenn Turner, took the Friday roll call very seriously, ticking off the names of the women on his list as they appeared to give him proof of life.

'Morning, Cynthia. How's your hip? Morning, Pat. Daughter coming to see you this weekend? Morning, Val. Your roses are looking lovely ...'

Once, Val went on holiday without telling Glenn she was going away. When she didn't answer her door that Friday morning, he had the police and an ambulance there in under three minutes. It was only thanks to Cynthia's quick intervention – 'She's gone to Torquay!' – that they didn't try to break down the door.

Only Jinx at Number Seventeen did not open up for Glenn's tenko. She'd had quite enough of those in her lifetime. Instead, she kept the well-meaning postman happy by adjusting the blinds at her kitchen window to give the impression of code as he walked up the garden path. On one occasion when Jinx did have to open the door for a parcel, Glenn told her, 'I like our secret signals, Mrs Sullivan. Makes me feel like we're spies. Were you a secret agent in the war?'

'In World War Two? I'm not quite *that* old,' Jinx responded.

What Jinx didn't tell Glenn was that every time she twitched the blinds to save herself having to have an actual conversation, she heard the same four words in her head – *Morse code for moron* – in the same cut-glass English voice, belonging to a real secret agent, or at least someone who claimed to have been one. And for a moment, she would feel an uncontrollable surge of annoyance that didn't dissipate until she had tapped out the Morse code for 'cow' on her knee. Only then could she get back to work at her laptop with a renewed sense of purpose. There were always plenty of messages from America to answer first thing in the morning.

'I'll bet you've been dreaming of me all night, Jenice ...'

Another name. Another secret.

On this particular Friday morning, however, Glenn would not take code for an answer. He rang the doorbell twice, three times, four ... With a flash of frustration, Jinx got up from the kitchen table to see what on earth the man wanted. She wasn't expecting any mail that couldn't be posted through the letterbox.

Out of old habit, Jinx paused by the mirror in the hallway to smooth down her thick white hair and check the front of her blouse for crumbs. When she turned back to the door, she saw through the frosted glass panel that there were now two people on her doorstep.

2

'Oh no.' Jinx groaned. Not him as well.

Standing next to Glenn was Malcolm Sanderson from number four – 'Colonel Mustard' as the ladies called him. An ex-military man, he liked to give the impression that he'd been in the Special Forces. 'What did I do in the army? I could tell you, but then I'd have to kill you,' was one of his favourite sayings.

Jinx plastered on a smile for Glenn's sake. Colonel Mustard grinned and tipped his slightly grubby panama hat at her, never quite letting the crown leave his head.

'Good morning, Jennifer,' the Colonel said. 'Looks like Glenn's got a stiffie for you.'

'A what?' The postman's eyes widened in horror.

Jinx plucked the crisp white envelope from his hand.

'Malcolm means this,' she explained.

'An invitation on card,' the Colonel elaborated. 'They used to be the norm for weddings, parties and balls et cetera, but very few people do things properly these days. Standards, like a pebble on a glacier, are forever moving, but only in a downwardly direction.'

Jinx and Glenn briefly pondered the Colonel's words.

'So, Jennifer, who's requesting the pleasure of your company?' the Colonel asked.

'I don't know. I haven't got X-ray vision.'

'Very sharp! Watch out, Glenn. She's a live one.' The Colonel gave Jinx an exaggerated wink.

The envelope remained unopened, as it would do until Jinx was safely alone, but turning it over in her hand, she surreptitiously glanced down at it for clues. Her name and address were typewritten. There was nothing on the back to give the sender's identity away.

'There's this too,' said Glenn, passing her a dull brown envelope with a clear plastic window. Printed on the back of this one was the address of the local hospital. The Colonel had already clocked that.

'Hospital appointment, eh? Well, I hope that whatever it is that has you under the doctor won't keep you from our VE Day extravaganza.'

Ugh. Jinx had forgotten all about that. She'd bought a ticket for the party back in January, just to keep the Colonel from haranguing her.

'I'm saving the first dance for you,' he said now. 'Glenn will be there. Won't you, boy?'

'Yes, of course.'

'We've got some good prizes for the raffle: cheese hamper, bottle of champers, funeral vouchers ... Butler's Funerals are sponsoring the event this year. We're raising funds for the youth club. Got to keep the youngsters out of trouble. If the government won't bring back national service ... Was the making of me, my national service.' The Colonel stood a little straighter, ready to expound on his theme.

Jinx slowly started to close the door on her unwanted callers. Glenn took the hint.

'I'd better be getting on,' he said. 'Post won't deliver itself.'

'I should be on my way too,' said the Colonel. 'I'm off to the shop to fetch *The Times*. They only get five copies in now. Can you believe that, Jennifer? Five copies for the whole of the village! If you're not up early, you miss out. They say everyone's going "on line" these days, but there's nothing like reading the obituaries with a cup of coffee in the garden and you can't see what you're supposed to be reading on a screen in the sunshine.'

'Yes, yes,' said Jinx impatiently.

Glenn was halfway back up the garden path. The Colonel quickly said 'Goodbye' – at last – and trotted after him.

'Do you read the obituaries, Glenn? You should, you know.

4

Sounds like a gloomy habit but it's actually life-affirming, that's what I always say.'

Jinx always read the obits too, though not for the same reasons the Colonel did. A month earlier, her heart had all but stopped when she read the obituary headline, 'Wartime SOE officer, who founded orphan charity.' But it wasn't her. *The wench was not yet dead.*

Alone in her kitchen, Jinx used her dagger-shaped letter-opener to slit open the neat white envelope. The Colonel was right. It did contain a 'stiffie'. But who from? No one who could possibly want to invite Jinx to anything smart knew where she lived, or even what surname she went by these days. She'd made pretty damn sure of that. All the same, Jinx found she was holding her breath as she pulled out the card.

'You are invited to the gala opening of The Meadows, Merevale's new premier assisted-living complex.'

It was junk mail. Jinx felt her shoulders creep back down.

'Come and join us for a guided tour and a glass of bubbles!' the invitation suggested.

Bubbles? Certainly not.

Jinx didn't open the hospital letter because she already knew what that would say.

Having despatched both the invitation and her hospital letter to the recycling bin, Jinx went back online to finish booking a flight to Florence. That done, she searched for a particular hotel just outside the city centre: the Hotel Regina.

Jinx was surprised to find that the old place was still in operation, though the photographs on the website suggested they hadn't changed the decor since her first stay in the 1950s. Looking at the available rooms, she guessed that the 'small double' was the one she'd been so thrilled to have when she was seventeen. If it was the right room, then the Juliet balcony looked down into the walled garden of a grand palazzo next door. Jinx remembered that garden. She remembered the scent of wisteria on the warm Italian air, so heavy you could almost feel it on your face. She could still hear the musical call of a hoopoe hidden in the trees and the bells of a dozen *campanili* sounding the hour in perfect asynchrony.

Jinx booked herself three nights in that old hotel. Three should be enough. With flights and accommodation in place, she set about looking for restaurants with excellent wine lists. Perhaps she should book a ticket for the Uffizi, too. And she must go to the Boboli Gardens and just stand among the orange trees and breathe in the smell of the leaves and the earth. Briefly closing her eyes as she thought about it, she was already there.

But Jinx's Italian break was not just about experiencing the treasures of Firenze one more time. There were more important things to do than sightsee: loose ends that must be tied up.

At the bottom of Jinx's wardrobe was a wooden box she'd found in India many years before. Made in the nineteenth century, it was the size and shape of a shoebox, carved from sandalwood with a bucolic scene on the lid. The trader she'd bought it from told her it had been made as a wedding gift for a princess.

'Perhaps it will make you lucky in love,' he said.

'I'm still not going to pay full price,' Jinx had responded, earning a delighted guffaw from her companion that day. From Penny.

The box closed with a tiny golden key that Jinx usually left in the lock. Sometimes, she'd gone from year to year without checking its contents, but lately she seemed to have checked it every day. Everything was still there: a wedge of cash, a small pile of treasured letters and photographs and the three things she would grab in the event of fire, flood or Armageddon.

That evening before bed she lifted the precious items out of the box again. The first was a porcelain mouse, pure white with a pink nose and painted whiskers as fine as a baby's eyelashes. It had a thin line of gold-coloured resin holding one of its big ears in place. The second was a ring — a narrow gold ring set with a murky diamond so wee it was more of a chip than a stone. The third was a small German-language guide to Florence with a fold-out map neatly annotated in fading pencil. The guidebook was coming to Italy, of course. The mouse and the ring? Well ... She still had to think about those. But Jinx slept quite soundly that night, satisfied that she would be able to get everything she needed to done before she bid this troubled world adieu.

Chapter Two

On Saturday morning, Glenn the postman was back, this time with his teenage daughter Thea in tow. Ahead of joining the team of villagers who would be tricking out the green for the VE Day party that evening, the pair called at Jinx's bungalow. Glenn had an idea that he ought to ask about the hospital letter. While he rang the bell, Thea stayed safely at the top of the garden path with her eyes firmly fixed on her phone.

'You again,' Jinx said when she opened the door.

Glenn took her grumpy greeting as a challenge.

'Good morning, Mrs Sullivan.'

'Glenn. Thea.'

Thea returned the greeting with an almost imperceptible nod.

Thea Turner was not an effusive sort of teenager. Jinx wasn't sure she'd heard her say a word these past three years, though as a small child she had been very different. She'd been the darling of the neighbourhood then, delighting the residents of the close whenever she joined Glenn for the Saturday round. ('Not strictly allowed,' Glenn would say. 'But I only let her deliver the birthday cards.') She loved to wear her dad's high-vis vest and told everyone she was going to be a 'post-lady' when she grew up. These days, Thea looked as though she would rather melt into the pavement than be seen in her father's company. Her way of dressing – black jeans and a hoodie – was the very opposite of high-vis now.

'I thought you might have opened that hospital letter,' Glenn said. 'If you need a lift to an appointment, you know I'd be happy to help.'

'Thank you, but I shan't be needing one,' Jinx told him.

'You're sure?'

'Absolutely.'

Jinx started to say goodbye, then remembered that she ought to let Glenn know she was going away. She didn't want to come home to discover that her door had been taken off its hinges.

'Glenn, I've booked a holiday. I'm leaving on Thursday for three nights, so you won't see me for the Friday morning *register*.'

Though the other women happily called it 'Glenn's *tenko*', Jinx couldn't bring herself to use that word.

'Oh. Going anywhere nice?' Glenn asked.

'Italy,' Jinx said.

'Italy?' Glenn echoed. 'You're going to *Italy*?'

'Yes. I'm going to Florence. Why?'

'But Mrs Sullivan, you could have come on the village coach trip. *We're* going to Italy. I thought you said you didn't have a passport.'

It had seemed simpler than telling Glenn that she'd rather boil her head.

Jinx thought fast. 'Back when you were getting the trip booked up, I didn't have a *valid* passport, and with all the news about delays at the passport office, I didn't think I had any hope whatsoever of getting one.'

'But you did.'

'Yes. I sent off four weeks ago on the off chance and it's just

9

arrived.' She started to close the door again, but Glenn was not stepping back.

'But wouldn't they have sent a passport "signed for"? I don't remember delivering that—'

'It came by DHL,' Jinx lied a little more.

'Right. DHL.' Glenn didn't sound at all convinced. 'But what a pity we didn't know you'd have a passport in time to join us. It would have been great to have you on board.'

'And I would have enjoyed it very much indeed,' said Jinx, lying so hard she half expected the bottom of her Marks and Spencer's slacks to start smoking.

Glenn organised a coach trip for the elderly residents of the village every year, and every year Jinx found a reason not to go. The itineraries were sometimes interesting – last year's was Highlands and Islands, the year before was Jane Austen's England – but Jinx could imagine nothing worse than a week on a coach with her neighbours. And when it came to the horror of forced proximity, Jinx knew what she was talking about.

Jinx was especially *not* sorry to have missed out on the previous year's Haggis night, complete with live bagpipe recital, for which the Colonel had sourced a dozen tam-o'-shanters with ginger wigs attached. However, the villagers who had taken part considered the Highlands and Islands tour such a success that they'd voted to be even more adventurous this year. It was to be the first time the village coach trip ventured overseas, on a bespoke itinerary entitled Tuscan Splendour.

'I'm so sad you're not coming with us,' Glenn said. 'You're going to be missing out. As well as all the usual sights – the Leaning Tower and whatnot – we're doing a visit to a vineyard and an afternoon in a cheese factory and having a private cookery demonstration from some real live Italian *nonnas*. We'll be making our own ravioli and eating it for lunch.'

'It all sounds tremendous fun.'

Glenn pulled a 'thinking face'.

'You know,' he said. 'I'm sure I could still get you onto our trip. There's room on the coach, and even if the hotels we've booked don't have availability, there's bound to be somewhere nice nearby. We could drop you off after dinner and pick you up for breakfast so you don't miss out on the camaraderie.'

It was the 'camaraderie' Jinx wanted to miss out on most of all.

'Perhaps you can get your money back on your flight and hotel? I'd be happy to check your Ts and Cs.'

'I wouldn't want to put you to any bother.'

'Well, next year you're coming with us. I won't take "no" for an answer. In the meantime, I'll make a note that I'm not to worry when you don't do our code on Friday morning.'

'Thank you, Glenn.'

'But you are still coming to the VE Day party tonight?'

'I'll be there,' Jinx promised, before faking a delicate cough into her handkerchief. *Foreshadowing*, wasn't that what they called it?

'Jennifer!'

Oh, no. It was the Colonel again, striding across the close with his newspaper aloft.

'Thought you might like to see this. You too, Thea. Come and have a look. Do you good to learn some history . . .'

The young girl did not budge from her place on the pavement, nor even glance up from her screen. The Colonel briefly frowned at her before barrelling on towards Jinx's doorstep.

'Fabulous piece here about some of our surviving World War Two veterans. Not many of them left now, but you'll love this pair. One was a Wren and the other one a Fanny.'

Glenn blinked.

'First Aid Nursing Yeomanry,' the Colonel quickly explained.

He thrust the paper beneath Jinx's nose and turned to address

11

his comments to Glenn. 'Of course, even the youngest people to have served in the war are in their late nineties now. These two sisters were still at school when the war started – not much older than you are, Thea,' he shouted back over his shoulder. 'They didn't have time to do anything terribly interesting, but they served, and that's what matters, eh? That generation was made of different stuff.'

Even before she saw the photograph, Jinx felt a shiver travel the length of her spine. A Wren and a Fanny? Sisters? It couldn't be . . .

While the Colonel extolled the virtues of the 'Greatest Generation', Jinx studied the photograph that accompanied the full-page interview. The two elderly female veterans sat side by side on a garden bench, framed by a trellis of roses. One wore a navy-blue trouser suit. The other, a smart brown jacket and skirt. Both had pure white hair, carefully curled for the occasion, and they were both wearing coral lipstick that drew attention to their bright false teeth. *There's never any excuse to let standards slip, Jinx.* Each held on her lap a framed black-and-white photograph of herself as a young woman in uniform.

'Still impressively sharp for their advanced ages, the Williamson sisters live together in South Kensington,' the interview explained. 'At 101 years old, Josephine, who served in the Women's Royal Naval Service, attributes her continued good health to a daily walk, oily fish and the company of her little sister. Meanwhile, 99-year-old former FANY officer Penny claims the secret to a long life is "a well-mixed Martini" . . .'

Jinx stared at the photograph, trying to reconcile the shrivelled women on the bench, both wearing their service medals so proudly, with the women she once knew. Was that really them? Was that really Penny and Josephine Williamson? Penny Williamson looked like a tortoise. And how could she possibly be ninety-nine when the day they met still felt like yesterday?

'Are you all right, Jennifer?' the Colonel asked. 'Only you've gone terribly pale.'

Chapter Three

Manchester, 1949

Jinx's mother Norma had been up since five, scrubbing every surface in their flat until it gleamed.

'What's the point?' Jinx asked. 'It'll only get dirty again.'

'We've got a visitor coming,' Norma told her. 'An almoner from St Saviour's. To see if they can find us somewhere else.'

'Why does the flat need to be clean if we want them to get us another one?'

'Because we want to look like we deserve the help. This place is filthy,' Norma cried.

It wasn't filthy. But even Buckingham Palace would be a pigsty by Norma Spencer's standards. She'd scrubbed at so much imaginary dirt since they arrived in England at the end of '45, that Jinx joked she must have scrubbed her fingerprints off. All the same, when Norma threw a duster in her direction, Jinx got busy. She knew better than to tease her mother when there was something important at stake.

It was half-term – Whitsun – so Jinx was at home when the almoner arrived at ten on the dot, knocking on the door with three sharp taps. While Norma checked that Jinx's little brother

Eddy was presentable in the hand-me-down clothes that made him look smaller than ever, Jinx went to let the visitor in.

The almoner – a slender woman in a smart blue raincoat – was standing with her back to the door. She was looking up the stairwell. It had poured with rain the previous evening and there were small rivulets of tea-coloured water still running down the walls.

'Good morning,' said Jinx.

The almoner turned towards her with a smile. She was much younger than Jinx had expected – perhaps still in her twenties – and as well as her briefcase and umbrella she was carrying a small posy of wild flowers.

'I picked these on my way to the station,' she explained, as she bustled on into the flat. 'Aren't they pretty? Do you have a vase?'

Did they have a *vase*? Jinx had to resist laughing at that. They barely had, as her father Maurice would have put it, 'a pot to piss in'.

'No vase?' the almoner continued. 'Oh well. They'll look just as good in a plain glass. No need to gild the lily.'

Making herself at home, the almoner found an empty glass on the draining board and filled it with water, frowning slightly when she saw the colour it came out.

'There.' The almoner put the flowers in the middle of the table, with its clean but greying tablecloth, and stood back to admire her handiwork. 'That's much better, don't you think?'

Norma had finished tidying Eddy's hair and brought him out to meet their visitor.

'Hello there, Mrs Spencer!' The almoner greeted Jinx's mother like a friend. 'I do hope you're expecting me. I'm Miss Williamson from the St Saviour's Society. Penelope Williamson. But you can call me Penny. And you two must be ... Edward ...' Penny pointed at Jinx.

15

'And Jennifer.' She pointed at Eddy, who giggled at the idea someone might mistake him for his sister. 'No!' he said. 'I'm the boy.'

'So you are,' said Penny.

'Jinx is the girl.'

'*Jinx?*' Penny tried out the nickname. 'Well, how do *you* do?'

While Norma made tea, Jinx offered Penny the best chair in the flat: an armchair that had seen better days. Every time Jinx looked at it, she remembered the afternoon they'd picked it out from the charity warehouse.

'That chair's infested,' Jinx heard one woman say as Norma tried it out for size.

'Won't matter to them, though, will it?' the woman's companion replied. 'Lord knows what they've brought back from Malaya. I heard about one of them what gave everyone in their lodgings ringworm.'

'I thought you got ringworm off cats.'

'And *forriners*.'

The chair was not infested. Norma had made sure of that, scrubbing the cushion covers until they were three shades lighter. But Jinx could not scrub away the memory of that afternoon in the charity shed, sifting through other people's cast-offs. And here they were again, three and a half years later, still having to ask for more. The sting of it never seemed to lessen.

Penny Williamson took the chair without hesitation. 'Oh, this is nice and comfy,' she said. 'Would you like to come and sit by me, Eddy, so we can have a little chat?'

Eddy looked as though he might leap into this Penny woman's lap on the slightest invitation. He settled instead for sitting on his little wicker-topped stool, and gazed up into her face while she took a notepad out of her briefcase.

16

'How old are you, Eddy?'

'Seven and a half.'

'That's a good age. And you, my dear?' She turned to Jinx.

'Fourteen. Nearly fifteen,' Jinx said.

Norma sat down opposite their visitor and wrapped her hands around her mug of tea. She had given Penny the least cracked of the cups and saucers, which Penny balanced on Jinx's stool, now doubling as a side table. Jinx could tell her mother was nervous. She was using her 'Hut Ten' voice, as they privately referred to posh accents. Penny had a 'Hut Ten' voice, too, but Jinx suspected she wasn't putting hers on.

'If you don't mind,' Penny began, 'I'd like to quickly run through the facts. You were in the Far East?'

'That's right. British Malaya.'

'And you were in the women's camp in Changi?'

'And at Sime Road, yes.'

'Awful place.' Penny shuddered, as if she knew. 'And you were interned when?'

'At the beginning of the occupation. We were rounded up in February '42.'

'When your children were ...'

'Jinx was seven. Eddy was six months.'

'Quite tiny, then. Malaria?'

'All of us.'

'Typhoid?'

'Thankfully, no.'

'Beriberi?'

'Yes,' said Norma. 'And all the usual skin conditions.'

'I had a boil as big as an egg!' Eddy piped up.

'Gosh,' said Penny. 'That must have been very sore.'

Eddy nodded solemnly.

Penny went back to her questions. 'Ongoing health problems?'

Norma raised her eyes to the ceiling. 'Where to start?'

Jinx sat on the floor on the other side of the room, pretending to be absorbed in her French homework, which she balanced on her knees. From time to time she sneaked a glance at their visitor, whose light brown hair and smooth skin seemed to radiate health and light, bringing sunshine into the dingy room that was always dark as winter. While the adult women were deep in conversation, Jinx made a quick pencil sketch of Penny Williamson, with her long neck and the pointed, upturned nose that gave her face an air of optimism no matter how miserable the conversation.

Norma was doing her best to make the family seem worthy of assistance. She told Penny how after their liberation from the camp, they'd wanted to stay on in Malaya but that was impossible. The house had been looted while they were interned.

'Not so much as a saucepan left.'

The 'Freedom Fiver' Norma had been given upon liberation didn't go far, and she couldn't get a job. Nobody wanted to take on an expat woman. Not even as a housemaid.

'Though I'd have done it, you understand. I'm not proud.'

They had no other family in the Far East so they'd had to come back 'home'. Home to a country that Jinx and Eddy had never seen.

All the way from Singapore, Norma told the children how wonderful it would be.

'England is beautiful,' she'd said. 'There are hills and dales and castles ... Just wait till you try a proper roast dinner.'

As soon as they docked in Southampton, Jinx knew they'd been sold a lie. Where were the green hills? The fairy tale castles? All Jinx could see were grey skies, grey bombed-out buildings and grey, grey people. And there was no heroes' welcome. Rather, Norma's older brother, their Uncle Ernie,

18

made it clear from the start that he was taking them in under duress. 'Because you got nowhere else to go.' Neither was there a proper roast dinner, whatever that was. Not even on their first Sunday. Rationing was still very much in force. When she reached for a second slice of bread on their first night at Uncle Ernie's, Jinx received a slap on the wrist.

'You've had your share,' her cousin Elsie admonished her. 'You can't just turn up and start eating all our food like you're in Singapore with your servants. You're not posh round here, you know.'

There was no point telling Elsie they weren't considered posh in Singapore either. Especially not in camp. Not by the women in Hut Ten.

The bread was stale anyway. All the food in England was terrible. The meat was stringy. Everything that had once been green was boiled to mush and there was no fruit to be had apart from wormy apples. Jinx's cousins had never even heard of a mango.

'Stop making things up,' said Elsie, when Jinx told her about durian fruit, and how its terrible smell belied the most amazing taste you could imagine.

Thankfully, they didn't have to stay at Uncle Ernie's house for long. He found them a flat – this flat – in a building owned by one of his friends. It was small and dirty and the water in the taps was dark brown no matter how long you ran it, but when Norma asked if their new landlord might have a look at the water tank, she was told, 'Beggars can't be choosers. You can't come over here and expect to live like Lady Muck. You don't know what we sacrificed in the war for the likes of you.'

The landlord himself had not served on account of his 'bad feet'.

*

19

'And there's just the one bedroom?' Penny Williamson asked.

'Yes,' said Norma. 'I sleep on a mattress in here.'

'So Jinx shares with Eddy? They're getting rather old for that.'

Jinx actually didn't mind sharing with her brother, though it meant neither of them got much sleep. While Jinx didn't think she ever dreamt any more, Eddy had nightmares. Bad ones. Every night he would wake up screaming and would not settle down again until Jinx had rocked him in her arms and sung the songs Auntie Ameera, their neighbour back in Johore, used to sing. Or else told him stories about the magical creatures that lived in the rainforest behind the house they'd once called home.

'Tell me about the night the tiger came into the garden.' Eddy asked for that one again and again. 'Is it true, Jinx? Is it really true?'

'It's all true,' she said. 'It was paradise.'

Having finished her questions, Penny Williamson had Eddy perform a number of exercises to ascertain the extent of his physical problems for herself. Jinx felt a pinch in her heart as she watched her little brother try to stand on one bowed leg and then the other for more than a couple of seconds. It was painful to see him struggle with such a simple task but Penny told him he was 'doing very well. Keep practising, Eddy.' Her jolly reassurance made him blush.

Penny turned to Norma. 'I'm certain we can make sure Eddy has everything he needs. The National Health Service is there to take care of us all.'

'God bless Mr Bevan,' said Norma.

'What a good man he is,' Penny agreed. 'I will help you sign up with a GP who understands the situation, and I will also be making a recommendation that you go straight to the top of St

Saviour's emergency housing list. This flat is very damp and cold, and that cannot be doing any of you any good. I suspect Eddy has asthma and I can hear that you're quite wheezy too, Mrs Spencer.'

'You can call me Norma.'

'Norma, then.'

Penny's warm smile made it seem a special kindness.

'I'm all right, Miss Penny. It's Eddy and Jinx that I worry about.'

'But you need to be well too, Norma, to ensure you can properly look after these fine young people. Though I must say you're doing a good job despite the circumstances. A very good job indeed. What a delightful son and daughter you have.'

Jinx and Eddy both got the special smile then.

Having checked her watch, Penny closed her notebook and slipped it back into her briefcase. Standing up, she paused to readjust the flowers in their water glass, then she looked straight at Jinx. Penny's bright eyes were clever. Curious. *Knowing.*

'Homework?' she asked.

'French irregular verbs,' Jinx responded, quickly folding the sketch and slipping it into her pocket.

'I know something about those. Would you like me to test you while you walk me to the station? It will give us a chance to get to know one another better, since we're going to be seeing quite a bit of each other for the next little while.'

Norma nodded her approval, so Jinx pulled on her grey coat. It was an old boy's coat, with sleeves that stopped halfway up her arms. Jinx noticed Penny watching and tugged the cuffs as far as they would stretch, but they still would not cover her wrists. It suddenly seemed such a shameful situation to be in – dressed in rags that didn't fit, begging for a new place to live – even though, as Penny Williamson would have told her, there was no shame in being poor. Not when the world was set up like it was, so that good people got left behind through no fault of their own.

Outside, Penny tested Jinx on her verbs. Which took *être* and which took *avoir*? Jinx got them all right.

But when they got to the corner, Penny asked a question that wasn't so easy to answer. 'May I see the picture you were drawing while I talked to your mother?'

'I wasn't—'

'You know you were. You put it in your pocket. Be a sport.'

Jinx unfolded the piece of paper. Penny looked at the drawing and laughed. Her laughter was instant and genuine.

'Ah! You've captured me quite wonderfully.'

'I'm sorry, Miss Williamson.'

'Why? It's a very good likeness. May I keep it? My sister Josephine will love this. She's always teasing me about my *questing* nose.' Penny took the sketch and tucked it into her briefcase. 'So, why are you called Jinx?' she asked then. 'Are you going to bring me bad luck?'

Chapter Four

Johore, British Malaya, 1941

To begin with it was *Jynx* with a Y, for *Jynx torquilla*, the wryneck bird. A relative of the woodpecker, the wryneck is brown and white with a little beak as sharp as a needle. It's a small bird. You might even call it nondescript. But it can turn its head through 180 degrees, twist its neck like a snake, and if you upset it, it will hiss at you. The ancients used it in their magical rituals.

For Jinx's father Maurice Spencer, a keen amateur naturalist, seeing a Eurasian wryneck in their garden in Malaya seemed an excellent omen. He'd last seen one in the garden of his childhood home in Sussex. It was at the very edge of its normal migration range there. Just as it was in their part of Malaya.

'But it's a sign that *we're* in the right place,' he said. 'That bird's our mascot.'

Maurice had come to the Far East to make his fortune. He had ideas for all sorts of businesses: import/export, sightseeing tours for rich Europeans, architectural services. Or perhaps he'd write a novel. He was the poetic type.

He said he nicknamed his only daughter 'Jynx' because, when she was a toddler, she hopped about him like a little

23

brown bird when he was working in the garden. 'And your head spins if you think there might be sweeties in the offing!' Plus, well, Jennifer and Jynx, they both started with 'J', so it sounded right. Jennifer Jynx. Jinx with an 'I' for short.

'But you're my lucky charm,' he always told her.

Jinx had nothing but happy memories of life before the war. Their village, on the outskirts of Kluang, was heaven for a child. When Jinx wasn't at school, she had the run of the place. She had friends in every house. Though their families came from all over the world and they spoke a dozen languages between them, the children could always make themselves understood in the games they played together.

Jinx especially loved living near the forest. On Sunday afternoons, Maurice would take her on 'adventures', naming the flora and fauna as they walked through the trees and spinning stories to help her remember them. He taught her to be respectful of it all. He also taught her to be fearless.

When the mangoes were ripe, flying foxes came in flocks to feast upon them. While many of her friends went shrieking indoors, Jinx would run in the opposite direction, fascinated to see the creatures, big as small dogs, that seemed to cover the sun with their wings. One day she climbed a tree and sat in it with a squishy mango balanced on her head, planning that if a flying fox tried to snatch the fruit, she would catch it for a pet.

Jinx sat in the tree for a whole afternoon before she got a bite. When a flying fox did come close enough, Jinx tumbled from the tree in her excitement and was scratched to bits on the way down.

After a bath in the tub on the veranda, Jinx snivelled as her mother tended her wounds, dabbing them with iodine.

'What's all this?' asked Maurice when he saw her tears. 'What do we say in this family?'

Jinx repeated a popular family mantra. '*We do not cry.*'

'Exactly. That's my daughter! Crying never solved a thing. And now you know how *not* to catch a fruit bat.'

A couple of days later, Maurice brought home a baby crocodile that he'd found in a puddle for Jinx to keep in lieu of her bat. Norma was not happy, but she supported her husband in most of his crazy decisions, including this one. They called the croc 'Mr Snappy' and kept him in a tub on the veranda until he was big enough to pose a danger to the cat.

Another time – it must have been late summer 1941 – playing in the garden at dusk, Jinx had seen a tiger, slinking through the trees at their property's boundary. She'd held her breath and kept perfectly still so as not to attract its attention, but it had turned and looked straight at her.

'It winked at me,' she told Norma, who all but fainted when she heard the tale.

'You're never playing out in the dark again, Jinx. You might have been killed!'

'No. It wouldn't have hurt me, Mummy. Daddy said so.'

Maurice was fond of the view that, so long as they were respectful to nature, no animal they encountered in the forest could ever be as dangerous as another human being. He repeated his theory at the dinner table that same night.

'It's men you need to look out for, Jinx. Rich men are worst of all.'

'You say that because you aren't rich,' said Norma.

'I say that because it's true, my love. To get rich in this world, you either have to be born rich or steal it. You can't get wealthy as an honest man. I've found that to my cost. And it's the wealthy as is causing this war. The ones who make their money from weapons and war bonds. The average man don't want it. They know they won't benefit, whether they win or lose. There's no animal as dangerous as a rich man.'

Jinx had heard about the war that was raging in Europe. Mrs Vickery, who ran the Sunday school from her drawing room, had arranged for a collection of unwanted clothes to be sent to the desperate people of London who lost everything in the Blitz. Jinx helped Norma package up some of her old dresses and added one of her least favourite dolls for some poor Cockney child who'd lost all her toys. But it seemed so remote, the fight with the Germans. It was easy to forget about it when life in the Far East went on much as before.

Then fighter planes started flying over Malaya, too.

Jinx was too young to have understood the implications of the Japanese signing the Tripartite Pact with Germany and Italy in 1940; that an attack on Britain was inevitably an attack on the British Empire, involving all the 'pink bits' on the map on the schoolhouse wall. When France fell to the Germans, its overseas colonies were suddenly undefended. Likewise the Dutch territories. The Belgian. All were ripe for the picking.

All the same, no one thought the Japanese would be the ones to do the picking in the Far East. They had been fighting the Chinese for a decade. They'd been humiliated by the Russians in Manchuria. Even Mr Takahashi, the Japanese tailor who made Maurice's suits and Norma's Sunday-best dresses, didn't believe his homeland had the might to carve out an empire of its own. And yet ...

'That plane was Japanese,' Norma told her husband, as a fighter flew right overhead. 'I saw the red circles. I thought you told me we were safe here, Maurice. I thought you said they couldn't get this far.'

'They can't,' said Maurice. 'You must have been mistaken.'

But Maurice was wrong. Norma wasn't mistaken, and soon the Japanese planes, with the rising sun painted on their wings, were being seen with alarming frequency.

In their sleepy village, the appearance of any plane was an event. Some of the older children climbed trees to get a better view. Jinx climbed with them. Though she was one of the smallest in the gang, she could climb as high as anyone. With bare feet she got right to the top of the rain tree in next door's front garden. She clung on tight as a plane flew by so low that it almost parted her hair.

It was far more unsettling than the tiger.

And yet Christmas 1941 was not so very different to the Christmas before, when war was still something that happened to other people. The news coming out of Borneo, Hong Kong and the Philippines didn't seem to rattle the Raffles set over the causeway in Singapore. When school restarted in January '42, however, Jinx's class had shrunk from ten to seven; two English girls and one Canadian were gone. The teacher, Miss Brooks, told the remaining pupils that their classmates had always planned to leave at Christmas. There was no need to worry about the 'foolish rumours' put about by Miranda Taylor's big brother that the Japanese were on their way to kill the men, ravish the women and eat any babies they found: white babies like Jinx's new baby brother.

'Miranda's big brother is talking nonsense,' Maurice told his daughter, but when Jinx woke in the night now, she would hear her parents arguing.

'Maurice, it's time to go, surely,' Norma pleaded.

'But where would we go *to*, my love? Back to England? And get bombed by Hitler there? Everything we have is here.'

'Until the Japanese take it. What then? We've Jinx and Eddy to think of.'

Hearing the anguish in her mother's voice made Jinx anxious. Mr Bins, the family dog, seemed to sense it too. The ragged mutt, so named because he'd been found as a pup scavenging on the town dump, would let Jinx hold him tight until she fell asleep. Mr Bins heard all Jinx's secrets and worries.

Then school closed 'because of the war' – no pretending this time – and Jinx's circle of expat friends dwindled further. And the Japanese planes coming over were suddenly too many to count. Jinx's mother looked to the sky every day and furrowed her brow so hard that the lines stayed put even when she was smiling at her children. Still, Maurice Spencer would not budge.

'Churchill is sending more troops,' he said. 'They'll sort it out. This is our home.'

Maurice remained optimistic until the day an Australian soldier arrived on their doorstep.

'The Japanese will be here in hours,' the soldier warned. 'You're being evacuated to Singapore.'

Norma looked to her husband for his answer.

'All right,' Maurice said, throwing up his hands. 'All right. I give in. Come on, Jinx. Pack your toys.'

Jinx packed her drawing paper and a little box of paints.

'And the animals?' asked Jinx. 'The cat and the lizards and Mr Bins? They're coming with us?'

'You can't bring animals,' the soldier told them. 'We're going over the causeway. Quarantine rules apply.'

It was easy to say goodbye to the lizards, which Maurice let loose in the garden. The cat always had other places to be. But in the years to come, the memory of Mr Bins, standing confused outside their locked front door as the army truck pulled away, would haunt Jinx as much as anything else. She sometimes wondered if that was the moment the first piece of her heart died.

Though it was heaving with Allied soldiers sent to defend the British Empire's Far Eastern jewel in the crown, Singapore did not stay safe for long. Everyone who could get out was going, until the Japanese fighters started picking off the evacuation ships the moment they were out of Keppel Harbour, making it more dangerous to flee than to stay. Then, on 15 February 1942, the unthinkable happened. After a week-long battle in the city's streets, the Allied forces surrendered Singapore to the Japanese. All European expats were immediately declared enemy aliens. The time to leave was long gone.

'It will be all right,' said Maurice. 'You'll see, Jinx. Everything will be all right.'

But it was not going to be all right. Not at all.

Chapter Five

The Cotswolds, 2023

Merevale had thrown a forties-themed party every May since 2005, the sixtieth anniversary of VE Day, marking 'Victory in Europe' at the end of World War Two. It was the Colonel, then recently retired, who planned the first party to honour the local regiment. The party had become an annual event thanks to Merevale's resident hero Roy Smith, who was among the British troops who had landed in Normandy on D-Day.

'We should celebrate Roy every year,' the Colonel said in 2005. 'Who knows how long he's got?'

As it happened, Roy Smith had until 2017, by which time the Merevale VE Day party had become a permanent fixture in the village's social calendar (and many of the villagers had forgotten its actual genesis).

Always a stickler for detail, in 2005 the Colonel found three black-and-white photographs of Merevale's 1945 party in the church archive and used them to draw a plan of the village, so that he might recreate that original shindig down to the very last piece of bunting. The original bunting was long gone, thanks to several generations of church mice, but the Colonel had been delighted to discover, beneath a pile of old cassocks, the Union Flag which had flown from a pole next to the war memorial back in the day. In the Colonel's timetable for the VE Day event, which was unchanging from year to year, 'raise the flag while playing the national anthem' always marked the start of festivities.

That year's party was slightly later than usual because the Coronation of King Charles III had taken place on 6 May, and the villagers agreed that to have two celebrations in one week-end was too much even for the biggest party animals among them. Jinx had skipped the 'Coronation Celebration', which had to be held in the village hall due to the inclement weather. She was no monarchist. She had no intention of joining that year's VE Day party either, just as she had swerved the pre-vious year's party and the one before that. It seemed to Jinx slightly sinister that her neighbours so gleefully seized upon any excuse to send the village back in time by dressing like their grandparents to queue for tea from an erratic urn. Jinx had better things to do.

When Glenn the postman knocked again at four o'clock to ask whether Jinx needed an escort to take her to the party and find her a spot at one of the long trestle tables, she faked another cough and suggested that it might now be bad enough to prevent her attendance.

'I don't want to give anyone a bug ...' she said, hoping that by the time the party started, Glenn would be too busy to check up on her. She'd already handed over twenty pounds for the buffet and a further ten for raffle tickets (funeral vouchers might come in handy). Surely that was enough of a contribu-tion?

At five o'clock, the Colonel and Glenn changed into the uni-forms of a captain and private of the Home Guard respectively (as they did every year – somehow Glenn was never promoted). Suitably attired, they started testing the sound system. Jinx jumped when she heard an air-raid siren, but thankfully the dreaded wail lasted for just a couple of seconds before the immortal voice of Vera Lynn crackled over the airwaves in its place.

'*We'll meet again ...*'

Jinx hated 'We'll Meet Again', which was a song that took her back to all the wrong places. Though right then the whole world seemed to be conspiring to take Jinx back to all the wrong places. The copy of *The Times,* that the Colonel had so thoughtfully brought over, lay on the kitchen table, folded open to that photograph of Penny and Josephine Williamson – a blast from the past as unwelcome as the sound of any air-raid siren.

When Dame Vera had finished her most famous song, there was a brief respite from the racket until half past six, when the partygoers started to gather. From every house in the village, guests emerged in their 1940s finery. The men wore uniforms hired from the fancy dress shop in Stratford or outfits cobbled together around their grandfathers' patched tweed jackets. Some of the women wore genuine vintage, but most had turned to faux vintage websites in search of more forgiving 'bombshell' dresses full of Lycra. Children were decked out as lovable East End evacuees, with dirt smudged on their faces.

Retired accountant Pat Robinson, who was dressed, as usual, as an Air Raid Precautions warden, ticked the guests off her list as they arrived, giving each attendee the three drink vouchers included in the price of a ticket. Any more than that, they'd have to pay for. Glenn was manning a barrel of 'Victory Ale', while his daughter Thea had been pressed into service to pour soft drinks for the children. There'd been some debate about whether to allow Coke and Sprite, just as there was every year.

'Wouldn't have been available back in the day!' the Colonel had insisted at the first planning meeting.

But once again it was decided that the twenty-first-century children of Merevale would not be fobbed off with water or squash, and keeping them happy (if hyperactive) was more important than historical verisimilitude.

While the villagers gathered on the green and drank the first of their three included beverages, the Colonel fired up the music again. An Andrews Sisters medley soon set toes tapping, and Glenn and Pat tested the specially laid dance floor with a quick foxtrot, much to Thea's embarrassment.

At Number Seventeen, Jinx remained at her laptop. She had work to do. She tried taking out her hearing aids, but the muffled sound that resulted was somehow more annoying than full volume. She put them in again just in time to hear Val Smith and Cynthia Pearson pause outside her house to squabble about their contributions to the party buffet. Val was wearing the WRNS uniform she always wore. Jinx could see her tricorn hat over the top of the hedge.

'All I'm saying is that a quiche *cannot* be vegan, Cynth. Not if you made it with eggs—'

'Well, what would I have made it with, if not with eggs? It wouldn't be a quiche.'

Jinx waited for Val's response – Val and Cynth didn't often miss an opportunity for an argument – but instead Cynth asked, 'Do you think *she's* coming tonight?'

Jinx knew exactly who 'she' was, given it was her hedge they were standing behind.

'I don't suppose she will,' said Val. 'She never comes to anything. Though she's the only person in the village old enough to have been at the original party, and you'd think she'd want to remember VE Day more than any of us.'

'Can't say she'll be missed,' said Cynth. 'Not exactly the "life and soul", is she?'

Then suddenly it was seven o'clock. The Andrews Sisters were put on pause while the Colonel gave another quick blast on the air-raid siren. The haunting sound, immediately recognisable even to those who had never had to fear it in real life, brought the laughter and chatter on the green to an abrupt halt. Parents held their children close as the wail faded away and the Colonel took up his microphone. His voice echoed, as though he were speaking from the past.

'Ladies and gentlemen,' he began. 'Welcome to Merevale's eighteenth annual VE Day jamboree. We're here to celebrate the end of World War Two.'

'In Europe,' Jinx muttered to herself.

'But we must never talk about victory without remembering the cost, the *terrible* human cost, of conflict. So, before we start our party tonight, I'd like to invite you all to join me in our traditional minute's silence as we remember the brave men and women of Merevale, commemorated on this very monument, who paid for our freedom with their *lives*. And,' he added, 'as we think about all those who protect that freedom today.'

Jinx imagined the Colonel keeping time on his watch, with its multiple useless dials. She imagined her neighbours, dressed in their retro finery and borrowed uniforms, bowing their heads. But Jinx kept her head high until the end of the minute was signalled by the start of the national anthem, which she could never hear without remembering a brave band of young British soldiers, that she'd watched marching off to engage the Japanese in the streets of Singapore, when she was just seven years old.

Chapter Six

Singapore, February 1942

They were prisoners on the island now. A week after the surrender was signed, Japanese soldiers came to the house where Jinx's family had been lying low and demanded that Maurice bring his wife and children to the *padang* – the playing field in front of the old city courthouse – so that they could be registered.

The walk to the *padang* that morning was like a walk through a nightmare. Singapore had been all but destroyed by the fighting. Hardly a building remained unscathed.

'Keep looking ahead,' said Maurice, trying to shield Jinx from the worst of it. 'Keep your eyes straight ahead and you'll be all right, sweetheart.' But the truth was there was no part of the horizon that provided a view suitable for children. Jinx would never forget seeing a dead arm the colour of cold marble that seemed to wave at her from the rubble.

The city's courthouse had been requisitioned by the Japanese for an administrative centre. Jinx followed her parents into a room where a senior officer sat at a desk, inscribing names into a logbook. They were told to bow and after they had bowed, they were told to bow again. Lower. When Maurice made a

35

quip about his poor old back not being up to it, the officer gestured to his sword and advised that further complaints would be remedied by death.

Duly registered, they were sent to wait outside on the field where once expat teams had played long games of cricket before retiring for high tea. The *padang* looked like a curious kind of market that afternoon. Jinx's parents had brought only three cases (one each and one for the children), but other people had brought the most extraordinary things – paintings, rugs and standard lamps. They set up makeshift living rooms on the grass between the wickets.

As they waited, Maurice did his best to keep Jinx distracted with comic monologues on their *padang* neighbours – Singapore's great and good, now much reduced in their circumstances. Norma sat silent with Eddy in her lap.

'They'll let us go home soon,' Maurice promised, but four hours after they'd been registered and sent outside, a Japanese officer gave the order that the expat men on the *padang* were to form a new line. They were being separated from the womenfolk and taken elsewhere.

When Maurice began to stand up, Norma grabbed for his hand.

'What are you doing? You can't leave us here.'

'I don't think I've any choice, my love.'

Japanese soldiers were already moving through the crowd, urging the men to do as they'd been instructed. 'Up! Up!' they shouted. Some used bayonets to underline the order.

'I'll see you soon,' Maurice promised. 'Just be good and do as you're told. It's not worth arguing with this lot.'

'Please don't leave us,' Norma begged him.

'My darling, it won't be for long. I bet Churchill is sending his warships already. They'll smash the Japs and we'll be home within a month.'

'With Mr Bins,' said Jinx.

'With Mr Bins,' Maurice assured her. 'He won't let the Japanese anywhere near our house.'

Then he kissed each of them in turn. Jinx and Eddy on the tops of their heads. Their mother on the lips – tenderly, so tenderly. In return, Norma laid her hand on her husband's cheek and looked deep into his eyes.

'Promise we'll be together again soon,' she said.

'I do, and—'

Jinx chimed in, 'We never break a promise.'

'And what else do we say in our family?' Maurice asked her.

'We do not cry.'

'That's right. Be brave, Jinx. Look after your mother and your little brother, too. You're in charge until I get back.'

'Now!' one of the Japanese guards shouted. He prodded Maurice with the barrel of his gun.

Maurice gave his family one last smile and a double thumbs up before he allowed himself to be pushed in the direction of the long line of civilian men already beginning a march to who knew where. Jinx and Norma watched until the line had taken him out of sight.

With Maurice gone, Eddy closed his eyes and opened his mouth as if to cry. Jinx, whose own eyes were not so far from spilling over, quickly wrapped her arms around him and, squeezing him tight against her, jiggled him up and down in the way that always made him laugh.

'Come on, Eddy,' she said. 'Daddy wouldn't want us to be sad. We do not cry. We. Do. Not. Cry.' She scrunched up her nose to keep her own tears at bay.

Norma sank back down onto their picnic blanket. She did not cry either. She was altogether too dazed.

*

Shortly after the men were marched off the *padang*, it was the turn of the women and children. While Jinx balanced Eddy on her hip and sang him a song about tigers and bears, Norma gathered their belongings for the walk. They didn't know when they set off how far they would have to go.

The mood of the line of women that shuffled off the *padang* was subdued. The Japanese guards carried sticks and swords and guns. No one argued as instructions were issued. No one complained about the heat.

They arrived in Katong on the island's south-east coast as the sun was setting. The beach resort, where Maurice and Norma had honeymooned eight years earlier, was unrecognisable. Many of the buildings had been shelled. Those that weren't shelled had been looted. The Japanese had commandeered the best that remained to accommodate their prisoners. Some of the men were being held in the cinema. A guard prodded Norma and Jinx towards a former guest house, already filled to bursting with women who'd been ahead of them on the march.

When they learned that all the bedrooms had been taken – 'It's eight to a room' – Norma put their cases on the floor and fell to her knees. Her face crumpled. Jinx was still carrying Eddy.

'She's got children with her,' the whisper went around. 'There's a baby. Make room, make room.'

A spot was found beneath the long staircase that had seen many a grand entrance in the hotel's heyday. Now it was pockmarked with bullet holes and covered in dust. In their tiny cubbyhole, Norma lay down on the blanket and closed her eyes. Jinx held Eddy until he fell asleep, but she stayed awake all night, watching and learning. Her father was gone and for the first time ever, she had seen her mother truly vulnerable. In that moment, Jinx realised that ultimately, she was going to have to rely on herself.

The expat prisoners were kept in Katong for around three weeks. During that time, routines were established, pecking orders determined; rumours abounded as to what would happen next. Where might they be taken? No one had any information – not even the guards – until one morning, the women were told to muster outside the guest house with their belongings. They were being moved.

They were ready to go before breakfast, but the order to march did not come until noon. Suggestions that they not start the walk until the merciless sun was beginning to go down again fell on deaf ears. An order had been given and they were only to obey.

The women carried everything they could: clothes and tins, but also those carpets and lampstands that Jinx had seen on the *padang*. The Japanese said they would take some of the bulkier items ahead in a truck, but who would trust their most precious belongings to the enemy? One woman wore a lampshade as a hat.

It was not an easy walk. In the midday heat, the bitumen road was tacky, sucking at their rubber-soled sandals with every step. They were given no food and no water, and were flanked by guards who made sure no local people tried to help. Eddy drooped listlessly against his sister's shoulder while Norma dragged their cases.

After a couple of hours, a whisper went down the line. *Changi.* They were going to Changi Prison. The men had already been moved there. Robbers and murderers had been set free to make room for the women and children.

At last the white walls of the notorious city jail loomed ahead of them. Japanese guards were stationed in the watchtowers around the perimeter, where once white men had looked out over Singapore's most hardened criminals. This was it, then. This was where they were going to be.

At the head of the line, one of the women began to sing. At first, her voice was wavering and uncertain, but slowly it grew in strength and the other women around her began to join in, until everyone was singing.

'There'll always be an England . . .'

Norma whispered the words through her tears. Jinx sang as loudly as she could.

Walking through the prison gates at her mother's side, with Eddy on her hip, Jinx cast one final look back over her shoulder at the outside world. Then the women were funnelled into a long concrete corridor and, as the last of them stepped into the prison, the heavy metal gates clanged shut.

Chapter Seven

The Cotswolds, 2023

After the solemn proceedings and the raising of the flag, the party on the village green was soon back in full swing. A special programme of live music had been organised by Merevale's very own songbird, Marilyn Butler, who liked to remind everyone that she might have been a professional singer had she not given it all up to join her husband Evan in the family funeral business (proud sponsors of the whole event). The villagers were largely in awe of Marilyn, but Jinx was sure that hell, if it existed, would take the form of eternity spent listening to that woman singing 1940s standards.

Dressed in a silver tea dress with her hair in victory rolls, Marilyn was always in her element on VE Day. Having introduced the crowd to her 'band', which comprised Dave, a retired auditor, on keyboards and John, a former publican, on drums, she began her programme with a rendition of 'Chattanooga Choo Choo'. The urchins of the village Sunday school provided an enthusiastic chorus of 'choo choos' while Pat Robinson, in her ARP uniform, added extra authenticity with the odd 'whoo-whoo' of a steam train whistle which she'd downloaded onto her iPad.

Though she closed her windows, Jinx could not escape the racket being broadcast over the loudspeakers. And now, it seemed, they were coming for her, fake cough or no. At half past seven, the doorbell rang. Jinx tried to ignore it. It rang again. If it was Glenn – and it almost certainly was – Jinx knew he would keep ringing until she answered, or he would decide she must be in trouble, in which case he would call for an ambulance and break down the door.

'I'm coming,' Jinx groaned.

But it wasn't Glenn. It was his daughter.

What little Jinx knew of Thea Turner, now that she was a teenager, was what Glenn had told her. Though she gave the impression that – like most teenagers – she had outsourced her brain to her phone, Thea was some kind of prodigy and had been pushed ahead at school so that she did her GCSEs when most of her peers were still learning to tie their shoelaces. How old was she now? Fifteen? Sixteen? Her face was young, but her eyes were somehow older. Her expression was usually pained.

That evening was the first time in a long time that Jinx had seen Thea *not* wearing some kind of hood that obscured her face. Neither was she in jeans. She was dressed in a 1940s guide uniform and she was holding a large plate, which she unceremoniously thrust in Jinx's direction the moment the door was open.

'Dad thought you should have some food from the buffet,' she said. 'Seeing as you've already paid for it.'

Jinx stared at the plate, which was loaded with all manner of things she would not have chosen for herself – everything was brown apart from a large dollop of coleslaw.

'It's a bit of everything,' said Thea. 'Though I wouldn't bother with the quiche. It's got mussels in it.'

'Mussels? In a quiche?'

'The original recipe included salmon, but Cynthia made it with mussels because they're "vegan".' Thea made air-commas around the word with her spare hand. 'She says mussels don't have a nervous system.'

'Don't they?' Jinx asked.

'Of course they do,' said Thea. 'Anyway, Dad says he'll pick up the plate tomorrow. There's no need to wash it. And he says, "Get well soon".'

'Oh . . .' Jinx almost asked 'why' before she remembered that she was supposed to be coming down with something awful.

Then Thea fished a quarter bottle of prosecco out of the brown satchel that went with her uniform.

'Dad said to bring you this as well, so you can have a drink when the Colonel does the official toast. You'll be able to hear it over the speaker.'

'I'm sure I will. Please thank your father,' said Jinx. 'And thank you, too.'

Thea shrugged. 'S'all right.'

Jinx wondered whether she ought to ask Thea about school, but decided that the ensuing conversation would bore them both. 'Thank you,' she repeated instead. Thea nodded and turned to go.

Jinx carried the plate of party food into the kitchen, determined to tip it straight into the bin. She wouldn't, though. Of course she wouldn't. Not without at least pretending she would get round to eating it at some point. She put the plate in the fridge.

Through the kitchen blinds, Jinx could see that Thea was still lingering at the top of the garden path, where the high box hedge, planted for exactly that reason, hid her from the view of the people on the green. Thea had her head bent over her phone and Jinx wondered what she was looking at on there. Responding to messages? On one of those occasions when she

43

couldn't avoid a conversation, Glenn had complained to Jinx that his daughter didn't seem to have any friends – in large part because she had skipped that year at school and her classmates didn't see her as a peer. Was she watching videos? Talking to strangers? Putting herself in harm's way? The Internet was full of crooks. Jinx knew that much.

Thea remained behind Jinx's hedge for at least five minutes before she straightened herself up, with a sigh that Jinx could see in the rise and fall of her shoulders, then let herself out through the gate.

After a short break, during which the Colonel played more Andrews Sisters and Glenn Miller's 'In the Mood', Marilyn Butler was back on stage to entertain the troops.

Since 2018, the Colonel had allowed disco lights to be incorporated into the 1940s theme and, as dusk fell, Jinx's kitchen was illuminated pink, green and blue in quick succession. The music was definitely getting louder. When she looked up the time, Jinx was disappointed to see that it was only nine. The noise and the lights would be going on until midnight. Jinx had seen the licensing application.

Most of the people on the green that night were post-war babies, but every one of them sang along with gusto when Marilyn segued into 'The White Cliffs of Dover', as though they, too, had been there on 8 May 1945, listening to Churchill's speech on the wireless. Jinx wondered how many of them even knew that the Second World War hadn't really ended on that sunny spring day. Not for some people. She put her hands over her ears.

But then ...

As though a needle had been lifted from a record, Marilyn Butler fell suddenly silent. Or, if not silent exactly, then she and her band were at least oddly muted. At the same time the disco lights stopped flashing through the kitchen blinds. Jinx dared to uncover her ears. This was a welcome development.

What Jinx didn't know in that blissful moment of relative quiet was that every house in the village but hers was experiencing a power cut.

In the village hall, Glenn and the Colonel flipped all the switches on the fuse board, but nothing they did could persuade the lights to come back on. A call to the National Grid went unanswered.

On stage, Marilyn continued to sing a cappella in the glow of a half dozen iPhones, but there were other more pressing things to worry about than restoring her spotlight. Without electricity, the chemical toilets wouldn't flush. The ice-cream stall was rapidly thawing. They couldn't allow anyone onto the dance floor in the dark.

'Health and safety,' said Pat, getting into the spirit of the ARP warden she was pretending to be.

Worst of all, the pump on the beer barrel wouldn't work.

'We're going to have to end the party early,' Glenn suggested. 'Everyone's had their three drinks.'

'I haven't!' Cynthia piped up.

'Finish early?' The Colonel would not hear of it. 'You're suggesting we finish *early*? On the seventy-eighth anniversary of the end of World War Two? Where would we be now if our forebears had not had the ingenuity and the guts to overcome such minor inconveniences as a total loss of power?'

'They weren't in danger of being sued by someone tripping over on the dance floor,' Pat observed.

Whatever, the electricity was not coming back on. Villager after villager confirmed that there was no electricity in any of the streets that radiated out from the green. Yet all the time, Jinx's bungalow glowed like a mirage.

'I don't understand why Mrs Sullivan still has power,' said Glenn.

'Witchcraft,' someone suggested.

'She's fed by a different substation,' the Colonel explained. 'It's because her house was built in the seventies.'

Jinx's bungalow was the youngest building in the village.

Everyone looked towards Jinx's windows.

'I wonder ...' An idea began to form in the Colonel's mind. 'If we could run an extension cable from Jennifer's garage for the ice-cream stall, the beer pump and the spotlights, it would make all the difference. We might be able to carry on the stage show without the speakers. Marilyn's got big enough lungs.'

'It would be a shame if we had to go home early tonight of all nights,' said Pat. 'When everybody's made such an effort. But who's going to ask her?' She looked at Glenn hopefully. They all did.

'She likes you,' said Pat.

The happiness of the entire village rested on Glenn's shoulders then. Months of preparation had gone into the party and they were still only a fraction of the way through the carefully curated programme. There was a dance competition to be won, the raffle to be drawn; Marilyn's husband Evan had promised to burp the national anthem if the crowd raised £100 in a whip-round.

'We've got to ask Jennifer. I'll be right behind you,' the Colonel told Glenn.

Like the village boy chosen as a tribute to the dragon, Glenn bravely headed for Jinx's front door, carrying with him two quarter bottles of Prosecco.

In her kitchen, Jinx was vaguely aware that something was going on. Glancing up from her laptop, she saw shadows at the end of her garden path, two of which were advancing together. Even in their 1940s outfits, she recognised them at once.

Jinx tipped the party food Thea had brought into the bin and took Glenn's plate to the front door.

'Thank you, Glenn. That was delicious,' she lied.

'Actually, Mrs Sullivan, we haven't come for the plate.'

The whole village stood in silence on the other side of Jinx's hedge as they waited for Glenn to present their suit.

'... just one extension lead, for the freezer ... all that ice-cream ... such a waste ... and perhaps one more, for the big light over the dance floor ... Everyone has worked so hard ... we'd be so very grateful ... Yours is the only house in the village with any power.'

What could Jinx do? The request wasn't really a request, was it? How could she say 'no', when every one of her neighbours was crowded about her front gate, peering at her with beseech-ing eyes? After Glenn's pre-emptive speech on the gratitude of the whole community, Jinx really had no choice at all.

'Electricity is expensive, I know,' the Colonel chipped in. 'We'll have a whip-round to cover your bill.'

For heaven's sake, Jinx muttered inwardly. Outwardly, she approximated a smile and waved Glenn in the direction of her garage door.

'I'll get the key,' she told him.

And the entire village sent up a cheer.

Moments later, an extension lead was plugged in and the lights came back on. Marilyn Butler launched into 'Happy Days Are Here Again' and the Colonel insisted that Jinx come out to the green with him to dance on the floodlit dance floor.

'One quick jitterbug?'

Jinx resisted. But four pints of Victory Ale in, the Colonel was not taking 'no' for an answer.

'Come on, Jennifer! You've saved the party.'

Then he took both her hands and pulled her out of her bungalow, like a blackbird tugging a snail from its shell.

'Three cheers for the Queen of VE Day!' the Colonel cried as he dragged poor Jinx out through her gate. He got her as far as the dance floor, where he tripped on the hessian underlay. He took Jinx down with him as he fell.

It wasn't until next morning that Jinx was seen by a frazzled young A & E doctor who diagnosed a fracture to her clavicle. Not a bad fracture, considering, but one that would require Jinx to wear her left arm in a sling to take the weight off until it healed.

'Everyone sends their best wishes,' Glenn lied when he returned to pick her up.

'And how is the Colonel?'

'Busy fighting off the ladies. He's a bit sore this morning, but nothing more than that. But you, Mrs Sullivan … You won't be able to catch your flight on Thursday.'

Jinx must have looked momentarily confused.

'To Florence, Mrs Sullivan. Your flight to Florence.'

Falling back against the pillows, Jinx closed her eyes and sighed. Her perfect Italian plan was foiled.

Chapter Eight

It took an age for Jinx to be discharged that day. A consultant did not arrive until lunchtime, and he left Jinx with a prescription for painkillers from the hospital pharmacy, which meant another long wait. Jinx told Glenn she could do without them, but he insisted.

'We don't know that they're just painkillers, Mrs Sullivan. The doctor wanted you to have those tablets for a reason.'

Jinx considered. She was certain they *were* just painkillers, but it was always worth having spares. Particularly heavy-duty ones.

Glenn settled Jinx in the pharmacy waiting area while he queued for the prescription, then he wheeled her out to his car in a hospital wheelchair. All the way back to Merevale, he was thinking aloud.

'You're going to need some help.'

'I'll be fine.'

'You've only got one good hand.'

'I can manage.'

Jinx continued to insist as much, though when they got to her bungalow, she couldn't even open the car door.

'I'm not happy about this,' said Glenn. 'You should come home with me.'

'No, thank you, Glenn. I'm a tough old bird.'

'I don't want to leave you.'

'But I very much want to be left.'

Jinx let Glenn make sure she got into her house without incident, but she refused his offer to make her some lunch. She was tired, and wanted only to be alone to work out what on earth to do about Italy now.

Jinx's suitcase, already half-packed, was still on the bed where she'd left it on Saturday afternoon. She tried to manoeuvre it back down to the floor with her right hand, her non-dominant hand, but it was awkward and, imagining herself trying to negotiate the cobbled streets of Florence, dragging it along behind her, she knew it would be difficult to the point of dangerous. Glenn was right. Jinx was not going to be catching that flight. Not on Thursday. Perhaps not ever, given what she knew.

Jinx tried to tell herself that it didn't really matter. No one was expecting her in Florence. And yet it did matter. It mattered very much indeed. The article about Penny Williamson and her sister Josephine, the significance of which the Colonel had no idea, had underlined to Jinx just how important it was to act now. The clock was ticking. Who knew how she would be feeling by the time her fracture was healed. She didn't know whether she would be able to get up the garden path in a month or two, let alone through an airport.

And it wasn't long before she wished she had let Glenn make her something to eat, because she couldn't bloody well do it herself. If only she hadn't thrown that buffet food into the bin. It would have to be biscuits for lunch. But trying to wrestle the lid off her biscuit tin one-handed, Jinx managed only to drop it on the floor – at which point the stupid lid sprang off, sending stale shortbread and Hobnobs skittering across the kitchen tiles in all directions.

Jinx felt that sharp, strange pain at the back of her eyes.

'No. I do not cry!' she reminded herself. 'I. Do. Not. Cry.'

But she couldn't even get down onto the floor to pick the biscuits up because, with one arm out of action, she knew she might not be able to get up again if she did. All she could do was sit on her kitchen chair and eat the solitary half Hobnob that had, by luck, landed on the kitchen table, right on top of yesterday's *Times*, still open to that awful picture of Penny and Josephine. Penny seemed to be looking straight at her.

'*Well, this is a mess, Jinx, isn't it?*' Penny's smug expression seemed to say.

Jinx grabbed the half biscuit and bit into it defiantly, but it felt wrong in her mouth and the unhappy, dusty flavour somehow made it even harder not to sob.

'I do not cry,' Jinx whispered.

Chapter Nine

Manchester, 1949

'I do not cry.'

Jinx walked across the playground with her second-hand satchel clasped tight to her chest like a shield, but the slings and arrows that came her way on that short walk, which always seemed to take forever, could not be stopped by physical means.

'Fleabag!'

The shouting started the moment she stepped through the gate.

'Good morning, *Smell-i-fer*!'

Doreen Hardy and her friends were delighted by the far from witty epithet.

'What's the matter? Don't know your name, Stinky Spencer?'

'She doesn't speak English,' someone else said. 'Try asking her in Chinese.'

'But I no speak Chinese,' said Doreen, mimicking Jinx's accent.

There was no point telling her that the accent she was mimicking was Malayan. 'Best to keep your head down, Jinx,' was her mother's advice. 'They'll get bored eventually. It'll be somebody else's turn.'

But six months had passed since Jinx started at the grammar school and nobody seemed to have grown bored of making fun of her in the least. If anything, it was getting worse: shouting in the playground, flicking paper balls at her head in class, tripping her up in the gym. There was nowhere to hide. And there was no point running to a teacher. Some of them were just as bad, asking Jinx to repeat herself endlessly.

Even when Jinx was talking to them in her own 'Hut Ten' voice, they claimed that her 'not quite British' accent made her incomprehensible.

'Speak the King's English!' was a phrase she heard a dozen times a week, particularly from Mrs Gilbert, the history teacher, who nonetheless had to admit that while Jinx spoke 'gibberish', her essays were flawless.

'As though they were written by someone else entirely,' Mrs Gilbert said.

Jinx hated school. She hated Manchester. She hated England. It was hard not to hate her mother for bringing them there. Would they ever go back home?

The almoner, Penny Williamson, continued to visit on Thursdays, though Jinx wondered how much more she could do for them. They didn't seem to be getting any closer to the top of the mythical St Saviour's waiting list, though Penny promised Norma on a weekly basis that things were happening. 'There are some pre-fabs going up near the park. I'm sure we can get you one of those.'

Penny had managed to sort out a few things. Eddy had calipers to straighten out his legs, and all of them had been given extra vitamins to compensate for the long-lasting effects of malnutrition. Jinx tried to be grateful for the tablets as big as marbles she had to take every morning with a glass of warm milk.

One winter afternoon, Penny was at the flat when Jinx got home.

'How's school?' she asked brightly.

'Bad.'

'You're still not having fun at the grammar?'

'I don't seem to have the knack for making friends.'

'I don't believe that,' said Penny. 'Though I didn't have many schoolfriends myself. Not until a soldier I met on a train at the beginning of the war gave me a pack of cigarettes. I invited the most popular girls in my class to come and smoke them in the sports hut. Then I was suddenly very well liked indeed.'

'So I just need to get hold of some cigarettes.' Jinx laughed, despite herself.

'That's better,' said Penny. 'Don't worry, be happy.'

'That's a very annoying thing to say. *Toujours gai?*'

Now it was Penny's turn to laugh, hearing her catchphrase parroted back at her.

'Why don't you think you have the knack for friendship, Jinx?'

'Everything is wrong about me. My voice. My clothes. The fact that I'm two years ahead of everyone else in the class in maths and Latin. And French. And English. And physics and chemistry and biology—'

'Even though you had those three and a half years in camp. And they tease you for it. Well, sticks and stones—'

'It's not just words.'

Jinx showed Penny the knees of her woollen stockings, both sporting big holes. As she did so, the memory of being tripped on her way into school that morning made her cheeks flush.

'I only want to be left alone,' she lamented.

'If someone bullies you, Jinx, it's because they secretly feel somehow inferior,' was Penny's opinion.

'Inferior to me?'

'Yes. You. You must make them feel quite thick, being so far ahead in your classes. You are intelligent and elegant and kind. I'm quite envious of you myself.'

Next day, Jinx arrived home to find a small brown paper parcel on the kitchen table.

'Penny came by,' said Norma. 'She said she promised to lend you a book.'

Jinx didn't remember that conversation, but a strange instinct told her to take the parcel into the corner to open it. Inside was a novel. At least, the dustcover suggested it was a novel. *Children of the New Forest* by Captain Marryat. Jinx had already read it. Eight times. It was one of the few books they had in camp. Penny probably thought Captain Marryat would be 'improving'.

However, Jinx soon discovered that the innocuous cover was hiding something quite different inside.

'*Self-Defence for Women and Girls* by Captain W.E. Fairbairn,' said the title page. Jinx flicked to the author's note. 'There are many persons with an erroneous impression concerning the Art of jiu-jitsu . . .'

And tucked between the last pages, Jinx found a note on a smart card headed with Penny's address.

'Dearest Jinx,' she'd written, 'It's time to take the battle into the enemy camp. As the good Major says, it's "kill or be killed".'

Kill or be killed? Was Penny talking about Jinx's bullies? She'd lost her mind.

But while Norma darned socks and Eddy played with his toy soldiers, Jinx devoured Captain Fairbairn's opinions on 'attack and defence'.

*

Jinx was fascinated by the book's contents. It was a strange sort of martial arts manual, illustrated with photographs of a young woman in a tea dress fighting off a man in a suit. There were defensive moves for a woman caught up in any number of situations: trapped in a car, molested in the office, set upon while walking down the street ...

'They are all practicable, and many are original, worked out in answer to the question: *What should I do if I were to be attacked like this?*' Captain Fairbairn explained.

Jinx was especially intrigued by the clever 'Defence against wandering hands', designed to fend off advances in a theatre or cinema. It basically involved knocking your date's nose against the back of the seat in front. *V useful*, Penny had scribbled in the margin. But what did Penny think Jinx could do with such information? What did she mean by giving Jinx this book?

'What do you think I meant?' Penny asked when Jinx next saw her. Penny had waited for her after school. 'I meant that you should learn how to defend yourself.'

'Where am I going to practise jiu-jitsu?'

Penny and Jinx fell into step as they walked towards Jinx's home.

'I used to practise on my little brother, but there isn't such a big age gap between me and George as there is between you and Eddy. You probably shouldn't ask Eddy to try to get you in a stranglehold. Poor little thing might get hurt.'

The thought of Eddy putting anything in a stranglehold seemed ridiculous. He was an exceedingly gentle child.

'I'll tell you what, why don't we take a walk to the park and you can try out what you've learned so far on me?'

'You're bonkers.'

'It's my best asset. Come on.'

Penny linked her arm through Jinx's and marched her through the park gates to a large patch of grass, away from the main thoroughfare. It was getting dark and Jinx was nervous, but Penny didn't seem to care.

'Now show me how that bully tripped you up. How were you walking?'

Jinx folded her arms across her chest as though she were carrying her satchel.

'And she put out her foot? Like this?'

'She must have done. I didn't notice.'

'You need to be more aware of what is going on around you, Jinx. The first rule of never being caught off guard is never to *be* off guard!'

'Wonderful,' said Jinx. 'I'll remember that.'

'Come on, Jinx. You're no sissy. You've been through things that those silly girls at school can't begin to imagine. I won't have you trying to slink by while they insult you. Let's get practising. Walk by me. If you can.'

'This is ridiculous.'

'Try.'

Jinx tried, but Penny marked her every move and Jinx simply could not get by her. Penny's arms and legs seemed to be everywhere at once. When Jinx did try to shove Penny away, it had no effect whatsoever. Penny pushed her straight back and almost upended her. With a fingertip. That was how it seemed.

'How did you do that?'

'Physics. You don't need force. You need to be clever ...'

They practised the same moves over and over until Jinx was so fed up that she wanted to plant Penny in a flower bed.

'Good,' said Penny when Jinx finally managed to dodge Penny's foot and turn the move back on her. 'We're finally getting somewhere. We'll make a fighter of you yet.'

'Where did you learn all this anyway?' Jinx asked.

'From the book I gave you. And perhaps a little bit of extra combat training.'

For just a moment, Penny's expression was far away. Jinx had heard all about Penny's wartime experiences as a junior officer in the First Aid Nursing Yeomanry. She didn't remember Penny mentioning combat training before.

'Why would you have needed that?'

Penny evaded the question. 'Gosh. It's six o'clock already. We'd better be getting you home. I won't see you next week because I'm going to London to see a great-aunt. But when I get back, I will visit and I will want to hear that you've given those bullies a taste of their own medicine.'

'I'll try to stay out of their way,' said Jinx. 'This stuff won't work on someone like Doreen.'

'It works on everyone,' said Penny, whose eyes were suddenly fixed on a spot in the bushes. Jinx couldn't see anything there.

'Get ready, Jinx,' Penny warned her, just as a man leapt out and made to open his coat to flash at them.

Penny had the fellow back in the bush – head first – before Jinx could see anything untoward.

'Now I suggest you go home and put some trousers on!' Penny told him.

Jinx gawped.

'Every woman should know how to defend herself,' said Penny simply.

Jinx was still shaking with adrenaline when she got back home, but Penny had brushed off the incident in the park as though it were an encounter with a badly trained dog. She'd barely flinched. For the rest of their walk she'd talked about the latest pictures and books, not mentioning jiu-jitsu again until they were about to part ways. Then she straightened Jinx's collar and told her, 'About those bullies, Jinx, as Fairbairn once said,

When it comes to defeating a ruthless enemy, there's no room for any scruple.'

Jinx concluded that Penny Williamson must have gone mad.

But she remembered the man in the bushes, and how easily Penny had fought him off. Penny knew what she was doing. While Norma and Eddy slept, Jinx secretly practised the moves in Fairbairn's book against her own shadow. And on Monday, she returned to school with darned knees and a determined expression.

Jinx had made a bargain with herself. Name-calling, she would not react to. Names were horrible but they were ultimately harmless, as the saying went. She would only retaliate if someone used physical force on her. If Doreen tried to trip her, for example. And even then, she would respond in the mildest way possible. Just enough force to put anyone off picking on her again.

As she approached the school gates, Jinx sent up a prayer that the circus would have moved on and she could cross the playground without anyone noticing. God, as usual, did not seem to be listening.

Doreen and her sidekicks, the Murray twins, were on the steps to the main school building. The moment they saw Jinx, it started. Doreen swaggered down the steps to meet Jinx in the middle of the playground. A hush fell all around as dozens of schoolgirls waited to see what would happen next. They were like the monkeys in the jungle back home, Jinx thought, falling quiet when they realised that one of their number was being stalked by a tiger, lest they, too, attract the hungry beast's attention.

'What's that smell?' Doreen began, theatrically pinching her nose. 'Seems to be coming from over here.'

Doreen marked Jinx as she tried to cross the playground. Each time Jinx moved to dodge her, Doreen got back in her face. Doreen played on the school netball team, so she was no slouch on that front.

Feint and block, feint and block. It went on like that for what seemed like hours, though it must have been less than a minute. Seeing from the corner of her eye that Doreen was moving to trip her, Jinx suddenly whirled about. Using her satchel to support and reinforce her folded arms, she turned and blocked Doreen halfway through her move, taking her by such surprise that it was easy to push her back onto her behind.

A gasp went up all round. No one was as surprised as Jinx was. But she managed to deliver the *coup de grâce* – a small shove to Doreen's chest with her foot that laid the bully flat out.

While Doreen lay on her back on the gravel, looking up at the sky with surprised-wide eyes, Jinx walked on into school and took her seat in the classroom moments before Miss Gilbert arrived to take the register.

Doreen would not call Jinx 'Smellifer' again. After her humiliation, Doreen found that suddenly *she* was the butt of all the jokes. The Murray twins asked Jinx if she'd like to sit at their table at lunchtime. She declined, instead joining, as usual, the table of girls who had lived in fear of Doreen, for whom Jinx was now a heroine. To whom she had given great hope.

'You're spectacular,' breathed little Edie Pope.

'*Kill or be killed*,' said Jinx, in what she hoped was an enigmatic sort of way.

Jinx couldn't wait to let Penny know how the glorious moment had unfolded.

When Penny next came to visit two weeks later, she was carrying an armful of parcels.

'A few little things from London,' she said, as she passed the gifts around. She'd been to visit relatives.

'Did you see the King?' Eddy asked her.

'Don't be silly,' said Penny, though later Jinx would find out that's exactly what Penny had been doing. She and her older sister Josephine had been presented to the King at an audience at Buckingham Palace, thanks to her well-connected great-aunt.

With that sort of family behind her, it seemed entirely feasible that Penny should be rich enough to buy Eddy a box of Turkish Delight as big as the battered suitcase Norma had carried back from Singapore with all their worldly goods inside.

The second parcel, for Jinx, was another large one. Inside was a blazer. It looked new.

'I hope it's your size.'

'Where did you get the coupons for this?' Jinx asked.

'Don't look a gift horse in the mouth.'

'Mummy, can I have some Turkish Delight now?' asked Eddy.

'After you've had your tea,' Norma tried, but Penny played devil's advocate.

'I'm sure a couple of tiny pieces won't spoil his appetite. Turkish Delight is terribly insubstantial.'

'Penny! You're the best.'

'You're not bad,' Jinx agreed.

Penny had Jinx put on the blazer to check that it fitted.

'Such a pretty girl,' Penny said. 'Even prettier when you smile. *Toujours gai!*'

'Why do you give us so much help?' Jinx asked when she and Penny were next alone.

'What did I say about gift horses?' Penny replied. But she carried on, 'Why do I want to help you, Jinx? Because I like you. You remind me of myself. The way you dealt with those bullies. Oh, how I wish I'd seen it! We're kindred spirits, you and I.'

Were they? Were they really? Jinx liked Penny, too, but it was hard for her to show it. The cost of getting it wrong was too high. While Penny's surprising martial arts skills had thrilled Jinx, they'd also frightened her a little, suggesting a certain volatility that might one day be aimed in her direction.

It was safer to maintain some distance. In every relationship. Jinx would never stop believing that. And that was why, almost seventy-five years later, Jinx was sitting hungry at her kitchen table, with the floor covered in broken biscuits that she could not quite reach.

Chapter Ten

The Cotswolds, 2023

When Glenn came to deliver the post on Monday morning —
another chirpy invitation from Merevale's premier retirement
complex — he was glad to see that Jinx was up and dressed. She
did not tell him it was only because she had not managed to get
undressed since he left her house on Sunday. Or that she had
barely slept, finding it next to impossible to sleep on her back,
which was the only position that didn't seem to hurt. She felt
too vulnerable, lying there, belly up.

'Have you had breakfast?' Glenn asked. 'I've brought you a
bacon bap.'

He passed her a brown paper bag that was soggy with grease.

'It's vegan bacon — Thea won't touch meat — but I've eaten
worse.'

So had Jinx. Much worse. And goodness, she was hungry.

'Mrs Sullivan,' Glenn continued, 'I've been thinking. You're
going to need some ongoing help. I thought I could send Thea
over. To do some cleaning and stuff.'

Jinx automatically shook her head. 'There's no need—'

'I'd actually be grateful if you would let Thea help you out.

She's at a loose end right now and I don't want her sitting at home all day.'

Jinx did not want the girl sitting in her house all day either.

But Glenn filled in the gaps in the face of her objections. 'She's taking some time off school, you see. She wasn't excluded or anything like that. You know how she did her GCSEs early, so she's in Year 12? That's lower sixth in old money. Well, now she says she doesn't want to do A levels after all. I've told her she can't just quit, and if she's not going to study then she's got to work but ... Could you use her help today?'

Jinx hated the idea, but as she stood there in the clothes she'd been wearing since Saturday evening, knowing that her kitchen floor was still covered in biscuits, she accepted she was going to need some assistance, and it would probably be better to have it from Glenn's daughter than from any of the cleaners her neighbours used. Before Glenn could say anything more, Jinx capitulated and said, 'Why not?'

Talking of neighbours ...

'Hello! Hello! Glenn! Jennifer!'

It was the Colonel, picking his way gingerly across the close towards them, carrying a bottle of sherry. Jinx noticed at once that he was wearing trainers.

'Not my usual style,' he admitted. 'But after Saturday night, I'm not taking any more chances with leather soles ... Jennifer, I am mortified that I've landed you in such a pickle. This is for you, with my apologies.'

He pushed the sherry bottle towards her before realising she didn't have a free hand with which to take it. He put it down on the doorstep instead.

'Now, Glenn has told me that our ill-fated tango rather put a spanner in your holiday plans. Italy, wasn't it? I've been giving some thought as to how I might rectify the situation, and I've decided that I would like to pay for you to join the village coach trip. What do you say to that? You'll be able to have your Italian jolly after all.'

Jinx groped for a tactful answer. 'I really couldn't—'

'*Insisto*,' said the Colonel in forceful Italian. 'That means "I insist". I had a nice win on the Premium Bonds last month ...'

'You must have many other things to spend the money on,' said Jinx.

'I'd like to spend it on you. I hate to think of you missing out on a holiday. And it will be a very good tour. I've been practising my Italian. Do you speak Italian, Jennifer?'

She did, but the Colonel didn't give her time to tell him.

'I signed up for lessons online,' he went on. 'I can't wait to try out my new skills. Or should I say "*Sono così eccitato*"?'

'Gosh,' said Jinx. The Colonel probably hadn't meant to say he was feeling extremely aroused, but with that man one could never be sure.

'One last chance to live the *dolce vita*. How could you resist?'

'Why don't you sleep on it?' Glenn interrupted.

Jinx nodded gratefully. 'That's a good idea.'

Satisfied that he had done all he could for the moment, the Colonel very slightly lifted his panama hat in farewell and set off again. Slowly.

'It's not a bad plan,' Glenn tried. 'Your coming with us. Pizza, Pisa, ravioli ... We're going to have a wonderful time.'

'Thank you for the sandwich,' said Jinx. 'Tell Thea I'd be grateful to see her as soon as she likes.'

Allowing anyone into her home was difficult for Jinx. Allowing someone in to *help* her was even harder. Jinx was determined that she would ask Thea only to do housework, but when she arrived at Jinx's bungalow that Monday afternoon, Thea was matter-of-fact about the things Jinx would *really* need help with.

'I'll get you some clean clothes,' Thea said as she swept up the broken biscuits. 'Do you need help to shower, too?'

It was the last thing Jinx wanted, but the one thing she needed most of all. Her distress at the idea must have shown on her face.

'I can help you get changed without it being embarrassing,' Thea said. 'I won't see anything.'

This was important to Jinx, whose old body told tales she didn't want anyone to know.

'I know what to do,' Thea assured her. 'I used to help my mum.'

Jinx knew that Thea had lost her mum, Glenn's beloved wife Lindsey, three years earlier. Lindsey's death had come after a long illness. All the same, Glenn had taken just a fortnight off on compassionate leave before he was back on his round and answering the villagers' gentle questions with, 'We're doing fine now, thank you.'

In the village shop, Jinx had overheard Val and Cynthia talking about it.

'He's back at work and Thea's at school. They're not grieving properly,' was Cynthia's firm opinion. Val was in agreement for once. But Jinx understood why Glenn wanted to be at work rather than wallowing at home. Jinx, too, was of the view that whatever tragedy befell you, life must go on. You couldn't bring the dead back by grieving. The sun would still rise and set without them, so you had to keep getting up each morning and find strength in routine. Why give in to grief if you could just ignore it? What was it Churchill once said? *Keep buggering on.*

Over the next two weeks, Thea came to Number Seventeen every morning and evening to help Jinx into her clothes and do various household chores. To minimise the amount of personal care she needed, Jinx let Thea into her wardrobe to find items she would be able to easily get on and off without disturbing her fractured clavicle. Jinx had a number of kaftans, bought on a long-ago trip to Morocco. A pair of old Scholl sandals saved any bother with laces.

Jinx soon got used to having Thea around, though even after a fortnight, she didn't feel she knew any more about the girl than she had that first morning. Their exchanges were always brief and to the point. Thea wore her headphones as she went about her work, taking them off only to ask Jinx for instructions or to let her know when she was leaving to go home. Thea's lack of interest in anything other than her phone was comforting, convincing Jinx that the young girl wouldn't be reporting back to her father or anybody else.

Jinx had not told any of the people in the village about her life before she came to Merevale. Had she ever invited them into her largely bare house, they might, if they were very observant, have guessed there was a Malaysian connection from the two framed black-and-white photographs on the mantelpiece. Jinx wondered if Thea had noticed the photographs as she dusted. If she had, she didn't mention it. Thea moved around the rooms with a perfectly neutral expression on her face. The only time Jinx saw her properly smile was when she handed over her wages on a Friday afternoon.

One surprising task with which Jinx needed help was plugging in her laptop. The plug fitted snugly into the socket, and it was difficult to do with one hand. The first time Thea did it, she struggled to conceal her surprise at the high quality of Jinx's tech.

'I only use it for checking the weather,' Jinx explained, and Thea seemed convinced by that.

But when Thea was gone, Jinx logged out of the BBC's weather page and into her email inbox, which was full of 'business' correspondence awaiting her attention. It was hard for Jinx to type with only her right hand but it didn't matter too much. These were emails from people who might benefit from having to wait a while for a reply.

Jenice, where are you? Mitch wanted to know. *It's been three days since I sent the money. Did you get it? Is something wrong?*

Mitch could definitely wait. There was, however, one email that Jinx was eager to read. This one came via an Internet forum for students of the Japanese language, which Jinx had joined under another alias. A couple of weeks earlier, Jinx had posted a picture of an old photograph she owned, asking if anyone might be able to translate the kanji script scribbled on the back of it.

Jinx knew she was going the long way round. She might simply have uploaded the photo to social media, explained how she had come to own it, and asked, 'Does anyone recognise these people? This house?' Somebody somewhere would know someone, she was sure. But Jinx did not want this very private story to become public property while she was still working out what it meant to her. She could not bear to see the heart emojis and the inane comments her search would inevitably attract. This was not a storyline for a TV documentary presented by one of those white-toothed young women who always made the show more about themselves than their subjects. Sometimes people were 'long-lost' for good reason.

Whenever Jinx looked at the photograph, which she had kept hidden away for so long, she felt a terrible mixture of emotions: sadness, sickness, tenderness and fury. And of course, she couldn't look at it without thinking of two moments in particular. The day she first saw it – presented to her by a proud father – and the day the print came into her possession. They were two very different occasions indeed.

It had taken Jinx a very long time to pluck up the courage

to post the picture on the forum, but now someone had obliged with a translation. A stranger called Ben Marwood wrote, 'The words say "Haruto, Aimi and Aiko Hinode, 1941, Osaka. Hinode is quite a rare name. It means "Sunrise". I know a Hinode who lives in Italy. Perhaps she knows the family. I could put you in touch if that might help.'

It might indeed. Jinx murmured the names aloud.

Aiko, Aimi and Haruto Hinode. Haruto. Her old friend.

Chapter Eleven

Two and a half weeks after the VE Day accident, Jinx was back at her laptop, slowly typing a message to her Facebook correspondent – Mitch in Seattle – who had kindly offered to buy her a red dress to wear to the airport when she flew over to see him. Thea had clocked off, leaving Jinx with a sandwich for her tea. The sandwich was tuna mayonnaise on brown bread, and very tasty. Jinx ate it as she read Mitch's latest DM.

Jenice, you've got to buy the more expensive dress. I insist. I'm sending the money, but I need pictures this time. For $500, I think I deserve to see you in the changing room.

Ugh. Jinx shuddered at the very idea.

'My camera's broken,' she was typing back when the doorbell rang.

This time it was Clive the window-cleaner, come to collect that month's fee.

'Heard you had an accident, Mrs Sullivan. Take more water with it next time!'

Jinx laughed, more from politeness than mirth.

'I'll get your cash,' she said. 'It may take a moment.'

'I've got all the time in the world for you, Mrs S.'

Clive the window-cleaner did not do digital payments. He was a big fan of conspiracy theories. His Facebook page – why did conspiracy theorists always have Facebook pages? – was littered with photographs taken from aeroplane windows, which Clive claimed to show that the earth was not round. It was all a big con.

'We're 20,000 feet in the air,' was a typical caption. 'So why can't we see any curvature? Tell me that, Bill Gates. #flatearth.'

Fortunately for Clive, Jinx liked cash, too. She kept a couple of grand in the house at all times – an old habit, though she hadn't had to do a moonlight flit in a while. She sometimes smiled to think of the people from the council – for it would have to be the council – clearing her bungalow and finding little (and not so little) piles of twenties and fifties here and there. She hoped it would make up for having to deal with the detritus of a long life ended alone.

That day she went for the stash in the airing cupboard, confidently reaching under the pile of towels with her good hand. But there was no cash there.

Strange. Jinx was certain there should have been at least a hundred pounds. Had she spent it without realising? She liked to think that she was as sharp as she had ever been, but perhaps ...

Not wanting to keep Clive waiting, she went instead to the bathroom cabinet and pulled a tenner out of the stash she kept in a box that had once contained haemorrhoid cream. Jinx had never needed the stuff, but such a box was an excellent place to hide anything you wanted to keep private. For some reason, the average burglar seemed to baulk at the idea of bodily functions.

Back at the front door, Clive was watching a video about the Illuminati on his iPhone.

'I'm sorry, Clive. I'm not as quick as I usually am.'

'Not with your arm in a sling, you're not. Don't worry, Mrs Sullivan. Why don't you have this month's clean for free. Call it a "get well" present.'

'That's very kind, but I have the money right here.'

Jinx did not want to be indebted to Clive, and he didn't protest either. The notion of a 'get well' present was soon forgotten.

'I'll see you next month, then,' he said.

'Perhaps,' was Jinx's distracted reply.

Jinx was disturbed by the idea that she might have spent all that money without keeping a proper account of it. She made a mental list of all the times she'd used cash in the past couple of weeks. Who had she paid? Glenn for groceries (he'd added her list to his 'big shop'). The milkman. The young man who mowed the lawn in the spring and summer. She'd given Thea her wages, but that cash had been from her purse.

Jinx went back to the airing cupboard and searched through the linen as best she could with one arm. Thea's neatly ironed pile was balanced on top of decades' worth of clean but crumpled bedclothes, under which Jinx usually kept her stash.

No. The money was definitely not there, and Jinx knew for certain she hadn't spent it. She just knew it. She was not losing her marbles. She knew what day of the week it was. She knew the name of the prime minister. She knew all the prime ministers going back decades, though with so many changes in 2022, she could be forgiven for getting the order of the last crop of no-marks wrong. And she knew she had not spent that cash, nor had she moved it from its hiding place. Which could only mean that someone else had.

Thea.

Where else had Thea been?

She'd ironed two of Jinx's blouses and put them in the wardrobe.

With difficulty, Jinx dragged out the Indian box, with the key still in the lock. She lifted the lid. There was the mouse.

There was the ring. There was the Florence guidebook, and there was the small pile of fifties.

One short. The implications were clear. No one had been in Jinx's airing cupboard or wardrobe but her and Thea. Case closed.

This was most unfortunate. It wasn't the money so much as the cheek of it. It was the fact that Thea obviously thought Jinx was a doddery old woman who wouldn't notice she was a hundred quid short. She felt her anger rising. No one ever got one over on Jinx.

She phoned Glenn. He picked up straight away.

'Mrs Sullivan. Has something happened?' he asked.

'Not exactly,' said Jinx. 'Could you ask Thea to pop round? I need help with a couple of things ...'

'I'm not far from you myself.'

'No, dear. I need help with a couple of things that ... that I would prefer to discuss with another woman.'

'Ah,' said Glenn. The hint of things feminine stopped him in his tracks.

Thea arrived an hour later, slouching up the garden path with her eyes glued to her phone. As she put her hand to the doorbell, Jinx was waiting for her. Having had time to consider her options, she was almost pleased to see the teen. This was going to be fun.

Jinx opened the door with a smile of welcome, but the minute the front door was closed, her demeanour was suddenly, shockingly, different. With her free hand, she grabbed Thea by the wrist. The young girl was startled by her strength.

'Where is it?' Jinx hissed. 'Where's my money?'

'I don't know what you're talking about.'

'Oh, I think you do. You may think I'm a helpless old lady, Thea. Won't miss a few quid here and there. But you've got me very wrong. I know that before you came into my house, I had eighty pounds in the airing cupboard. Afterwards, nothing. And there were nine fifty-pound notes in the wardrobe, where now there are only eight.'

'I didn't take it.'

'Then who did? Apart from your father, you are the only person who's been inside my house this year. Should I be asking him where my money is?'

'No,' said Thea. 'No.' The anguish in her voice was all but an admission of guilt. 'Please. I've got your money in my bag.'

'Why did you take it?'

'Why did you leave it lying around?'

'Victim-shaming?'

Jinx held out her hand. Thea handed over four twenties and the fifty, all crumpled. It was quite something to crumple one of those new plastic notes, denoting a special level of careless-ness, Jinx thought.

'What did you want the money for anyway?' she asked. 'Am I not paying enough?'

Thea had seemed pleased with the rate they'd agreed, which was far more than minimum. 'No. It's just ... I wanted to buy some clothes.'

'Another hoodie?'

Thea shrank into the one she was wearing.

'Are you going to tell Dad?' she asked Jinx desperately.

Jinx could already imagine the disappointment on Glenn's face, and knew she couldn't bear it.

'I'm not,' Jinx said. 'I can think of a far better punishment.' She couldn't keep the smile from her lips.

'Don't go to the police,' Thea pleaded.

'I won't go to the police. But you are going to make it up to me ...'

Thea groaned as Jinx revealed the terrible cost of her silence.

'No way. You have got to be joking.'

'Not a bit am I joking,' said Jinx.

Glenn could not believe what he was hearing. Was Thea really telling him she wanted to go on the coach trip? He'd long since accepted that she would not be joining him on the Italian jaunt, just as she hadn't joined him the year before or the year before that. Instead, they'd made arrangements for her to stay with her Aunt Jess, whom she professed to find even more annoying than her dad. Glenn had been upset to think that Thea would rather stay with Jessie than go to Italy with him. But now she was telling him she'd changed her mind.

'Why?' Glenn asked.

'Because Mrs Sullivan wants to go and she needs someone to help her. And ... I don't know ... Because I've never been to Italy before and I want to see it?'

She didn't sound or look convinced. Her entire body was a shrug.

'Even on a coach trip? Even on a coach trip with a load of old duffers?'

'Yes. Mrs Sullivan says if there's still space on the coach, she's up for it, and she'll pay for me because I'm going to have to help her get dressed and all that.'

'And she's taking up the Colonel's offer? Of paying for her?'

'She says she is categorically *not* taking up the Colonel's offer.'

What Jinx had actually said was, 'My number one rule in life is never to put yourself in a position where someone else has power over you.'

'Like forcing you to go on a coach trip,' Thea had responded.

'Exactly.'

'Blimey. You and Jennifer Sullivan on my coach trip,' said Glenn. 'I am honoured.'

'Shut up, Dad. Don't make me change my mind.'

Glenn wasn't about to risk that. He called the coach company right away and was delighted to find there was room for two more passengers on the executive 34-seater. A little later, the lovely woman from Capstan Coaches confirmed that the hotels they'd be stopping at in France and Italy had space, too. Getting Thea and Mrs Sullivan on to the excursions would be no bother at all. When Glenn explained that Mrs Sullivan had a broken clavicle, the coach company said they would arrange for the hire of a foldable wheelchair, so Mrs Sullivan would not risk tripping on the cobbled streets of Tuscany. With everything in place, Glenn printed off another copy of the itinerary and instructed Thea to take it round to Jinx's house right away.

'Tell her the coach people are happy to take a cheque if she doesn't do internet banking.'

Of course she wouldn't do internet banking, was Glenn's guess.

'Thea, I can't tell you how much it means that you're coming away with me.'

'Don't get soppy, Dad.'

'Of course not.'

'You are getting soppy. Your eyes are doing that weird sparkly thing. If you cry about this, I am straight out of here. I'm not joking, Dad. Don't risk it. It's just a coach trip. It's no big deal.'

She had no idea just how big a deal it was.

When Thea left to take the itinerary to Jinx, Glenn went straight to the mantelpiece and pressed a kiss to a framed photograph of Thea's mother Lindsey, eternally suntanned and smiling as she raised a pina colada to the camera on a long-ago holiday. Glenn missed her every day. She was the love of his life. He was sure she must have helped bring about this turn of events somehow.

'Thank you, sweetheart,' he said. 'I'll make sure Thea has a good time.'

Glenn could have sworn that when he put the picture back in its place, Lindsey's smile seemed somehow brighter.

'We're going to Italy!' Glenn punched the air.

Chapter Twelve

The news that Jennifer Sullivan was going to join the coach trip soon went around the village. Nobody could believe it. Jinx couldn't believe it herself, but time was running out and she wanted to be in Italy more than ever. Especially since Ben Marwood's email.

It would be difficult, Jinx knew, doing everything she needed to do with just about every pensioner in Merevale in tow, but not impossible. She studied Glenn's itinerary to work out when she might be able to enact her plan. There were a great many stops on the tour and only two days and three nights in Florence itself, which were timetabled from dawn till dusk. Still, beggars could not be choosers. How many times had she heard that in her life?

The night before departure, Thea came over to help her pack.

'Dad says it's going to be really hot.'

Jinx had already checked the forecast. An average of twenty-five degrees for the days they were going to be away. Glenn's idea of hot weather differed greatly from her own. Mid-twenties was a cool day in Johore.

Thea carefully packed Jinx's case and left it open on the bed in the spare room so that Jinx could throw in anything she might have forgotten. Jinx knew exactly what was left to pack. She would not forget.

'Are you looking forward to this trip even a little bit?' Jinx asked.

Thea shrugged in response.

For a moment, Jinx wished she could tell the teenager how little she wanted to go on a coach holiday, too. Why, like Thea, she was compelled to take the journey. She wondered whether the aches and pains she had been feeling that day were the lingering effects of the fall or the signs she had been warned to watch out for. Drinking, though of course not recommended, seemed to take the edge off.

'If you could make me a Martini before you leave, I'd be most grateful,' Jinx said. 'Make one for yourself as well.'

'A – I don't know how to make a Martini. B – I'm only sixteen.'

'I was your age when I had my first one.'

Jinx remembered the way Penny had watched her, to see what she would make of the taste. Jinx had hated it, the first time – it tasted like petrol – but she licked her lips and said, 'Hmmm. Not bad.' She knew even then that she had to play the game.

Alone again, Jinx finished putting the last few things into her bag. Would she need reading material? The Colonel had dropped off a book that afternoon. He was still pretending to be put out that Jinx was refusing to let him pay her passage.

'Jennifer, I bear responsibility for your fractured collarbone,' he'd said. 'If you won't let me pay your fare, you will have to let me make it up to you in other ways.'

'Please, consider all debts discharged,' Jinx had assured him. A book, though, she could accept. The Colonel had insisted on that. As he handed over the Waterstones bag, she could tell he was excited to see her reaction.

'You remember those sister veterans in *The Times*? This is their memoir. Published yesterday.'

Jinx pinned a smile to her face as she looked into the bag.

Penny and Josephine Williamson had been all but unrecognisable in the photograph in the newspaper, but there was no mistaking the women on the cover of this book, which was called *Sisters at War*. With her FANY cap perched on top of her curls at a particularly jaunty angle, young Penny Williamson was unmistakable.

'You can bring it on the tour,' the Colonel suggested. 'It's an interesting read.'

Not half so interesting as it might have been had Penny told the truth about her war years, Jinx suspected. Not to mention what she did afterwards.

Though Jinx knew she had an early start, she could not resist cracking open the Williamson sisters' memoir that night. She guessed it was ghostwritten. There was not a semicolon to be found, and both Penny and Josephine had always been fond of a semicolon. As for the subject matter, a 'fine work of fiction' were the words that came to mind, as Jinx read Penny's account of her wartime service as a junior officer with the First Aid Nursing Yeomanry, 'providing administrative support at a commando training facility' before she trained in code and cipher and was sent overseas. Yet even that was closer to the truth than the penultimate chapter, which was a canter through Penny's post-war career.

Penny wrote, 'Tired of being so far from home with my work helping displaced people in Germany, I returned to England in 1948 to take up a position as an almoner with a charity called St Saviour's. I loved my work in Manchester, which brought me into contact with many lovely people from very different backgrounds to my own. Spending time with them in their cramped and often unsanitary homes, I was humbled by their unstinting generosity and kindness. Though they had next to nothing, they never failed to offer me a cup of tea or a sandwich, albeit served on broken crockery.'

Jinx bristled, remembering her mother's cracked teacups. Norma would be turning in her grave at the idea anyone thought their flat was 'unsanitary' when she worked so hard to keep it nice.

And after that? After Manchester? Jinx silently asked her long-ago friend. What did you do then, Penny?

'In 1951, I left the north of England for London, where I worked in the antiques business for a while before setting up a charity of my own, building schools and children's homes all over the Third World.'

No mention of how the money for these good works was raised, of course. Or of how much of it was spent on the charity and how much on 'administration'. Penny was in self-congratulatory mood.

'As I enter my twilight years, I continue to be deeply concerned with helping and inspiring the underprivileged to achieve their highest potential. It gives me great satisfaction to have been able to mould so many young lives over my century on this earth. I'm proud to have been able to make a difference.'

There was no doubt that Penny had made a difference to Jinx. Alone in her Cotswold bungalow, with no family and no real friends to call on, Jinx often wondered how her life might have looked had she never met her erstwhile mentor.

Snapping the book shut, Jinx took a last slug of her second Martini (she'd had Thea make two). Now she was more determined than ever that she had to get to Italy, if only to send one last postcard to Penny Williamson: war veteran, charity worker, national treasure. Liar to the back of her bright false teeth.

Chapter Thirteen

Thea was not wrong about the early start. The seven o'clock ETD on the coach tour itinerary had been brought forward by an hour. For the past few days the news had been dominated by dramatic footage of queues for the Chunnel snaking all the way back to the M25 thanks to striking border guards.

Glenn knocked on Jinx's front door at a quarter past five in the morning. Still frustratingly incapacitated, Jinx had no choice but to let Glenn zip her case shut and carry it out of the house. Jinx had at least managed to flip the lid over so that no one could see what she'd packed. Not that the most important things were in her case. The old German guidebook and the porcelain mouse were both nestled in her favourite brown handbag with the cross-body strap. Snatch-proof, it was, with that strap. Thanks to Penny, Jinx had always been alert to the risk of petty crime.

Thea was waiting at the top of the garden path, eyes on her phone as ever, though she did look up long enough to say, 'Morning, Mrs Sullivan' in a quiet voice.

'We need to be careful not to wake the neighbours who aren't joining us today,' Glenn explained in a stage whisper as he guided Jinx towards the village hall.

Everyone in the close was going on the trip apart from the

Arnolds at Number Seven. They were being taken on holiday to Mallorca by their son, Julian, 'the international lawyer', as they told anyone who cared to listen.

'This is going to be a real adventure,' Glenn said. 'I've never been to Italy before, though I've wanted to go there ever since I saw *Under the Tuscan Sun*. I saw that film on my first date with Thea's mother ...'

Glenn smiled at his daughter but she did not even look at him.

The other travellers were already at the village hall. A tattered paper banner proclaiming 'Team Merevale', which was brought out every year, hung from the front of the 34-seater executive coach. The driver, who introduced himself as Ivor, to much hilarity – 'Ivor the driver! We won't forget that!' – was loading luggage on board. Heavy negotiations were underway regarding where everyone would sit. It threatened to cause a mutiny before they even set off. Fortunately, Glenn had a plan.

'In the interests of fairness, I have made a seating chart for every day of the trip, so everyone gets a turn by a window and everyone gets a turn near the front.'

'It's the back seat I'm interested in,' said the Colonel, causing the four women vying to sit next to him to giggle like teenagers. The Colonel was dressed like an extra from *A Room with a View*, in a pale lemon linen suit and his grubby panama, though the weather in the Cotswolds that morning was cold and grey. No one would have been in the least bit surprised had it snowed. The jet stream had gone AWOL for the season, meaning Europe was toasty but the UK distinctly not. Pat Robinson was wearing a navy-blue anorak with a fur-lined hood, which she'd zipped up so it looked like a funnel.

Glenn consulted his diagram. 'Actually, Malcolm, I've got you at the front next to me today. Mrs Sullivan, I thought you should stay at the front for the whole trip, so you don't have to risk bumping down the aisle with your bad collarbone.'

Jinx predicted it would not be long before other passengers tried to pull rank. She might have been wearing a sling, but there were a great many blue badge holders on the passenger list, and who was to say that a fractured clavicle trumped an arthritic hip long overdue replacement or a knee that made a sound like a Labrador eating an ice cube?

'Just take the front seat,' Glenn whispered. 'It's my experience that people don't really want to change seats as much as you'd expect. Tomorrow morning, everyone will get on the bus and take the seat they choose today, I bet you. Oh, and I meant to say we've got you a wheelchair for the excursions.'

'A wheelchair? I don't need one of those.'

'I'm afraid you do. For our insurance.'

'Never get old,' Jinx told Thea.

'It's better than the alternative,' Thea replied.

Using Glenn's seating plan, the Colonel directed everyone to their seats, while Glenn beetled up and down the aisle helping people stow smaller items of luggage on the parcel shelves. Jinx would be next to Thea in the row behind the driver. Glenn and the Colonel were across the aisle from them. Behind Jinx and Thea sat Val and Cynthia, who had already come close to falling out that morning when they discovered they were wearing identical Marks and Spencer's sundresses underneath their raincoats.

'I didn't know you bought that dress. I thought you said green wasn't your colour,' Cynthia complained.

'Well, it isn't yours,' said Val.

'Actually,' Marilyn Butler announced in a loud aside to Pat, 'neither of them should be in that shade. Val's a summer and Cynth's a winter. They both need something with a bluer tone.'

When she wasn't singing or tidying up corpses, Marilyn was a 'colour consultant'.

Pat and Marilyn were seated together behind Glenn and the Colonel. Marilyn was travelling without her husband Evan because 'people won't stop dying just because we want a holiday'. Evan had been on the Highlands and Islands trip and was still fuming that Butlers had missed out on the funeral arrangements of a former local mayor because he and Marilyn were in Scotland when said dignitary popped his clogs.

As Marilyn took off her coat, Glenn struggled to get her vanity case onto the parcel shelf.

'Gosh, that's heavy,' he said.

'And he's surprised,' Val hissed to Cynth. 'Takes a lot of plaster to keep that façade together.'

Val, whose hearing aids needed adjusting, was not speaking as quietly as she thought. Marilyn, who did not need hearing aids, gave her a look that put Jinx in mind of a particularly malevolent dachshund she'd once known.

When at last everybody was seated and more or less happy with their lot, Glenn stood up at the front of the coach and, activating the tour guide's microphone, gave a short speech of welcome.

'Ladies and gentlemen—' he began.

'You can't say that any more,' said Cynthia in row two.

'Ladies and gentlemen,' Glenn persisted. 'Welcome to the fifth annual Team Merevale coach trip. I hope you're all as excited as I am about the next nine days.'

'You bet your life we are, Glenn!' The Colonel led a cheer.

'We've got a fantastic itinerary ahead of us. You should all find a printout in the seat pocket in front of you to refresh your memories. The printout also contains essential safety information regarding this coach, such as your nearest exits, which I'm pointing out to you now ...'

'Doors to manual!' the Colonel joked.

'Thank you for that, Malcolm, but no, I won't be coming through with a refreshments trolley ... As I was saying, the printout contains essential information including emergency numbers to call should you get separated from the party at any time. I suggest you tear off that part and keep it safe in your handbag or wallet ...'

Glenn's speech continued for what felt like another ten minutes, but was probably only one. 'Thank you for your attention, everyone.'

Then he looked to Thea, as if for reassurance, and Jinx could see from the expression on his face that he was disappointed, if not surprised, to see that Thea's attention had long since drifted back to her phone.

At six o'clock exactly, Ivor the driver gunned the engine – waking the Arnolds at Number Seven. Mrs Arnold snapped her bedroom curtains open furiously. The coach party cheered again.

'Shall we start with a sing-song?' somebody suggested as they hit the ring road. 'Marilyn?'

'It's very early,' Marilyn protested.

'Oh, go on!' someone said.

'If you insist ... la la laaaaaa ...' Marilyn piped up in her thin soprano warble.

Jinx tapped Thea on her knee and asked her, 'Those headphones of yours. Do they cut out *all* the noise?'

Jinx would never have chosen to be sitting on a coach listening to Marilyn Butler singing 'The White Cliffs' at six o'clock in the morning, but she was going to Italy and that was all that mattered.

Chapter Fourteen

Penny, Italy, 1944

After six weeks in the Special Operations Executive facility
known as 'the cooler' at Inverlair, failed F Section agent Penny
Williamson was ready to get back to the action. There was no
hope whatsoever that she would be going behind enemy lines in
France now, but the mysterious 'powers that be' had arranged
for her to slip back into her former FANY role. Furthermore,
thanks to some behind-the-scenes manoeuvring, she was at the
front of the queue for an assignment overseas, should she want
one. Of course she wanted one! Having spent the 'summer' in
Scotland, Penny was ready for some proper sunshine, so she
was pleased that, ahead of deployment to a 'top secret' location,
she was issued with a lightweight uniform.

'Not Norway, then,' she observed as she took possession of
her new khakis and smart brown shoes.

'I can't tell you,' said the officer handing over the clothes.

'Be like Dad, keep mum, eh?'

It was Penny's least favourite slogan from the Ministry of
Information's jolly posters. Four years into the war, there were
plenty of women keeping official secrets very well indeed.

It was testament to Penny's own ability to keep a secret that Cecily Williamson still thought her younger daughter had been working in the officers' mess at a commando school, pouring drinks and flirting. She had no idea that Penny had spent the spring of that year training with the Special Operations Executive in surveillance, sabotage and spycraft.

But because she was still under twenty-one, Penny had officially to seek permission from her parents to be posted overseas. It was faintly ridiculous, given where she might have been had things gone according to plan and she'd managed to jump out of that blasted plane into France, but those were the rules. Penny's father was away with his regiment, so Cecily had agonised over the papers alone.

'Overseas? I'm not happy with the idea of you being on a ship full of young men,' Cecily told her. 'What if one of them tries to take advantage?'

'I know a couple of good moves for that,' Penny thought.

Cecily gave her consent, of course – she couldn't stand the sight of her younger daughter sulking – and two weeks later, Penny was on her way.

The voyage from Liverpool was a bore. Penny and her fellow FANYs were all given officer status so they could use the upper decks of the ship, rather than mix with the low-ranking servicemen below (the senior FANY officers were as worried for the girls' virtue as their mothers had been) but the ship was dry – even the officers' mess – and the tuck shop ran out of sweets long before they reached their destination.

The endless sea days were dull. There were entertainers from ENSA, the Entertainments National Service Association, on board, but they more than lived up to their nickname – *Every Night Something Awful*. Penny thought that if she had to hear 'We'll Meet Again' one more time, she might pitch the company's bright-eyed Vera Lynn wannabe over the guard rail next time they met on the deck.

Much had changed since the beginning of the war. When Chamberlain first made the declaration in September 1939, Penny was still at boarding school and it had all seemed very exciting. She couldn't wait to 'do her bit'. The moment she was old enough, she'd joined the First Aid Nursing Yeomanry and was chosen to be trained in code and cipher. It was very much more interesting than the post-school career she'd expected to have, when secretarial college, *cordon bleu* school or an early marriage were the choices. Then things took an even more exciting turn.

Having been spotted dispatching an amorous army man with W.E. Fairbairn's 'Defence Against Wandering Hands' during a performance of *Blithe Spirit*, Penny was called to meet the shadowy recruitment team of the SOE, who offered her the chance to become an agent – 'not a spy, Miss Williamson' – embedded with the French Resistance.

It felt like destiny. Penny excelled in training. She was best in her cohort at coding, she took naturally to the art of disguise, and her ability to turn a house over without leaving a speck of evidence was exemplary. She particularly enjoyed the SOE's training module on housebreaking, which might come in handy should she ever need to steal something from an enemy stronghold.

As well as the 'soft arts', Penny was also surprisingly good at unarmed combat for one so small, easily despatching male trainees twice her size with a judiciously placed elbow. It was all going so well ... But Penny had failed at the final hurdle. When it came to jumping with a parachute from the Halifax bomber taking her to France, she'd found herself paralysed with fear. She simply could not be persuaded to leave the plane and, instead of being deployed, had to be taken back to the air station where she and her fellow F Section agents had been given a heroes' send-off less than three hours earlier.

It was a disaster. There were endless debriefings, but while everyone agreed that Penny Williamson might still be a valuable asset in the field, no amount of pleading would persuade her superiors that she should be allowed to go into France by less dramatic means than a parachute drop – by boat, say, or in a smaller plane that would actually land. Instead, that moment of hesitation in the belly of the Halifax cost her the chance to be the heroine she was sure she might have been.

Penny could not help but feel she'd let everybody down. Not least Frank, her trainer in unarmed combat. She was especially embarrassed to have failed him. Her secret lover Frank had always believed in her. She was certain that he must have fought for her to be allowed on another mission when the SOE panel was deciding her fate.

Penny was furious when she was booted back into the FANY rank and file, but at Inverlair, she'd had time to cool down and re-examine her motivations for wanting to go to France in the first place. From imagining the war as a Hollywood picture in which she was the star, Penny now saw it the way most people did. She only wanted it to be over before any more people she loved – especially her little brother George – were asked to risk their lives. If by serving as an ordinary code and cipher officer Penny could still do something to speed the Allies to victory, she would be happy enough with that.

At last Penny's convoy reached Algiers. A small number of FANY officers had already been posted there, working to support the brave men and women embedded with the partisans all over southern Europe.

Penny liked Algiers. It was unlike any place she had ever been before. After three years of rationing in Britain, the markets overflowing with food and clothes, and noisy with people and livestock, seemed almost unreal. Even the sandstorms felt romantic. Penny would have been happy to stay there, but in July 1943 the Allies retook Sicily and soon after that mainland Italy began to fall back into Allied hands, inch by painful inch.

'You're going to Italy,' Penny's senior officer told her in early 1944. It made more sense for the coders working with the Yugoslav partisans – such as Penny was – to be on the Adriatic coast, closer to the action. Penny didn't argue.

If she had liked Algiers, Penny fell in *love* with Italy. It was *amore a prima vista*. From the moment the troop plane touched down in Bari, she was enchanted. Oh, the beauty of the landscape! The smell of jasmine on the warm air! She had smelled jasmine before, of course – in the garden at home – but somehow it was different here. Headier, warmer, lovelier. And the broom, too. Broom was a very plain name for such a wonderful plant.

Genista, the Italians called it. That was better.

Penny had never been taught Italian – not formally – but she'd sat through many Latin lessons at school and that gave her a head start. The SOE had not been wrong about her facility for languages. She was soon translating Italian to English for Allied officers who'd been in the country for months, yet picked up no more than '*si*' or '*grazie*'.

Though the local Italians had very little after the German occupation, they were generous with what they had, and when they had nothing to share, they still had a way about them that made you feel as though you had been given a great gift in a smile. How different they were from the people back home, Penny thought. Rationing had brought out the mean side of so many.

Perhaps if they had grapes and olives growing in their gardens,

91

they might feel differently, Penny's sister Josephine pointed out.

Penny wrote to Josephine almost every day – long letters about the landscape and the music and the wine.

And figs straight from the tree.

Lucky old you, Josephine wrote back from her dingy digs in Plymouth. *What I wouldn't give for a fig. The food in the Wrens is marginally worse than at school.*

How is that possible? Penny responded. *The food at St Mary's was the worst in the world.*

They never wrote about their actual work. That wouldn't get past the censors. What a strange job that must be – reading about the lives of strangers and deciding whether their private letters were anodyne enough to be passed on. Penny wondered if the censors ever discreetly lost correspondence that might cause the intended recipient too much pain at a time when morale was especially important.

Love you, sis, Penny finished every letter. *Keep your chin up. Toujours gai.*

Chapter Fifteen

The Coach Trip, 2023

Team Merevale reached the Channel Tunnel at around nine o'clock on the morning of their departure. The queues were not as bad as expected, leaving just enough time for everyone to make a dash for the loo before the coach was loaded onto the train.

'Do not dawdle in the gift shop!' was Glenn's final instruction as the majority of his passengers disappeared into the terminal. Only Thea and Jinx remained on board.

'I'll get you two some breakfast,' Glenn suggested. 'What would you like?'

'Anything,' Jinx and Thea answered, simultaneously and with similar disinterest.

Unfortunately for Jinx, 'anything' ended up being a 'Breakfast King' bun from the Chunnel terminal's Burger King concession, which meant that Jinx got to cross off a second thing from her very short list of 'things I will never do', the first having been 'go on a coach trip'. She had sworn she would never eat anything from a fast-food restaurant, yet there she was, unwrapping a brioche bun, still slightly chilled in the centre and oozing with radioactive-looking ketchup.

Half an hour later, everyone was back on board and Glenn was walking up and down the aisle making sure they all had their passports ready and open at the photograph page for border control. He could only hope everyone had taken seriously his reminder – sent two months earlier – that they needed to be sure their passports had enough time left on them to be EU-compliant. Too late now if they hadn't.

'Oh, Glenn!' Marilyn twittered. 'I can't let you look at my passport. It's got my date of birth.'

'She's fifty-two,' said Val. 'Plus VAT.'

Jinx hoped Glenn wouldn't look too closely at her own passport, which would disprove her story that she'd not had a valid passport when the trip was first announced. Luckily, when he got to the front of the coach, Glenn said, 'I know yours will be valid, Mrs Sullivan, since you've only recently got a new one.'

Jinx held her breath while the border guard examined her passport. She didn't know why. There was no reason for her to be nervous. All the same, when the guard looked from her photograph to her face and back again more than once, she couldn't help but think back to the first time she had travelled on a passport under an alias.

'It will be fine,' Penny had assured her then. 'You have such a pretty face, Jinx. If the guard looks at your documents for more than a minute, it's only because he's fallen in love.'

Jinx very much doubted that the border guard had any such thoughts on this occasion. He stamped one of the middle pages. Why did they always do that? Stamp the middle pages, instead of working from the front in an orderly fashion?

'Enjoy your holiday, madame,' he said. 'And you, mademoiselle,' he added to Thea.

'With this lot?' Thea muttered to herself as she glanced back into the bus.

*

Then they were off again. The coach was loaded onto the train that would whisk them to 'the Continent'. Most of the passengers were excited and impressed by the sleekness of the operation, but Cynthia was worried at the prospect of going under the Channel. Marilyn suggested a singalong to take Cynthia's mind off the trial ahead.

'Let's all sing "I Whistle a Happy Tune" from *The King and I*. Someone once said I looked like Deborah Kerr. My family does hail from Scotland.'

'So does Wee Jimmy Krankie,' Val heckled from behind Thea and Jinx.

'I'll start,' said Marilyn, ignoring the insult. 'And you can all join in whenever you like. We all know the words, I'm sure. *Hmmmmmm. La la la la la la laaaa*.' She sang a few random notes as a warm-up.

'It's no good,' said Cynthia. 'Ever since I watched *The Poseidon Adventure*, my biggest fear has been death by drowning.'

'You've made it my biggest fear now,' said Pat. 'I wasn't even thinking about it before. We're going under the sea in a train carriage! What happens if there's a leak?'

'What's *The Poseidon Adventure*?' Thea asked.

'It was a film they showed every other Christmas when I was a child,' Marilyn explained. 'It's about trying to escape a sinking cruise ship.'

'Festive,' said Thea.

'My biggest fear has always been finding myself stuck in a coach, in a tube, below the ocean, full of pensioners singing songs from *The King and I* ...' Jinx thought. Thea, wisely, had put her headphones back on.

The sun on the other side of the Chunnel seemed much brighter than it had been in Dover, though perhaps that was only the effect of having been in the gloom for half an hour. Now that they were on French soil, the Colonel immediately began speaking in an extravagant Franglais accent, straight out of *'Allo 'Allo* – 'A television series that wouldn't get made today,' Cynthia explained to Thea – adding in the obligatory *'he-hon, he-hon'* at the end of every sentence. Jinx wondered how a French pensioner would impersonate them. *Les Rosbifs.*

There was to be no stopping in Calais, since Ivor the driver was on a tachograph and there were still many miles to go before the first hotel. But Pat was worried about toilet breaks. She wasn't the only one.

'We'll be stopping every hour or so,' Glenn assured her. 'And don't forget there's a WC at the back.'

That wasn't comforting to anybody. No one wanted to have to use the loo on the coach. Everyone who had been on the Highlands and Islands tour was still scarred by the memory of having to detour via Raigmore Hospital in Inverness after Eileen Griffiths was injured when the coach had to make an emergency stop for a deer while she was having a wee. She didn't break any bones in the incident, but she was wedged into that chemical toilet for more than an hour. She had a stroke a couple of months later. Val and Cynthia were certain the timing was not unrelated. 'Stress can bring these things on,' said Val.

Even the thought of a rest break in just over an hour was no comfort to Pat, who'd heard that French motorway rest stops didn't have proper toilets. 'Just a hole in the ground.'

'When did you last go to France, Pat?' Glenn asked.

'They have proper toilets,' Ivor the driver assured her.

Still Pat worried all the way to Reims where, much to her relief, the toilets were distinctly British in style.

'And they had toilet paper.' Not that that would have been a problem, since Pat was carrying three rolls of her own in her capacious tote bag, along with four sets of disposable cutlery, two packs of Rennies and a large pack of flushable moist wipes. Pat, who had spent two decades leading Merevale's Brownie pack, knew the value of being prepared.

With four 'comfort breaks' en route, Team Merevale arrived at the first hotel on the Tuscan Splendour tour just before tea-time. It was not going to trouble many of the establishments in the Michelin guide, but everyone was glad to get there after what felt like a very long day on the road. As they piled off the coach, Glenn proposed that everyone find their room, settle in, then reconvene in the hotel garden for a welcome drink.

'Chablis o'clock,' said the Colonel. 'Splendid idea.'

Only Jinx and Thea didn't join them. Thea helped Jinx to her room, then gratefully skipped off to commune with her phone while she had access to free wi-fi – her father had refused to move her on to a package that would allow her to use local 4G.

Jinx realised she was more tired than she'd thought when she lay down on her bed for what was supposed to be just a short nap before dinner. The bed was hard, with scratchy sheets, and the pillow was too thin, but she had slept in far, far worse. And she'd made it to France, when so recently she'd thought she might never leave England again. She would make it to Italy, too, she felt sure now. She would be able to carry out her plan.

Before she closed her eyes, Jinx turned her head to look at the porcelain mouse, which she had retrieved from her handbag and put on the bedside table. His tiny black eyes seemed to sparkle at her.

'Not long to go now, Mousey,' she said.

Chapter Sixteen

Changi Prison, Singapore, 1943

'By next month it will all be over ...'

At first, that was a familiar refrain about camp but, as the weeks turned to months turned to years, a sense of optimism was increasingly hard to come by. All but the most delusional internees had long since stopped pretending it was a matter of days before the Allies stormed the island and they all went home.

Perhaps it was easier for the children. Eddy was so young when they went into the prison that Jinx doubted he could remember anything else. To him, Changi was the world. He'd never enjoyed the freedom of walking in the jungle with their father, listening to the calls of the birds that Maurice knew as well as the voices of his children.

'What does a jynx sound like?' Jinx would ask, and Maurice would impersonate the rising peeps of a wryneck's song.

'But my favourite Jinx sounds like you,' he would tell her then. 'Let's sing a song, my little songbird. Anything you like except "Run, Rabbit, Run".'

Which, of course, would be Jinx's cue to launch straight into the song Maurice hated, while he chased her around the garden, growling like an ogre and making her giggle so much she could hardly breathe.

Maurice Spencer had a wonderful voice – a smooth baritone like his hero Bing Crosby. Jinx loved it when Maurice sang 'May I?', the Crosby tune that was the soundtrack to her parents' first dance.

'When we were courting,' Norma would say.

'We're still courting,' Maurice would always reply, before taking Norma into his arms and sweeping her into a back bend, to Jinx's wide-eyed delight. Maurice and Norma were every bit as in love as they had been when they first met. When Norma was in her husband's arms, the years fell away and she was a giddy young thing again, waiting at the edge of the dance floor for someone just like him.

Maurice would dance with Jinx, too. She would take off her wooden-soled sandals – her *terompah* – and stand on the tops of his big feet as he waltzed her round the room to the sound of more Crosby on the gramophone.

'*You must have been a beautiful baby ...*'

That was their song.

But by the early autumn of 1943, it had been a very long time since they'd heard anything from Maurice. The first Christmas after the surrender, the Japanese guards had allowed the male internees to send gifts to their loved ones on the women's side of the prison and Maurice had sent a melon, that probably cost him his pocket watch (many of the prisoners were swapping jewellery for food by then). There was a letter, too, written in blunt pencil on the back of an old receipt. It didn't say much – '*Hello my dears, I miss you terribly. Food's awful. Company's worse*' – but they read it over and over. There had been nothing since. No gifts. No news. Maurice was never among the male prisoners who brought the food over from the kitchens on their side of the jail.

Norma remained stoical. If Jinx's lip ever wobbled, Norma would only have to ask, 'What would your father say?'

'We do not cry.'

There was just one afternoon, when Norma lay down on the piece of bug-ridden sacking that constituted her bed and covered her eyes with her arms, and Jinx thought her mother might be weeping. That afternoon Mrs Mulvany asked Jinx to help her tidy the 'silence hut' – the specially built shack where the adult women could escape the chaos of the prison for an hour or two. Jinx was excited. The children weren't normally allowed in there. Meanwhile, Eddy was whisked away by beautiful young Mrs Ennis, who said she would look after him until bedtime.

'What's wrong with Mummy?' Jinx asked Mrs Mulvany.

'Same as what's wrong with all of us. Sometimes life in this place gets a bit much. She'll be all right again soon enough.'

Jinx had already sensed that it was important that she not lean too heavily on her mother, but keep her own worries pressed down inside. She remembered her father's words to her on the *padang*: 'Look after your mother.' She was protective of Eddy, too, making sure the other kids knew that if they picked on her little brother, they would have her to answer to.

Jinx had her own small circle of friends – girls she might not have met on the outside. Olga was one of her favourites. They'd had the same sort of upbringing. Neither of their fathers was in Singapore on 'Empire business'. Olga wasn't stuck-up and she could speak Malay. Many of the kids could, unlike their expat mothers, who had never bothered to learn. It was fun to have a secret language, in which they could talk privately about the adults as they went about their work in the camp's vegetable garden.

*

100

Jinx would always sing as she worked the vegetable patch alongside the wall that divided the men from the women, hoping that her father could hear her. Once, when she was singing 'You Must Have Been a Beautiful Baby', a couple of male voices joined in from the other side of the wire, but she didn't think either one of them was Maurice, and they were soon silenced by a guard.

You didn't ever argue with a guard, any guard, but some of them were worse than the others. The women gave them nicknames. There was *Blue Stocking*. He got that name because, bizarrely, he wore a blue bird's feather tucked into the top of his sock. *Balsam*, his sidekick, was the very opposite of calming, and would walk around the prison whacking his stick against everything and anything: walls, bars, any poor internee who happened to get in his way. *Artichoke* was so-called because of the shape of his ears.

The children had their own names for some of the guards, too. *Goofy* was one of the younger officers at Changi. He earned his nickname because of the particular way the flaps on the sides of his cap hung down around his long face, giving him the look of the floppy-eared dog in the Disney films the children knew from before the occupation. But Goofy was not as stupid as he looked, as the children quickly learned. They could not get anything past him. And as the war went on longer, the guards got meaner.

Jinx kept her head down. She did not cry.

Chapter Seventeen

The Coach Trip, 2023

Having risen at sparrow's fart to join the coach at the village hall, Glenn's merry band of travellers had an early night in northern France, turning in after just a couple of glasses of the local plonk (or a bottle, in the case of the Colonel). They had another early start on their first morning on 'the Continent', in order to be in Italy that night.

As per previous coach trips, breakfast was a flashpoint. The early birds went through the hotel buffet like the proverbial plague of locusts. When Cynthia, Val and Pat got to the hot selection, they found there was nothing left but a couple of dubious-looking button mushrooms and half a ladleful of scrambled egg.

Evil looks were cast in the direction of those coach party passengers – especially the perpetually behatted Colonel – who had loaded their plates with more than their fair share. The Colonel had three sausages.

'More sausages are coming.' The restaurant manager did his best to avert a riot.

'None of us is going to suffer if we miss out on a couple of bangers,' Pat suggested.

'Speak for yourself!' said Val, who had been on the 5:2 diet since the day the Tuscan trip was first announced. That day was one of her unlimited calorie days, and woe betide anyone who got between her and a cooked breakfast.

Cynthia agreed it was imperative that Val get her sausages. 'You know what she gets like on a fast day. Don't want her to get so upset she knocks the Colonel's hat off!'

Rumour was that the Colonel had had a hair transplant. Jinx had once heard Val and Cynth gossiping about it.

'He went to Antalya,' said Val. 'Same place he had his teeth done.'

The Colonel's teeth were already the talk of the village. They were perfectly even and *Love Island* white. Apparently they'd cost twenty grand.

'He spent the rest of his savings on a hair transplant. In Turkey, where I've heard they use horsehair, not human.'

'Ah well,' said Cynthia. 'He can enter the Grand National and win his money back.'

'It can't have taken properly,' said Val. 'That's why he's always wearing that hat.'

It was true what they said about village life, Jinx often thought. The gossip was horrendous, far worse than in the city where people had less room, and maintaining one's psychological space was a matter of survival. In London, where she had lived for many years, Jinx had barely known her neighbours and that suited her just fine. In the Cotswolds, she had done her best not to get to know her neighbours, but she'd soon come to realise that they would talk about her anyway. And what they didn't know, they would make up. Like the Colonel's hair transplant. 'One hundred per cent Shetland pony.'

As it was, Jinx missed out on most of the buffet excitement, having decided she would not go down for breakfast. While this was not the sort of hotel that provided room service, the manager had made an exception for Jinx, agreeing that he would bring coffee and rolls to her room to save her from having to negotiate the buffet with her arm in a sling.

By the time Thea knocked at eight, Jinx had already managed to dress herself in another wide-sleeved kaftan, but she needed Thea to help fasten her sling over the top. Thea did so without a fuss, with the air of someone for whom it was no big deal.

'Did you sleep well?' Jinx asked.

Thea answered with a shrug.

'On to Italy today,' Jinx pressed on. 'Are you excited?'

'A whole day on a coach,' Thea responded. 'Wonderful.'

'Well, it's a means to an end,' said Jinx.

She found herself tempted to say, *'Toujours gai!'*

At half past eight, Team Merevale mustered in the car park. Glenn had his clipboard out and was trying in vain to count people onto the coach.

'Best wait until they're all on and count them then,' was the Colonel's advice. 'Like herding fish, this lot. No discipline.' Discipline was very important to the Colonel.

'Everybody, please get on board.' Glenn raised his voice just a little.

'Come on, Glenn. No one's listening. You've got to show you mean business. Would you like me to call them to order?'

Glenn didn't have time to reply before the Colonel boomed in a voice trained for the battlefield, 'Aten-shun!'

'Who put him in charge?' asked Val.

'Come on, you horrible lot. Everybody on board. Now!'

Even with the Colonel deploying his best military tactics, it took a while to get everyone loaded. There was panic when Glenn asked his passengers to 'please check you've got all

104

your medication with you *before* we set off'. He did not want a repeat of the situation on the Jane Austen's England tour of 2021, when they had to make a four-hour detour to fetch Cynthia's heart meds. A half day's drive was less onerous than trying to get through to her GP surgery to ask if they could send a prescription to a pharmacy near their next stop, but it did mean that everyone had to miss out on the scheduled visit to the Clarks Village outlet shopping centre. Val still hadn't forgiven Cynthia for that.

After the Colonel reiterated Glenn's instructions, 'Check your medications now!', thirty handbags and bum-bags were duly checked for supplies. No one had forgotten anything, though Pat was anxious that she might not have packed enough Gaviscon for the whole trip. She had double-dosed the previous night.

'You'd think you'd be safe from spices in France,' she'd complained after dinner, having finished a large portion of boeuf bourguignon and wiped the bowl clean with half a baguette.

Then, when Glenn thought that he could safely ask the driver to close the doors and start the engine (the engine was in fact already running, for the air con), Val announced that she needed a pre-emptive widdle. And when she came back, Cynthia felt inspired to do the same. 'Just in case.' As did Pat. So that Glenn felt forced to make another announcement: 'Ivor informs me we're going to be driving for two hours before the first rest stop today, therefore I ask you, please, to ensure you are well prepared.'

'Remember the five Ps,' echoed the Colonel in his battlefield voice. *'Proper Planning Prevents Piss-Poor Performance.* If you'll pardon my French,' he added for the benefit of the more easily shocked.

'That's six Ps,' Marilyn pointed out.

'Are we ready yet?' Ivor the driver asked.

The Colonel stepped in once again. 'Team Merevale, it is almost nine o'clock Central European Time. Any further delay could jeopardise our endeavour to be in *Toscana* before sunset. Buckle up!'

Jinx sent Glenn a small smile. She could tell he wasn't entirely happy to have been usurped so early in the tour. Glenn cleared his throat.

'That's right. As Malcolm says, we really do need to get going. Seat belts on.'

Luckily, they had only gone half a mile before the Colonel realised he had left his own 'days of the week' medication box in the hotel's breakfast room.

Glenn had spent many hours preparing for this coach trip. He'd studied the route with the attention of a London cabbie preparing to take 'the Knowledge', back in the day when you couldn't just type an address into your phone. He'd bought a huge paper map of Europe from a local camping shop and spread it out across his kitchen table, turning the room into a control centre, plotting the coach's predicted daily progress with red string and marking points of interest with chess pieces and old Connect Four tokens.

For each point of interest, Glenn had prepared a little speech to be delivered as they drew near. An hour out of the car park, he drew the passengers' attention to his first POI for the day, which was a church tower on the right.

'Coming up on the starboard side is the medieval church of St Jean ...'

It was a very interesting little speech, all the passengers agreed. Unfortunately, the fascinating medieval tower of St Jean was no longer visible from the road, having been obscured by a gigantic electronics warehouse.

'Never mind, Glenn. I'm sure we'll be able to see some of the things you're going to talk about,' the Colonel reassured him.

As promised, two hours into the trip, Team Merevale reached the first rest stop, where everyone planned to buy supplies to supplement the skimpy-looking sandwiches the hotel had prepared for their packed lunch. No one had ever seen Val move so quickly as she did once the coach was parked up. Her new knee was working out.

Glenn had shaved five minutes off the planned rest time, fully expecting that Team Merevale would lose at least one of its members in the surprisingly well-appointed gift shop-cum-*supermarché*.

Val was back first, laden with a baguette and pots containing various sandwich fillings, which she asked Glenn to translate. Glenn was lost at *'jambon'*. He had to ask Thea to take over. She turned the pots over in her hand.

'This one is duck,' Thea said.

'Duck!' Val exclaimed. 'I didn't want that.'

'And this one is snail.'

'That's disgusting. They ought to put a picture on the lid.'

Jinx turned her face towards the window so that she didn't laugh. She knew, as Thea did, that the pot of 'snail' in fact contained rillettes of mackerel.

'I can't eat this,' Val complained.

'Are snails suitable for vegans?' Pat asked Cynthia.

'Snails definitely have a nervous system,' Thea interrupted. 'And so do mackerel. It's fish in that pot, Val. I was joking.'

'I don't think it's very funny,' said Val. 'We didn't all have the advantage of an education in the languages.'

'No, but you did have the advantage of forty-odd years as an actual European,' Thea said under her breath.

There was a blast of feedback as Glenn turned his microphone back on.

'Is everybody on the bus?' he asked. 'I'm going to do the head count. Please sit down and stay sitting down until I've finished.'

He started from the front, where the Colonel was wielding a baguette as he recreated an incident from his youth that had the women around him rapt.

'The bugger didn't know what hit him ...'

'You knocked him out with some bread?' Marilyn was confused.

'Not bread, Marilyn. I used an umbrella. The bread is only a metaphor.'

'It's not a metaphor for anything,' Thea muttered.

'So you didn't kill anyone with a French stick,' Marilyn qualified.

'Of course not.'

'I was going to say. Even sourdough's not that hard.'

By now Glenn had counted all the way to the back of the coach, but Cynthia was on her feet again.

'I left my sunglasses in the shop!' she cried.

And with that, she clambered down into the car park.

Glenn climbed down after her.

'Cynthia, hold on. Wait! They're on top of your head. I can see them!'

'Is it going to be like this all the way to Italy?' Thea wondered aloud.

'Almost certainly,' said Jinx.

Despite a further number of unplanned pit stops, they did make it to Italy that day. By the time they got to their hotel just outside Viareggio, everyone was ready for a drink. They were also ready for a bit of personal space. Cynthia and Val were barely talking. Their rapid-cycling love–hate relationship was in a hate phase, thanks to a disagreement about Low Traffic Neighbourhoods.

Marilyn, who had tried to keep spirits high with a non-stop singalong, was complaining of a sore throat.

The Colonel remained chipper. 'I think we all deserve an Aperol spritz,' he said. 'Especially our driver.'

But Ivor the driver declined to join his passengers for an *aperitivo*. He'd need danger money for that.

Glenn was worried that relationships on the bus were already starting to fracture. Pat tried to reassure him. 'We always knew that the first two days were going to be the hardest. We're in Italy now, Glenn. We've got five lovely days ahead of us.'

'Five days of Aperol spritzes and sunshine. Last person to the bar buys first round,' said the Colonel, as he disappeared into the hotel.

'Not fair,' Cynthia shouted after him. 'I've been waiting for a new hip since before the pandemic!'

Jinx was the last off the coach. Risking a big bar bill, Glenn waited to help her down. Thea already stood on the tarmac, with her own bag and Jinx's, facing the hotel.

'What a dump,' Thea said.

Glenn didn't hear it. Or at least he pretended not to. 'This place looks all right, doesn't it?' he said to Jinx instead.

Jinx agreed, though she could see Thea's point. The hotel was far from a Tuscan treasure. It was a low-rise building of the kind you see on the outskirts of towns all over the world. The photograph provided by the coach company had been misleading, showing only a heavily cropped view of the hotel's faux Palladian entrance, which was flanked by two potted bay trees. Though it was called 'The Palazzo', this place had more in common with a motorway service station than a Florentine palace. And it was to be home for the next three nights.

Jinx could tell Glenn was nervous that his fellow travellers would think he had messed up with the booking, so she told him, 'It's the perfect spot for seeing the sights.'

Thea's body language expressed her view.

They had to rush straight to dinner that evening, because the hotel kitchen was closing. In the dining room, Jinx found herself sitting next to Marilyn, who was wearing a chiffon scarf around her throat.

'Are you enjoying yourself, Mrs Sullivan?' Marilyn raised her voice and leaned in, perhaps thinking that Jinx, like many of the people on the trip, was hard of hearing. Jinx was not that hard of hearing thanks to her tiny modern hearing aids. She wished she'd taken them out before Marilyn started speaking at her.

'I'm a bit hoarse,' Marilyn said, indicating her scarf. 'Singing and air conditioning don't mix. I need to save my voice, so I shan't be singing tonight. Unless ...' She gave Jinx a conspiratorial smile. 'Unless I get any special requests.'

'Oh no,' said Jinx. 'Even if you do get a request, you must not give in. Don't let anyone persuade you not to give your vocal cords the rest they deserve. I knew a soprano once,' Jinx lied. 'Gave in to the clamour of her fans always wanting to hear "just one more", and ended up not able to sing a note.'

'I wouldn't want that.'

'Exactly. So how is the funeral business these days?' Jinx changed the subject.

'We did Mr Jones last week, as you probably heard. That was a lovely do.'

Marilyn explained that Mr Jones' wicker eco-coffin (three thousand pounds with a locals' discount) had been lined in ecru satin. 'His daughter is a colour consultant, as am I, so she was quite particular about it. And she was absolutely right.

It makes an amazing difference to the complexion, the colours you wear. Autumns should never be buried in white.'

Having made sure everyone was happy, Glenn sat down next to Jinx in the seat that Thea had vacated for 'just a minute' a full half an hour before. Jinx could tell Glenn was not yet in the holiday spirit. His wide smile was let down by the strain around his eyes.

'Do you think everyone's having a good time so far?' he asked Jinx, with such an air of desperation that what could she say other than, 'Absolutely'?

'And you, Mrs Sullivan?'

'I am.'

'And Thea? Do you think she's happy? I couldn't believe it when she said she wanted to come on the trip. I hope she's not regretting it.' As he said that, Glenn's eyes drifted towards the door, where Thea had reappeared, head still bowed towards her phone – there but not there, as usual.

'Well, perhaps she only came along to help me, but I'm sure she'll fall in love with Italy before the week is out,' Jinx said.

Team Merevale was already beginning to disperse in the direction of the hotel bar.

'We need Marilyn,' said the Colonel, coming to fetch her. 'There's a piano.'

'I can't sing tonight, Malcolm. I've been singing all day.'

'How can we go to bed if you don't sing us off to sleep?'

Marilyn purred. 'Just the one, then.'

'"Lili Marlene"?' the Colonel suggested.

'In which language?' Marilyn asked. She could sing it in English, Italian and German.

Italian would have been the obvious choice, but Cynthia jumped in with a request for German.

'*Vor der Kaserne ... vor dem großen Tor ...*' Marilyn sang.

She mangled the accent. Cynthia did likewise as she sang along. Cynthia enjoyed an excuse to show off her German language skills. Her grandfather was Prussian. 'Came over with the Kaiser, but he was on the right side in both wars!'

'Oh Lili Marlene'. Jinx had often wondered what the young people of today would listen to when they were consigned to their care homes? Would they still be listening to grime in their eighties? Singing along to Stormzy while their carers mouthed 'Ah, bless' to each other above their banging grey heads?

While Marilyn sang, Thea helped Jinx to her room. The young girl was monosyllabic. She'd obviously decided that she was not going to pretend she was enjoying herself. Indeed, when Jinx tried to make conversation about the days ahead, Thea said, 'I should have let you tell Dad about the money. I can't believe I've got a week of this.'

'I suppose you made your choice that day in Merevale,' Jinx said. 'Try to pretend to be happy for your father's sake. He's put a lot of effort into this trip.'

'I didn't ask him to. I don't know why he does it. He gets himself into a complete state every year setting up a trip so that Val and Cynth can spend a week complaining about the hotels, the food, each other ...'

'So we ought to make up for their rudeness,' Jinx suggested. 'Look like we're having fun?'

'This is a terrible hotel,' Thea said to herself. 'It's like a prison.'

It's nothing like any prison I know, thought Jinx.

Though the windows were shut and the air conditioning was on, an hour later Jinx could still hear plenty of noise drifting up from the hotel bar, whose doors opened onto the garden beneath. When Marilyn, whose voice had obviously fully recovered, trilled the first few bars of 'Somewhere Over the

112

Rainbow', Jinx hunted about for the television remote control in the hope of finding something to watch that would distract her.

There were few stations in English, but one Jinx did find was a history channel. Of all the cheery subjects, it was broadcasting a documentary about the design and development of the atomic bomb.

'The bomb was an invention that would alter the course of the Second World War and, ultimately, the course of history . . .' said the American narrator in portentous tones.

Jinx didn't need to be told about that.

Chapter Eighteen

Sime Road Internment Camp, Singapore, 1944

Life in Changi was terrible, but worse was yet to come. In September '43, the Japanese High Command was rattled by a successful guerrilla attack on their ships in Singapore's harbour. Their vengeance was terrible. Fifty-seven people were rounded up on 10 October – the 'Double Tenth' – and taken to be questioned by the *Kempeitai*, the military police. Three women from Changi – Dorothy Nixon, Dr Cicely Williams and Freddy Bloom – were among their number. Local civilian Elizabeth Choy, who together with her husband had secretly passed food, medicine and messages to the internees, was also taken into custody and tortured for nine months.

Early the following year, having failed to find the perpetrators of the sabotage, the Japanese decided to move the majority of the Allied military prisoners in Singapore to the jail, where it would be easier to maintain maximum security. That meant moving the civilian men, women and children who had been interned there since '42 elsewhere. Elsewhere was a former RAF station at Sime Road in the middle of the island.

If any of the residents of the women's camp were excited about the move (though who had the energy to be excited after two and a half years on starvation rations?), that feeling was squashed the moment they saw their new accommodation. Since the RAF had abandoned the site, it had been used to house POWs too sick to work. The POWs had been too sick to take much care of the place either. The large huts that were to house the women were falling down, with big holes in the ceilings that let in the monsoon rain.

The 'upper-class' women, the self-appointed camp leaders, who had been at the very top of British colonial society before the war, moved themselves into Hut Ten, the less tumbledown of the two biggest huts. Jinx and her family were billeted in Hut Sixteen, where white women were in the minority. The majority of the women in Hut Sixteen were Eurasian or Chinese. Some had been the mistresses of expat white men. Others were the children of mixed relationships. There was even a Japanese woman in the camp, interned because she had been married to a European. She seemed to be most despised of all, by the guards and by some of her fellow prisoners.

Now ten years old, Jinx was starting to understand how the world worked and where her family was in the pecking order. People from Hut Sixteen did not mix with the people in Hut Ten, with their fancy posh voices. It didn't matter that in the eyes of the Japanese guards, they were all – ex-charladies or real 'Ladies' – the lowest of the low. The unspoken rules of the British class system were inescapable, even in hell.

At night it was so hot inside Hut Sixteen – built for sixty men but now home to more than twice that many women – that Jinx often couldn't sleep. Curled into a ball on the bug-infested hessian sack that comprised her bedding, she tried to shut out the night-time sounds of 130 sleeping women: the snoring and the coughing and the occasional cry from the depths of a bad dream. When the sun went down, it was usually too dark in the hut to see even as far as the end of your nose, but on this particular night a full moon shone through the gaps in the asbestos roof, illuminating the bodies below with an eerie blue light.

Jinx was drawn outside by the lunar glow. Careful not to disturb the sleepers around her, she picked her way across the floor with the high-stepping gait of an egret. If any of the adult women saw her go, they didn't try to stop her. Outside, she found a spot out of sight of the hut and sat down on the dirt with her back against the trunk of a papaya tree. She traced patterns in the dust with her fingertips as she sang quietly to herself.

She sang 'Tudung Periuk', a song by Miss Dinah from the movies that she'd heard their old neighbour, Auntie Ameera, sing. *'Pot lid, pot lid.'* The words made no sense in English, but Jinx knew what they meant in Malay. The cooking pot was a metaphor for protection, for the warmth of the family.

As Jinx softly crooned, she was suddenly aware of a second voice joining in. Sometimes Olga or Eileen would come out to sit in the cool night with her, but the voice she heard was not that of one of her friends. It was male. Jinx jumped up, ready to skitter back to the hut, but it was too late. The guard they called Goofy was blocking her way. He may have been named after a cartoon character, but he carried the same big stick all the guards did and he wouldn't be afraid to use it.

'Stop! Stop!' Goofy said, but quietly. He didn't shout like he usually would. 'Stop.'

Jinx was frozen in flight. This was it. She was going to get a proper beating now. She gave up any thought of escape and bowed deeply, hoping that a suitable show of contrition would save her a couple of whacks. She stayed bent forward at the hips, waiting to be told to straighten up again. Goofy put his hand gently on Jinx's shoulder.

'You sing,' he said. 'Know sing.'

Jinx was confused now. She came out of the bow and stared at him.

'Know sing,' he said again.

He was smiling. Jinx didn't dare return the gesture.

'Know sing,' he repeated. He hummed a couple of bars. Did he mean he knew the song too?

He reached into the pocket of his shorts and pulled something out. In the light of the moon, Jinx saw it was a photograph. The young guard thrust it closer to her face so that she could see it better. There were three people in the picture: Goofy, a woman and a little girl. 'She sing,' he said, as he tapped the face of the girl.

Jinx nodded.

'Look, look.'

Jinx took the photograph. Her hands were shaking. Examining the picture more closely, Jinx saw that the adults were gazing down at the child with adoration.

'Is this your daughter?' she asked. She searched her brain for the Japanese word. Could only find the Malay. Tried that instead. '*Anak perempuan?* Daughter?'

She handed the photo back. Goofy held it with two hands and looked at it with softened eyes.

'Daughter,' he nodded. 'You age.'

'My age?'

'Yes.' He made 'ten' with his fingers. Then he tucked the photo away, rearranged his face from soft to stern again and said, 'Inside. Quick.'

Jinx didn't wait to be asked twice. She vanished into the darkness of the hut just as two other guards came round the corner, their torches strobing the ground ahead of them, their voices loud, not caring who they woke up. Jinx lay down again between her mother and her friend Olga's mum and closed her eyes tightly, feigning sleep.

Jinx didn't tell anyone what had happened under the tree that night, and by the time the sun rose again, it was as though she had dreamt it. Goofy didn't even look at her during tenko. They'd had tenko every morning since the Double Tenth. Sometimes the roll call, during which they had to stand, could last for hours in the heat of the sun.

Goofy strutted along the lines of women as he usually did; as all the guards did. He prodded Mrs Morris with his stick when she didn't bow low enough. He shouted at one of Eddy's little friends. Perhaps it had been a dream. There was nothing about Goofy's demeanour that matched the soft-eyed dad of Jinx's memory – the man who had so proudly shown her his daughter's photograph. He was just like the rest of them. The rest of the guards. He thought the captive women and children were dirt. Why would he ever be kind?

After tenko, Jinx joined the queue for breakfast. Sometimes she wondered if the breakfast they got in camp was worse than not eating at all. Thinking about food sent Jinx's stomach into action. To eat so little after such painful anticipation often made her nauseous. All those digestive juices sloshing around with nothing to digest but hopes and dreams.

'They've cut the rations again.' The word went around the camp. They hadn't seen a green vegetable or piece of meat in weeks. Lots of the children had swollen stomachs, caused by a lack of protein. Beriberi was increasingly common, caused by a deficiency of vitamin B1.

Sometimes, when she was working in the field, Jinx would wait until the guards were looking elsewhere and pull off the tiniest part of a sweet potato leaf, just to feel something in

118

her mouth other than the saltless starchy tapioca paste they were now eating morning, noon and night. The vegetables the prisoners grew were strictly for the guards' consumption. Some of the children had resorted to eating snails. The reviews had not been good.

Everyone was ill all the time now. Everyone was covered in sores. Soap was a distant memory. When you went to the stinking latrine, you were as quick as you could be so the flies didn't have time to land on you. They would lay their eggs in an open wound.

Norma did her best to keep their spirits up. She shared what little food she had for herself with Jinx and Eddy, of course, determined that they would survive. Eddy was a blessing. Though there wasn't much to laugh about, he was still a natural clown. He could always make his big sister smile, and in turn she could usually comfort him when his stomach growled and his own smile faded.

Every night Jinx would tell Eddy a bedtime story. His favourite was about the tiger Jinx swore she saw in their garden in Kluang, back when the world was a nicer place to be.

While Eddy dreamed of tigers, Jinx lay awake again. It was another sticky night. The air in the hut was thick with the smell of unwashed clothes and skin. Jinx tip-toed her way to the veranda. If she couldn't sleep, she wanted to be outside, looking at the stars. She wondered if her father ever looked up at the stars from the men's side of the camp and thought of them looking down on her. If she sent a message via the Southern Cross, would her father receive it?

She was sending up a whispered prayer when she felt a moon shadow fall across her face. It was Goofy. Jinx hastily scrambled to her feet and bowed, but he waved the gesture away.

He got the photograph out again. 'You sing me,' he said.

'Which song? Same as last time?' Jinx began in a tiny voice.

'Thank you,' Goofy said, when the song was done.

As he walked away, Goofy paused to retie the laces of his boots. When he carried on without looking back, Jinx saw that he had left something behind him. At the base of the tree was what looked like a tin.

Jinx blinked, fully expecting that the tin would have vanished when she opened her eyes again. But it was still there and Goofy had not returned to retrieve it. Then, just he was about to go round the end of Hut Ten, he briefly looked back at Jinx and nodded urgently. It was the signal she needed. The tin was meant for her.

Jinx darted forward, quick as a lizard, and snatched it up. Condensed milk! That condensed milk was more wonderful than anything Jinx had seen in a year, two years, three ... She hurriedly tucked it into the waistband of her shorts. Goofy might have left behind a casket stuffed with gold.

'Where on earth did you get this?' Norma asked when Jinx showed her in the morning.

'I found it,' Jinx said.

'You found it?'

'Yes. It was under a tree.'

Norma hid the tin in her petticoat. She had sewn a secret pocket there for exactly this kind of situation.

'Don't tell anyone,' she instructed Jinx in a whisper.

'I'm not stupid, Mum.'

Over the next week, Norma eked out the tin's contents, giving Jinx and Eddy a spoonful each day. She didn't declare the bounty to Hut Ten, as she was supposed to under the rules set by the grand ladies. And at tenko each morning, Goofy still stared through Jinx as though he had never seen her at all.

*

Then one day, the camp woke to terrible shouting. The noise immediately put Jinx on edge. A young guard, whom some of the children called Sweet Pea, came through the hut, thwacking the air with a long cane, demanding that everyone go outside at once. There was going to be a search.

The women lined up in their tenko order and bowed and stayed doubled over while the commandant marched up and down between them, shouting so hard that specks of spittle flew from his mouth. He was so angry that morning that the children dare not even share glances with one another. In a situation like this, staying still and silent was a matter of self-preservation.

It felt like an age until the guards who were searching Hut Sixteen came back out empty-handed. The commandant couldn't believe they hadn't found anything. There was more shouting. He waved his stick in the air, threatening to bring it down on each of their backs in turn.

Eventually, the women were ordered to file down to the sandy patch of land that had been a football pitch for the RAF officers before the war, but which now was the very opposite of a place for games. There was a rope hanging from a tree and in the middle of the dirt sat a cage made from bamboo. It was a small cage, that perhaps had been made for taking chickens to market. Jinx found her eyes were drawn to it, imagining herself inside. Other children had been put in that cage before.

When the women were all assembled, two guards came down from the guardhouse with a third man between them. Jinx could feel the collective holding of breath as the women tried to work out who it was. They dare not look openly. Was it one of their loved ones from the men's camp? Someone's husband, father, brother? It was not. The women quickly realised the guards were bringing out one of their own.

Goofy was not wearing his uniform that morning, just a pair

of shorts and a grubby vest. His feet were bare and his hands were tied together in front of him. He stood straight and still as the commandant barked what had to be insults in his face. At the end of his speech, he knocked Goofy to the ground, then roughly dragged him to his feet, only to knock him down again. Goofy did not cry out, but Jinx could barely contain a gasp as she watched him being struck about the face.

The women continued to watch in silence as Goofy was hung by his thumbs from the tree. Though his face was contorted, he did not cry or complain, which only seemed to enrage the commandant further. After what seemed like forever, but was probably only twenty seconds, he was cut down again. Goofy spent the rest of the day bent double in the bamboo cage, without food or water. The prisoners were forbidden from talking to him.

Rumours quickly spread around the camp about the reason behind Goofy's punishment.

'He's been sleeping with the commandant's mistress,' was the most popular.

There was little sympathy for the man, though everyone acknowledged of the guards: 'When it comes to punishment, they're even worse to their own.'

Then a Japanese woman who had recently been brought into the camp reported back what she'd understood of the commandant's rant.

'Some food was stolen from the officers' stores. They think Goofy took it to give to one of us in return for favours.'

After that, the gossip turned to who might have been the recipient of Goofy's largesse. All the adult women were talking about it. Someone – one of them – must have been letting Goofy have his way with her.

'Whoever it is, I don't suppose he'll be in a hurry to help her again.'

*

At dinner that night, Jinx ate her tapioca but she saved the tiny scrap of bread she would normally have gobbled down.

All day the children had been dancing around Goofy's cage, while the other guards turned a blind eye, perhaps believing that the children's games only amplified Goofy's humiliation. But it gave Jinx the chance to get close enough to do the only thing she could think of to repay the poor man's kindness. She dropped her scrap of bread just outside the bamboo bars, where Goofy could reach it with his fingers. Their eyes met briefly, and Goofy nodded ever so slightly in thanks.

The very next day he was back in uniform and walked by Jinx as though she wasn't there. She could hardly blame him.

But three nights later, there was another tin under the papaya tree. And when Jinx sang a snatch of Goofy's favourite song the following morning, defiantly loud, so that he might hear her, she felt as though she was a skylark, soaring high above the camp and singing for joy.

Chapter Nineteen

The Coach Trip, 2023

It was day three of Team Merevale's Tuscan Splendour tour, and Glenn was tentatively pleased that the fractious atmosphere that had developed on the coach between France and Italy seemed to have dissipated. Val and Cynthia had put aside their squabbles over their first Aperol spritz. Pat was satisfied with the new hotel's 'facilities', despite being confronted with the horror of a bidet in her en suite bathroom.

'People's bottoms go on those things. They should have lids,' was her opinion.

'Very useful for washing one's feet,' said the Colonel.

Marilyn had donned the first of a series of sequinned kaftans and sashayed around the breakfast room singing 'That's Amore', briefly duetting with Ivor the driver over a stick of celery.

'Salad for breakfast,' said Val. 'Why would anyone want that?'

'It's good for your biome,' said Cynthia.

'Not at breakfast time it's not.'

The Colonel had loaded his plate with cold meats.

'Terrible for your hair,' Val said wickedly.

Only Jinx and Thea were late to breakfast on day three.

'My fault, Glenn,' Jinx said. 'I couldn't decide what to wear.'

In reality, Thea had woken late and Jinx was mostly dressed by the time her young helper arrived.

'I suppose you're going to tell Dad,' said Thea.

'That's not the kind of person I am,' said Jinx.

All the same, they travelled down in the lift to the breakfast room in silence. At the buffet, Thea pushed Jinx to the table, then went up to the buffet to load a plate for her. To a casual observer, it seemed as though Thea was being very solicitous, but she banged Jinx's plate down so that a cherry tomato jumped off onto the tablecloth. Jinx chose not to mention it. Sometimes the only way to react was not to react. Jinx had learned that much in camp.

Back at the buffet with her own plate, Thea drifted along as though she had her own weather system: a black cloud perpetually threatening heavy rain. Jinx wasn't the only one who had noticed.

'She could be so pretty if she only smiled,' said Marilyn.

'Perhaps she's not a morning person,' Jinx said.

After breakfast the coach party was going to visit San Gimignano, the small Tuscan hill town famous for its medieval towers. While his travellers finished getting their things together for the day, Glenn swotted up. Never one to choose the easy option, he had decided to do all the tour-guiding himself, researching the 'must-see' sights on the Internet and preparing a walking route accordingly.

Though Glenn was nominally in charge of Team Merevale, the Colonel was finding it very hard not to help/take over. He sat down beside Glenn as he was studying his map in the hotel lobby and starting firing questions and suggestions.

'Well, that looks like a very interesting route, Glenn, but

have you considered the gradients? Cynthia won't get up a slope with her hip, and Val will have trouble getting down one even with her new knee.'

'I specifically looked for routes around the town with the minimum number of steps,' Glenn explained.

'Good, good. Don't want to have to get behind the ladies and push, now, do we?'

The Colonel wandered off, leaving Glenn worrying. He put the carefully planned route around San Gimignano into his phone for the tenth time to check that the gradients were as gradual as he hoped.

Glenn had set an alarm on his phone to alert him when it was ten minutes to the day trip's departure. When it went off, he headed out to the front of the hotel, where Ivor the driver was waiting with the coach. The Colonel was already there.

'Morning, everybody,' Glenn began, as Team Merevale drifted outside. 'We're going to be leaving in ten minutes, so if you could please make sure you have everything you need for the day ...'

Those people who were by the coach continued chatting.

'Ahem!' Glenn coughed. Ineffectually.

'Aten-shun!' The Colonel summoned Team Merevale to muster. 'Places, please.'

Glenn had to admit that Team Merevale moved when the Colonel said so.

'Thank you, Malcolm,' he said quietly. Only Jinx noticed how crestfallen he seemed.

As Glenn had predicted, after the first morning, there had been no complaints about seating positions on the bus. Everyone had settled into their places and now they refused to budge, having all convinced themselves that the front, the back or slap-bang in the middle with no view whatsoever was the very best place to be. As a result, boarding was, thankfully, a little faster every time.

Once the doors were closed, Glenn picked up the microphone to issue that day's instructions. For some reason, the microphone was not working and Glenn's voice couldn't seem to cut through the chatter at the back of the bus. The Colonel stepped in again. He didn't need a microphone.

'All right, you horrible lot.'

Glenn reluctantly handed the Colonel his prewritten speech for that morning. 'Let's see what we have in store today,' the Colonel read from Glenn's notes. 'San Gim. That's the place with all the towers. And an afternoon's cheesemaking near Volterra. What a treat for all you cheese lovers on the coach, and I know there are a few! Now it's time to hit the road. I'll give you a heads-up when there's something you need to take notice of ... *Head's-up*, Glenn? What does that mean? In the meantime, sit back and relax and enjoy the Tuscan countryside.' The Colonel paused for a moment, then said, in what was meant to be a comic aside. 'Who wrote this tosh?'

From the second row Pat instigated a polite round of applause. Glenn muttered 'Thanks', then turned his attention to fixing the microphone.

The microphone was not fixed by the time they arrived at their destination, so it was down to the Colonel to announce, 'San Gimignano, the Town of Fine Towers!' above the noise of the coach's engine and Marilyn's singing. There followed a small tussle as Glenn wrestled back his papers, determined at least that he would be leading the actual tour. Once Team Merevale was off the coach, however, confusion ensued when both Glenn and the Colonel raised folded umbrellas in true tour guide style. Most of the ladies mustered around the Colonel.

'Tell you what, Glenn,' said the Colonel. 'I'll hold the

umbrella. It'll be easy for me. My arms are used to holding a ceremonial sword aloft for hours on end.'

'Like that Penny Mordor at the Coronation,' said Cynth.

'Mordaunt's the name,' said the Colonel. 'But yes, just like that. Fine woman, Mrs Mordaunt. Shades of Lady T.'

'Was that when you were in the SAS, Malcolm, that you had to hold a sword aloft?' Cynth asked.

The Colonel leaned in close and whispered, 'I could tell you, but then I'd have to kill you,' which set Cynth off in a fit of the giggles.

'Oh, you do talk some nonsense,' she said, swatting him with her sun hat.

Jinx had seen San Gimignano before, and knew that the town's narrow streets were going to be too steep and narrow for the wheelchair Capstan Coaches had insisted she use for excursions. Glenn promised he would be perfectly happy to push the chair, but Jinx suggested it made more sense for her to sit in a café, well known to Ivor the driver, while the others saw the highlights.

'I'll stay with Mrs Sullivan,' said Thea.

'Don't you want to see the towers?' Jinx asked.

'I'm not really interested in history.'

Jinx said nothing, but her expression must have said it all.

'I'm just here to make sure you can get dressed every day, like you asked me,' Thea responded to the unspoken rebuke. 'I don't have to take any flak.'

'Quite right.' Jinx pulled a five-euro note out of her purse. 'Fetch us both a coffee, then I shan't talk to you and I shan't expect you to talk to me either. Deal?'

Thea hesitated before she took the note, as though sure there must be some catch. 'All right, then. Cappuccino?'

'Espresso.'

Thea returned and put the coffees down with a clatter. Having thanked her, Jinx kept true to her word and said nothing else, concentrating instead on the comings and goings around the café.

Since Team Merevale had arrived in San Gimignano, the coach park had really filled up. Busloads of tourists followed their tour guides in crocodiles like schoolchildren, chattering with excitement as they filed through the town's ancient walls. They were doubtless all heading for the Piazza della Cisterna with its medieval well, around which the Guelphs and the Ghibellines had competed to build ever taller town houses, until San Gim looked like a medieval Manhattan, with several of the towers nearly seventy metres tall.

Now that she was there, Jinx wished she could see inside the town's walls one more time – the fourteen remaining tower houses were remarkable – but she accepted that wasn't going to happen. She couldn't expect Thea to try to negotiate the streets with the wheelchair, and while she felt a little sad that Thea had decided not to join the rest of the group, Jinx wasn't going to tell her she should catch up with them either. She and Thea weren't going to talk. That was the deal.

Yet out of the corner of her eye, Jinx could see that Thea was watching her. She must be wondering why Jinx *really* wasn't trying to engage. There was no point being in 'a flounce', as Penny would have called it, if no one was paying attention, was there? When Thea asked, 'Do you need another coffee?' Jinx knew she'd won this little match.

'Were you OK in that café?' Glenn asked when the others returned from their mostly flat tour.

'Oh yes,' said Jinx. 'Thea and I had a very nice, *quiet* time.'

The Colonel counted everyone back onto the coach. Val was the straggler on this occasion, having decided at the last minute that she did want to buy a scale model of the town houses after

129

all. Back on the bus, she showed the people in the seats around her what she'd bought.

'I think this will look really nice on my rockery,' she said. 'A little piece of Italy.'

'Made in China,' said the sticker on the bottom.

Next stop that day was the cheese factory.

Team Merevale arrived for their cheesemaking session near Volterra at around midday. While Alessandro, the factory owner, explained health and safety rules in perfect English, the Colonel made interjections in what the ladies of Team Merevale were already calling his 'Dolmio voice', after the pasta sauce brand. Even after several dozen online lessons, the Colonel's knowledge of Italian was shaky and his pronunciation worse. However, that didn't stop him from acting as though he might have been a translator at the UN.

When Alessandro explained that the cheese would be made from unpasteurised milk, the Colonel wisely agreed that the best cheese did not contain '*preservativi*'.

'Indeed,' said Alessandro. Condoms were not something that anyone should expect to find in their *formaggio*.

Togged up in their white overalls and hairnets (Jinx noticed that the Colonel stepped away from the rest of them to put his net on), Team Merevale took their places at a workbench and set about making their very own '*caciotti*'. Only Jinx and Thea did not join in. Jinx because making cheese with one hand was not for beginners. Thea because, as she told her dad, 'This place smells rank and I'm going to throw up if you make me.'

'You'll get used to it,' Glenn suggested.

'Not before I hurl,' Thea replied.

Val and Cynth heard the painful exchange between father and daughter. There were mutterings of 'in my day' and 'ungrateful', to which Thea responded with a scowl.

Jinx was glad to have an excuse to wait outside. There was a garden behind the factory where three large chestnut trees provided shade.

Jinx had not brought her laptop with her to Italy, but she did have her tablet and, while Thea was busy catching up with news from home on the cheese factory's wi-fi, Jinx decided she probably ought to do some work. She hadn't checked her emails or DMs since leaving the UK. Her married Facebook 'friend' Mitch had messaged again. He said he was ready to leave his wife. Jinx suggested that if he was really going to do that, then he ought to start making an 'escape fund'. If he transferred a lump sum to the usual account, she would, of course, keep it safe.

Mitch replied at once, agreeing that an escape fund was an excellent idea. In a matter of moments, another payment had been made to Jinx's special account.

'I can't wait until we're together,' he messaged.

Jinx gave the message a thumbs up. Poor sap.

Ordinarily, Jinx felt no compunction whatsoever about separating a man intent on cheating with a younger woman from his money (Jinx had chosen some very good pictures for her alter ego Jenice's profile), but glancing up from her phone, she saw Thea give another of her soul-racking sighs and was struck, for the first time, by the irony of the situation.

Thea was only on this trip because Jinx had caught her stealing. Jinx couldn't exactly claim the moral high ground on that. But she'd needed to get to Italy, and for that she had needed Thea's assistance. At the time, she could think of no other way to persuade Thea to join Glenn's trip than blackmail. Would the end justify the means? Feeling an unwelcome flash of guilt that she was taking advantage of her young companion, Jinx deleted Mitch's messages and transferred £500 from her bank account to Save the Children.

131

As if to reward Jinx's uncharacteristic altruism, Thea glanced up from her phone and gave Jinx what looked like a smile, though it was more likely a squint in the sunlight.

While Team Merevale waited for their little baby cheeses to form and dry, a buffet lunch was served outside under the trees. The Colonel engaged the three women who had prepared the lunch in his very best Italian. The women smiled and nodded graciously as he practised all his best phrases.

'*Il mio nome è Malcolm. Vengo dai Cotswolds. Mi piace molto il formaggio.*'

'*Cosa vuoi mangiare?*' one of them asked.

The Colonel was very happy to tell her. He already knew the answer to this one. He said, '*Vorrei un po' di pene.*'

'I want *un po' di pene* too!' the woman responded, much to the delight of her cackling colleagues. 'I'll give you extra for that,' she added. '*Il tuo italiano è eccellente, caro signore.*'

The Colonel was pretty pleased with himself when he got to the table.

'Got a double helping of pasta for my Italian,' he told Thea. 'It's always worth learning a language. Goes a long way to helping international relations.'

When the woman who had given him a double helping came to the table to refresh the water jugs, the Colonel took great pleasure in telling her, '*pene delizioso.*' He was rewarded with a wink.

'Fabulously flirtatious people, the Italians,' the Colonel said.

Though Team Merevale's cheeses looked nice enough, in the end no one wanted to take one home. That was because Marilyn had lost a false eyelash and couldn't be sure it hadn't fallen off before lunch. Possibly even while they were all leaning over the huge vat in which the curds were separated from the whey.

Nobody was too worried. Lunch had been generous and dinner at the hotel that night was another enormous pasta buffet.

The hotel buffet, like the one at the cheese factory, featured *penne al pollo*, offering the Colonel a chance to asked for '*un po' di pene*' once more. The young man with the serving spoon answered the Colonel's request with a beaming smile.

'Of course,' he said. 'I get off my shift at ten o'clock.'

'*Bene, bene*,' said the Colonel. Sitting down next to Jinx and Thea, he said, 'I don't know why he thought I'd be interested in what time he gets off tonight. I suppose he was just practising his English.'

Later, the young man came to their table to gather up empty plates. He leaned across Jinx's shoulder to take the Colonel's plate with a wink.

'I seem to be getting all the winks today,' said the Colonel, somewhat bemused. 'I don't understand it.'

Jinx wondered only briefly whether she ought to tell him about the very subtle difference between ordering *penne al pollo* and, well, cock.

Jinx put Thea out of her misery early that evening, asking to be taken to her room the moment dinner was over.

'Three days down,' Jinx said.

'Six to go,' sighed Thea.

'Would you plug my tablet in, please?' Jinx asked.

Thea connected Jinx's tablet to its charger.

'You've got a message,' Thea said, surprised no doubt to see it. 'From someone asking about a payment to your bank account. Does that sound right, Mrs Sullivan? You know about banking scams, don't you? You mustn't give your banking details to anyone who contacts you out of the blue. Even if they say they're from your bank.'

Jinx was amused by the sudden rush of concern. For a moment, she could see that Thea was 100 per cent her father's daughter.

'Your dad posted a leaflet through everyone's door back in February,' Jinx told her. 'After Val gave her debit card to those people who claimed to be from Lloyds.'

'That was horrible,' said Thea.

It was. Poor Val had received a phone call, telling her that her account had been compromised. The callers told her they needed to send a courier round to pick up her bank card so it could be safely destroyed. Having asked her to confirm her PIN before she handed the card over, they cleaned out her account within minutes of leaving her bungalow.

'Don't worry. I won't send anybody any money,' Jinx assured her young helper.

'Good,' said Thea. 'Sleep well.'

Alone in the ugly yellow glow of the bedside lamp, Jinx opened her handbag and took out the ceramic mouse, which she placed once again on the bedside table. Then she fished out the old German guidebook to Florence. It wasn't easy to open out the folded-up map in the back with her collarbone complaining every time she moved, but she managed it somehow.

Putting on her glasses, Jinx peered at the map as though if she just looked at it for long enough, the tiny notes upon it might start to make sense, but they hadn't made sense in 1951 and they didn't seem about to give up their secrets now. It was a German book about an Italian city, belonging to one Axel Durchdenwald. Once again, Jinx read the incongruous English inscription inside the front cover. *Besides, the wench is dead.* What did that mean? With just a couple of days to go, Jinx very much needed to know.

Chapter Twenty

Italy, May 1945

Penny Williamson had fallen in love with Italy. The landscape, the people, the food ... The only fly in the ointment was that she was billeted in a hamlet just outside Brindisi with three other FANY officers in a tiny house that was not what you would call 'well-appointed'. There was no boiler, so Penny and her housemates had to wash in an old metal tub in the kitchen, taking it in turns to heat water in a huge pot on the stove. To make a change from this miserable situation, from time to time they would club together to take a room at the Imperiale in Bari. The Imperiale was one of the few places around where you could usually get hot water. Newly washed, the FANYs would then head to the Allied Officers' Club to flirt and dance with whoever was in town.

On the first Monday in May, Penny and her friends Jean and Judy pooled their wages and took a room at the Imperiale for the usual reasons. Judy, who had a date, took first bath. Jean went second, Penny third. While Penny was in the tub, Jean tapped on the bathroom door and announced that she had to go back to Brindisi to cover a missing colleague's shift in the watch room.

With Judy romancing and Jean back at work, Penny found herself at a loose end. Bathed and dressed, she headed to the club. The usual crowd was in its usual corner. Penny waved a greeting but didn't join them straight away. She went to the bar and ordered herself a Scotch and soda, briefly thinking that her father would have been horrified to see her with a 'man's drink'. That made it all the more delicious. She wondered if he would also have been horrified to see her in the Scottish Highlands, learning how to silently kill an enemy combatant with her bare hands. Happy days.

When Penny went to pay for her drink, the barman told her, 'It's been taken care of.'

Across the bar, an American airman gave Penny a small salute. Penny raised her glass towards him, rather hoping that would be enough, but the airman took it as a signal that he should join her.

'Jimmy Noone,' he introduced himself. 'Just got into town. Nobody told me the crusty old Brits turned out such pretty girls. What should I call you?'

For a moment Penny considered using an alias, but the bar was full of people who knew her as FANY code and cipher officer Penny Williamson. People such as Judy and her boyfriend Bobby, who chose that moment to reappear.

Judy's cheeks were bright pink with excitement. She waved her left hand in front of Penny's face. 'Look! Look what happened! Bobby has asked me to marry him.'

Bobby was busy accepting the congratulations of his colleagues in the RAF.

'Drinks for everyone,' Jimmy announced, pulling out his wallet.

The newly engaged couple were astonished. 'You don't have to do that,' Bobby said.

'But I want to,' said Jimmy. 'Hell, hasn't the war taught us all that we need to celebrate every bit of good news when we can? I want to celebrate you two lovers. Tell the barman what you want.'

No one needed persuading. The bartender lined up drinks for all, and someone started belting out old favourites on the piano. Judy and Bobby were a popular couple and everyone was pleased to toast their happiness, especially with free booze. The only recompense Jimmy required was a turn around the dance floor with Penny.

'I'm not much of a dancer,' she said.

'I don't believe that at all. Come on.' He offered her his hand.

'Don't be a spoilsport, Penny.' Judy poked her towards the floor.

As Jimmy held her close and told her that she looked like Gene Tierney, Penny had already decided that after this one dance, she would head off to 'spend a penny' and not come back. Jimmy wasn't her type – there was something slightly slippery about him, she thought. Something too showy about the way he had insisted on buying all the drinks. Besides, a bed with clean sheets awaited her at the Imperiale. The hotel's beds were almost as big a draw as the bath.

The following morning, Judy left early to get back to Brindisi for her shift, leaving Penny to enjoy another soak in the tub.

'How will you get back?' Judy had asked her.

'I'll get a lift with someone,' Penny shrugged. It was usually easy enough. But for some reason, that day it wasn't. No one was heading her way. All the same, she wasn't entirely pleased when Jimmy the American sidled up in the hotel lobby and said, 'I hear you're looking for a ride.'

'I don't want to take you out of your way,' Penny said.

'I'm taking Lieutenant Ludovico in the same direction. Meet me out front at midday.'

Safety in numbers, Penny thought. Plus, there were no other options and she had to be back in Brindisi. Her commanding officers would be unimpressed to hear she'd got herself stuck in Bari. You didn't rock up late during a war.

Thus, Penny was ready at the rendezvous at 1200 hours exactly. Jimmy was there in his jeep. There was no sign of his friend.

'He's still asleep.' Jimmy shrugged. 'Can't take the cheap wine.'

'Shouldn't you wake him up?'

'I gave him the same instructions I gave you. A man can't follow orders, that's on him ... Means you get to sit up front.'

It was a small silver lining – Penny had never been good in the back seat – but she was careful to arrange her skirt so it covered her knees, and tucked her bag down the side of her body to form a barrier between her and Jimmy. She wasn't sure why she didn't like him, but she knew, from her SOE training, that one's gut instinct was usually right. If someone gave you the creeps, it was because they were creepy.

Jimmy chose the coastal road, past Polignano a Mare and Monopoli. As he drove, he told Penny about his life before the war. He'd studied at Yale, then joined his cousin's brokerage business in New York.

'Never been there? You haven't lived.'

Penny offered the minimum of information in return. Jimmy didn't seem to mind. He was on a riff.

When he'd finished telling her about home, Jimmy told her about his war. There was a sense all around by now that victory was a matter of days away. The Soviets had stormed Berlin and

Hitler had committed suicide in his bunker. The Allies were closing in on the Germans from all directions. All the same, Penny was surprised when Jimmy described his own role in detail. He told her he spoke German, and had been involved in the interrogation of a number of high-ranking enemy officers captured as Rome and Florence were cleared out.

They stopped in a tiny hamlet outside Monopoli to buy lunch. Jimmy may have been fluent in German but Penny's Italian was better, and so she did the honours, finding bread, dried tomatoes and hard-boiled eggs. It also gave her a chance to ask if anyone else might be driving south. Of course not, the villagers laughed. Who had petrol? She could borrow a donkey?

The only option was to get back into Jimmy's Jeep.

'Light me a cigarette,' Jimmy suggested as they set off again.

Penny plucked the box of cigarettes from Jimmy's hatband and tapped out two. She searched her bag for her matches but couldn't find them.

'Do you have a lighter?'

She'd already started to look in the glove compartment.

A small parcel, swathed in cloth, fell out, becoming partially unwrapped in the process. It was an oil painting – a Madonna and Child. Even a quick glance told Penny it was a very fine piece.

'You might want to put that back,' Jimmy said.

But Penny had never been one for following instructions. Not unless it suited her. Instead, she looked at the painting more closely.

'This is beautiful.'

'Uh-huh,' said Jimmy.

'Where did you get it?'

'A village in the north. Some old lady was selling a load of junk to buy food. I didn't want any of it but she wouldn't take my money if I didn't let her give me something in return. I felt bad for her. She needed the dough.'

Junk? This wasn't junk. Though her boarding school education hadn't prepared her for much beyond conjugating Latin verbs, Penny knew enough about art to know that this painting was special. It was church altar special.

'How much did you pay for it?'

Jimmy named a laughably small sum.

'I love it. Can I have it?'

'I'm taking it home for my mom.'

'I'll give you twice what you paid.'

'I'm taking it home. Look, just put it back, will you? You shouldn't be poking about in glove compartments anyway.'

'I was looking for a lighter.'

'And if you'd waited, I'd have told you it's in my pocket.'

Penny carefully rewrapped the painting. She knew plenty of well-to-do Italians had been forced to sell their most treasured possessions to get by, but there was something about Jimmy's story that didn't quite ring true. For the amount of money he was talking about, you would expect to get some old pan with a hole in it, not an oil painting of such quality.

Penny had heard that the Germans had requisitioned a great deal of Italian treasure as they occupied the country. They'd cleared out museums, palazzos and churches. Had Jimmy in turn liberated this Madonna from one of the German officers he'd interrogated? However he had come across that painting, it was special and he knew it. There had been no disguising his irritation when Penny asked if she might buy it off him.

'Put it back,' he said again.

'Are you really going to take this painting to the States? Perhaps it should stay here. Given you paid so little, it seems a shame to take it out of the country.'

'If the Italians wanted to hang on to their stuff, they shouldn't

140

have backed the wrong guy. They support Hitler, then expect to be bailed out for free? That painting is my retirement fund.'

Like the good trainee agent she'd once been, Penny pretended not to have noticed that Jimmy had changed his story within a matter of minutes, or that he was getting angry. But she had noticed. Just as she noticed that after his little outburst, Jimmy subconsciously tapped his breast pocket, where the corner of a small red book poked out. As he did so, Penny remembered her former SOE trainer and lover Frank telling her, 'People can't help pointing to the things they're trying to hide.'

They drove on through the heat of the day. At points, the cicadas were loud enough that you could hear them over the Jeep's noisy engine. Penny felt like she could use a quick nap, but didn't feel comfortable enough in Jimmy's car.

The map suggested they were still ten miles from Brindisi when he pulled the Jeep off the main road on a 'scenic diversion' down a dirt track that led to the coast.

'My watch starts in three hours,' said Penny.

'This won't take long.'

Jimmy parked the Jeep facing the sea and got out. He took off his jacket and draped it across a fallen tree, with the lining down, so that he could sit on it without getting his trousers dusty. Penny did not sit down next to him.

'Come and look at the view,' Jimmy said.

It was the best kind of early summer day. The sea glittered as if it had been sewn with sequins in the sunlight. On the horizon, a number of large ships – Allied ships – were peacefully at anchor.

'Beautiful, huh?'

Penny agreed.

'Like you,' Jimmy said, standing up.

When she turned to respond to that, Jimmy grabbed Penny's

face, pulling her to him for a kiss. It wasn't a romantic gesture; it was one of entitlement, and Penny didn't like it one bit.

'Please let go,' she said, with lips tight and straight.

But while he let go of her face, Jimmy did not let go of Penny. Instead, he grabbed her by the waist.

'C'mon. I've driven miles out of my way to get you back to work on time. The least you can do is—'

'Let me go.'

He pulled her closer still and tried to get his hand inside her blouse. When Penny batted his hand away, Jimmy laughed and told her not to play 'hard to get'. But Jimmy had picked on the wrong girl. It had been a while since Penny had used her unarmed combat training, but it came back to her in an instant, with an added dose of fury that made her especially effective. Seeing that he wasn't going to back off, she easily broke his hold with a textbook Fairbairn move.

'How dare you?' Penny snarled at him.

'Think you're too good for me, is that it?'

'I *know* I'm too good for you.'

Jimmy's eyes flashed anger and he drew back his fist, but before he had a chance to swing at her, Penny used both hands to push him hard in the chest, so that he tipped backwards over the log. That wasn't entirely what Penny had wanted. She wanted only to make her point, not risk him dashing his head open. But he didn't hit his head and he came at her again, and then she *had* to punch him. Just once, with her small fist perfectly rolled and her thumb on the outside as she'd been taught by Frank at the training camp. Penny had a beautiful right hook and she knew exactly where to aim it.

Jimmy collapsed against the bonnet of the Jeep, holding the side of his face in disbelief.

'What the hell was that for?' he asked.

'I told you to let me go.'

'And I woulda done, you crazy bitch. You misunderstood my intentions.'

'I'm not sure I did at all.'

'You are crazy. Nuts. Sicko.'

'You're not the first person to say that ...'

Penny smoothed down her skirt, thinking that now she had made her point, they could carry on to Brindisi. Had there been any other way to get back, she would have taken it, but she told herself it would be OK and if it wasn't OK, then she knew how to throw herself from a moving car. The SOE had prepared her for that, too. *Elbows in, fists under chin, legs together and roll ...*

Jimmy grabbed his jacket, which had slipped from the log, and got into the Jeep. Before Penny could get the passenger door open, he had started the engine and threw the Jeep into reverse, almost upending the vehicle as he drove it backwards over rocks in his haste to get back onto the road.

'Hey! Wait! Where are you going?' Penny shouted.

As he swung the Jeep in a wide circle, Jimmy tossed Penny's overnight bag out onto the dirt.

'You bastard!'

He didn't stop to hear it. Penny ran after him for a while but he wasn't coming back. Jimmy was no gentleman. He was gone, leaving nothing behind him but dust.

Cursing her rotten luck, Penny retrieved her bag and sat down on the fallen tree to gather herself. What now? Where the hell was she? She had to get back to the road.

At least Penny's sensible FANY shoes were made for walking. She tightened her laces and readied herself for a hike. As she did so, she saw that Jimmy had dropped something in their tussle.

It was the book he'd had in his top pocket: a little red

guidebook to Florence, in German of all things, with a fold-out map in the back. The map was not much use in Puglia, but Penny picked the book up all the same, out of an instinct that Jimmy had not meant to leave it behind. She flicked through the pages. Here and there a few words were underlined in pencil and on the inside cover was written a name, Axel Durchdenwald, and single sentence in English. *Besides, the wench is dead.*

Marlowe. Penny recognised the quotation from *The Jew of Malta* at once. A guidebook in German with an English inscription? How strange. But just as a man with a hammer sees everything as a nail, Penny, trained in code and cipher, spied a code. Tucking the book into her pocket, she resolved to work it out.

Thankfully, Penny was further south than she'd thought and the gods were with her. It didn't take long to get back to the main road, where a lorry driver, who'd stopped to change a tyre, told her he was heading in the right direction. For a handful of lire, he was happy to take Penny all the way to Brindisi.

'Where have you been?' Jean asked as Penny walked into the house. 'I've been waiting for you all day.'

'I'm not late,' Penny responded defensively.

'No, but haven't you heard the news?' Jean grabbed Penny's hands. 'You must have done. It's over, Penny. The war is over. The Germans capitulated. Eisenhower took the unconditional surrender from Jodl this morning. Europe is free again and we're going home.'

In the excitement of VE Day, Penny forgot all about her brush with Jimmy Noone and his German guidebook. Though all leave was cancelled in an attempt to stop celebrations getting out of hand, everyone was euphoric. The Nazi menace was defeated. Peace had come at last.

Sitting in the watch room on the evening of 8 May, Penny tuned in to the King's broadcast from London, while out on the sea Allied ships sounded their sirens and let off flares in lieu of a victorious firework display.

Today we give thanks to Almighty God for a great deliverance ... Germany, the enemy who drove all Europe into war, has finally been overcome. In the Far East we have yet to deal with the Japanese, a determined and cruel foe. To this we shall turn with the utmost resolve ... But at this hour, when the dreadful shadow of war has passed from our hearths and homes in these islands, we may at last make one pause for thanksgiving and then turn our thoughts to the tasks all over the world which peace in Europe brings with it.

It was a quiet shift, so Penny had time to write a letter to her sister Josephine.

'*I can't quite believe it's over. Can you? It's as if the past five years were a terrible dream. I can't wait to see you, my dearest sister (my only sister). What fun we'll have when we're all together again with George and Ma and Pa. I'm even looking forward to Mrs Glover's cooking.*'

Of course Penny was happy that Hitler and his cronies were finished, but over the next few days she couldn't help but feel a little melancholy too. Victory over Germany had not been without cost. She'd lost friends and colleagues. The names of the airmen shot down over the Adriatic during her time in Brindisi were engraved on her heart. She'd coded messages for agents and Yugoslav partisans who would never be going home. And she still had no idea whether Frank, the love of her life, had gone to the front line since they said 'goodbye' in Scotland. She did not know if he was dead or alive.

*

145

A couple of years later, Jimmy Noone made a reappearance. Not in person. He was smirking out from the pages of a newspaper, in which it was announced that he had been promoted to a senior position in US government intelligence. By coincidence, in that same paper, Penny read about the shocking number of valuable works of art that had disappeared from Italy during the war and were still missing. Looted by the Nazis? Hidden for safekeeping just a little too well? Or taken home as souvenirs by Allied servicemen who should have known better?

The article prompted Penny to pull out the box of letters and other mementoes she'd brought back from Brindisi, and there it was: the little red guidebook – *So besuchen Sie Florenz und seine Umgebung* – with its curious inscription. *Besides, the wench is dead.* All of a sudden, Penny thought she might know how to find Axel Durchdenwald's looted treasure, which her old acquaintance Jimmy Noone had intended to go into his retirement fund. Now Penny was determined that it would fund her own happy ever after instead.

Chapter Twenty-One

Manchester, 1950

On Jinx's sixteenth birthday, Penny Williamson arrived at the Spencer family's flat with another enormous parcel, wrapped in brown paper and tied with thick white ribbon. Eddy's eyes bugged out of his head at the size of it. Meanwhile, Jinx could tell that her mother was nervous as to what the parcel might contain. Penny had been so generous to them over the past year. There was no way they would ever be able to repay that generosity. However, Penny had a way of minimising her gifts, framing them as 'little things' that it gave her great pleasure to pass on. Like the dresses inside the parcel Jinx unwrapped that day.

'They're not new,' Penny said. 'They belonged to my sister Josephine. She wanted me to have them but they're really not my style.'

Jinx had heard all about Josephine, Penny's big sister, who had served in the Women's Royal Naval Service during the war, had studied English literature at Cambridge, and was now engaged to be married to a former submariner called Gerald. Gerald was flying high in the diplomatic service.

Norma hovered as Jinx pulled out three dresses, each one

more lovely than the last. She was no doubt wondering whether such outfits were suitable for a schoolgirl.

'They're beautiful,' Jinx said. 'Not that I have anywhere to wear them.' If she wore any of those dresses in Manchester, she would look as out of place as a blue-tailed bee-eater in a British park.

'But you will have somewhere to wear them,' Penny assured her. 'Norma, darling, I'd like to take Jinx to London when she finishes her exams.'

Jinx was to sit her School Certificate in a couple of weeks.

'She should visit the National Gallery.'

On the strength of her sketches, Penny seemed to think that Jinx had a career ahead of her as a great artist. It was a nice idea, but even at sixteen years old, Jinx was far more realistic. She knew that once she'd finished her School Certificate, she would need to get a job. There could be no art school for her.

Given her work as an almoner, which brought her into contact every day with people who had less than nothing, Penny Williamson seemed to have very little idea what it really meant to be poor. She didn't seem to understand that the opportunities she and her sister Josephine could claim as their birthright were not for the likes of Jinx.

With all this in mind, Jinx expected Norma to turn down the trip on her behalf. No point showing Jinx a world she could never be a part of. Instead, Norma said, 'Would you like to go to London, Jinx?'

'Oh yes!' For once, Jinx didn't hide her enthusiasm. 'Yes, please.'

What Jinx had forgotten was that Norma was not always a poor single mother raising two children in a crumbling flat. Once upon a time, she, too, was sixteen years old and desperate to run away from the grey world she'd grown up in. Once upon a time, Norma was brave enough to take a job as a lady's maid in Birmingham, where she worked so hard that when her employers announced they were moving to Singapore, they insisted that she should come too.

'I couldn't wait to go,' said Norma. 'And I shall always be glad that I did.'

Three and a half years of internment were forgotten as Norma remembered the first time she laid eyes on Maurice Spencer, the first time he asked her to dance, the day he asked her to marry him ...

'And you two. My children. You two were my reward for being brave. Be brave, Jinx,' said Norma. 'Go to London. The world won't come to you.'

The London trip was scheduled for the day after Jinx's last exam. Penny met Jinx at the station and gave a satisfied nod when she saw that Jinx was wearing one of the three dresses she'd given her on her birthday. The plain blue cotton brought out the colour of Jinx's eyes. Penny explained that they would be staying at the home of her great-aunt – the one who'd arranged for her and her sister to have an audience with the King.

'She's a little old-fashioned, but her house is three minutes from Fortnum's.'

They travelled first class, and when they stepped onto the platform at Euston, Penny summoned a porter to carry their bags. Jinx instinctively clung to her tatty old suitcase – one of the cases she and her mother had taken into Changi, all those years ago.

'Let the nice man carry it for you,' Penny insisted. 'A lady doesn't carry her own bags.'

As Penny wove through the crowd with head-turning confidence, Jinx straightened up and tried to follow suit.

*

The great-aunt was not at the house in Mayfair that day. She was in the country. A housekeeper let Penny and Jinx in, telling them tea would be ready the moment they rang.

'Do you need any help?' Jinx asked instinctively.

'Jinx,' Penny tutted. 'You're a guest!'

'I don't want to get used to it,' Jinx said later.

'Why ever not? I think you should get *very* used to it, because you, my dear, are going to go far.'

When they did have tea, they were joined by Penny's sister. Jinx could tell that Josephine and Penny were related at once. They shared the same fine-boned features and soft brown hair. From a distance, you might have thought they were twins. But Josephine, though less than two years older than Penny, was much more serious. She asked Jinx about her schoolwork. What books had she studied for her English exam?

'Josephine is the world expert on boring poetry,' Penny mocked her.

'I wrote my dissertation on T.S. Eliot,' Josephine explained. 'Do you know Eliot's poems, Jinx?'

'I know *Old Possum's Book of Practical Cats*,' Jinx replied.

'Oh, good.' Josephine seemed pleased. 'But there's so much more to him than that.'

'If you two are going to talk about Eliot,' said Penny, 'then I am going to open the sherry.'

Penny poured three glasses and insisted on a toast. 'To my big sister, Josephine, and to Jinx, my honorary little sister,' she said.

'What have you let yourself in for, Jinx?' Josephine laughed.

The following day, Penny and Josephine took Jinx to the National Gallery, where they viewed the treasures that had spent the war years hidden from the Germans in a Welsh coal mine. Jinx was able to tell the sisters about the work they were

150

seeing. Not just the history of the artists, but things about the techniques they had used to create transcendent paintings that still had the power to move a viewer centuries after the paint had dried. Jinx knew all about the first women admitted to the Royal Academy and the famous female painters who had been changing the art scene since the war.

'Jinx could be one of them,' Penny said proudly.

Josephine seemed impressed.

'I don't have a generous benefactor,' Jinx said after Josephine had left them to meet Gerald. 'Well, you've been very generous, of course, but I have to make my own way now I've finished school. I have to find a job, so Mum doesn't have to work so hard. She's not well.'

'I have noticed,' said Penny. 'And I understand. But for you to end up in some awful service job would be a travesty. That's why I've been thinking you should come to London too, Jinx. I'm moving down here to set up my own antiques business and I'm going to need a secretary. Would you like that? To come with me?'

'Would I like that? Oh yes!'

'Wonderful. Your first duty will be to mix me a Martini. Drinks cabinet is over there.'

Penny shouted the instructions. 'Make two.'

They were joined by one of Penny's friends, an art dealer called Cecil, who dressed like Oscar Wilde. He was smoking a cigarette in a long old-fashioned holder. He looked Jinx up and down, as coolly as a racing trainer inspecting a horse.

'Is that one of your sister's dresses?' he asked Penny.

'How did you guess?'

'It's very Josephine. She looks like Shirley Temple. How are your sister and the young fogey?'

'Happy but boring, *comme d'hab.*'

Over the course of the next hour, Jinx made nine Martinis altogether. By eight o'clock, she had double vision.

'But where will I live if I come to work in London?' she asked Penny.

'With me,' Penny told her. 'I'll sort everything out with Norma.'

It all seemed terribly simple. Even if Jinx did feel a little uneasy when, on her way back from spending a penny, she heard the others laughing.

'My goodness, Penny. Where on earth did you find your funny little pet?'

'She's hilarious, isn't she? But I've bet Josephine ten pounds I'll pass her off as an Hon at Dickie Mortimer's Christmas party.'

'I'll help. I love a wager,' said Cecil. 'And I know a thing or two about fakes.'

Though she wanted her daughter to have all the opportunities she hadn't, Norma wasn't entirely happy with Penny's plan to take Jinx to London. Luckily for Jinx, Penny was persuasive.

'She'll have no chance to get into trouble with me around.'

Eddy was excited at the prospect of having a room to himself. Penny never had managed to get the Spencer family moved into better accommodation. And now she was leaving the St Saviour's Society. 'Before I leave,' she promised, 'I will make certain your situation is at the forefront of my colleagues' minds.'

Two weeks later, Norma and Eddy had still not moved, but Penny and Jinx were installed in a mansion block near Sloane Square, within walking distance of the Mayfair gallery Penny would share with Cecil. Jinx would be secretary to them both.

Penny had decided it was time for her protégée to acquire some polish. Jinx's accent was almost RP now, but she needed to know how to carry herself as if she had grown up among the

Raffles set, not among the working-class kids of her ragtag gang back in Johore. That meant no more sitting cross-legged on the floor. No more crossing her legs, full stop. Penny showed Jinx how to sit on the edge of a chair, put her knees together and arrange her legs slantwise to form a pretty angle, with her skirt at the perfect height to be distracting but not indecent. Talking of skirts, Cecil gave Jinx an advance to 'buy something that doesn't make you look like such a goody two shoes. It reflects very badly on me.'

Jinx's role at Cecil and Penny's gallery was not too onerous. The place was very rarely actually open, though neither Cecil nor Penny seemed too worried that they had many fewer customers than their neighbours. Those customers they did have seemed to spend vast amounts of money. Jinx was astonished by the figures that went through the books. At least once a month, Penny would declare that she'd sold 'some Renaissance thingumajig' and hand Jinx a pound note from a thick wedge of cash. Jinx sent the extra money straight to Norma.

Jinx received another bonus in December, when she wowed the crowd at Dickie Mortimer's Christmas party and Josephine duly paid Penny £10 upon hearing Dickie tell Cecil, quite sincerely, that 'the Honourable Jennifer Spencer' had more class in her little finger than Princess Margaret had from head to toe.

'Jinx,' Penny declared, 'I wouldn't be surprised if Dickie decides he has to marry you. Remember your old friends Penny and Cecil when you're chatelaine of Mortimer Hall.'

Penny herself had many admirers but didn't seem interested in any of them, so Jinx began to wonder if Penny was an 'invert', such as Cecil described himself.

But then one day Penny did bring a man back. He was sitting at the kitchen table, smoking Penny's cigarettes, when Jinx walked in after work. He didn't have a jacket on; just a white shirt, which was open at the neck.

'So this is the famous Jinx,' he said. He held out a hand as big as a bear's paw.When Penny appeared seconds later, her cheeks were pink and her hair was a mess.

'You're back early,' she said, almost accusingly. 'I see you've met Frank.'

Frank was still smiling at Jinx warmly.

'He's just about to leave.'

Frank sighed. 'Make me a cup of tea first.'

'Jinx will do it.'

Jinx assessed the situation while she waited for the kettle to boil. Frank's coat was hanging on the back of the door. Plus his hat. A policeman's hat. He was a copper! And he was obviously Penny's lover. Jinx knew Penny well enough by now to know when something mattered to her, and this man clearly did.

Penny was in a very strange mood that evening, smoking one cigarette after another.

'In case you're wondering, Frank and I met during the war,' said Penny.

'In Italy?'

'No. Before then. In Scotland,' said Frank.

'A training thing,' Penny said dismissively. 'Anyway, we bumped into each other last year. We're friends catching up, that's all. He just popped by for tea.'

'Of course,' said Jinx.

Frank was *definitely* Penny's lover.

Later, Penny dragged Frank through into the sitting room and Jinx could hear a hushed argument, too quiet to make out the words. Except for 'Pygmalion'. She was sure she heard that.

Chapter Twenty-Two

Though Penny had not particularly wanted Jinx to meet her lover Frank, once they'd run into each other in the kitchen that day, there was little point in keeping them apart. Jinx often came home from the gallery (where Penny was rarely seen) to find Frank at their table, smoking cigarettes that he lit with a match from an engraved silver matchbox that he wouldn't let out of his sight. 'It's my lucky matchbox,' he told Jinx.

Jinx liked Frank. He knew about the Far East, having been a policeman in Shanghai before the war. He'd worked alongside Captain Fairbairn, the man who wrote the self-defence book that helped Jinx defeat the school bullies. Frank knew Singapore and Johore too. He understood why Jinx missed her faraway home. Jinx loved it when she and Frank were alone and able to talk about Johore without Penny interrupting with some piece of boring gossip about a duchess Jinx had never heard of.

Frank understood what it was like to be an outsider in Penny's rarefied world. His background had much more in common with Jinx's than with Penny's. Frank hadn't come from money. He admitted to Jinx that he didn't like most of Penny's posh friends.

'But then, they probably don't like me either,' he said. Not that it bothered him. Even if, whenever one of those posh friends was around, Penny seemed to be suddenly spikier towards Frank, goading him about his clumsy manners.

'You're setting a bad example for Jinx,' Penny would tell him if he waved his knife while talking at the dinner table or tucked his napkin into his collar.

Penny would always apologise afterwards and blame her sour mood on an overly strong Martini. 'You know I love you, Frank,' she'd tell him, and he would fold her in his arms and kiss her on the top of her head and they would dance around the room in the way that reminded Jinx of her mother and father. Though Frank was very much married to someone else, his love for Penny, and hers for him, was clear.

Jinx didn't remember much about her father any more. Except when Frank lit a cigarette. He bought the same brand Maurice always had, and as the first wisps of smoke curled into the air, they could take Jinx back to before the war, and if she closed her eyes quickly enough, she might catch the memory of Maurice for just a couple of seconds.

'What are you thinking, Jinx?' Frank would ask her then. 'You were miles away.'

'I was. I was back in Johore ... Oh, I miss mangoes,' she once said.

When she next saw him, Frank brought her a mango that he'd found on a stall in the East End. It was on the turn by the time it got to Jinx, but she held it to her cheek and breathed in the sweet scent and decided it was the best gift she had ever received. Frank was delighted to see how happy it made her. He really was the kindest sort of man.

For her seventeenth birthday, Frank gave Jinx an antique print of a wryneck bird. She loved it. Not least because it showed that he had listened to her when she told him about the origin of her nickname. She wasn't sure Penny ever had.

'Ghastly,' was Penny's opinion on the picture, expressed only once Frank had gone home. 'You'll have to hang it in your bedroom. I think you'll find my birthday present much more interesting.'

Penny jumped up and went to the bureau, which she usually kept locked. She took out an envelope and handed it to Jinx.

'Open it.'

Penny seemed excited.

Inside the envelope was a passport. The only thing missing was the photograph.

'What's this?'

'It's your new passport. We just need to get a picture.'

'But it says Julia Farquharson. That's not my name.'

'I know. But it sort of suits you, and if we wait for the Home Office to sort out your real papers, we'll be waiting forever.'

All Jinx had was the scrap of paper that had allowed her to travel as a refugee from the Far East to England. She was still waiting for confirmation of her official status as a British citizen. Whatever application her mother had made was still lost in a maze of bureaucracy.

'And we don't have forever as we're going to Florence next week.'

'Florence?'

'Yes. You've always wanted to go, haven't you? I'm visiting an old friend who might have some pictures to sell. You're coming with me, of course.'

Jinx stared at the passport. 'Is this a forgery?'

'A pretty good one,' said Penny.

'I can't go to Italy with a forged passport.'

'Darling, no one in Italy knows who you are,' said Penny. 'If you say you're Julia Farquharson, why wouldn't they believe you? Now a "thank you" wouldn't go amiss.'

Jinx went to bed that night in a terrible quandary. She could not believe that Penny was proposing she pretend to be Julia Farquharson – whoever she might be – for a trip to Italy. It seemed to her to be a very risky enterprise, though Penny told her that since the war all sorts of people were without official paperwork, and a great many of them had jumped at the opportunity to change their names.

'We'll never know how many,' Penny said. 'I'm sure there are even SS officers out there, pretending to be nice Jewish schoolteachers. In the scheme of things, your passing yourself off as this Julia girl is a very small crime. In any case, if we do get into trouble, we know a policeman.'

When at last Jinx agreed to pose for a passport photograph, Penny had her put on some make-up first, to make her look as though she might have been born three years earlier, as per the fictitious birthdate. Once the photograph was stuck in place and overlaid with a stamp that Penny handily kept in the bureau, it looked fairly official.

Still, all the way across Europe on the recently inaugurated BEA flight from Northolt to Rome, Jinx was nervous. Not least because it was the first time she had been on board a plane.

'Shouldn't we have parachutes?' Jinx asked.

'You can't just put on a parachute and jump without training,' Penny said, somewhat irritably. 'And even with the training, it isn't easy, you know.'

Penny was right about one thing. When they arrived in Rome, the border guard who inspected Jinx's passport spent far more time looking at her face than at her paperwork. His eyes flicked between the two, but lingered on Jinx's nervous smile rather than on the solemn face in the photograph.

'*Bellissima*,' he said, as he stamped a page and handed the document back to her.

Jinx blushed and rushed by him before he could change his mind. She felt jittery until a porter had reunited her and Penny with their identical cases (Jinx was borrowing one of Penny's) and they were on their way into the city.

Penny had allowed for just one night in Rome, dismissing the ancient wonders around every corner with a wave of her white-gloved hand.

'Romans, Romans, Romans. Didn't you have enough of them at school?'

Jinx was enchanted, stopping to read every Latin inscription they came across. She was pleased that her schoolgirl Latin went some way to making it easy for her to understand the Italian of the porters, the waiters and the staff at their hotel, and make herself understood in turn.

Penny, of course, was fluent in Italian, thanks to her time in Brindisi with the FANY. She was fluent in several languages. French was probably her best, she explained.

'My Uncle Godfrey was a wine merchant in Paris. Josephine and I would often stay with him before the war. I've only been once since '45, though.'

As they walked around the Forum, Penny told Jinx about that last visit to Paris, with Josephine, and how they had learned the fate of the Jewish family who had been living in the building in 1939. August and Lily Samuel, the family's children, had been Penny and Josephine's friends.

'August joined the Resistance. Got himself shot on his way to blow up some Gestapo officers. His sister and their mother were rounded up in the Vel' d'Hiv'.'

Jinx had heard about the Vel' d'Hiv' round-up of July 1942, when Parisian Jews were taken from their homes and held at the city's velodrome, the Vélodrôme d'Hiver, before they were transported to the concentration camps. She wondered if, like her parents on the day they were summoned to the *padang* in Singapore, they'd thought they would be going home again after they'd been registered.

Now she and Penny were standing in the shadow of the Colosseum, another great monument to man's inhumanity to man.

'Lily would have been about the same age as you, Jinx. Had she lived.'

Penny was momentarily miles away, her eyes soft and sad. Then she rearranged her face and said, 'We've got so much excitement ahead of us. This trip is going to be very *gai*, Jinx. *Toujours gai.*'

'Why do you always say that?' Jinx asked. 'What does it mean?'

'It means everything.' Penny flourished her hand in the air. 'It's a rule for life, Jinx. Act happy, be happy. It's something Josephine and I have said to one another since we were children. Don't you know the Archy and Mehitabel books?'

Jinx didn't.

'Then that's another area of your education we must address. But you can borrow our motto in the meantime. It means pull your socks up and put on a smile, there's nothing to be gained by being miserable.'

'You are relentlessly cheerful, Penny. Occasionally it can be quite annoying.'

But even Jinx, for whom the glass was usually half empty, could not be miserable that day. She felt lighter somehow, away from England. In the Italian sunshine – even in a borrowed dress – she could be anyone. She didn't feel pity in the eyes of the strangers who looked at her. In England, she felt it was always so obvious she didn't really fit in. In Rome, it was different. She felt the admiring glances of men and women. The possibilities for transformation weren't limited to going by an alias in her passport.

They were up early the following morning to catch a train to Florence. Penny bought first-class tickets, naturally.

'Few things in life are worth the money, but travelling comfortably is one of them.'

As the train tracked the Apennines up the spine of Italy, Penny pulled a guidebook out of her handbag. It was small and thin – pocket-sized – with a graphic red-and-white cover. It was tattered and it looked well used. And it was in German.

'That looks old,' said Jinx.

'It was printed just before the war, if you can call that old, but I don't think Florence will have changed much, do you?'

'Why didn't you get an English edition?'

'I like to keep up with my languages.'

Penny unfolded the map that was tucked into the back of the small volume and Jinx leaned in to look. Penny pointed out where their hotel was. A small pencil 'X' already marked the spot.

'We're going to be staying here. I think it's best to be away from the *duomo* and the rest. The city will be full of tourists.'

'Aren't we tourists?'

'Certainly not. We're adventurers.'

Then Penny pointed out the landmarks every first-timer in Florence must see before she tucked the guidebook back in her handbag without letting Jinx take a closer look for herself.

'Look out of the window,' Penny said. 'It's far more interesting to see the world with your own eyes than to read about it. And you'll never see Italy for the first time again. You must *live* every moment of your life, Jinx. Every single moment. Not everybody gets the chance.'

Penny's words came back to Jinx seventy-two years later, as she watched Thea once again choose her phone screen over the exceptional view from the window of their coach.

Chapter Twenty-Three

The Coach Trip, 2023

Day four of the Tuscan Splendour tour saw Team Merevale headed for Siena. Watching the landscape roll by, Jinx was in a contemplative mood. She'd woken that morning with a pain in her ribs that she didn't think was a hangover from her fall or caused by the lumpy bed at The Palazzo. She'd been warned that it might happen, that it was one of the many ways her illness might manifest itself – these random aches and pains. She had briefly pondered staying in bed, but she knew that if she told Glenn she didn't feel up to leaving the hotel, Thea would use it as an excuse not to see Siena and everyone, in Jinx's view, needed to see Siena at least once in a lifetime. Jinx took three painkillers and boarded the coach.

When they got to Siena, Team Merevale was grateful for the escalators carefully positioned to take visitors from the coach park to the city. An excellent idea, which Pat said she would suggest at the next parish council meeting as a solution for the uphill walk from Merevale village hall to the bus stop. This, even though, as the council's treasurer, she knew only too well that the council barely had money to have the churchyard mown.

Glenn had prepared an excellent itinerary for the morning,

beginning in Siena's Piazza del Campo, site of the famous Palio horse race. Pushing Jinx's wheelchair, he led Team Merevale on a circuitous route, so that the impressive shell-shaped piazza would come as a surprise at the end of a dark narrow alleyway.

'Ta-daa!' Glenn said as the piazza opened out in front of them.

'And why is this special?' asked Cynthia, who was distracted by a blister that had formed beneath the strap of one of her sandals.

'Why is this special? It's just pretty amazing, isn't it?' said Glenn. 'And it's where the crazy horse race at the beginning of *Quantum of Solace* happens.'

'Ah, yes,' said the Colonel, before adopting a Sean Connery accent to tell the ladies, 'The name's Bond, James Bond,' despite the fact that the actor who played Bond in *Quantum of Solace* was Daniel Craig.

That year's Palio had taken place a week before, and there was still sand and sawdust on the floor of the piazza. Glenn continued, 'As we walk around the town this morning, you'll see flags hanging from some of the buildings. Those are the flags of the city's seventeen *contrade* or districts. Each year, ten of the districts are drawn in a lottery. Each of those ten *contrade* fields a horse and jockey and yes, before anyone asks, some of the jockeys are women. The first woman to ride in the Sienese Palio was Virginia Tacci, in 1581. She's believed to have been just fifteen years old at the time. Quite an achievement.'

Glenn looked at Thea, who glared back at him.

Not many people were paying much attention to Glenn's carefully written speech. The Colonel was still treating Pat, Val and Cynth to his best Sean Connery impression.

'*I shay, Misch Moneypenny.*'

Pat was barely able to control herself as the Colonel directed his faux Scottish smoulder straight at her.

163

'Why is the Colonel speaking like his teeth are loose?' Thea asked Jinx.

'Ahem ...' Glenn tried to bring everyone's attention back to the beauty of Siena, but the Colonel had moved on to misquoting George Lazenby in *On Her Majesty's Secret Service*.

'*Just a bit of stiffness coming on ... in the shoulder.*'

'Oh, gross,' said Thea, pulling a face that could have turned the Colonel to stone.

Holding aloft his furled umbrella to signify his position in the pack, Glenn tried again.

'Now, who's up for a little climb?' he asked, gesturing towards the Palazzo Pubblico, with its iconic bell tower – the Torre del Mangia. 'It's three hundred steps, but according to all the guidebooks it's worth it. The view from up there is one of the best in all of Tuscany.'

He had only two takers: the Colonel and Pat. Cynthia, Val and Marilyn were intent on tracking down a discount shoe shop that Marilyn had seen mentioned on Instagram. Jinx would have liked to see the view, which she had seen many years before, but three hundred steps up was out of the question.

'You mustn't stay down here with me,' she told Thea, but Thea said she would rather sit with Jinx than see a 'stupid view'.

'I definitely don't want to be around the Colonel,' Thea told her.

'*My name is Pussy Galore ...*' Pat was attempting her own impersonation.

Thea covered her ears with her hands and did not uncover them until Glenn, Pat and the Colonel were far, far away.

Thea had not, as Jinx hoped she might, shown any sign that she was warming to the idea of being in Italy, however she had ended up there. She could have been in a hospital waiting room for all the enthusiasm she showed for the Piazza del Campo, with its intricate fishtail paving in red brick and travertine, designed, according to legend, to represent the folds of the Virgin Mary's cloak. She didn't look up when the broken-sounding bell in the Torre del Mangia chimed midday. Neither was she interested in seeing the famous black-and-white Gothic *duomo*, the cathedral of Santa Maria Assunta, with its strangely poignant unfinished wing, abandoned when the town's population was decimated by the plague. If it wasn't on a screen, Thea didn't seem to want to know.

'Where do you want me to put your wheelchair?' Thea asked.

Jinx chose a table in the shade at one of the overpriced cafés overlooking the piazza. When the waiter came, she pressed Thea to have an ice cream.

'I don't want one,' Thea said. 'Just water for me.'

Jinx took Thea's choice of refreshment as the rebuke she was sure it must be. It said, as Thea had already said in so many ways, 'You can make me come here but you can't make me enjoy myself.'

Jinx found she didn't want an ice cream either after that.

If the waiter was disappointed that these customers occupying one of the best tables were having only an espresso and a glass of water, he didn't show it. He set Jinx's coffee down with a wide smile, then shot a glance towards Thea that seemed to ask, 'What's up with her?'

'You really don't have to sit here with me all the time,' Jinx reiterated. 'You're missing all the sights.'

'I'm missing *home*,' Thea replied.

'I see. But you're in Italy and you're stuck here for another four days. Why don't you make the most of it?'

'Because I don't want to? Because I didn't want to come in the first place? The deal was that I came on this trip to help you out as punishment for stealing your money. Which I gave back, by the way. There was nothing about me having to enjoy myself.'

'No, as you've told me before, and that's your choice. Though I had hoped that your being here would benefit us both.'

'I don't know why you wanted to come on this trip anyway. You can't do half the activities,' Thea said.

'That's true. But it was the only way I could get to Florence, and I want to see Florence one more time.'

'Why? It's just another old town.'

'I hope you'll change your mind when you see it.'

Thea's sigh was audible to the whole piazza.

'It's one of the world's most lovely cities,' Jinx persisted. 'When I was your age, it was top of my wish list.'

'When you were my age, when you were my age … Everyone on this trip keeps going on at me about what they wished they'd done at my age. I get the point. You old people couldn't just jump on a plane and go on holiday because of the war or something, right? And I'm sorry that was the case, but it's not my fault. Maybe I don't want to see Florence, no matter how lucky everyone seems to think I am to be here. And, you know what, it's my life.'

With that, Thea got up, pushing away from the table so abruptly that she almost knocked it over. Other customers in the café tutted as Thea brushed by them on her way out into the campo. Val and Cynthia, returning from the shoe shop laden with glamorous sandals they would never be able to wear with their bunions, had seen it all.

'That girl needs a proper talking-to,' said Val. 'She's a selfish little madam. Flouncing about like a toddler when there are other young people who would love to be here.'

'Like my granddaughter,' said Cynthia.

'Like your granddaughter, Cynth,' said Val. 'She would

have loved to see Siena.' Nothing brought those two together like casting judgement on a third party.

'It's nothing to worry about. I think I may have touched a nerve, that's all,' said Jinx.

'You're too generous, Jennifer. We've all seen how she talks to her father. You've paid for her to come on this trip, and see how she talks to you too! My granddaughter would never speak to her elders like that,' said Cynthia.

'Glenn should know about this,' was Val's view.

'I'd rather he didn't. Least said, soonest mended,' said Jinx.

Val and Cynthia didn't hear her. They had segued on to one of their favourite topics: people who don't know how to behave. Subsection: the youth of today.

'I don't know what they teach them in school these days,' said Val, 'but it certainly isn't manners.'

Though they were itching to tell him about his daughter's rudeness, Val and Cynthia did as Jinx asked and refrained from relaying the incident to Glenn. They agreed it would have been a shame to spoil his day too. Glenn finally seemed to be relaxing into the holiday mood. When the small intrepid party that had climbed the three hundred steps of the bell tower joined the others at the muster point, he was full of the wonder of the view.

'You can see for miles. I could totally imagine what it was like here in medieval times. You would have loved it,' he told his daughter, when she reappeared (eyelids slightly puffy, Jinx noted).

Back on the coach, Thea took her place next to Jinx at the front of the bus. Their conversation did not stray beyond the essential.

'I'll fasten your seat belt, Mrs Sullivan.'

'Thank you.'

'Shall I put your handbag on the parcel shelf?'

Then they both went back to watching the view. Thea to a soundtrack of sad songs on her headphones and Jinx to a soundtrack of Penny Williamson classics.

'Seize the day, Jinx. *Toujours gai!*'

Chapter Twenty-Four

From Siena, Ivor the driver took the coach due north to the heart of Tuscany's 'Chiantishire', where Team Merevale was booked onto a wine tasting at Poggio Mendini, a vineyard specialising in organic Chianti Classico.

As the coach wound through the Tuscan countryside, Glenn hoped that he'd chosen the right place for a tasting, out of the many tastings he'd researched online. The Colonel reassured him, 'As long as there's alcohol on offer, you won't get any complaints from this lot. You've seen what they're like at any village celebration. Enthusiastic but undiscriminating.'

Poggio Mendini was certainly beautifully situated. It stood on a hill – hence the *poggio* – surrounded by acres of vines, which were an astonishingly bright green in the sunshine; the bright green of leaves drawn by children. A long tasting table, laid with a dazzling white cloth, all the better for seeing the colour of the wine against, had been set up under a pergola, with a canopy of yet more vines dotted with tiny grapes. The Colonel chanced a taste of one of those grapes and discovered, to his disgust, that it was far from ripe.

'I need some wine to get rid of the taste!'

'I can help you with that,' said the vineyard's chatelaine, Giovanna, appearing with two bottles dangling from each hand.

Together with her assistant, Giovanna poured out tasting portions of four different wines into the glasses arrayed in front of Team Merevale and launched into her spiel about grape varieties and the characteristics of the land that made a Chianti Classico.

'The wine in the glass on the left is our most recent vintage,' Giovanna explained. 'It's 100 per cent pure Sangiovese. The grapes were picked during the pandemic, and I think you'll agree that you can taste all our hopes and dreams in every sip.'

Team Merevale nodded along, sniffing and swirling and comparing the aromas and colours.

'Can you smell the pandemic?' Cynth asked Val and Marilyn.

'The pandemic smelled like face masks and hand sanitiser to me,' said Marilyn. 'This wine is nice, though.'

At the far end of the table, Jinx sat in her wheelchair with Thea by her side. Thea was too young to take part in the tasting, so she munched on breadsticks and sipped a Diet Coke. She was sceptical when she heard the tasting notes.

'How can grapes taste "like red fruit"? They *are* red fruit,' she said.

'Can you tell the difference?' Glenn asked the Colonel. 'I mean, can you really tell the difference between the wines?'

The Colonel assured him that there really was a difference.

'By the time the Colonel gets to the fourth wine, he won't be able to tell the difference between Chianti Classico and cat's pee,' was Val's opinion.

Jinx took a contemplative sip.

'There is a hint of cat's pee there.'

She had hoped to amuse Thea with her comment, but Thea did not respond. Instead, the young girl crunched another breadstick in a raging kind of way.

But Glenn need not have worried that anyone else would be disappointed by the tasting. Giovanna and her team kept

170

everyone well topped up, so that as it came to an end the Colonel said to Glenn, 'After drinking all this wine in the sunshine, I think I'm going to need a little nap.'

It was such a nice thought that the Colonel decided to repeat it, in Italian, for Giovanna's benefit. '*Mi servirebbe un pisellino, Giovanna!*'

He raised his glass at her.

Giovanna kept a straight face, but her assistant had to walk away from the table to compose herself. It wasn't often a visitor told them that he needed a little penis. She thought perhaps the Colonel had meant to say *pisolino*.

That afternoon saw a definite shaking off of inhibitions for Team Merevale. Giovanna was generous with her tasting pours and was very happy indeed to open further bottles, which she sold to her visitors at a significant discount. The delicious wine and the sunshine worked magic on the spirit.

'This makes me want to sing,' said Marilyn, swirling her glass so hard that the contents flew out and drenched Pat. Fortunately, Pat's dress was already purple and she found it funny, as did Val and Cynthia, who had long since given up the pretence of sipping and sniffing. They were glugging it back.

With the official tasting over, everyone found themselves a spot in the shade to enjoy a picnic lunch.

'I could live here forever,' said Val.

'If you hadn't voted Brexit, you could,' said Marilyn.

'May I pour you two another glass?' asked Glenn, keen to avoid another heated debate.

The Colonel stepped in to back him up. 'What are you ladies most looking forward to for the rest of the trip?'

Marilyn jumped to answer the question. 'Lucca,' she said. 'I'm looking forward to Lucca. Home of Puccini. You know, when I was a younger woman, my singing teacher suggested I consider a career in the opera.'

'My arse,' muttered Val.

Marilyn turned towards her with narrowed eyes.

'My arse is flat from all that sitting on the coach. That's all I was going to say.'

Jinx and Thea had found their own spot, away from the others in the shadow of the tall stone house with green shutters that stood at the very top of Poggio Mendini.

'It's rather lovely here, isn't it?' Jinx tried to start a conversation.

Thea shrugged. 'I suppose.'

'It's probably more fun for those of us who are drinking.'

Thea agreed. 'It's really boring to be around drunk people when you're not.'

'I won't argue with that. But this view—'

'Why are people so obsessed with views?' Thea asked.

'Doesn't it lift your heart?'

'Not really.'

Jinx pushed on. 'When you get to my age, you seize life's joys where you can, by taking in the world around you, trying every new thing, seeing every view. Life is short.'

'You don't think I know that? That life is short?'

Jinx realised she had trodden on a landmine, but there was no time to backtrack because suddenly there was a commotion further down the lawn.

The Colonel, standing up too quickly, had had a dizzy spell, lost his footing and ended up doing a forward roll across the grass. Unfortunately, he had taken his tumble on a surprisingly steep slope, and he had rolled another twenty metres before he came to a stop against a drystone wall, causing a statue of the

Three Graces of ancient legend to topple off the wall and land on top of him.

A collective gasp went up.

Glenn was the first to take action. He raced down the slope to administer first aid. The Three Graces were only half life-size but they still looked bloody heavy. The Colonel lay groaning beneath their full weight. He must at least have broken a couple of ribs.

'Someone call an ambulance,' Glenn cried.

Glenn braced himself to lift the statue off the Colonel's chest, but before he could do so, the Colonel suddenly bench-pressed the three Roman goddesses skywards.

'Well, would you look at that?' he said.

Giovanna, who had sauntered down the hill herself, joined Glenn and the Colonel by the wall.

'Ah yes,' she said, lifting the Three Graces with one hand. 'They're not real. They're polystyrene. They were left over from a film shoot. I'm very sorry all the same.'

She helped haul the Colonel up to standing.

'No need to be sorry,' said the Colonel. 'When I woke up this morning, I prayed to end the day flat on my back beneath three beautiful ladies.'

'Can't say that sort of thing, Malcolm,' Glenn reminded him. 'Perhaps he has concussion?' he suggested to Giovanna by way of an excuse.

'*Si! Domani ho mal di tetta,*' said the Colonel.

Giovanna struggled to hide her smile at the thought of the Colonel having 'tit-ache'.

The Colonel strode back up the slope. 'False alarm, every-body. I'm perfectly fine. Nothing broken. Just need to take more water with it next time.'

'He needs to get himself a stick,' said Thea.

'Yes,' said Jinx, looking ruefully at her sling.

And all the time he had managed to keep his hat on.

More than half of Team Merevale fell asleep on the drive back to the hotel that afternoon. Those who weren't asleep shared confidences they'd never shared before. Chianti Classico was a great loosener.

'There should be a disclaimer at wine tastings,' said the Colonel. 'Dark secrets may be unearthed.'

But nobody would have guessed that Pat Robinson, who *never* took off her cardigan, even when the temperature was nudging thirty degrees, had supplemented her student grant by working as a life model in the 1970s.

'When you say "life model",' the Colonel probed, 'do I take it you mean "*life model*", Pat?'

'I do.'

She did.

'That's with no clothes on,' Cynthia mouthed at Val.

'I posed for some rather good artists, actually. There's a portrait of me in a municipal gallery in Nottingham.'

'There never is,' said Marilyn. 'In the buff?'

'Completely starkers.'

'You are a dark horse, Pat.'

'I've had my moments.'

Pat asked Glenn to look up the painting in question on his phone, so that everyone could see it.

'Are you sure?' Glenn asked.

'Yes, please. It's called "Pat by the window, reading *Jane Eyre*." The artist's name is Simon Fletcher. R.A.,' she added. 'That's R.A. for Royal Academy.'

'I hope the book is covering her you-know-what,' Val mouthed at Cynthia.

In the end, no one could tell what *Jane Eyre* was covering. The painting was an abstract affair with Pat's best assets

174

represented by two blancmange-pink squares and a large black triangle.

'Perhaps the triangle is meant to be the book?' suggested Glenn hopefully.

'I think I've had too much Chianti,' said the Colonel, looking at the painting upside down.

At the front of the coach, Jinx and Thea sat side by side in silence. Thea was listening to her music again, and Jinx was wondering how she had managed to throw at Thea exactly the same sort of nonsense which Penny had so often thrown at her? Seize the day? *Toujours gai*? She couldn't blame Thea for turning away from her.

Back at the hotel, Jinx eschewed the Colonel's *aperitivo* hour. Safely alone in her room, she tipped the contents of her handbag out onto her bed as usual. She put the mouse on the bedside table, then sat down to look at the old German guidebook. As she unfolded the map in the back, the scent of old paper drifted up and she remembered again the first time she'd seen it in Penny's hands.

Starting in the piazza where Team Merevale's Florence hotel was located, Jinx traced her finger along the *lungarno* to the smaller square on which stood the Hotel Regina. The pencil mark Penny had made to mark the old hotel's location was still just about visible.

She heard Penny's voice in her head.

'I don't think Florence will have changed much, do you?'

Would that still be the case? The following day she would find out.

175

Chapter Twenty-Five

Florence, 1951

The Florentine hotel Penny had chosen – the Hotel Regina – was not terribly grand, and it smelled strongly of old dog. They were greeted at the door by landlady Signora Bianchi and her doddery dachshund, Romeo.

Penny had booked Jinx her own room for their stay – a narrow single, but her own nonetheless – with a Juliet balcony that looked out over a beautiful garden. The beautiful garden, alas, did not belong to the Hotel Regina, but to the large house next door, which was hidden from the road by tall walls covered in trailing wisteria and headily fragrant jasmine.

The Regina's own garden was nothing more than a narrow strip of grass along the back of the building, scratched almost bare by Romeo the dachshund's claws. In the middle was an unhappy potted olive tree with just a few shrivelled fruit clinging to its branches, and the 'lawn' was edged by a macabre row of tiny graves with elaborately carved headstones. The headstones were dedicated to Signora Bianchi's previous canine companions. All of them *bassotti*, she explained. 'Better company than a second husband.'

'I can imagine. We're dog people, too,' said Penny. 'Aren't we, Julia?'

Jinx was examining a painting on the lobby wall. She didn't respond to Penny at first, having completely forgotten she was Julia for this trip.

'Oh, that girl,' said Penny to Signora Bianchi. 'Absolutely obsessed with art. We're talking about dogs, Jinx. Don't we love them?'

Jinx thought of Flaubert, the dachshund puppy they'd left behind with Cecil in London. The antipathy between Flaubert and Jinx was mutual.

'Are you here for the museums?' Signora Bianchi asked.

'Yes,' said Penny. 'And a little work.'

On the train ride from Rome, Penny had outlined the plan for their time in Florence. They would be visiting Penny's friend, who had some old paintings to sell, and they had tickets for the opera. Other than that, Jinx would be at leisure, though Penny had a couple of meetings in the diary.

First, however, Penny promised to give Jinx a tour of the city's most celebrated sights.

Leaving their suitcases still packed, they headed straight out. They wiggled their way in single file down the city's narrow pavements towards the Ponte Vecchio, which was lined with jewellery shops that seemed to be doing a brisk trade. The tourists were back in force that summer.

'The Germans destroyed every crossing in the city except for this one,' Penny explained as they crossed over the famous medieval bridge, with boutiques across its length. 'Apparently, Hitler was rather fond of it. You know, it used to be entirely covered in butchers' shops.'

Jinx had not known that.

'Must have smelled appalling.'

Though the war had been over for six years, there was still a lot of construction work going on in the city, as the Florentines worked on the bridges and buildings Adolf Hitler hadn't held so dear.

Once across the Ponte Vecchio, Penny and Jinx turned right and headed for the Piazzale degli Uffizi and the Uffizi gallery.

'I imagine you'll want to pop in there at some point,' said Penny, waving her hand dismissively towards the buildings which housed so many of the world's artistic treasures. 'But there's plenty of time for that. I think we want to see *David* today.'

They paused in the Piazza della Signoria, in front of Michelangelo's impressive young warrior, who gazed impassively over the heads of the tourists crowding for a photo opportunity.

'It's not the real one,' Penny reminded her young companion as she gazed up at the naked statue, which was much bigger than Jinx had imagined. 'But worth a picture all the same. Go and pose in front of him. I'll take a snap for your mother.'

Penny took out her Box Brownie again.

'Come round to the other side, so I can get his bottom in.'

'Penny! I won't be able to show Mum that.'

'Don't be silly, Jinx. That bottom is Michelangelo's finest work.'

They left the piazza via the Via dei Calzaiuoli, where they were beset by hawkers thrusting flowers, scarves and hand-tinted picture postcards in their faces. Penny soon put them off with a phrase or two in Italian.

'What did you say to them?' Jinx wanted to know.

'I told them I was delivering you to a convent. You have no need for material things.'

'You didn't say really that.'

'No. You're right. I told them to bugger off. I should probably teach you how to say it yourself. Except that I don't think Julia Farquharson is the type of girl who swears.'

'You're quite right, Penny.' Jinx hammed up the Hut Ten accent that had won Penny a tenner from Josephine after dreadful Dickie Mortimer's Christmas do.

It was coming up for four o'clock, and all around the city various bells were signalling the hour in a delightfully un-synchronised way.

'Isn't that a wonderful sound, Jinx?'

Jinx had to agree.

On the corner of the Via del Campidoglio, Penny stopped and said, 'Now put your arm through mine. From here on, I want you to keep your eyes firmly shut until I tell you to open them. No peeking. We're following the sound of the biggest bell.'

Jinx closed her eyes and allowed herself to be led for the last few feet. She felt Penny position her so that she was facing in the right direction, then heard her say, 'Here we are. Open your eyes now. And look straight up.'

Jinx's mouth dropped open as she tipped her head back to look at the cathedral – the celebrated Duomo di Santa Maria del Fiori – which suddenly loomed before her. The towering marble-clad building, topped off with Brunelleschi's terracotta cupola, seemed too big for the square into which it had been dropped. Jinx was lost for words.

'Isn't she lovely?' said Penny. 'Luckily, the Americans were *very* precise with their bombing.'

'It's beautiful,' said Jinx.

'Wait until you see inside.'

Penny took her arm again and they headed for the huge bronze doors. Before they stepped in, Penny made certain that Jinx's hair was properly covered by the scarf she had been wearing around her neck.

179

'Now look innocent or something. Yes. That's your best expression. No wonder poor Dickie was fooled.'

They stepped into the cool darkness of the nave. Outside, a cloud had passed over the sun, but as soon as that cloud had wafted on, the dome itself was lit up. Jinx was open-mouthed again as she gazed up at Giorgio Vasari's frescos of the Last Judgement circling the dome's interior.

'Not bad, eh?'

'It's ... It's better than I ever imagined.'

Jinx knew what she was looking at. In the days leading up to the trip, she had pored over an art book that Penny had given her back when they first met. She pointed out the scenes for her now, naming the saints and the sinners who played out eternal stories of salvation and damnation above their heads.

Penny took her hand. 'I'm very glad to be here with you, Jinx. There's something about seeing this place with you by my side that is very special indeed.'

The heartfelt nature of Penny's words was at odds with her usual arch humour and insistence that everything should be 'toujours gai'.

'I'm going outside for a ciggie,' she said then, as though even that tiny hint of sentimentality had been too much for her.

While Penny went for a smoke, Jinx walked around the cathedral, taking in the treasures she had previously known only from the pages of a book. She could hardly believe she was in Florence. She tried to imagine herself centuries earlier, standing in the same spot alongside the men and women who had brought the Renaissance into being. Did they have any idea, she wondered, how their work would endure? Would she ever create any work of her own that endured in the same way? That was the ultimate human impulse, wasn't it? To leave something important behind. To not be forgotten. To live for ever in the minds of the people who came after you.

Jinx did not know how long she stood and gazed up at the dome, not minding that it hurt her neck to have to look up so high. She was as happy as she had been since before the war. She only wished that her father might be standing alongside her. He would have liked this place.

When Penny rejoined Jinx beneath Vasari's dome, she was entirely her usual self again and suggested, '*Aperitivo*?'

While it was still not the done thing for women to go into bars, Penny Williamson didn't care, and in her company neither did Jinx. They were modern women with modern ideas. In fifty years' time, no one would bat an eyelid when two women bought themselves drinks, Penny assured her.

'Only the bourgeois care now,' Penny asserted, as she guided Jinx towards Il Bottegone. She ordered for both of them. A negroni for herself and an Americano for her young companion.

'Because you are still a beginner, and two types of liquor is quite enough for you.'

'Tell me about your first time in Florence, Penny,' Jinx asked.

'It was right after the war. The whole place was in a bit of a state. As were the poor Florentines. I'll never forget one child I saw. No shoes. Ribs sticking out like a xylophone.'

'Like me and Eddy in Singapore.'

Penny briefly pressed Jinx's hand. 'My dear Jinx, I hate the thought of you and Eddy in that awful place with nothing to eat for years on end. I don't like to think of any child going through hunger and deprivation thanks to some stupid grown-up fight. It's why I want to start my own charitable foundation. For you and Eddy, and children like Lily Samuel, too.'

Lily Samuel's story had stuck in Jinx's head, just as it obviously haunted Penny. Jinx imagined the poor girl heading off to a German camp and put her glass back down.

181

'You're a very good woman, Penny,' Jinx said.

'I try to be.'

Chapter Twenty-Six

That evening, Penny and Jinx were invited to a party. Their host was an American called Tony, whom Penny had met during the war. Tony had fallen in love with Italy and, after VE Day, had gone home to Chicago only to collect a few belongings before making his home in Florence. Now he worked at the city's American consulate.

Penny picked out the dress that Jinx should wear. It was another old frock of Josephine's, a pink silk number, with stiff cap sleeves and a nipped-in waist. Dior's New Look, no longer all that new. Penny loaned her a double string of pearls with an elaborate clasp to go with it. Looking at herself in the mirror, Jinx wondered how Josephine would have worn the dress herself. It seemed at odds with Josephine's serious demeanour and the gloomy poetry of which she was so fond.

'She's nothing like Penny,' Cecil had agreed when Jinx talked about Josephine with him. 'Probably never said "fuck" in her life. Or had one.'

'But she's recently married,' Jinx said.

'And?' Cecil raised an eyebrow at that.

That evening Penny wore a black silk number, off the shoulder.

'You look like a Singer Sargent portrait,' Jinx breathed.

Penny was a chameleon, and with the black dress and a pair of discreet diamond earrings she had made herself truly beautiful. She could do that. There were moments when Penny looked so plain you wouldn't have glanced at her in the street. On other occasions she drew the light and glittered like a film star, and you couldn't take your eyes off her. It was as though she had different faces hanging up in her wardrobe as well as different outfits.

They were right to dress up. Penny had taken Jinx to a few parties in London, but nothing to compare to this one. The guests were drawn from the very best of American society, in Europe doing the new 'grand tour', visiting Paris, Rome, Florence and Venice. Perhaps the American section of Berlin if they were daring. The Americans were the new aristocrats. The men had made their money in manufacturing (arms and oil, mostly). The women were the very best of their breed, with legs as fine as any racehorse. They were all of them richer than Jinx could possibly have imagined.

Jinx was terrified at the prospect of saying the wrong thing. Fortunately, there was no opportunity for *faux pas*. At dinner, Jinx found herself seated between two middle-aged men who were far more keen to know what she thought of their achievements than to hear anything about hers. It was easy enough to look interested. Cecil had taught her how to do that. Everyone who stepped into Cecil's gallery left with the impression that he thought they were wonderful. Jinx had picked up the knack.

The women guests, for the most part, were less friendly. Jinx was far younger than all of them and they made a point of seeming uninterested in her, though each of them was watching to make sure their husbands were not being charmed. Only one woman – perhaps a little more savvy than the rest – did make the effort to speak to Jinx. 'To know her enemy,' as Penny might have said.

The woman held out her hand to Jinx, and Jinx noticed at once the thick diamond line bracelet glittering on her wrist. She couldn't miss it. Each of the perfectly cut stones was as big as a pea.

'I'm Clementine Wilde,' the woman said. 'This is your first time in Italy?'

'It is.'

'Well, I'm sure it won't be the last. Who are you anyway?'

Jinx found herself saying, 'Julia Farquharson. The Honourable,' she added. 'From London.'

Jinx cringed inwardly at that 'Hon'. You probably weren't supposed to mention your title if you really had one.

'I don't believe I know your family,' said Clementine. There was something pointed about the observation. Was it so obvious that Jinx hadn't been born to this kind of life?

'Well, I don't believe I know yours either,' Jinx said in response. 'So I suppose that makes us quits.' She could see from the flicker in Clementine's expression that it was the wrong thing to have said. Penny, standing just behind Clementine, stifled a laugh.

If Jinx had felt uncomfortable when they arrived at the party, her sense of unease only grew as the evening went on. These were not her people. She wondered if it showed.

'Darling, of course not,' Penny said when they were back at their hotel. 'You are as good as any of them and far more intelligent. That witch Clemmie Wilde isn't worth worrying about. She acts like a duchess, but her grandfather was a farm boy who got lucky in the Gold Rush. Go back four generations and her family were poor as dirt. *She ain't no Medici,*' Penny added in an American accent designed to make Jinx laugh.

The following day, their host Tony invited them to join him for lunch at the consulate.

'The night ended rather badly,' he told them. 'Clemmie Wilde lost a diamond bracelet.'

'Oh, really?' said Penny, eyes on her plate.

'Seems it was rather a good one. We searched high and low but couldn't find it anywhere. Her husband wasn't even sure she was wearing it, but she insisted she was and that it must have fallen off and been purloined by one of my staff. She's demanding I sack the entire household if the bracelet isn't returned by tonight.'

'How unfortunate,' said Penny.

Tony briefly left his guests to accept a telegram. While he was gone, Jinx told Penny. 'She *was* wearing that bracelet last night. I saw it when she shook my hand.'

'Clever sausage,' said Penny. 'How very observant you are.'

'The diamonds were enormous.'

Tony was on his way back.

'I was telling Penny—' Jinx began.

Penny gave Jinx a kick under the table before changing the subject to the possibility of a trip to Fiesole.

'Oh yes,' said Tony. 'Can't come to Florence without going to Fiesole. The view! And you've got to see Pisa. Are you taking this charming girl to Pisa, Penny?'

'I'm sure we'll find a moment,' Penny said.

'You must.' Tony turned to Jinx. 'Leaning Tower et cetera. She will love it ... Say, do you ladies have plans for this evening? We're throwing a party here tonight. Some bigwig called Jimmy Noone is in town.'

For just a second, Jinx thought Penny's face registered surprise at the name.

'What a pity we're going to be at the opera,' Penny said. 'Some other time.'

*

That same day, Penny took Jinx to see the paintings she had thought she might try to sell.

'Not worth a thing,' was Penny's opinion on the distinctly pedestrian landscapes. 'Or the *soprintendenza* wouldn't be letting them out of the country.'

After that, Penny left Jinx more or less to her own devices for the afternoon. Jinx didn't mind. She felt very grown-up as she navigated the city on her own, using a map provided by Signora Bianchi, who seemed to have taken a liking to her guests after discovering that Penny had been with the FANY in Brindisi. Signora Bianchi shuddered as she told Penny and Jinx about the German officers who had used the Hotel Regina as a knocking shop during the occupation.

'I couldn't refuse them a room, no matter how much I wanted to. They would have killed me!' the old woman claimed.

As she struggled with Signora Bianchi's street plan, Jinx briefly wondered why Penny didn't just lend her the pocket guide. Even if it was printed in German, it would have been much easier to have that book than the unwieldy map, which was as big as an issue of *The Times* and just as difficult to fold.

Jinx decided she would buy herself an English copy of the little red guide if she found one. If Penny wasn't going to accompany her to the Uffizi, it would be useful to have a description of the work she might see there, so she didn't waste too much time on endless medieval Madonnas and miss out on hidden treasures. Jinx wanted to see the Botticellis, of course, but most of all she wanted to see the *Doni Tondo*, which both Penny and Cecil had described so lovingly.

'Michelangelo truly understood the human condition,' Cecil had told her. 'And he was every bit as good a painter as Leonardo. Better, in my opinion.'

Gosh. They were right. Jinx was astonished by the painting:

the brightness of the colours and the natural beauty of the composition. The Madonna, interrupted in reading, reaching up to take the Christ child from Joseph, looked as weary as any real human mother, trying not to be annoyed that her child's father couldn't seem to take him long enough that she might finish reading a chapter of her book.

Standing in front of Michelangelo's masterpiece, Jinx wished she was not alone in the gallery, so that she might turn to a companion and share her feelings of awe. It would have been especially lovely to have Eddy with her. The baby in the painting reminded Jinx of Eddy when he was small, before they were taken prisoner by the Japanese and his chubby little legs got all thin and spindly. She had written a postcard to Norma and Eddy that morning, excitedly describing her first flight and the Duomo, which seemed equally miraculous. She still had to find a suitable gift for her brother. He would be happy with sweets, she was sure, but she wanted to get something special. Penny had unhelpfully suggested Jinx bought her brother a stuffed dormouse from the taxidermist's shop near their hotel.

'That he would love.' Penny was certain.

Next day, Jinx took herself to the Pitti Palace, enormous and austere on its sloping piazza. She wandered through the Boboli Gardens behind the palace, in hope of finding some of the fruit and flowers she knew from home inside the greenhouses. She found her way to the orangery. Most of the orange trees had been brought outside for the summer. Wandering between their serried rows, she breathed in the scent of warm earth and thick green leaves.

It was not quite the smell of home – of Johore – but it was closer than anything she had found in an English garden, and while the tiny white flowers that dotted some of the trees weren't the same as the ones she and her friends used to plait into their hair, they were similar enough to bring a smile to her lips. When no one was watching, Jinx pinched a sprig and folded it inside her handkerchief. She would press it between the pages of a book later.

Oh, it was heaven to be in Italy that day. Jinx had all but forgotten how anxious she'd been when Penny first presented her with that fake passport. Thank goodness she had allowed herself to be persuaded to come. The city was beautiful, the people were charming, the food was straight from Heaven. Everything was perfect. Until Penny returned to meet her at the hotel, seeming more than usually agitated ...

Signora Bianchi had laid out afternoon tea on a dusty iron table in the hotel's scrubby garden, among the dachshunds' tomb-stones.

'Would you look at that,' said Penny. 'They're all named after characters from Shakespeare. *Helena. Desdemona. Giulietta.*' Penny was trained to spot patterns and prided herself on being able to do so. 'And you, Romeo. I suppose you'll end up there one day, too.' She gave the hotel's current canine incumbent a scratch between the ears.

'Did you go to the Pitti?' Penny asked Jinx as they sipped the too-strong Darjeeling and ate the stale cakes.

'I did.'

'Good, good. See everything you needed to see?'

She didn't seem to want any detail.

'I've decided we're going back to Rome in the morning,' she announced.

'I thought we had another two days,' Jinx said.

'Yes, but you've seen pretty much everything you wanted to, haven't you?'

'What about Fiesole?'

'That's just another view. I was wrong to have dragged you

away from the Eternal City so quickly. You can't come to Italy without seeing Rome properly. Pack your bag tonight, Jinx. We need to be ready before breakfast, so an early night, I think. Will you need any more food today? No? Wonderful.'

With the prospect of missing supper, Jinx had another slice of cake.

Both women retired to their rooms. Jinx packed, as Penny had suggested, then got into bed with her book. Concentrating on the complicated story after a long day spent sightseeing sent Jinx to sleep. When she woke again, the room was completely dark. Lying on soft down pillows looking up at the ceiling, she heard the bells of a distant campanile sound two.

Jinx was sad to think they would be leaving Florence so soon. She would have been happy to stay. Perhaps she would be back before too long. There were many opportunities for an art restorer in a place like Florence. Cecil had been teaching her some of the tricks of the trade.

These were the thoughts that were going through Jinx's mind when she heard a sudden crash from outside her window. Jinx jumped up to look. It sounded as though the noise had come from the palazzo garden, but it had set Romeo the dog barking so loudly you'd have thought that a herd of wild boar had breached the wall and was rampaging in his direction.

Signora Bianchi opened her bedroom door – just along the corridor – and shouted, 'Stai zitto, Romeo.' The dog modified his bark to a disgruntled-sounding growl.

While Signora Bianchi went back to bed, Jinx remained on her Juliet balcony, listening carefully to the sounds from the garden over the wall. Whatever or whoever it was that had made the initial racket was silent. Jinx could hear only the cicadas and the occasional whirr of a nightjar's call. Romeo the dog gave one last defiant bark, before he, too, settled down.

Jinx looked out over the palazzo's garden, searching for movement as her eyes adjusted to the dark. She saw nothing but she stayed there, leaning over the balustrade, breathing in the scent of the night. Wearing her long white nightdress and with her hair loose, Jinx fancied she looked like Shakespeare's most famous heroine. She leaned her cheek on her hand and sighed, '*Ay me.*' Where was the brave lover who would climb up a creeper for a kiss?

'Jinx.'

Jinx was in a dream world.

'Psssst. Jinx.'

A pebble flew past Jinx's head and landed in the room behind her, clattering across the terracotta tiles.

'Jinx! For heaven's sake.'

The voice was coming from right underneath. A shadowy figure stepped into the square of light cast by Jinx's open windows. It was Penny. She was in the palazzo garden.

'What are you doing down there?'

'Go downstairs and distract the dog. Stop him barking. Take biscuits.'

'What? Why?'

'Because I'm stuck down here. I have to climb this wall and come in via your balcony, that's why.'

'I—'

'Just bloody do it, Jinx. Quick as you can.'

'I haven't got any biscuits.'

'Then improvise, darling! Give him your arm.'

Jinx crept downstairs, trying not to set the staircase creaking. Fortunately, Romeo rather liked Jinx and needed no persuading to follow her when she beckoned him in to the hotel's small lounge. Jinx kept him in there, talking to him softly and scratching him between his ears. He didn't even need a biscuit.

An entire band of robbers might have walked right past while Jinx was tickling his tummy.

Jinx wasn't sure how long Penny needed her to provide a distraction, but her mission had to be aborted in any case when Signora Bianchi came downstairs, with her hair in a net, and asked if there was a problem. Why was Jinx creeping about in the middle of the night?

'*Mi scusi. Ho avuto un ... un incubo?*' said Jinx, unsure she had the vocabulary. 'I was sleepwalking?'

'Oh, *bella.*'

Seeing that her old dog was in heaven thanks to Jinx's attentions, the expression on Signora Bianchi's face softened. She went into the kitchen and returned with two biscuits. One for the dog and one for Jinx. 'This will give you sweeter dreams.'

Romeo got back into his basket. Jinx took her biscuit upstairs to her room. When she got inside, Penny was sitting on the bed, arms folded, looking cross as two sticks.

'Why on earth did you lock the door? I couldn't get out.'

'I didn't think—' Jinx began.

'No, well. There we are. Next time use your brain. Good night.'

'Penny! Wait! Aren't you going to tell me why you were stuck in the palazzo garden in the first place?'

'Not tonight, no. We've got an early start.'

When she went to the bathroom the following morning, Jinx saw that Penny had left muddy handprints all over her towel.

Chapter Twenty-Seven

The Coach Trip, 2023

Having helped Mrs Sullivan get ready for bed, Thea went straight to her own room. She was scrolling through old photos on her phone when a WhatsApp message came through from her dad.

'You OK?' Glenn asked.

'Yes,' Thea replied.

'Long day! Want to come and watch a film with me?'

'Why?' was Thea's response.

'Thought it would be nice. Haven't seen much of you.'

'We've been on the same coach all day.'

'Yes. But no chance to talk.'

'Too tired,' Thea texted. 'Need to sleep.'

'OK. Night.'

At the top of Thea's screen, she could see that her dad was typing something else. *Dad is typing, Dad is typing* . . . It seemed to go on for ages. He was either writing a very long message or he was struggling to get the words right. Please, get the words right, Thea silently begged. Please be typing what I want you to type right now. But after a full minute, no new message came through and Glenn went offline.

Thea stared at the chat, which was just like a hundred other exchanges they'd had over the past year. Nothing different about it. But there should have been, shouldn't there? Had he forgotten? How could he have forgotten?

All day, Thea had been waiting for Glenn to mention that today was the third anniversary of her mum's death. All it would have taken was a simple acknowledgement of the fact. One line. Recognition of the fucking big red cross in Thea's mental diary. But he had said nothing. Just like last year. Just like the first year after she died. As if not mentioning the date could make the memory of it go away. As if Thea would ever see the date on her phone and not be hit by thoughts of all those last times: the last kiss on her mum's soft warm cheek, the last smile, their last goodbye.

Why didn't her dad understand? If he did understand, he would never have arranged a coach trip to Italy. Alone in her bedroom, Thea pressed one blade of her nail scissors against the inside of her thigh.

Chapter Twenty-Eight

On day five, Team Merevale was very slow to muster in the car park for the departure to Pisa. The Colonel felt particularly unwell.

'It was the pasta sauce.' He was certain. Definitely not the two bottles of Chianti he'd put away at the wine tasting, or the Aperol spritzes he'd downed in the hotel bar afterwards. 'Never trust a buffet, Glenn. Lord knows how long those *pene* had been there.'

Glenn had heard by now from several of the hotel staff that the Colonel's pronunciation of *penne* wasn't quite right but, like Jinx, he'd decided it wasn't the time to try to correct him.

Since it was a 'moving' day, Glenn did his best to impress upon Team Merevale that they needed to be sure they had all their belongings with them when they left the hotel that morning: hats, bags, medications, etc.

'We won't be coming back here tonight,' he reminded Val and Cynthia.

'Attenshun!' the Colonel shouted over the breakfast buffet hubbub. 'They're not listening to you, Glenn. Tell them again. This time with a bit of authority, man.'

Glenn opened his mouth to begin, but the Colonel spoke right over him.

'Glenn wants you all to be sure you have everything, and I mean everything, with you. Except the hotel towels, Val. You're not meant to have those in your bag.'

'Well, I never!' Val protested. 'Accusing people of thieving. It isn't on.' But she blushed as she thought of the two mini soaps she had pinched from an unattended housekeeping trolley.

The Colonel's announcement did the trick, and everyone made certain to 'do a nervous' when they got back to their rooms.

'Nervous wreck,' the Colonel explained to Thea and Jinx. 'Cockney rhyming slang for "check".'

'Why don't you just say "check"?' Thea asked.

'Where's the fun in that?'

The Colonel took charge again for the loading of the coach and the head count.

'All present and correct,' he assured Ivor the driver. 'Let's hit the road.'

Three miles down the motorway towards Pisa, the Colonel realised he was missing his phone.

After a detour to retrieve the Colonel's enormous mobile, at last Team Merevale arrived in Pisa, where everyone took the obligatory 'holding up the Leaning Tower' photographs in the town's Piazza del Duomo.

'Otherwise known as the Piazza dei Miracoli,' Glenn announced at the beginning of his carefully prepared tour.

Only Thea and Jinx stayed in the shade of a café terrace, rather than join the scamper round the monuments.

Nobody tried to persuade Jinx that she should allow herself to be wheeled around the tower, but Glenn did try to coerce Thea into posing with him for a tower pic.

'Dad. It's *lame de la lame*. It's what everyone does. If you type "leaning tower" into Instagram, you get about a million pictures of grinning idiots pretending they're the only thing stopping the tower from falling down. You couldn't be less original if you tried.'

Glenn did get his Leaning Tower photo, though. One on his own and another one with the Colonel, who pretended to be pushing the tower into Glenn's hands. It took a while to get the perfect shot, with the Colonel resolutely stage-managing all the way.

'Say *formaggio*!'

He got that bit of Italian right, at least.

Tower photos taken, Team Merevale had a quick spin around the cathedral before it was time to get back on the bus for Lucca, the charming walled town to Pisa's north-east. Arriving at the birthplace of Giacomo Puccini, Marilyn was prompted to entertain her fellow travellers with a quick burst of 'Un Bel Di', Cio-Cio-San's famous aria from *Madam Butterfly*, in the coach park. Marilyn could not quite make the high notes – or the low ones, for that matter – but most people seemed impressed.

Jinx applauded politely, remembering the first time she ever heard *Madam Butterfly* performed live, at the Teatro della Pergola in Florence. Jinx had thought it magical, but Penny had been dismissive of the soprano and disappeared during the interval, leaving Jinx alone.

'Life is too short for bad opera,' Penny had said when she reappeared at the hotel hours later, having been who knew where. Jinx still didn't really know what had really happened in Florence; only that whatever Penny got up to had made it a trip to remember.

*

In Lucca, some of the younger and fitter members of the coach party hired bicycles to cycle around the city's ancient walls. Jinx had expected Thea would join them – who wouldn't like a bike ride around a high city wall? – but she claimed she didn't want to.

'Someone has got to stay with you,' she said. 'In case you need something.'

'Don't make me your excuse to miss out again,' said Jinx. 'I am perfectly happy in the shade with a crossword.'

'So am I,' said Thea.

The Colonel had found a printed edition of that day's *Times* in a tobacconist in Pisa. Having read the obituaries – 'No one I've heard of. It's been a long time since anyone interesting popped their clogs' – he'd passed the paper on to Jinx, telling her that she could do the crossword if she liked. He'd already done the sudoku. Well, nearly done it. He didn't seem to have noticed that he had two nines in the top row. Jinx spotted that right away.

Jinx had not done the cryptic crossword for a while. When she and Penny shared a flat in London, they did the cryptic every Sunday evening in the winter, when there were no parties to go to and Frank had to be with his official family. To begin with, the clues had seemed impossibly hard to Jinx. Penny found them easy. She explained her methodology.

'They're all written to a formula, Jinx. The first thing to do is find out who set the puzzle. Each setter has a particular style. You'll soon start to see patterns. They all have their own obsessions.'

Week on week, Jinx's crossword technique improved until soon she was almost as good as her mentor. After that, she and Penny didn't do the cryptic together any more, but sat in armchairs on other sides of the room, each with their own copy of *The Times* on their laps as they raced to be the first to finish.

'You'd have made a good code and cipher officer,' Penny told Jinx. 'We could have used you in Italy.'

Jinx had quickly picked up Morse code. She and Penny used it to send one another covert messages, tapped out on the table or on their knees, when they were in the company of people who bored them.

One weekend, when the weather was too awful to leave the house and Frank had family obligations, Penny tried to teach Jinx how to code a message using a poem as a cipher. Penny had known Leo Marks, the genius who told the SOE they should have people in-house writing bespoke poems for their agents that the Germans couldn't easily guess.

As Penny explained, 'The Germans are very cultured people, Jinx. Shakespeare, Marlowe, Webster ... They knew it all. If you used a line from *Hamlet* or *The Jew of Malta* as your cipher, the Germans would have the code cracked in a minute. So Marks brought in unknown poets, who wrote brand-new poems for each agent, and they helped us to win the war. Let it never be said that poetry, and the knowledge of it, is not a useful thing.'

Penny wouldn't have said that in front of Josephine, of course.

Despite the way she teased her sister for being a swot, Penny also knew a lot of poems. She had a favourite: 'Invictus' by William Ernest Henley. Sometimes, when something had put her into a sad or bad mood, Jinx would know that Penny was coming out of it when she muttered, 'bloody, but unbowed' in response to Jinx's polite 'How are you?'

Sitting outside the café in Lucca, Jinx asked Thea to fold the paper so that the puzzle page was uppermost. It was hard to do that with only one hand. It would be hard to write neatly in the crossword boxes, too.

'I could do the writing for you?' Thea suggested to Jinx's surprise.

'I can manage.'

Thea took out her phone. Jinx knew that Thea appreciated that Jinx didn't question out loud whether the amount of time she spent scrolling was excessive. Glenn did, of course. But though Thea could usually find plenty to amuse her on that little screen, Jinx became aware that her young companion kept glancing in the direction of Jinx's paper and the words she was fitting – or rather, not fitting – into the boxes. What a mess it was looking already. And Jinx realised that perhaps Thea's suggestion was an olive branch of sorts after the previous day's awkward exchanges.

Thea cleared her throat.

'Number two down, Mrs Sullivan. Is the answer to that one "hippopotamus"?'

Jinx quickly reread the clue. 'Yes. I think it is.'

'And number eight across ... I think you'll find the answer is "Where Eagles Dare".'

It was.

'You're good at this.'

Thea shrugged the compliment off.

'I used to do the crossword with Mum. She was *really* good at it. She could work out a puzzle faster than anyone. Words, number, pictures. She knew every reference you could think of. She could crack any code. She was going to work at GCHQ after she left university.'

The Government Communications HQ in Cheltenham was not that far from Merevale.

'Mum wanted to go into cybersecurity, but then she got pregnant and that was the end of that. I guess I ruined everything, coming along like I did ...'

'I'm sure she didn't see it that way,' said Jinx.

'I would have done,' said Thea. 'She could have done anything, but she got stuck with me and Dad.'

'Weren't you thinking about doing something similar, Thea? Going into cybersecurity, I mean. I seem to remember your father telling me you were. That you were doing A levels in maths and sciences?'

'Yeah. But I wasn't good at it like Mum was.'

Before Jinx could ask her anything more about it, Glenn and the Colonel came wobbling round the corner on a tandem. The Colonel was in front, of course, though Glenn was doing most of the pedalling.

'Thea!' the Colonel bellowed. 'Swap places with me and go for a ride around the city walls with your father. It's great fun. You really mustn't miss it.'

'No thanks,' said Thea.

'Come on, girl. Do you good to get a bit of exercise.'

'I'm fine, thank you.'

The Colonel dismounted, suddenly leaving Glenn in charge of the bike, which immediately dropped to the floor with a clatter. The Colonel walked across to Jinx and Thea, swaying a bit as he did so. He was red-faced from the ride, or perhaps from the wine he'd put away at lunchtime. He stopped in front of Thea and wagged his finger at her. At first, Jinx thought the Colonel was joking about, so silly was the gesture. But the Colonel was not playing.

'Now look here, young lady,' he began. 'I haven't said anything up until now because I didn't want to spoil the holiday for everyone else, but the fact is you're spoiling it all by yourself, sitting there with a face like a wet weekend, making snide remarks all the time. Your father has put a great deal of effort into this trip, and the least you can do is get on the back of that tandem and look like you're having fun for half an hour.'

'Thanks, but no thanks,' said Thea.

'Thanks, but no thanks?' the Colonel echoed. *'Thanks, but no thanks?* Who on earth do you think you're talking to?'

Jinx held up her hand and tried to stop the Colonel mid-flow.

'No, Jennifer. I've had enough of holding my peace. You're spoiled, Thea Turner, that's what you are. You're an entitled little madam, and it will get you nowhere in this world.'

'Malcolm!' Having untangled himself from the tandem, Glenn tried to intervene. 'I don't think—'

'You should be saying this yourself, Glenn. Your daughter has cast a shadow over the whole tour. Ask any one of the ladies here and I'm sure they'll agree with me.'

There were murmurs of agreement from Cynthia and Val. Pat, wisely, quickly excused herself to look at a nearby display of postcards. Marilyn hurried after Pat.

The tandem lay on the ground while Glenn and the Colonel had a brief but increasingly heated debate about Thea's behaviour.

'She's sixteen years old. That's plenty old enough to act like an adult, Glenn. I was in the army at her age!'

'Malcolm, I don't think it's your place to tell Thea how to act—'

'Then whose place is it? Come on, man. You're her father.'

'And as such, I'll thank you to leave the parenting to me.'

'Parenting? You call letting her act like she owns the world parenting?'

'Malcolm, I don't think we should be having this conversation right now.'

'Then when will you be ready to have it, Glenn? When she's twenty and no bugger wants to give the sulky brat a job?'

'Shut up!' Thea shrieked. 'Shut up! Shut up!'

Jinx reached to grab Thea's hand, but Thea shook her off and ran away from the café, in through the town walls. Glenn ran after her, leaving Team Merevale agog.

'It had to be said,' the Colonel insisted.

'No,' said Jinx. 'It really did not.'

The Colonel blushed with a mixture of fury and shame. Jinx didn't have to say any more to him. And when Val and Cynth started muttering again about 'the youth of today', Jinx fixed them with a basilisk glare.

'You two,' Jinx said, 'would do well to keep out of it.'

'Hear, hear,' said Pat and Marilyn.

Team Merevale did not see Glenn and Thea again that afternoon. Marilyn pushed Jinx's wheelchair to the car park where they were to meet the coach.

Glenn and Thea arrived five minutes after the agreed muster time, by which point the rest of the group was already on board. Everyone was quiet. Even Val and Cynthia. Battle lines had been drawn, with the coach splitting into Team Glenn and Team Colonel.

'What's happened to you lot since I dropped you off?' Ivor the driver wanted to know.

'Best not ask,' said Pat.

All eyes were on Thea as she took her place next to Jinx. Glenn sat down next to the Colonel, but did not so much as glance at him. The Colonel did not acknowledge Glenn either.

The atmosphere was heavy on that coach. The events of the past few hours had left the coach party too subdued for a sing-song, though Marilyn, who was listening to *Tosca* on her headphones, still occasionally burst out with an operatic trill. *'Mario! Mario! Ma-ri-oooo!'* Pat quickly shushed her.

Glenn did not bother to draw Team Merevale's attention to the various points of interest he had researched for the next leg of the journey, such as San Miniato, 'the Truffle Town', with its charming hilltop tower. Instead, he leaned his head against the window and fumed inwardly, composing the witty comebacks he should have made when the Colonel started on Thea outside the café. How dare that stupid man talk to Thea like that! And yet, to Glenn's great sadness, he couldn't help but think that the Colonel had a point. Thea had been terrible company on the trip. Sullen and sulky and altogether not the sweet and charming Thea she could be. But then, that Thea hadn't been around for a long while. Not since they lost Lindsey.

Glenn sneaked a look at his daughter on the other side of the coach. With her headphones back on, she was in her own little world again. He wished he could be there with her. Why was she still so sad when he thought he'd done everything he could to make her life happy and exciting since Lindsey died? Where was he going wrong?

'Is that the Duomo?' someone shouted from the back of the bus, bringing Glenn out of his reverie.

They were driving into Florence at last, heading across a bridge to the hotel on the Lungarno Vespucci, carefully chosen for its combination of accessibility (vital for seniors) and proximity to the medieval city's main sights.

Glenn snapped back into tour-guide mode before the Colonel could beat him to it. He snatched up the microphone, even though it wasn't working, and shouted: 'Ladies and gentlemen, boys and girls, welcome to *Firenze*!'

Chapter Twenty-Nine

'Mrs Sullivan? Mrs Sullivan? We're here.'

Thea gave Jinx a nudge. Jinx had fallen asleep with her head against the coach window not long after they passed San Miniato. She seemed to need to nap all the time these days. Waking suddenly, for a moment Jinx had no idea where she was.

'We're in Florence,' said Thea quietly.

The coach was parked with its nose towards the Arno. Jinx looked out at the square in which they had stopped, trying to place it on the map in her head. She felt an odd sense of calm excitement as the coach doors opened with a pneumatic hiss. She'd made it to Florence. Even as recently as that morning, she hadn't quite believed that she would.

'Do you want to get off right away or wait for the crowd to get off first?' Thea asked.

It made more sense to wait as Cynthia and Val and Pat and Marilyn and the Colonel and the rest all disembarked – still sticking to their 'teams' – and headed for the cool lobby and, more importantly, the toilets of the Hotel Fiesole. A week into the tour, no one had yet dared to use the toilet on board the coach. Meanwhile, three hotel door staff rushed forward to load Team Merevale's cases onto trolleys. Jinx winced as she watched her own case being thrown on top of the pile. Thank goodness she had her real valuables on her, in her handbag.

Once the crowd had gone, Thea and Glenn helped Jinx down to the pavement. Glenn pushed Jinx's chair into the lobby, where the hotel manager and her reception staff were busy taking photocopies of passports and handing out room keys.

Glenn, Jinx and Thea handed their own passports over for check-in. The receptionist tapped on her keyboard, then furrowed her brow.

'Mrs Sullivan and Miss Turner,' the receptionist said. 'Might you have been booked into the hotel under other names? I don't have rooms for you.'

'What?' Glenn and Thea said at once.

'I have a room for you, Mr Turner,' the receptionist told him. 'But not for the two ladies. I can't find their names on the system. Are you sure they're supposed to be here?'

'We're a coach party,' said Glenn. 'And this is my daughter. Of course they're supposed to be here.'

'There is nothing on my screen. No Jennifer Sullivan. No Thea Turner.'

Glenn embarked on another conversation with the hotel manager, which involved much arm-waving and exaggerated facial expressions. The manager said she understood that the two guests needed rooms, but there was no record of their ever having booked them.

'But we can book two rooms now?' Glenn suggested.

'I'm afraid not,' said the manager. 'There are no rooms to book.'

It was the height of the summer season, she patiently explained. The Hotel Fiesole was completely full. There wasn't even a cupboard to be had this side of the Arno.

A small Team Merevale contingent gathered to find out what was happening.

206

'Perhaps the Colonel could give up his room and share with someone?' Pat suggested.

Neither Jinx nor Thea could share with the Colonel and, after that afternoon's row, Glenn definitely didn't want to. Even if the Colonel did give up his room, it would only free up one bed. They would still be one short.

But where Glenn saw disaster, Jinx saw opportunity. She could not have planned the situation better. In fact, she *had* planned the situation, when she called the Hotel Fiesole from Merevale to cancel the rooms Glenn had booked for her and Thea.

'There is a place,' she said. 'It's only a little way from here but I've stayed there before. It isn't smart, but it will be good enough. If they had space, Thea and I could go there together.'

Jinx gave him the name of the hotel where she had stayed all those years ago with Penny – the one in which she had planned to stay again when she thought she would be in the city under her own steam: the Hotel Regina.

The name made the manager of the Hotel Fiesole pull a face that said everything. 'The Regina?' She grimaced. 'You want to stay there?'

'If we can,' Jinx told her. Though she knew they would be able to, because she'd already checked. 'Please give them a call.'

The manager made the call. 'The Regina has one room free,' she said. 'A double with twin beds.'

'Thea,' said Glenn, 'you and I will have to share. Mrs Sullivan can have my room here.'

'No. Mrs Sullivan needs me,' said Thea. 'I'll share with her at the Regina. If that's all right. I don't want to stay here with this lot,' she told her father *sotto voce*. 'They all hate me.'

'They don't,' Glenn insisted.

'It feels like they do. Mrs Sullivan and I will be OK together in that other place. Let me go, Dad.'

'It's not the Ritz,' Jinx agreed. 'But I'm sure we'll muddle through.'

The Hotel Regina was close by. Having had their evening meal in the Hotel Fiesole with the others – Glenn insisted on that – Glenn, Thea and Jinx left for their new lodgings. Thea pulled two wheelie cases. Glenn pushed Jinx in the wheelchair.

Glenn was worried. 'I can't imagine what kind of tip this place is, if they've got room at such short notice.'

'It really isn't bad,' Jinx reassured him.

But as they waited in the Regina's lobby to be checked in, Glenn's doubts only increased. Thea, too, looked disappointed. To say the Regina looked 'tired' was an understatement. There was an air of Miss Havisham's boudoir to the public areas, which were decked out with vases of dusty polyester flowers, faded from many, many long Italian summers.

'Are you sure this is the place?' asked Glenn. 'When were you last here?'

'1951,' said Jinx.

There were no dogs to greet them at the hotel that day. Signora Bianchi was long gone, too, of course. However, the hotel still had many of La Signora's old-fashioned touches. The paintings were exactly the same, if a little dingier from decades of dust and neglect.

Jinx wondered why, unlike so many other places in the city, the Regina had escaped renovation. Perhaps it was stuck in an inheritance tangle. Why else wouldn't the place have been stripped to its bare bones and recreated as a boutique hotel with an Illy coffee machine in every room and an extra nought on all the prices?

But there wasn't even a charming, old-fashioned welcome any more. The Regina's manager, a man in his fifties, seemed annoyed to have to deal with them. He handed over the room key and nodded towards a tiny lift, just big enough for Jinx in her wheelchair with Thea squished up against the mirror. Glenn carried their cases upstairs.

The moment Jinx was through the door, she knew that this was 'her room', though the hotel management had shoehorned in an extra bed since she was last there. It was going to be a squeeze. Thea was clearly having second thoughts. She chose her bed and sat down upon it. The springs sagged to the floor. She looked as though she might cry.

'It's only for sleeping,' Jinx said. But even she was suddenly nervous that she'd made the wrong decision when she cancelled those rooms at the Hotel Fiesole to make sure they ended up here.

Jinx suggested they stay downstairs until bedtime. Glenn insisted on staying with them until they were ready to turn in. He was not happy to leave Thea and Jinx alone, while he stayed down the road at the altogether better-appointed hotel with Team Merevale.

'I've got my phone, Dad. What can possibly happen?'

'Put the chain on the door and don't let anybody in. Call me if you're the least bit worried. I will be here in two minutes.'

But as soon as Glenn left, thinking that the two women were safely tucked up in bed, Jinx and Thea came downstairs again.

The sky was still just about pink, fading to purple, and outside the air had finally cooled down enough to be pleasant. Jinx asked Thea if she wouldn't mind sitting in the Regina's garden for a while. It was too hot to sleep in that tiny room without air conditioning.

The manager grudgingly brought a couple of drinks out – a negroni for Jinx and a Crodino for Thea – and reminded them that he would be clocking off soon.

'This isn't a Holiday Inn,' he said.

'Miserable old git,' said Jinx.

'I agree.'

It was almost a toast. They clinked glasses and Jinx sipped her negroni. It was very watered down. Penny would have sent it back.

'Is it like you remember?' Thea asked. 'This place?'

'Well, they've hardly changed a thing about the garden,' Jinx observed. 'Except for the grass.'

The scrubby old lawn had been replaced by a patch of lurid green artificial turf, that was rolling at the edges, and the original olive tree had been replaced by a similarly pathetic-looking new tree in a terracotta-coloured plastic pot, but the old pet gravestones still lined the wall. Romeo, the long-ago dachshund, had joined his predecessors in 1953. Jinx explained the stones' provenance.

'They were the landlady's pets,' she said.

'Horrible,' was Thea's view.

'Gives the place character,' Jinx suggested.

'Gives me the creeps. They've all got human names. Helena and Giulietta. That's Italian for Juliet, isn't it? Makes it look like little people are buried there, not dogs.'

Beyond the garden wall, the bells of the city's many *campanili* sounded the hour – eleven o'clock – and the manager made a point of coming out to tell Jinx and Thea that if they wanted anything else to drink, they would have to help themselves and write it down in the bar's honesty booklet.

With the manager gone, Jinx sent Thea to add a shot of gin to her weak negroni.

'Should I write it down?' Thea asked.

'Top the bottle up with water,' was Jinx's suggestion.

'That's not very honest.'

'It's only making up for the alcohol that man didn't put in my drink in the first place.' Jinx took a sip. 'Another slug, I think.'

'What if they've got CCTV?'

'They haven't,' Jinx assured her. She'd checked. She always checked for that.

Outside with their drinks, Jinx and Thea fell silent and listened to sounds of the night. A familiar whirring came from the garden of the palazzo next door. Familiar to Jinx, at least.

'Is that a toad?' Thea asked.

'It's a nightjar,' said Jinx, remembering the first time she'd heard one. 'It's a bird.'

'How do you know so much stuff?'

'My dad used to tell me about birds. He knew a lot about the natural world. He let me keep all sorts of pets.'

'What kind of pets?'

'Once he let me have a crocodile.'

Thea laughed. 'Yeah. Right. You had a crocodile.'

'I called him Mr Snappy. But he was a very boring pet. You can't teach a crocodile tricks. And we had to get rid of him once he was big enough to eat the cat.'

Thea shook her head. She didn't believe it. But it made her smile.

The conversation lapsed again, but the silence was less uncomfortable than it had been and it was Thea who broke it this time.

'My mum had cancer,' she said suddenly. 'A kind of leukaemia. She was diagnosed when I was ten. She was OK for a while and we thought she'd get through it.'

Jinx nodded and Thea carried on.

'We made lots of plans for when she finished her treatment. Dad bought a globe with loads of stickers and we all took it in turns to spin it, shut our eyes and put a sticker where our fingers landed. I went first and I got Italy. Then Mum had a go and she got Italy, too. And so did Dad. It was probably only the way the globe was made that meant it always stopped facing the same direction, but we thought it was fate. Dad went to a travel agent's and picked up a load of brochures. We cut out pictures of the places we'd visit and stuck them on one of those "vision board" things. Siena was on there. And the Leaning Tower of Pisa. And Lucca. And Florence. Florence was on there, too. Mum wanted to see the Duomo. She told me it was a miracle of engineering. She was interested in that sort of thing.'

'And that's why you didn't want to come here?' Jinx read between the lines.

'Yes.' Thea sniffed. 'Italy was meant to be the trip we did to celebrate Mum being well again. We were meant to do loads of things here. I don't want to do them without her.'

'She wanted to see Italy so much. She loved the idea of this place. Even before Dad bought that stupid globe, she used to go on about it. We watched *Under the Tuscan Sun* and *Letters to Juliet* about a million times. Mum got an olive tree and put it on our patio, but it died when she couldn't look after it. I was going to get a new one. When I took that money from your house, that's what I was going to spend it on. How stupid is that?'

'It's certainly not what I imagined,' Jinx said.

'And that's how I ended up here. Ironic, eh?'

Thea wrinkled her nose in a gesture that Jinx recognised as an attempt to stop tears because she'd done it so many times herself.

'This is Mum's place,' Thea said. 'She was meant to be here with us.'

Jinx reached across the table and laid her free hand on Thea's arm, but Thea shook her arm free and furiously dabbed at her eyes. 'Nothing is right. But I'm not going to cry,' she said. 'I never cry. I can't. There's no point, is there? It won't change any-thing.'

'It might,' Jinx said, surprising herself. 'Let the tears come if they want to. There's nothing wrong with crying, Thea.'

Now it was Jinx's turn to wrinkle her nose.

It wasn't until one o'clock in the morning that Thea and Jinx went up to their small twin room. With her usual casual care, Thea helped Jinx out of her clothes and into her nightdress. This time, however, Jinx could feel Thea's eyes upon her – on the tattoo on her arm and on the thin white scars that criss-crossed the brown skin of her back – but Thea didn't mention them, so Jinx didn't mention them either.

Thea turned out the light and was soon asleep. Jinx lay awake, listening to the sounds of the garden next door. The scent of jasmine drifted through the open window and she was back in 1951 once more.

Chapter Thirty

Florence, 1951

Penny and Jinx did not have time for breakfast on their last morning in Florence. Penny had booked them onto the very first train out of Santa Maria Novella. She was still in a strange mood, and for that reason Jinx hadn't dared to ask if they might stop to buy supplies for the journey. However, as the train made its first stop outside the city, Jinx spotted a man with a trolley coming down the platform.

'He's selling pastries. I'll get some,' Jinx said.

They had ten minutes before the train was due to move again, so Jinx jumped off to chase the vendor. The platform was crowded with people trying to find their carriages or saying 'goodbye' to loved ones. While Jinx queued for breakfast, she gazed absent-mindedly at the hustle and bustle and found her attention drawn to two large men, both wearing suits and grey stetsons, who were walking the length of the train, looking in at every window. After a minute or two, they got on at the opposite end of the train to Jinx and Penny's carriage.

With her paper bag full of pastries, Jinx returned to the compartment where she had left Penny reading a day-old copy of *The Times*. But Penny wasn't there. Jinx wondered if she'd got the carriage number wrong, but soon decided she hadn't. Their twin cases were still tucked under the seats.

Jinx sat down to wait for Penny to return, hoping she wouldn't be long. Manners dictated that she should wait for Penny before starting to eat, but Jinx was so hungry. She picked at the corner of a cream-filled cornetto, doing her best to leave it looking more or less intact. As she was nibbling away, like a very polite mouse, the two suited men looked into the carriage from the train's corridor. They seemed to be searching for someone. They didn't look too friendly, but Jinx gave them a smile all the same.

'*Buongiorno*,' she said.

They moved on to the next carriage without returning her greeting.

Moments later, they came by again and once again they peered at Jinx closely. Disconcerted by their interest, she waved her cornetto at them.

'*Delicioso!*' she said.

The larger of the two men shook his head and they carried on.

Manners be damned. Jinx took a bigger bite of her pastry. It was then that someone hissed at her from the luggage rack above her head. Jinx almost hit the rack when she jumped up with fright, to find that Penny was stretched out upon it, as though it were a bunk bed. She had covered herself with her pink Hardy Amies duster coat and Jinx's blue raincoat, so that she looked like a bundle of clothes.

'Watch your head,' Penny said as she swung back down to the floor.

'What are you doing up there?'

'We have to get off the train.'

Penny dragged their cases out from beneath the seats. On the platform, the guard was blowing his whistle and checking the carriage doors were closed. As the last door was slammed shut, the train began to shift forward, with a laboured creaking sound.

'It's too late. We're moving,' said Jinx. 'We can't get off now.'

'We can, but we have to be quick. Put your coat on, Jinx. Do it up tight.'

'It's hot.'

'Put your coat on. You'll need it for protection. We have to get out of here.'

Jinx started to protest, but Penny mimed the pulling of a zip across her lips.

'Shut up, Jinx. There's a good girl. Now I need you to listen very carefully. This train will not start to really speed up until we're outside the town limits. Right before it does, we're going to throw our bags off and jump straight out after them.'

Jinx's instinct was to laugh.

'Darling, I'm not joking. Those men—'

'The men in suits?'

'Yes. Those are bad men, and if I stay on this train, they will try to hurt me. When they realise you're with me, they'll want to hurt you, too.'

'Why would they want to hurt me?'

'I'll tell you everything the moment we're nice and safe again. Suffice to say it's to do with my war work. Coat on? Good. Now, when the moment comes I want you to jump as far as you can, straight out at ninety degrees to the side of the train, cover your head and tuck your knees and roll away on landing.' Penny briefly demonstrated the correct arm position. 'Protect your head at all costs. Got that?'

There was something about Penny's manner that drove home to Jinx that she wasn't playing a prank. The train was going at quite a lick now. Penny pulled down the window in the door and stuck her head out.

'Good. There's a curve coming up. Should slow us down for a moment or two.'

Then Penny pitched the cases out through the window.

'Right. Let's go.'

'You're bonkers. We'll die!'

'We'll die if we stay in this carriage.'

Seconds later, Penny opened the door and threw herself out after her luggage. The carriage door slammed shut behind her. Jinx stuck her head out through the window, hoping to see that Penny had landed safely, but she could see no sign of her. She couldn't possibly have landed without injury.

As Jinx was wondering what on earth she should do, the suited men returned. And this time one of them was holding a gun.

Perhaps Penny wasn't entirely mad after all.

'Get her,' Jinx heard one say in an American accent.

Without waiting to give them a chance, Jinx wrenched the carriage door open and paused in the frame for the longest two seconds in her life before she jumped out after Penny, sailing through the air with her arms and legs akimbo to land on a fortuitously placed pile of straw with a heavy 'whumpf'.

'That was a bloody terrible jump, Jinx.'

Penny hauled her young friend to her feet. 'You looked like a windmill coming out of that carriage. You're lucky you didn't break both legs.'

Jinx just stared at her.

'Come on, you goose. Look sharp. We can't hang around. They'll be back to find us before you know it.'

'You ...' Jinx's voice shook as she found her words at last. 'You ... You made me jump from a moving train.'

'And aren't you glad you did?'

'I could have been killed. A man waved a gun at me.'

'So isn't it better to have taken your chances than to have been shot in the back of the head? Come on.'

'Who were they?'

Penny dusted Jinx down and pulled a piece of straw from her hair. As she did so, her face softened.

'Thank you for being so brave, Jinx. I knew you would be. Now we need to get somewhere safe.' She looked at her watch. 'Assuming those goons didn't jump off moments after us, they'll have to get off the train at Arezzo. My guess is they'll immediately catch the next train heading north to find us, so our best bet is to head south to Arezzo by road.'

Penny handed Jinx one of the suitcases, which she had retrieved before coming to find her.

'You made me jump from a moving train!' Jinx complained again.

Penny snorted. 'Are you going to keep going on about that? It saved your life, Jinx. *Toujours gai.'*

Landing on straw had saved Jinx from terrible injury, but half an hour after the jump, as she followed Penny down a farm track, she was still shaking from the shock. Penny, by contrast, seemed energised by the whole affair, as she had that long-ago evening in the park when she dispatched the unfortunate flasher. She strode along ahead of Jinx as though they were walking off Sunday lunch in Hyde Park.

'They had a gun! I want to know why they were after you,' Jinx insisted.

'Darling, I could tell you, but then I'd have to kill you,' Penny said.

'Given that you think my simply knowing you makes me a target, too, I think I deserve to know more.'

'You wouldn't believe me if I did tell you. And anyway, I signed the Official Secrets Act.'

'Why? Were you a spy?'

'Not exactly. But I did have an exciting war, and during the course of it, I may have made a few enemies.'

'The men in suits?'

'Someone higher up the chain than that ... but we definitely want to avoid his goons.'

A car was coming up the road towards them. Penny pulled Jinx down into a ditch so they wouldn't be seen as it motored on by in a cloud of dust and tiny stones that spattered Jinx's face.

'I want to go home,' Jinx cried, as Penny dragged her along a farm track.

'For goodness' sake, Jinx. I thought your time in the camps had made you tough.'

'Don't you dare use that against me.'

'Oh, look!' Penny exclaimed. 'I spy a truck.'

Outside a small stone farmhouse was parked a beaten-up Lancia 3Ro. The farmyard in which it stood was deserted, apart from a couple of scrappy-looking chickens, but as Penny and Jinx drew nearer, they heard the sound of energetic love-making coming from an open window. Jinx blushed.

'Perfect,' said Penny. 'Sounds like they'll be busy for a while.'

Jinx watched in confusion as Penny tossed their cases into the back of the truck and jumped up into the driver's seat. The truck's keys were dangling from the ignition.

'Bingo.'

'Now you're stealing a truck?'

'Yes. Are you coming? Get in.'

Penny had to sit right on the edge of her seat to reach the truck's pedals, but she soon managed to get it started and they were out of the farmyard and away down the white road before the poor unsuspecting farmer could get his trousers back on.

They abandoned the truck, which stank of animals and earth, down another track half a mile outside Arezzo. The rest of the way, they walked. They tied two grubby blankets, found in the truck, around their heads and shoulders in an attempt to blend in with the local farm-workers, and Penny did that thing she could do – twisting her body so that she suddenly looked completely different, ten years older, unrecognisable as the young woman who had jumped from the train.

In Arezzo, they headed for a small *pensione* Penny knew, situated behind the cathedral. When an elderly man opened the door, he did a double take before he grabbed Penny's bag and ushered her inside.

'*Bruna*!' he cried.

Penny nodded.

'*Dai, dai.*'

Without asking any questions, the man took Penny and Jinx straight to the third floor, where he showed them two rooms. Jinx was given the smaller room, with a sloping ceiling and a window that looked out only onto the back of another building.

'Now I need a little rest,' said Penny. 'Have a wash and a little sleep yourself. You'll feel much better when you do.'

But Jinx did not feel like resting. Her veins were still coursing with pure adrenaline. 'How did you know to come here, and who is that man downstairs? Penny, you need to tell me what's going on.'

'And I will, dear. Little sleep first.' Penny closed her bedroom door in Jinx's face.

The old man knocked on the door to Jinx's room a few moments later, with a plate of cheese and charcuterie and some slices of dry Tuscan bread. Shortly afterwards, he came back again with a bottle of wine and a jug of warm water to wash in.

'*Bruna*,' he said. He tapped his heart as he did so and smiled.

'Yes,' said Jinx. '*Bruna*. Whoever *she* is.'

Jinx wanted to know why on earth the man was being so kind to his mysterious *Bruna*, but her Italian wasn't good enough, so she settled for saying, '*Grazie*.'

An hour later, Jinx had stopped being afraid and was starting to be angry. Very angry indeed. Her shoulder ached from where she had landed on it. She had grazes on the heels of her hands and her knees. There was a rip in her new nylon stockings. Bloody Penny. What on earth was she thinking, jumping from a moving train? Stealing a poor farmer's truck? And what did she mean when she said, 'It's to do with my war work'? Why would two American henchmen be after a former FANY coder?

Jinx tried to regain her composure as she waited for Penny to finish her nap. It was hot in that attic room. She washed herself with the tepid water from the jug, then opened her case to find something to change into. Except that it wasn't her case. Penny must have mixed them up.

Oh, well. Given the circumstances, Jinx felt entitled to put on one of Penny's frocks. She pulled out a yellow dress that she had always admired. As she did so, a small velvet pouch came with it and some of the contents of the pouch spilled out onto the floor.

Jinx did a double take as she watched glittering gems roll in all directions. She jumped to stop one from rolling through a gap in the floorboards. It was a green stone, as big as a marble. Was it an emerald? Jinx quickly gathered the stones up so that they formed a sparkling rainbow in her hand. What on earth was Penny doing with so many loose gems?

Jinx picked up the velvet pouch and shook it to see if there were more. As she did so, a diamond rivière bracelet tumbled out. It looked awfully familiar, and when she picked it up, Jinx recalled Tony's words over coffee in the garden.

221

'The night ended rather badly. Clemmie Wilde lost a diamond bracelet ...'

This diamond bracelet. The one Jinx now held in her hand.

Chapter Thirty-One

It was a couple of hours before Penny finished her nap and knocked on Jinx's door that afternoon. Jinx was waiting for her, sitting on the edge of the bed in Penny's favourite yellow shirt-waist dress. She had no smile of welcome for her friend. But Penny swept into the room as though nothing much had happened; as if a quick stop in Arezzo was always part of the plan.

'Hello, darling. I see you've changed. Is that my dress?'

'You took my case,' Jinx said. 'What's going on, Penny? Why are we here? Why did we jump off a moving train? We could have died!'

'Not that again. Jinx, don't be a fusspot. That train wasn't going any faster than a bus on Regent Street.'

'It bloody was. And why are those men after you?'

'It has to do with my war work,' Penny insisted. 'As I said, I would tell you more, but I've signed the Official Secrets Act.'

'I don't believe you.'

'That is actually true. I have signed the Official Secrets Act.'

'To be a FANY officer?'

'I was trained in code and cipher. You have to be able to keep a secret for that.'

'That doesn't explain why anyone would want to kill

you now. Six years after the end of the war? And they were American, too. The Americans were on the same side as us. Who were those men?'

'Can I trust you, Jinx?' Penny asked.

'I don't think I'm the untrustworthy one here.'

Jinx slowly opened her hand to show Penny the diamond bracelet.

'Whatever happened today, I don't believe it had to do with "war work" at all.'

'Give me that,' said Penny, as Jinx held the glittering bracelet to the light.

'Is this Clemmie Wilde's?' Jinx asked.

'Yes, it is.' Penny didn't seem particularly bothered that Jinx had found the thing. 'Who cares? She won't miss it.'

'Your friend was going to dismiss half his staff because of this bracelet.'

'He won't. Clemmie's husband will have bought her another by now and the whole incident will be long forgotten.'

'But how did you get it? And the rest? You've got hundreds of loose gemstones in your bag.'

'A dozen,' Penny corrected her. 'Though they are quite big ones, I must admit.'

She sat down on the edge of the bed next to Jinx and let out a deep sigh, like a child being questioned on some minor piece of bad behaviour.

'Did *you* steal this bracelet, Penny?' Jinx asked.

'Depends what you mean by steal.'

'We jumped from a moving train because you were being chased by two American henchmen. We're in what I assume to be a "safe house" with a bag full of diamonds and you're travelling under an alias. I'm travelling under an alias, too. What on earth is going on?'

'Nothing! Jinx, you've read far too many novels.'

'Enough to know fiction when I hear it!'

'Oh, I knew I shouldn't have brought you here.'

'I'm beginning to wonder why you did.'

Now Penny lolled on the bed, like a teenager. 'Jinx, there are a few things you probably ought to know about our life.'

'*Our* life?'

'Yes. Our life. Our apartment in London. The parties. The outfits. This trip. How they're paid for.'

'By your antiques business.'

'Sort of. I know bugger all about antiques. Cecil sells fake old masters and I'm a professional jewel thief. The business launders all our cash.'

Penny's explanation was so ludicrous that Jinx laughed out loud.

'I don't think it's funny,' said Penny, sitting up again.

'It's hilarious. You're a professional jewel thief?'

'I am.'

'You steal jewels for a living?'

'Not just for a living.'

'For fun?'

'I do it because I believe there should be a redistribution of wealth. Jinx, do you remember the day I brought you that school blazer?'

'With your birthday money. From your great-aunt.'

'I didn't have any birthday money. My great-aunt is as mean as they come. I bought your blazer with the cash I made by selling a bracelet not dissimilar to the one you hold in your hand now, except that one was from Devrey.'

Jinx knew the society jewellers well. Their shop was not far from Penny and Cecil's offices.

'I don't believe you.'

'Perhaps it's better if you don't ... Have you finished with that cheese?'

225

Penny reached for Jinx's plate. Jinx pushed Clemmie Wilde's bracelet into her face again.

'OK. Then if you are a jewel thief, how did you steal this? She had it on her arm.'

'Well, that was *very* simple.'

Penny seemed happy to tell it, as though Jinx had just asked her for the secret to her recipe for rock buns.

'As Clemmie held my hand when saying goodbye, being ever so *sincere,* though I knew she absolutely hated me from the off, I closed my other hand around her wrist in an equally friendly gesture and flipped the catch so that the bracelet fell into my hand as she moved away.'

'She would have noticed.'

'She was too busy being charming. Oh, Jinx, don't be a bore. Clemmie Wilde deserved to lose that bracelet.'

'Theft is ... It's wrong.'

'And so is getting rich off the back of other people's suffering, like Clemmie Wilde's husband did when he supplied weapons during the war.'

'For our side.'

'He didn't supply them at a discount, did he?'

Penny took a bite of some bread.

'Oh Jinx,' she said when she'd swallowed her mouthful. 'Didn't you ever see something you really, really wanted in the hands of someone who didn't even know what they had? Didn't you ever think about stealing that thing, knowing that you could make better use of it? That you deserved it more? You must have.

'The money I make supports our little London home, and your mother and Eddy up in Manchester, and a number of other good people who deserve to have much better lives. I'm talking about people whom Clemmie Wilde would not give so much as the time of day. She simply strides through life with her nose in the air and her thoughts only on her next trip to Paris to see Monsieur Dior.'

Penny held out her hand and motioned to Jinx to give her the bracelet.

'I'm going to turn that bracelet into several winter coats and pairs of shoes for people who don't have them. It's my way of redressing the balance. Like Robin Hood. Isn't that a much better use of Clemmie Wilde's blood money? I doubt she'd have worn the silly thing again anyway. It only highlighted how coarse her wrists are. No breeding, that woman. It must have broken Dior's heart to see his New Look on such an old haggis.'

Penny reached for the rest of the half-eaten plate of cheese and charcuterie. 'Pass me that. I'm ravenous.'

'Mum would be disgusted to think you helped us with stolen money.'

'Which is why I hope you won't tell her. Your mother is a good woman. Decent and proud. You are decent, too, Jinx. And you should be proud. You moved to London because you wanted to support your family. It's simply that honest jobs don't pay terribly well. Not enough to pay for our lovely flat, or the house in Manchester where Eddy has a bedroom of his own and it isn't damp, so his chest is getting better ... Oh, Jinx. What a dilemma, eh?'

Penny held out her hand for the bracelet again and Jinx finally passed it over.

Chapter Thirty-Two

In light of events Penny changed their itinerary, and later that day, instead of going south to Rome to catch a plane as originally planned, they went north again to Genoa, in a car provided by Penny's friend in Arezzo – 'Someone I met while I was in Puglia,' was all she would say about her old pal. Next day they headed directly west into France. They took the train from Marseilles to Paris, where there was just enough time for a meal at *Le Train Bleu* in the Gare de Lyon before they transferred to the night ferry for London at the Gare du Nord. They had long since shaken off the men in suits, who Penny explained were associates of an old acquaintance called Jimmy Noone, who *might* think Penny had something that belonged to him.

All across France, Penny continued to act the part of a decent upper-class English woman, part of the Establishment, but now Jinx knew she was a thief she could hardly stand to look at her. Yet already a little voice was reminding Jinx of the other facts. Penny's ill-gotten gains had made their lives so much better. It would kill Norma to know the truth. It would also kill Norma and Eddy to have to move out of the house they couldn't afford without Penny's assistance. With her 'good deeds' Penny had tied them all up in a knot.

That didn't mean Jinx couldn't untie it. As they crossed the Channel, Jinx was making calculations. She did not need to be associated with Penny's lies and deceit. As well as sending money back to Norma this past year, Jinx had been putting a little aside on a regular basis. She had enough to pay for a room in a boarding house for a week or two, during which time she could look for a new job. She had experience and skills now. But what if she needed a reference? Penny wouldn't give her one.

Jinx's hand shook as she held her false passport out to the guard when they got back to Dover. He barely looked at it, but Jinx still felt sick all the way to London on the train.

When they got back to the flat in Sloane Square, Penny asked her, 'Have you had enough of punishing me yet, Jinx? Finished your flounce? Can we go back to being friends and put it all down as a fabulous adventure?'

Jinx had steeled herself for this moment.

'No,' she said. 'We can't. I'm sorry, Penny, but I want no more to do with you. I want to live an honourable life, even if that means being poor.'

Penny was stung, Jinx could tell, but she did not try to change her mind.

That night, Jinx packed her bags. She wished she could talk to Frank about the situation, but she didn't know where to find him except at the police station. When morning came, Jinx left the flat. She did not say goodbye to Penny, who'd had a skinful the previous night and was snoring so loudly Jinx could hear her from the hall. Jinx walked to Euston station and boarded a train back to Manchester.

She arrived just as Eddy was getting home from school. They walked into the house he and Norma now shared together.

Seeing her daughter for the first time in a year, Norma was

delighted. But over the course of the evening, her delight turned to concern.

'You've given up your job? And the flat you shared with Penny?'

'I'll find a new job,' Jinx promised. 'And I can live here with you.'

Norma waited a week before she told Jinx that she was under the doctor. 'They think I might need an operation. I won't be able to go to work for a month.'

Without Norma's income, the rent on the flat was too expensive. And Eddy's teachers thought that if he carried on doing as well as he was, then he might get a place at the grammar school. The cost of the uniform was ruinous.

Until that moment, Jinx had not appreciated quite how expensive a modest life was. She was quickly running through the money she had saved in London, and there was no well-paying work to be found up in Lancashire.

'Telephone Penny,' said Norma. 'See if you can go back to your job. Eddy and I will be OK up here.'

Jinx missed Penny and Frank – even Cecil just a little bit – although she'd never admit it. Needing to provide for Norma and Eddy gave her the perfect excuse.

'For the right reasons?' Jinx said when she and Penny next met at a restaurant near Euston station.

Penny looked up from her plate. 'What was that, Jinx?'

'You do it for all the right reasons?'

'If you're referring to what I think you're referring to, then yes, I believe I do.'

'And Frank knows about it?'

'Darling, Frank is my fence.'

'He's a policeman.'

'If you want access to anyone in the criminal world, a police-man is the best person to ask.'

'So Frank's a thief, too?'

'Think of him as Little John to my Robin.'

By the time they had paid for lunch, Jinx was decided.

'I want in on it.'

'Bother,' said Penny. 'Frank told me this would happen. Are you sure, Jinx?'

'I'm sure.'

'Good girl.'

Penny really hadn't intended ever to tell Jinx how she made her living, but reflecting on events at leisure, she realised everything had already started to unravel when Jinx found her down in the garden of the palazzo in Florence. At least the adventure on, or rather in getting off, the train had saved Penny from having to explain why she'd had to climb through Jinx's bedroom window with her dress covered in dirt that night. Had Jinx looked out a few minutes earlier, she might have seen Penny digging a hole with her bare hands, according to co-ordinates which she now knew were wrong.

'Besides, the wench is dead.'

Penny had been so certain that that single line, scribbled in the front of the old German guidebook to Florence, was the key to a poem code using a passage from Marlowe's *The Jew of Malta,* which directed the clever reader to a spot in the palazzo's garden. When she found out that the palazzo had been used by high-ranking German officers before the Allies liberated the city, it all made perfect sense. Axel Durchdenwald was a German intelligence officer. He must have hidden looted treasure in the palazzo's grounds, intending to pick it up later. Jimmy must have worked that out, too. It was why he was in Florence. It was why he had sent those henchmen after her

231

when he found out – through dear old Tony – that Penny was in Florence, too.

As soon as she'd solved the puzzle – or rather, thought she'd solved it – Penny had booked the Hotel Regina for its proximity to the grand house, thinking that it would be easy to shimmy over the wall under cover of darkness and do a bit of digging.

But Penny had found nothing where 'X marked the spot', and she couldn't go back to work on the code again because now she had lost the guidebook, too. It wasn't in either of the cases she and Jinx had taken to Italy. She could only think that it had been lost when they jumped from the train. Jinx didn't have it.

Except that Jinx did have it. Penny had accidentally put the book in the outside pocket of Jinx's case rather than her own as she was preparing to jump. When Penny started fussing about the guidebook on the train from Genoa to Marseilles, Jinx was immediately intrigued. She didn't trust Penny at all any more, and the fuss seemed to suggest that the guidebook was worth much more than she had paid for it. *If* she had paid for it. Jinx determined that she would take a closer look. She hid the book in a pocket of her handbag, and there it stayed until Jinx moved back into the London flat and stashed the book under her bed.

Chapter Thirty-Three

Back in London, Jinx held Penny to her promise: that she would tell her the 'tricks of the trade'.

It turned out that Penny's method was quite simple.

'Being able to get away with stealing anything depends mostly on appearing as though you don't need to,' was her philosophy in short.

Thus, Jinx's education in the art of the steal was really another lesson in etiquette. Though Jinx didn't always like to wear them, gloves were a necessity in this new line of work, ideal as they were for hiding bracelets and rings. Penny showed Jinx how to take them off and put them back on without drawing attention to their presence.

'You must not leave the shop assistant with any lasting impression at all, except that he has met one of any number of beautiful young girls from good families.'

'But you are from a good family. Have you always done this? Steal things?' Jinx asked her. 'How on earth did you start?'

Penny recalled her own first steal as though it were a particularly happy story.

'When I was a teenager, I tried to buy a bracelet in Galeries Lafayette in Paris for my sister's birthday, but the assistant abandoned me when a wealthy customer walked in. She didn't know she hadn't taken back all the bracelets she'd been showing me. Neither did I, until I was halfway back to my godfather's apartment. When I realised I was still wearing one, I was shocked, but later I thought how easy it had been to walk out of the store without anybody knowing I hadn't paid. I gave the bracelet to Josephine and she was delighted. And I had still had my pocket money. The next time I did it was deliberate. It was after the war, when I was working for the Refugee Commission. I stole a ring to raise the money to help a young Jewish woman and her children find a new home.'

'Like Robin Hood,' Jinx said before Penny could make the comparison herself again.

Then came the first time for Jinx to try out her new skills in the field. Penny chose the target. A soft one. An easy one. They travelled out of London to a small provincial town, to a jewellery shop that sold engagement rings and christening presents to well-heeled local farmers. Penny gave Jinx her instructions as they got off the train, then went ahead to the target shop. Jinx should follow precisely three minutes later. By the time she arrived, Penny would have assessed the situation.

'If I have my handbag on my right arm when you come in, you are free to go ahead with the mission. If it is on my left arm, then you should abort.'

'And just walk out?'

'Yes. But best have a reason why you came in in the first place. Ask for directions to the post office or the market. You'll think of something. Good luck, Jinx. Try not to live up to your name.'

Penny clipped away down the train platform. Jinx watched her go and waited another three minutes – counting the time on the watch Frank had given her for her seventeenth birthday (which she was no longer 100 per cent sure he'd actually *bought*). Then she followed.

It started to rain on the walk into the town centre. That was a good thing. An umbrella gave Jinx extra camouflage, helped her blend in.

There was the shop: 'J. Toomer and Sons'. Jinx paused to look at the items in the window, though really she was looking beyond them, through the glass, to see if Penny was already inside. She was.

Jinx pushed open the door and the bell attracted the attention of the grey-haired man who was showing Penny a watch. There was one other assistant there. A young woman, not much older than Jinx was, who stood to attention as Jinx walked in.

Penny's handbag dangled from her right hand. When Jinx stepped up to the counter alongside her, Penny gave Jinx a polite smile before turning back to the watch that the man had brought out of the cabinet so she could get a better look. The smile was so perfectly dismissive, no one would guess that the two women knew each other, but Jinx could read all sorts of things into it. It was a smile that said, 'Go ahead'.

Jinx already knew that while Penny seemed to be giving the man on the other side of the counter her full attention, she was doing nothing of the sort. From the corner of her eye, she would be watching Jinx's every move.

'How may I help you?' asked the young woman.

Jinx asked to see some bracelets. 'For my sister.'

Now she knew the story of Penny's accidental first steal at Galeries Lafayette in Paris, it had to be a bracelet Jinx took first, too.

'Do you have a particular style in mind, miss? Gold or silver? With stones or without?'

'Would you bring me a selection?'

Eager to please, the young woman loaded a velvet tray with

three silver bracelets in varying thicknesses. Jinx held each one in turn.

'Could I see some in gold, please?'

The assistant went to tidy the others away.

'But keep these silver ones here so I can compare?'

It wasn't long before there were nine bracelets on the tray. Far more than the maximum allowed for insurance purposes. Jinx looped two on one wrist and three on the other, then slowly took four off while she engaged the assistant in conversation.

'I couldn't help but notice your beautiful ring,' Jinx said. 'Are you engaged?'

'Just last week.'

'Did you choose the ring?'

'My fiancé did.'

'What good taste he has.'

'Do you think so?' The young woman held out her hand so she could look at the ring herself. Which gave Jinx an opportunity to put her gloves back on and over the last remaining bracelet. By the time she had finished admiring her own ring, the assistant had all but forgotten what Jinx had come in for.

'I think my sister would like this one,' said Jinx, touching the finest of the gold chains. 'But I'd hate to get it wrong, so I'm going to ask our mother what she thinks. She's shopping elsewhere at the moment, but we're meeting for a cup of tea and I shall bring her back here afterwards.'

'We're open until five o'clock.'

'Congratulations on your engagement!' said Jinx as she left the shop.

Penny caught up with Jinx at the train station.

'Your sangfroid! No fear at all. Most girls your age would be afraid of going to jail.'

Jinx reminded her, 'You know I'm not afraid of jail.'

Though Jinx was a natural, Penny was not entirely keen for her to follow in her footsteps. She advised Jinx to continue to work with Cecil. There was plenty of *almost* honest work to be done in the gallery. On the surface, Jinx agreed, but she couldn't resist finding out if what she'd experienced so far was beginner's luck.

A month later, she went into a jewellery shop alone and managed to come out with a plain gold ring worth three pounds. After that, she was hooked. Eventually, she persuaded Penny that they should work as a team. It was always useful to have a lookout.

Penny had rules when they were working together. They never stole from anyone who would really miss what they took. They didn't steal from individuals (Clemmie Wilde had been asking for it) or burgle people's houses. Of course it wasn't the case that their crimes were without victims. The jewellery shops they had targeted had owners, who had insurance premiums to pay. It was inevitable that the staff who had been on duty when she or Penny made a steal would have had to answer difficult questions. And they were perpetuating something unjust on a much bigger scale, weren't they? As long as people thought diamonds were worth buying – or stealing – there would be those who suffered in the pursuit of them, not least the children who were sent to dig them out of the earth.

'Our charitable contributions make up for that,' Penny claimed. At least 60 per cent of the proceeds of each steal went towards 'good works', Penny assured her. The rest?

'Well, we have to look the part, dear.'

Jinx enjoyed the work. It made her oddly happy. Any psychologist would have been able to see what was going on. Having spent three and a half years in prison camps, where concealing valuables was a matter of life and death, Jinx needed the adrenaline she got from stealing jewellery to feel half normal. With no real threat hanging over her, life could sometimes feel strangely dull. Her brain had become accustomed to the constant hum of stress, so that it was a life *without* stress that felt uncomfortable now. And who didn't need extra money?

Though Frank disapproved wholeheartedly of bringing Jinx into the business – Jinx had heard him rowing about it with Penny – he could always find a buyer. And there was nothing Jinx liked more than taking the train to Manchester and pressing crisp banknotes into her mother's hands. Eddy got into the grammar school. Jinx made sure he never had to wear a second-hand uniform.

Ten years passed in the blink of an eye, with both Penny and Jinx becoming ever more daring in their heists. They egged each other on and delighted in outdoing each other. They kept a box of newspaper cuttings, detailing their most outrageous capers. The police didn't know whether they were looking for one woman or ten. They had a trunk full of wigs and disguises. Frank continued to find safe buyers for their bounty.

Jinx had a few boyfriends over the years, but never anyone worth giving her heart to. Meanwhile, Penny was always faithful to her true love. Jinx knew by now the real story of Penny and Frank's meeting in the war, at the SOE commando training school in the Scottish Highlands, where Penny went by the code name Bruna. Frank had taught Penny how to kill with her bare hands.

'He got me in a stranglehold,' said Penny.

'And I knew it was love when she landed me on my arse,' was Frank's response.

When Jinx found someone who looked at her like Frank looked at Penny, then she might believe in love, too. She couldn't help but be a little jealous of her friends' relationship.

No matter how badly Penny behaved towards him, it seemed Frank would always love her. And no matter how close Jinx and Penny had become over the years, Jinx would always come second to Frank in Penny's heart.

Chapter Thirty-Four

The Coach Trip, 2023

Though Jinx and Thea had escaped Team Merevale's hotel, they were not excused from the tour itinerary. Glenn called Thea from the breakfast room of the Regina at half past seven.

'Why aren't you downstairs? You're going to be late for the Highlights of Florence tour.'

'Mrs Sullivan has already seen the highlights of Florence,' Thea tried.

'You haven't. And I'm sure she'd like to see them again. What else are you going to do today?'

Thea could think of a thousand things she would rather do, but sensed that her father wouldn't approve of any of them.

'Tell your dad we'll be downstairs in a minute,' Jinx mouthed.

But before they left the room, it was time for a conversation.

'I thought you would get me out of the tour today,' Thea complained. 'After what I told you.'

'Why?'

'You know. I don't want to spend the day looking at the things my mum never saw, in the company of the Colonel, Val and Cynthia.'

240

'I'll give you that second part,' said Jinx. 'But I've been wondering ... Thea, do you believe your mum loved you and your father.'

'Of course she did.'

'Then here's another question. Would you want someone you loved to be unhappy and miss out on something rather special, just because you couldn't be with them?'

'Of course not.'

'Then by definition, your mum would want you and your dad to be happy today. And what do you think might make your dad happy?'

Thea knew she'd been talked into a corner.

'He'd want me to go on the tour.'

'Exactly. Apart from anything else, I think we have to show Val and Cynth that they're wrong about the pair of us. Don't you?'

Though Glenn had researched that day's itinerary with his usual thoroughness, he was not going to be leading the tour. His liaison at Capstan Coaches had explained that it would be easier to get inside the crowded museums and galleries with an official tour guide, who could also ensure that the route Team Merevale took around the city was accessible for those with limited mobility. While Luca the guide led Team Merevale in a crocodile, Glenn joined Thea and Jinx in her wheelchair at the back, well away from the Colonel and Val and Cynthia, who were naturally at the front.

First stop on that day's itinerary was the famous Piazza della Signoria, where Luca found a shady spot where Team Merevale could stand as he drew their attention to the historic riches to be found around them.

'This square has been the centre of Florence since the four-teenth century,' Luca told them. 'It was here that preacher

241

Savonarola instigated the "Bonfire of the Vanities", ordering the burning of all those things he thought might lead one to sin – the books, the jewels, the fine ladies' dresses – only to be burned at the stake himself a few years later. I will show you the marble plaque that indicates the very spot.'

Luca had plenty of historical detail to impart, but for the most part, Team Merevale was more interested in taking pictures of the gigantic model of Michelangelo's *David*, in front of the Palazzo Vecchio. And the café. There was pastry to be had.

From the Piazza della Signoria, Team Merevale took the Via dei Calzaiuoli. Luca pointed out the beautiful church of Orsanmichele, with its pillars topped by copies of the statues of the fourteen patron saints of the Florentine guilds.

'Created by Verrocchio, Ghiberti and Giambologna ...' Luca made the words sound like music, '... and Donatello, who sculpted San Marco, patron saint of the linen weavers, and San Giorgio, commissioned by the guild of armourers.'

While Luca asked his audience to imagine Florence in the 1400s, when Donatello had his workshop there, Jinx was imagining a nearer past. She saw herself walking this street in 1951, with Penny beside her.

'Close your eyes, Jinx.'

She closed them again now, as Glenn pushed her wheelchair, and kept them closed until they reached the Piazza del Duomo and she tried to see the cathedral again as though for the first time. Standing behind her, Thea murmured 'Wow.' And at last Jinx was glad that she had compelled Thea to come on that bloody coach trip after all, if only for that wow.

'You must live every moment of your life, Jinx.' Penny's words echoed in her head. 'Every single moment.'

Chapter Thirty-Five

Team Merevale eagerly followed Luca into the Duomo, not least to find shelter from the sun. While Luca answered questions about the cathedral's great treasures, from the marble floor to Lorenzo Ghiberti's enormous rose window, Glenn slipped away on his own. He found a rack of candles in front of a friendly-looking saint, pushed a folded ten-euro note into the offertory and took a candle for himself. Fixing it to a spike on the top row, he decided to have a little word with the saint while he lit it. No, not with the saint. With Lindsey, his late wife, Thea's mum.

'So here we are in Italy, Linz. We made it. You were supposed to be with us, of course. We didn't go to Verona. Probably a good job, because I don't think I would have been able to keep from crying, seeing what was supposed to be our special place without you. You would love it here, though, in Florence. Aperol spritz everywhere you go. They drink it like water. Well, the tourists do.

'Are you looking down on us, Linz? If you are looking down, then you'll have seen me argue with the Colonel about Thea, about the way she's been behaving. He thinks I'm a bad dad. Am I, Linz? Am I getting it wrong? I feel like I'm always getting it wrong somehow. I know Thea's a good girl. The way she's been with Mrs Sullivan is remarkable. But she just doesn't seem happy. How can I help her be happy, Linz?'

Glenn heard no reply. Not that he'd expected one. But he had expected to feel something. A sense of comfort or peace. Nothing. The saint looked down, impassive. Glenn took himself back out into the piazza for a quick cry.

But Glenn was not the only one feeling a little overwhelmed by emotion in the Duomo that morning. Stepping outside, he found himself standing right next to the Colonel, who was cleaning his glasses with a grubby-looking handkerchief. The Colonel nodded in acknowledgment and made it clear that he'd not been crying. Not at all.

'Pollution,' he muttered.

Glenn and the Colonel stood side by side, saying nothing, for a short while, then both began to speak at once.

Glenn demurred, as he usually did when it came to his old friend. 'You go first.'

'Glenn,' said the Colonel, 'I want to apologise. I spoke out of turn in Lucca, and I fear I have caused you and Thea a great deal of unhappiness.'

'Thanks,' Glenn said. 'Please don't worry about it.'

Don't worry about it? Why did he say that? Glenn wondered. Because batting the apology away seemed like the only thing to do. It would be too excruciating to let the Colonel say any more.

But the Colonel was determined to say his piece.

'I'm afraid I do worry about it. I'm an old fool, Glenn, and too often in my life I have opened my mouth before I've engaged my brain.'

Glenn made to protest.

'No, it's true, Glenn. I don't always think before I start giving my opinion. Especially when it's an opinion on something I know nothing about. Such as raising a child. I should not have made a judgement about your parenting skills.'

'I guess they have been lacking,' said Glenn.

'Glenn, that could not be further from the truth. I shouldn't be pontificating on anyone's parenting ability, because not only am I not a father myself, I never even had one. At least not one that I knew. I didn't know my mother either, if I'm perfectly honest.'

This was news to Glenn.

'Were you an orphan, Malcolm?' Glenn asked.

'Might as well have been,' said the Colonel. 'Might have been better. I was illegitimate. I was born in 1944. My father was a GI. By the time my mother realised she was pregnant, he'd been posted to France and she never saw him again. She couldn't raise me on her own, so she put me in a home. I think she thought that one day she would come back for me. She never did.'

'Malcolm, that's terrible.'

'It was just the way things were. When I left the home, I went into the army and that was my family. So I know a lot about following orders and next to nothing about love. If I thought that Thea was being ungrateful, it's probably because I can see that she has what I never had. A father who loves her.

'I should have kept my mouth shut. Your daughter is grieving, Glenn. Pat and Marilyn put me straight about that last night, after you went to bed. They put Val and Cynth straight about a few things, too. Including those horrible green dresses.'

'They never did?'

'It was Defcon 1 there for a moment.' The Colonel grimaced.

'I wish I'd seen that,' said Glenn.

'A dressing-down was no less than we all deserved. But can you forgive me, Glenn? I'm going to apologise to Thea, too, of course. As will Cynthia and Val. I have made sure of that. Thea is a wonderful young woman. Caring and sensible. She's a chip off the old block. You should be proud.'

'Malcolm, thank you. I really am.'

The Colonel nodded. 'You've been a good friend to this silly old man over the years,' he said. 'To all of us. We're grateful, you know, for all that you do for us. We may not always remember to show it, but we are. You mean the world to Team Merevale. And especially to me,' he added.

Glenn suddenly enveloped the Colonel in a hug that took him by surprise, knocking his panama hat off.

Glenn rushed to retrieve it, to cover the Colonel's 'hair transplant'. But there was no hair transplant. Just a common or garden bald patch, that made Glenn love the Colonel even more.

While the Colonel wandered off to look into a shop window – 'Not crying. It's the pollution, of course.' – Glenn spotted Jinx and Thea emerging from the cathedral's accessible door. As they crossed the piazza, they disturbed a little group of pigeons that scattered skywards, narrowly missing their heads, making them both rock with laughter. Glenn had never seen either woman laugh like that before.

'Did you see that, Dad? I wish you'd got a photo.'

'I could take one now?' Glenn suggested. He fully expected a 'No'. But Thea let Glenn take a photograph of her in front of the Duomo, then asked Jinx if she might take a photograph of her together with her dad. Inspecting the snap on Glenn's phone screen afterwards, she even said, 'We can get this one printed out when we get home, Dad, and put it in a frame.'

Glenn had to work very hard not to burst into happy tears at the thought.

'Would you believe Val and Cynthia apologised about yesterday while we were in the cathedral?' Jinx told him, as he pushed her wheelchair towards a patch of shade. 'They have promised to buy us all ice cream.'

'I like Italy,' Thea said then. 'I'm glad we came.'

Chapter Thirty-Six

Team Merevale had a very busy day in the city. After the Duomo – no one wanted to climb to the top of the dome, thank goodness – they marched to the Accademia to see the real *David*. From there to the Uffizi for a quick glance at Botticelli's Venus on her half-shell through the selfie-taking crowds. Jinx was glad to have an excuse to leave the chaos and return to the old Hotel Regina, with the dog cemetery for a garden. She suspected that Thea was, too.

They persuaded the grumpy manager to bring drinks out to the plastic grass lawn, and Jinx told Thea more about her first trip to the city.

'Who did you come with?'

'With someone called Penny Williamson.'

'How did you know her?'

'Oh, she was a mentor of sorts.'

Jinx didn't go so far as to tell Thea in what field.

'Penny was an extraordinary woman. Unusually liberated for the time. She really opened my eyes to what was possible. We had a wonderful time together. Crazy, you might even say. I remember so clearly the moment I saw the Duomo. Penny made me close my eyes as she led me towards it, so that the scale and magnificence of it would come as an even bigger sur-prise. Afterwards, I had my first negroni ...'

It felt strange to be talking so warmly about Penny after all the years of estrangement, and yet there had been good times, hadn't there? A very long time ago.

'Do you think she's still alive?' Thea asked. 'Your friend.'

'I'm not sure,' Jinx lied.

In the copy of *The Times* procured by the Colonel just that day, Jinx had found the smallest note towards the bottom of the register pages. Not a death notice, but a 'very much still with us' notice.

'Happy birthday to Josephine Naiswell (née Williamson) of South Kensington, 101 years old today. With love from your little sister Penny (99) and all the family.'

The wench was still not dead.

At ten o'clock, Jinx decided it was time for bed.

In her usual calm way, Thea helped Jinx get undressed. While Jinx didn't ever look forward to this moment, which underlined her fragility, she was grateful for Thea's discretion. However, this time, as she helped Jinx into her nightdress, Thea read aloud the words woven into the tattoo on Jinx's arm. The tattoo Thea had hitherto pretended not to have seen.

'*Kill or be killed*,' Thea murmured.

'Ah,' said Jinx. 'That old thing.'

Thea stepped back.

'I'm sorry. I didn't mean to—'

'It's OK. One doesn't get a tattoo imagining that nobody will ever see it.'

'But why *Kill or be killed*?'

'Youthful exuberance.'

'And is that a sparrow?'

249

Thea referred to the bird which hopped across the top of the words.

'It's a wryneck bird, actually. A *Jynx torquilla*.'

'I've never heard of that.'

'You don't see them much in England.'

'So why one of those?'

'I just rather like them.'

Jinx's nightdress was loose and gaped at the back of her neck. She could almost feel Thea's eyes on her scars, which crossed her brown skin like silvery snail trails. Though age had definitely withered Jinx, those scars would never fade away.

'What happened to you, Mrs Sullivan?' Thea asked at last.

On the day in 1966 when she last saw Penny Williamson, Jinx had promised herself that she would never be so vulnerable again. No one would ever know her so well as Penny had.

Staying invulnerable meant keeping one's weak spots, one's tender points, safely hidden away. For Jinx, that meant not talking about things like the scars on her back. But she was almost ninety now, and if the last couple of weeks had shown her anything, it was that she could no longer operate in the world entirely alone. And though Thea probably hadn't done it consciously, she had acted in such a way that Jinx had come to like her these past few weeks. Thea was as closed to the world as Jinx had tried to be. Where was the harm in telling her the truth about this one thing?

'I took a beating as a child,' said Jinx. 'In a World War 2 prison camp.'

At last, Jinx told the story that she hadn't told in decades. She hadn't spoken about the war with anyone since Eddy died in 1981. Just forty, he was. Much too young. Jinx had stayed with him during his last few weeks, and he asked her to tell him about camp again and again. He could barely remember

250

it, though it had shaped his entire life. It was standing in the sun through endless tenkos which caused the skin cancer that killed him.

'But how were you in a prison camp?' Thea asked. 'Are you Jewish?'

'The Japanese weren't after the Jews,' Jinx explained. 'Not at first, anyway. My crime was simply to be a British citizen, though I had never been to England in my life. Not then. When the Japanese occupied Singapore, we were lumped in with the rest of the expats out there on British Empire business, rounded up and put in Changi Jail.'

'Were you really young?'

'I was seven when I went in. Ten when I came out.'

'I can't believe I didn't know this.'

'Why would you?'

'I saw the photographs in your living room. I knew you didn't grow up in England.'

'You could tell it was me in the photographs?' Jinx asked.

'Yes, of course. You look the same. I mean, it's obviously you.'

That news made Jinx's heart hurt, because the photographs were taken before the war, when she was last truly herself.

'That little girl seems like another person altogether now,' Jinx said.

As she told Thea the story of her childhood, Jinx realised that she was saying names she hadn't spoken in years. The names of her friends in camp, of the Hut Ten women, of the Japanese guards. Of her father. Her mother. Eddy.

'My little brother was just a baby ...'

'God, Mrs Sullivan. How did you live through all that?'

'It never occurred to me not to.'

'But why don't you tell everyone?'

'Because I don't want anyone to see me as a victim, and some people, if they knew my story, would treat me differently.'

251

'Better, perhaps?'

'I don't know. When we came back to England, people did know our story and they treated us like dirt.'

'I'm sorry,' said Thea.

'There's no need to be sorry for something you're not responsible for.'

I sound like Penny, Jinx thought.

'No, I'm sorry because I thought you were a cynical old witch for no reason.'

'And now you think I have a reason?'

'Yes!'

'It's true it isn't easy to love your fellow man when you know what he's truly capable of.'

'I can't believe you were beaten so badly.'

Jinx's eyes softened and grew sad as she remembered the day she took the thrashing that marked her for life. It had to happen. One of the guards had found her with an empty condensed milk tin. She was dragged before the commandant and Goofy was ordered to administer the lashes. Goofy's senior officers knew it was the best way to punish him, too, to persuade him that it wasn't worth it, trying to help any of the prisoners.

'People are fucking terrible,' said Thea.

'Language.'

'They are, though.'

'You're fucking right,' Jinx said. 'But most of the time it's because they're scared. And I'm still here. That's the best revenge.'

'But those scars ...'

'Are a part of me. People have worse on the inside.'

Thea suddenly turned her face away like a much younger child, who thinks that if they can't see someone, that someone can't see them either.

'Let me show you something,' Jinx said.

Jinx asked Thea to go into her handbag. 'There's a little black velvet pouch. Be careful with what's in there. It's very old.'

Jinx was nervous as Thea tipped the white mouse out of the pouch into the palm of her hand.

'Is this valuable?'

'Only to me.'

Jinx held out her palm so that Thea could rest the mouse there.

'See its right ear? See how it's been glued back into place.'

'You can see the join.'

'You're meant to. The Japanese have a tradition. It's called *kintsugi*. You've heard of it, I'm sure. Everybody has these days. When they mend an ornament like this, they don't try to hide the join. They don't use invisible glue, like we would, to try to make it seem as though it was never broken in the first place. They mix their glue with gold so it stands out. Because as far as the Japanese are concerned, the cracks are part of the broken thing's story, and fixing them with gold reminds us that even broken things can have value and beauty. The man who fixed this little mouse understood that.'

Jinx wondered where it had come from, this speech, and why it felt so urgent.

'Who was he? The man?' Thea asked.

'I'll tell you another day. For now, all you need to know is that we're beautifully broken, you and I. I know you have your scars, too.'

Thea tugged at the hems of her baggy black Bermuda shorts.

'Our scars are part of our story. We don't need any new ones – don't get me wrong – but we have no need to be ashamed of those we do have.'

'Then you should show yours and tell everyone what happened.'

'Not everyone understands *kintsugi*, Thea. Not everyone deserves to know our whole stories, yet. But you know mine, and I'm starting to understand yours, and we can share our stories with each other whenever we want. For now, I think that's enough.'

Thea nodded.

'Shall I put the mouse back in your suitcase?'

'No,' said Jinx. 'For tonight, Mousey can sit on the chest of drawers between us and watch over us both.'

Thea didn't tell Mrs Sullivan anything more about her own scars that night, but knowing that the older woman had noticed them was a comfort. It was a promise that when she finally felt like talking, really talking, Thea would be heard.

Chapter Thirty-Seven

On their second morning in Florence, the coach party were due in the *'nonnas' kitchen'* for their Italian food class. The Colonel was especially excited.

'Oggi, facciamo una torta,' he told the hotel manager when she asked him what his plans were for the day.

'I see,' she said in English, wondering if she should let him know that he'd unwittingly happened upon the Florentine slang for a 'threesome'.

With her arm in a sling, Jinx didn't think she would be much use when it came to making pasta. Thea was only too happy to bunk off with her.

'Don't you want to make some pasta?' Glenn asked.

'Someone has got to keep Mrs Sullivan company,' said Thea, making her excuses from the moral high ground. 'She'd never say that she'd prefer to have company, but I know she would really. I don't want to leave her alone.'

Glenn was prouder than ever of his daughter in that moment.

So the majority of the party set off to meet the *nonnas*, leaving Jinx and Thea behind with the wheelchair.

'Shall we take this thing for a spin?' Jinx suggested to her young friend. 'There is a place near the Via Romana I'd like to

255

go back to. It used to be a junk shop, full of the most extraordinary things. The man who owned it was an amateur taxidermist, I think. You've never seen such weird and wonderful stuffed animals. Looked nothing like they must have done in life.'

'Dead things. Sounds great,' said Thea. 'Let's go.'

The two new friends set off. It was no easy feat, dodging the summer crowds in the centre of the city, though they did their best to take backstreets that weren't clogged with tourists taking selfies in front of buildings the significance of which they would have forgotten well before they got home.

The crowds thinned out as they got further away from the river, but gentrification had reached far into the city's outskirts and the shops Jinx vaguely remembered as being hardware stores or butcher's shops had been replaced by fancy boutiques and galleries. The junk shop with the stuffed animals was long gone.

Where once the window of the tiny boutique off the Via Romana had been full of badly stuffed roadkill fresh out of a nightmare, now it contained a single display case, and in the display case was a single beautiful piece of jewellery – a gold ring, engraved with a delicate, twisting garland of leaves and flowers. The work was so fine, it was hard to imagine any human hand small or dextrous enough to have been able to create such a thing.

'What a pity,' said Thea. 'I was looking forward to seeing the strange stuffed animals all twisted up in their death throes.'

'Ha! Would you mind if we went inside anyway?' Jinx asked. 'I should like to try to remember the old place.'

But this was not a shop that you could just walk into. The jewellery for sale there was expensive. Thea buzzed the doorbell and the proprietor – a Japanese woman in her forties

– peered out to make an assessment of her would-be customers before she opened the door.

'Can I help you?' she asked in English, perhaps knowing from the way they were dressed that her visitors couldn't possibly be Italian. She seemed wary, but warmed up straight away when Jinx greeted her with a little head bow and a small snatch of Japanese.

'*Kon'nichiwa. Haitte mo īdesu ka*?'

'You speak Japanese!'

'Only a few words.'

'Your accent is very good,' the woman assured her, as she opened the door wide enough for Jinx's wheelchair to come through. 'Where did you learn?'

'Here and there,' Jinx said. She quickly changed the subject. 'You know, I came to this place as a young woman. When it was a junk shop. It certainly looks different now.'

'I've been here for three years,' the woman explained. 'Before that it had been empty for some time. It was in a mess. The walls were damp and the ceiling was coming down.'

'But you saw the beauty in the bones and you've transformed it. What a pretty shop. What lovely jewellery. May I have a closer look at a few things?'

The woman, who introduced herself as Hikari Hinode Mancini, pulled a velvet tray from a drawer and laid it on top of her desk.

'Are you looking for something in particular?'

'I'll know it when I see it,' Jinx said. 'Sometimes the strangest little thing will speak to you and tell you that you must take it home at once.'

Hikari seemed to like that idea.

'Perhaps I could see the ring in the window first,' Jinx said.

Thea browsed the cabinets while Hikari gathered baubles she thought might intrigue or inspire her customers.

257

Jinx exclaimed with delight as she held the ring from the window in her hand.

'This is quite the most beautiful thing I have seen in a long while.'

'Thank you. The winding flower is jasmine.'

Hikari explained the method she had used to create it: a mixture of Japanese and Italian metalworking techniques. 'Very time-consuming, which is why it is expensive.'

The ring was priced at five thousand euros.

'And how did you come to be in Italy, dear?' Jinx asked.

Hikari explained that she had come to Florence as a student, fallen in love and never left.

'With an Italian?'

'With the city,' Hikari corrected her. 'And with an Italian man after that. The very first time I walked through the Piazza della Signoria and saw all those statues – so much beauty, so casually placed – I knew Florence would steal my heart. Places have a soul just as much as we humans do, I believe. In this city, you can still feel the energy of all those wonderful artists of the Renaissance, finding their inspiration here.'

As Hikari said that, Jinx thought of Sime Road. When she'd last been in Singapore, in 2005, she had visited the site of her former 'home'. The only thing indicating that the prison camp had ever been there was a plaque. But pulling down the huts had not cleared the atmosphere of the place. She felt cold the whole time she was there, though the temperature was thirty-five degrees. She felt cold now, just thinking about it.

'You are from England?' Hikari asked.

'Not originally.'

Should Jinx just tell her? No. She didn't want to.

'But I have been in England since I was quite a small child,' Jinx said. 'I live in the Cotswolds now. Perhaps you know the area?'

'Oh, yes. Beautiful countryside.'

Jinx asked Hikari to slip the jasmine ring on to the middle finger of her right hand.

'I'm a bit incapacitated, as you can see.' Jinx indicated the sling.

With the ring on her finger, Jinx held her hand away from her face to better admire it.

'A little big for me, I think. Do you have anything else?'

'I may have the perfect thing for you in the back of the shop.'

By the time ten minutes had passed, Jinx had persuaded Hikari to lay eight different pieces out in front of her. She kept picking rings up and putting them down again, talking all the while. Thea was fascinated by the whole performance. The Mrs Sullivan she knew was not one for small talk, and now that Thea knew why her friend had every reason to dislike the Japanese, the bonhomie seemed especially odd.

With so many items out on the tray, it was hard for Hikari to keep track of what was where. Ordinarily, she was very careful about such things, but the old lady with the smattering of Japanese phrases was so sweet, Hikari let her guard down. She wasn't always so charmed by her customers. The rich ones in particular often forgot their manners.

'Manners are very important,' Jinx agreed, when the subject came up.

'I can tell how people will be the moment they say "Hello",' Hikari said.

'Oh, yes. First impressions count.'

After ten minutes of toing and froing, Jinx told Hikari that she would have to go away and think about the jewels over-night. They were expensive.

'I'm sure I'll be back for something, though. Come along, Thea. Time to go.'

*

259

Having locked the door behind her customers, Hikari went to tidy the jewels Jinx had tried on away. When she picked up the velvet tray, she did a double take. It no longer contained the number of items she thought she had laid out upon it.

Hikari ran to the door. She fumbled to open it, dropping her key twice before she got it into the lock. By the time Hikari was out on the street, the old lady and her young companion were long gone. The summer crowds had closed around them again like the sea.

Chapter Thirty-Eight

Sime Road Camp, Singapore, 1945

By the spring of 1945, Jinx had given up imagining a life out-side camp. It was an abstract thing to her now.

'I can't remember Daddy's face,' she whispered to Norma one night. 'Do you think he's forgotten us, too?'

'Of course he hasn't. You'll see him soon enough,' Norma promised.

It was harder than ever to get news from the outside world, but thanks to the Japanese-speaking prisoners who eavesdropped on the guards, they had heard about Iwo Jima and the month-long battle in which the United States Marine Corps and the United States Navy wrestled the island from Japanese control. And in May 1945 rumours started going round that the war in Europe was over. Hitler was dead and the Germans had surren-dered.

Was that good news or bad? Good news, surely, that the Germans were defeated and the Allies could concentrate on the Far East instead. But perhaps bad news, too. As the weeks passed the Japanese guards seemed more jumpy than usual, more likely to lash out. Rations at the camp had been cut again, so that there was hardly any point turning up for mealtimes. Was it because there was no food left, or because the Japanese wanted to punish their prisoners for Allied successes, as had happened on the Double Tenth?

'The Japanese won't give up easily,' was the considered opinion of most of the adult internees when they talked about how the war might end. 'Fight to the death is their rule.' And if the fight didn't go their way, would they take the POWs with them? Everyone kept their heads down. When planes flew over, the children rushed outside to see whether it was true – that they were Allied planes, not Japanese – but their mothers pulled them back into the safety of the hut. There was no point enraging their captors. They were still a very long way from being free. They might still starve to death.

There was no rice any more. Only tapioca, and very little of that. Goofy hadn't left condensed milk under the tree since the day Jinx had been caught with a tin and he'd been instructed to give her ten lashes. Everyone was listless. The children no longer had the energy to play like they used to. Jinx earned an extra spoonful of mush each day by joining the party of women and girls chosen to dig a new storage tunnel in the hillside. There were those who thought that doing anything for the Japanese was treachery, but no one begrudged the children their extra rations.

At night, the internees listened to the sound of fighter planes engaging in the dark sky above the Singapore Strait, and hoped and prayed that the ones that tumbled into the unforgiving sea were not 'our boys'.

On one occasion, shrapnel fell into the grounds of Sime Road and Norma told Jinx that she must not go outside after dark, in case it happened again. Not that it was very much safer under the battered asbestos roof of Hut Sixteen, more holes than ceiling now.

July came and went. The guards were more agitated than ever. Jinx narrowly escaped another beating when she was found chewing a blade of grass. Then on 6 August 1945, the unimaginable happened. The unconscionable.

Hiroshima.

Three days later, Nagasaki.

And on 15 August, Japan's Emperor Hirohito announced Japan's surrender in the strange high-pitched voice that seemed so at odds with the image of the bogeyman who'd had the power of life and death over the internees for so long.

The internees found out a couple of days later, when Allied planes flew over the island, dropping leaflets as they passed by. As the leaflets drifted down from the sky, the children ran to the top of the hill to grab them by the handful.

Jinx stood and read her leaflet as others continued to fall around her, like flakes of ash from an enormous bonfire, for that was what they seemed to be.

'Read it to me, Jinx,' Eddy begged her. 'Tell me what it says.'

'*To All Allied Prisoners of War. The Japanese Forces Have Surrendered Unconditionally and The War Is Over* ... The war is finished,' Jinx said. 'We're going to see Daddy again.'

There was no real jubilation. There was relief. There were tears. There were prayers of thanks offered up to the God who had been absent for so long. But there was no jubilation, because how could they celebrate when they were all so tired and hungry, and there was still no food but a single loaf of bread dropped from a plane shortly after the leaflets, to be shared between twenty. And a day after that, half a pound of butter per person, presumably to go with the bread. The leaflets warned them not to eat too much, but no one took any notice. Jinx poured warm butter into her mouth until she was sick.

The leaflets had also told them to stay where they were. More help was coming. In the meantime, the Japanese High Command had agreed that their guards would stay on in the camps, to ensure order while they waited for the liberating troops to arrive. That news prompted an outburst of rare bad language from Norma.

'What? They're expecting us to continue to answer to those bloody monsters? I'm not having that. Any one of those men tries to tell me what to do, he's going to get his stick up his own arse. And about time, too.'

In the event, the confrontation Norma half-hoped for didn't happen. The Japanese guards regarded the idea that they stay on to keep order as just as ludicrous as the women did. They soon made themselves scarce. The senior officers locked themselves away in their quarters. The most junior disappeared, taking off their uniforms and melting into the crowds outside the prison gates.

Goofy was among the last to go. Jinx saw him on the path to the officer's house, that was still strictly out of bounds under orders from the women of Hut Ten. Jinx stood in front of him without fear and, daring to look straight into his face at last, saw that he was almost as thin as the prisoners. More haunted now, for sure.

'Goofy.'

He smiled at the sound of his nickname and responded with a half-hearted 'Woof'.

'I suppose this is it for you, too,' Jinx said. 'The war's over.'

They still only knew the bare minimum of each other's language, but they both understood this was 'goodbye'.

'You'll be able to go home and see your daughter,' said Jinx.

Goofy nodded. 'Daughter' was a word he knew very well now.

'You must be happy about that,' Jinx chatted. 'And I will be able to see my father at last.'

Goofy nodded again. Then he reached into his pocket. When he opened his hand, it was to reveal a small porcelain mouse. White with pink-tipped ears.

'You,' he said, as he pushed it towards her.

Jinx instinctively shook her head. 'I can't.'

Goofy put the mouse away again.

'Goodbye, then,' said Jinx.

'Goodbye,' said Goofy.

He bowed low. From the waist, showing the maximum respect.

Jinx briefly bowed her head in return.

When Goofy straightened up again, she could see that the light had gone out in his eyes. She had the urge to say something else, something comforting, but Norma was suddenly there shouting, 'Come away from him, Jinx. Come away from that bastard.' And she knew there was no point telling Norma that this was the bastard who had left condensed milk under the tree and risked his life to help them survive, because he was also the bastard who had covered Jinx's back with bright red scars on the day she got caught with one of those blasted tins. Jinx turned away and walked back to Norma, knowing that she would not speak to Goofy again. Not in this life.

A week later, they were still in the camp and they were still half-starved. The Allied food drops were sporadic and random. Their troubles were far from 'packed up in an old kitbag'.

'When can we see Daddy?' Eddy asked several times a day.

Other children in the camp had already been reunited with their fathers, but Maurice was never among the smiling men who met the women by the gates each morning. The Allies were still insisting that the men and women were back in their separate camps by nightfall.

265

'He must be in the sick bay,' said Norma.

'Can't we ask someone?' Jinx suggested. 'Perhaps we could go and see him?'

Norma couldn't keep up the pretence. Not now.

'Jinx, your dad ... Your dad wasn't ever here at Sime Road. He died in Changi.'

Norma's voice cracked as she told her children what had happened. Maurice had contracted malaria. He was too weak from malnutrition to survive it. It happened in '43. When Norma got the news, she had asked Mrs Mulvany to keep Jinx occupied while she tried to work out how to tell her. Jinx remembered that day.

'But I decided I couldn't tell you because things were already so hard, and you were both so small and we had to keep going. I had to keep you both alive. I didn't think you could carry any more sadness. You do understand that, Jinx, don't you?'

'Daddy's dead?' Eddy burst into tears. His loss was no less keen for his not being able to remember much about their father. Jinx and Norma's memories had given flesh to Eddy's image of the man they called 'Dad'.

Jinx did have memories, a great many of them, and nearly all of them – right up until the soldier came to tell them to evacuate – were happy. She could still hear her father's voice in her head.

'What do we say in our family?'

'We do not cry,' Jinx murmured to herself. 'I do not cry.'

'You're my brave girl, Jinx,' the voice said. 'Daddy loves you.'

'Can you forgive me, Jinx?' Norma asked her.

Jinx did not cry then, either.

With nothing to eat and no money to buy any food, in some ways the situation seemed more desperate than before. Norma bartered her last valuable possession, her wedding ring, with one of the locals who came to the camp each day, to buy both her children new shoes. She was horrified to discover that her sacrifice could only buy shoes for Eddy. She and Jinx would have to stay barefoot.

What Jinx wanted more than anything was soap. She wished the Allies would drop some of that along with the bread and too much butter. She wanted to be able to stand outside in the rain and feel the suds washing away the tiny biting creatures that had made their home in her hair, which hung down her back like a thick, matted rope. When she saw herself reflected in a piece of old tin, she thought she looked like the illustration of a Stone Age child she'd once seen in a history book, a child from a time before people knew about shampoo and showers. Her gums were sore. How long before she got to see a toothbrush again?

Each day, Jinx and some of the other girls would go out foraging, though there was rarely anything new to find. The camp had been comprehensively picked over the moment the guards left their posts.

Only the guards' house itself remained off limits. The adult women were wary, not knowing what might await them inside. Were there Japanese men still in there with their guns trained on the doors? The children had no such worries. They'd grown up inside a nightmare. No bogeyman could scare them now.

To the side of the house was a garden – a beautiful garden, built and tended by prisoners – where the guards had escaped their daily duties. The children all wanted to see it. Defying her mother's insistence that she stay away from the place, Jinx followed her friends inside.

You could hear the buzzing of the flies before you saw them. It was a moment or two before Jinx realised that the objects floating in the ornamental pond were bodies – Japanese guards,

267

still in their uniforms. They'd taken their own lives rather than wait for the victors to arrive.

'Jinx! Come over here!' Her friend Eileen was down by the water.

Eileen was standing over a body.

'It's Sweet Pea,' she said, scorn curling her lip. 'Cowardly bastard. Didn't want to have to face the music when the Allies turned up, did he? Help me get him out.'

Jinx and Eileen took a leg each and pulled the body of the dead guard onto the land, where it settled in a puddle of bloody ooze that had them both skipping backwards. Jinx clapped her hand to her mouth to keep herself from retching.

'Come on, you chicken.'

Tiptoeing back to the body, Eileen crouched down and started going through Sweet Pea's pockets. She found a half-full packet of cigarettes, but they were too waterlogged to be of any use. She found a condom, too.

'Filthy beast,' Eileen sneered.

Back then, Jinx didn't know what a condom was, but she followed Eileen's lead in finding it disgusting.

'Hold your nose, Jinx.'

Looking for gold teeth, Eileen opened the dead man's mouth with the nonchalance of a vet checking a lamb. Sweet Pea's mouth fell open easily. Rigor mortis had been and gone. The muscles and tendons around his jaw were loose and liquefying.

'Three,' said Eileen, taking the tweezers she'd borrowed from her mother's precious manicure kit. 'One for you and two for me, because I suppose I'm going to have to take them out. Here goes.'

Eileen dropped the first gold molar into Jinx's palm.

'Should we be doing this?' Jinx asked. 'Is it wrong?'

Eileen shrugged. 'They'd have done the same if they won, wouldn't they? To the victors the spoils!'

They found Goofy that same afternoon. When Jinx rolled him over, he looked up at the sky with unseeing eyes. His blackened lips had peeled back from his teeth, in a parody of the smile he used to flash in her direction when none of the other guards was looking.

Holding her breath, Jinx reached into Goofy's breast pocket and found the little porcelain mouse that he had tried to give her; the mouse she had refused. She would take it now, though. It wasn't stealing, was it? He had wanted her to have it once.

Checking another pocket, she found the photograph he'd shown her on that night when the full moon drew her outside. There was his best smile on a day when he had never been happier, when he could not have imagined what was to come over the next few years. Jinx sat down on one of the rocks that had been so carefully placed when the garden was dug and examined the photograph carefully. It was creased and smudgy from being taken out and looked at many, many times. When tears pricked Jinx's eyes, she reminded herself, 'I do not cry.'

'Poor Goofy,' she murmured.

'Daughter.' She heard his voice as he tried out the word she'd taught him. She saw the way his eyes creased whenever he spoke about his little girl. 'Daughter.' Now that little girl had no father. Just like Jinx and Eddy.

Jinx took the photograph, too.

From that day forward, Jinx didn't give the gold teeth a second thought – though Norma had refused to touch such hideous spoils of war and gave her hell for even thinking about selling a dead man's teeth, no matter what they were made of. Jinx never felt a moment's guilt. You do what you have to do to survive. Her only feelings of having taken something she shouldn't were reserved for the photograph and the porcelain mouse, which she did not mention to anybody. Used to having to hide things from the guards and other desperate internees, Jinx kept the mouse safe all the way back to England in the secret pocket she had made inside the waistband of her shorts. The mouse was hers. A talisman. She would not give it up. Not ever.

Chapter Thirty-Nine

Italy, 2023

Back at the Hotel Regina, Jinx felt a sense of peace that she had not felt in years. With Thea's help, she had managed to do all that she could realistically hope to have done in Florence. It had never been realistic, her plan to find Penny's hidden treasure. Though she had spent many long hours staring at the pencil marks in the German guidebook, running the underlined words through every classic code formula she could think of, she had only ever come up with gobbledygook. And if Penny had got it right, and the code pointed to a spot in the garden of the palazzo behind the Hotel Regina, how could Jinx ever have hoped to get over the wall and dig up the bounty at eighty-nine years old and with one arm in a sling. Far better to believe that the code was not a code at all, just random scribbles. *Besides, the wench is dead.* Just a phrase a German officer liked, with no more meaning to him than the cod German phrases Penny sometimes liked to use for comic effect. *'Picnic ist verboten.'*

While Thea went to ask the hotel manager if it might be possible for her and Jinx to have tea in the garden, Jinx's mind drifted to a different hotel, in the shadow of the Taj Mahal, in the early sixties. She remembered an evening when she and

271

Penny talked about Florence as they shared a bottle of moonshine in their room. It wasn't hard to get hold of alcohol in this dry state, not if you were ex-SOE. Penny Williamson knew dodgy people everywhere.

'Is everyone you know a crook?' Jinx had asked her.

'All the interesting ones,' was Penny's response.

They were in India to meet an especially big crook and hand over a fistful of diamonds that Penny and Jinx had picked up in Mayfair in an extraordinary heist that was still all over the papers. Fortunately, the Metropolitan Police were looking for two redheads and Penny and Jinx were currently both brunette.

They made a formidable team, Jinx and Penny. Their shared house in London had a room full of disguises (Eddy thought it was because they worked as film extras in their spare time). In India, they were brown-haired missionaries, dressed in the drabbest outfits at their disposal, and both wearing glasses they didn't need.

'People trust the short-sighted,' was Penny's point of view.

'Didn't Hitler wear specs? Hirohito definitely did.'

'They trust *women* in glasses, then.'

Neither one of them was wearing their fake glasses in the hotel bedroom, where Penny divided moonshine into teacups.

'God, this stuff is rough.'

Penny could take her liquor, but it wasn't long before she started to get maudlin. And whenever she got maudlin, she went back to that night in Italy, when she failed to find treasure in the Florentine palazzo's garden.

Jinx knew all about Penny's brief, failed career as an agent with the SOE's F Section now. Official secrets be damned. Penny had told Jinx everything about her war years.

'F stood for France. I was going to be embedded with the Resistance, but I couldn't do the parachute jump. I'd have been a bloody good agent, Jinx. Frank told me.'

Jinx also knew about Brindisi, and the day Jimmy Noone had assaulted her friend.

'I knew he was trouble the moment I saw him.'

And Penny thought Jinx had told her everything, too. That was her mistake. At that moment, the German guidebook to Florence was still safely hidden under a floorboard in Jinx's bedroom back in South Kensington.

'I can't have got it wrong,' Penny wailed. 'I was famous among my colleagues for being able to decipher the indecipherables. Everyone brought the messages they couldn't decode to me. I could always make a stab at what was missing, or mixed up, and I was usually right. But that bastard got one by me. It all made sense that it led to the palazzo. German intelligence officers were stationed there. The garden was an obvious place to hide looted treasure.'

Jinx agreed. But perhaps the German book was just a guide to nothing more than the jewels of Florence that anyone could see in the Uffizi or the Accademia. Its only real significance was as a souvenir of the time Jinx jumped from a train to avoid being shot by two CIA operatives sent by Jimmy Noone to ensure that Penny hadn't found what he obviously thought of as *his* treasure.

'Oh, I read too much into it,' Penny sighed.

Turned out neither Penny nor Jinx had read quite widely enough.

Jinx and Thea took up their usual spot in the garden at the Hotel Regina with the Colonel's copy of *The Times*. Thea folded the paper so that the cryptic puzzle was on the outside and started to read the clues aloud.

'Mind if I fill some in?' she asked.

'Your handwriting is better than mine,' Jinx agreed.

'Three across is "Lily of the Valley".'

273

'Hmmmm.'

'I think four across is "pantechnicon".'

Jinx nodded.

'Eight down. "The wench is dead." That's from a T.S. Eliot poem, isn't it?'

'What?' asked Jinx.

'The wench is dead?'

That phrase again. It was a good one, Jinx supposed.

'It's Christopher Marlowe,' she told her young friend. 'From *The Jew of Malta.*'

'No, it's T.S. Eliot. Mum had me read some poems to her when she was dying. I remember it really well because it was so weird. I mean, who says "wench"?'

'Christopher Marlowe did.'

'And T.S. Eliot.'

'You're mistaken.'

'Honestly, Mrs Sullivan, I'm so not. How much do you want to bet me?'

Thea snatched up her phone. The Regina's free wi-fi was patchy, but by standing up and moving closer to the doors that led back into the building she got enough of a signal to look up the phrase.

'We're both right,' Thea announced happily. 'It is from a play by Christopher Marlowe, and it's in a T.S. Eliot poem, too. "Portrait of a Lady". He used it as a ... What do they call it when you use a quote from something else at the beginning of a poem?'

'An epigraph. Show me.'

Thea enlarged the words on the phone screen. T.S. Eliot. How had Jinx never come across this poem before? She scanned the words. Like so many of Eliot's poems, it was a long one. But why didn't she know it? Why had she never read it?

Jinx realised it was because she had never looked up the

sentence on the internet, having always assumed, always *known*, that it was Marlowe; having spent so many hours going through an old copy of his play, using the phrase as a cipher code, trying to fit Marlowe's words to her purposes.

'So can I write "Eliot" in?'

'For goodness' sake,' Jinx muttered.

'What's wrong?' asked Thea. 'You don't think I'm right? It fits.'

'I do think you're right,' said Jinx. 'In fact, I *know* you are. Thea, I think you may have solved a very old puzzle.'

'Can I write the answer in, then?' Thea still thought Jinx was talking about the crossword.

'Yes. Then we need to get a printout of that poem. Ask the manager.'

'That git?'

'Tell him it's important. Don't worry about the cost. Stick it on the room.'

'You can read it on your tablet.'

'I need it on paper.'

'Are you going to tell me why we're doing this?'

'Because, my dear Thea, it might just make us rich.'

Half an hour later, Jinx and Thea sat on either side of the small dressing table in their shared hotel room, with the printout of the poem between them. Jinx had shown Thea the inscription in the guidebook and the places where the book's original owner had underlined the text; now she explained how she thought a poem code should work.

'There are five pencil marks on the first page, under five individual letters – JEOMR. The first thing to work out is at what position in the alphabet the letters appear.'

Thea started to try to work it out on her fingers, but Jinx was already there. 'Ten, five, fifteen, thirteen, eighteen. And those are the words in the poem used for the transcription key, with the added complication that we're skipping the epigraph.'

Jinx picked out the words from the poem and had Thea write them down.

'*Afternoon fog arrange the will.*'

'That doesn't make sense,' said Thea.

'We haven't finished yet.'

Jinx described how Thea should give each letter in the chosen words a number, and those numbers would help them discover the real meaning of the message.

Except it made no sense when set against the grid.

But it must make sense. Jinx went back to the beginning and started again. Were the underlined words the message? The tiny pencil marks on the map? She had Thea draw out the grid again and again, but they could make nothing from the material they had except nonsense.

'Penny would have been able to do this,' Jinx muttered. Yet Penny hadn't found treasure either, though she had got as far as a square on the map.

Jinx turned letters into numbers into letters into nonsense again. Thea watched, unable to see any pattern at all. After an hour, she was ready to give up. Or perhaps just give up on a code.

'Maybe it's not that complicated,' Thea suggested. 'Maybe the final clue isn't in code. It's in plain sight. There's a place in the first verse of the Eliot poem.'

'What place?'

Thea pointed it out. 'There. "Juliet's tomb." Isn't that in Verona?'

Certainly the most famous one was. But they were miles from Verona.

'Well, that's it, then,' said Jinx. 'We're in the wrong city.'

Then a dog barked somewhere outside in the street, and it

came to Jinx that it just so happened that another tomb for 'Juliet' was hidden in the scruffy little garden of a hotel in the Oltrano that once smelled of an old bassotto called Romeo.

Penny had often said that one could be 'too clever for one's own good', but Jinx doubted that Penny had ever felt the maxim referred to her. Yet it all made sense now. Penny had got so far, using Marlowe for her code, but she had ended up digging on the wrong side of the wall. Jinx explained the whole strange story to Thea.

Thea took only one thing from it.

'You want me to dig up a *grave*?'

Chapter Forty

A plan was made. The grumpy manager would clock off at eleven, leaving the reception unmanned until the following day, when someone would arrive at six to start setting up the breakfast room. As soon as the coast was clear, Thea would go down to the scrubby little garden and find out whether her hunch, that Juliet's Tomb was the real clue, was right. They had no spade, but Thea liberated a large serving spoon from the breakfast room that would do just as well.

The night was warm, just as it had been back in 1951, when Penny got stuck in the palazzo garden. Right then, 1951 might have been only yesterday. The city's bells sounded as they had always done. The hotel garden looked the same in the moonlight. The same night birds called to one another from the darkness of the trees across the wall.

Jinx and Thea waited patiently for the eleven o'clock peal and another fifteen minutes after that before Thea went down to the garden. There was no dog to keep quiet. No landlady with her ears pricked for the sound of guests sneaking down to the kitchen or, worse, into each other's rooms.

'But what do I say if someone wants to know what I'm doing?' Thea had asked.

'Pretend you're sleepwalking. Say you had a nightmare.'

Thea crept downstairs. Jinx leaned over the Juliet balcony rail to watch Thea come out into the garden. Even though it was past one, music drifted over the wall from the palazzo, which was now a conference centre and wedding venue. It was difficult, Jinx supposed, to keep such a grand old building going otherwise.

Jinx heard the door to the garden creak as Thea stepped out and swept the phone's torch over the small, sad stones by the wall. Thea soon found Giulietta, beloved companion to Signora Bianchi, and got down on her knees. It was time to dig for treasure.

Jinx found it hard to lean over the rail for too long – vertigo was one of the more unpleasant consequences of ageing – but she tuned in to the sound of Thea digging, of the little metal spoon cutting through tangled roots beneath the earth. Then ... was that the sound of metal on metal? Jinx dared to look again. Thea was standing, looking up at the balcony. She gave a thumbs up, then got back down to keep digging until, at last, she had liberated a small metal box from the dirt.

Thea brought the box up to the room. It was the size of a man's shoebox, made from painted black tin. Though it had rusted in places, it was largely intact.

Jinx had already unfolded that day's copy of *The Times* on top of her bed, to protect the sheets from any dirty marks. Thea laid the box down reverently in the middle of the paper and they both stood back to look at it.

While the box was still unopened, their imaginations ran wild with the thought of the treasures it might contain. Money (though Italian lire wouldn't be much use now, would they)? Jewellery? Gold bars? A small Renaissance painting?

'Shall I open it?'

'Go ahead,' said Jinx.

Thea used the spoon to lever off the tin box's lid.

Jinx dared not look. Thea hardly dared look either.

'Tell me what's inside it.'

Thea drew breath. Surprise? Delight? Disappointment?

'Bones,' Thea told Jinx. 'Animal bones. I mean, I hope that's what they are.'

Jinx opened her eyes to see Thea wincing at her discovery.

'Just bones?' Jinx asked her. 'Are you certain? Is that all?'

Jinx and Thea stared at the dirty yellow relics in the box with heart-deep disappointment. Animal bones, for sure. A dog's, by the look of the long-nosed skull. Giulietta, the ever-faithful dachshund. Just as the headstone proclaimed.

Thea grimaced at the 'treasure' her hard work had unearthed.

'I can't believe you made me dig up an actual grave. I've probably picked up a curse.'

But the bones weren't the only thing in the box. There was something that had been added more recently, too. Tucked down the side was an envelope, stained brown by who knew what over the years.

'Could you pull it out, please?' Jinx asked.

'Oh my God,' said Thea. 'I need gloves for this.'

Thea wrapped one of the hotel bathroom's shower caps around her hand in lieu of anything better.

'For goodness' sake.' Jinx did the job herself, with her right hand. 'This isn't *The Mummy*, dear.'

It would have been difficult to open the envelope with one good hand, but the passage of time had left the paper so fragile that the postcard inside just fell out. The front was printed with a black-and-white photograph of the Imperial Hotel in Bari. Written on the back were three little words in an elegant hand, in black ink turned sepia by the passage of time. All the same, they were perfectly readable.

The three little words were, 'Fuck you, Jimmy.'

'What does that mean?' Thea wanted to know. 'Is it another code?'

Jinx shook her head.

'I think it's plain English for "Fuck you, Jimmy".'

Someone, a long time ago, had decided to have a little joke.

'I can't believe there wasn't anything valuable after all that searching,' Thea complained. 'What a total waste of time. Do you think there ever was anything exciting in there? Did someone else get to it before us? Or was there never really anything there but a dead dog and a nasty postcard? Who would have dug up a dead dog to leave that postcard? I mean, it's rank enough now, but it must have been putrid when they put the note in. Who messes about with a dead body?'

Jinx looked again at the handwriting. Could it be?

Of course it was.

But when had she done it? And what had *she* found?

Chapter Forty-One

On their last morning in Florence, Jinx and Thea took breakfast in the hotel's garden. Thea had done a very good job, filling in the hole she'd dug and replacing the fake grass with care. It was impossible to tell that a grave-robber had been by in the night.

Glenn was already up, of course, and had walked across to the Hotel Regina to meet them. He'd learned from past coach trips that the day you left any hotel, it was extremely important to be methodical when helping your passengers check out. He had already cleared out of his room.

'Don't forget to do the nervous,' he warned his daughter.

'Why don't you just say "check your room"?' Thea asked him.

'Because nervous is how I feel when I'm in charge of seeing that everyone gets back onto the bus without forgetting anything important.'

He went into full tour guide mode.

'Be especially vigilant for medications you might have left in the bathroom.'

'I haven't got any medications, Dad,' said Thea.

'And I will be responsible for mine,' said Jinx.

'And valuables on the bedside table.'

Glenn had a flashback to the Jane Austen's England tour, when one of his ladies thought she'd left her wedding ring in a bedside cabinet, only to remember – just as Glenn was about to ask the hotel manager to quiz the housekeeping staff – that she had in fact left it in her safe back home in Merevale.

Though Thea had scoffed at her father's diligence, when she and Jinx were getting ready to leave, she did do her own version of the 'nervous', even getting down on her hands and knees to check under the beds and wardrobe. The bathroom shelves were empty but for the hotel toiletries they hadn't used. How about the bedside table?

Thea opened the drawers. There was nothing they'd put in there, though she did find an old map of the city a previous guest must have left behind. It was one of those maps you see in hotels, a sheet from a huge pad of the same, upon which someone had marked out a route from the Hotel Regina to the perfumery of Santa Maria Novella.

'Do you think this will lead us to treasure?' Thea asked Jinx, her voice full of sarcasm.

'I am very sorry I made you dig up a box of bones,' Jinx replied.

Thea flashed a smile. 'One day, it will make a good story.' Then she asked, 'Have you got everything, do you think, Mrs Sullivan? Passport? Money? What about your mouse?'

It was the first time Thea had noticed that the mouse which had watched over them as they slept wasn't there any more.

'He's safe,' said Jinx. 'He's where he should be.'

At eleven on the dot, Jinx and Thea were at the Hotel Fiesole in time for the head count. Team Merevale's luggage mountain had grown considerably over the past couple of days, as everyone made the most of Florence's reputation as a place to shop.

Val, Cynth and Pat were all carrying smart new Italian hand-bags. The Colonel was sporting a new panama hat. Marilyn Butler had a new pair of boots. Team Merevale also had some new friends. Thea and Jinx had missed out on a great final evening at the Fiesole. Team Merevale had joined a coach full of American World War 2 history enthusiasts for a sing-off in the hotel bar, pitting Marilyn against Ralph from Maryland.

The travellers mustered in the hotel lobby for a last good-bye. Numbers and addresses were exchanged. Hugs were given. Kisses were stolen (from and by the Colonel).

The goodbyes went on until Ivor and the driver of the Americans' coach started to become impatient. Tachographs wait for no one, not even romantic octogenarians snatching the opportunity for one more squeeze.

'Wait!' said Marilyn. 'We've got to do this properly.'

Jinx's heart was already sinking at the thought of what 'properly' might mean for Merevale's favourite (OK, it's only) songbird.

'Ralph, will you accompany me in an a cappella version of "We'll Meet Again"?'

Marilyn stretched out her hand, with the air of Barbra Streisand inviting Frank Sinatra to join her on stage.

'How could I refuse?' Ralph said.

'Oh, please try,' Jinx muttered. Low enough so that only Thea could hear.

Marilyn took a breath and drew her hand upwards in front of her chest, as though gathering enough wind to blow the Duomo down.

'*We'll meet again ...*'

Her audience allowed her two bars before they all joined in.

Emotional farewell completed, it was time to get back on the bus. The Colonel took his place. Val, Cynth and Pat made space for Marilyn, eager to know whether Ralph and Marilyn would meet again. They all knew by now that Marilyn and Evan's marriage was in the doldrums. (As it turned out, Evan would meet the coach with armfuls of flowers – over-ordered for a funeral – and Marilyn would fall in love with him all over again.)

While all this was going on, Thea and Jinx were waiting on the pavement for Glenn to help them board. As they did so, two *carabinieri* in shining knee-high boots swayed over to Thea and Jinx in her wheelchair.

'*Inglese?*' they asked. 'We have been looking for you.'

Chapter Forty-Two

Hikari had no idea how the old lady in the wheelchair, with one arm in a sling, no less, had managed to get away with such sleight of hand. Upset and embarrassed to think she had not been paying enough attention, she called her husband Tommaso, who immediately dispatched two of his police officer colleagues, who were patrolling nearby, to Hikari's shop. She started to cry as she told him what she thought had happened.

She had CCTV, of course. Tommaso had insisted upon it. He'd insisted she always kept the door locked, too, only letting in a maximum of two customers at a time and locking the door behind them so they couldn't grab what they wanted and run. Tommaso had been called out to too many robberies to allow his darling Hikari to take any risks.

'She was in a wheelchair and she had a broken arm, I think. She was a very old woman.'

For once, Tommaso didn't repeat his maxim that 'Old thieves never die, they just pick softer targets.'

'And you're sure that everything else is as it should be?'

'Tommaso, that's what I've been trying to tell you. Everything is fine.'

'So we're not looking for a thief?'

'No. We're looking for the opposite. She didn't take anything. It's what she left behind.'

When they arrived, Hikari showed Tommaso's colleagues the porcelain mouse the size of a thimble and the envelope that had been left beneath the velvet tray. Opening that envelope, she'd found a black-and-white photograph that made her cover her mouth with shock because she recognised it at once. An identical photograph lived in her grandmother's photograph album in Japan. Because the little girl in the picture was Hikari's grandmother, and the man looking down at her with so much love was Hikari's great-grandfather, Haruto, the young soldier who never came back from the war. It was the only photograph of Haruto that Hikari had ever seen.

But how had the old woman known to bring the mouse and this photograph to Hikari's shop?

After she'd posted about the photograph online and found someone who was able to translate the kanji for her, Jinx had searched for 'Haruto Hinode' – the man she knew as Goofy – on Google. Prompted by her email correspondent's revelation that he knew a woman with the surname Hinode in Italy, it wasn't long before Jinx thought she'd tracked down a descendant – Hikari, the jeweller in Florence. Hikari's smile in the picture on her website was strangely familiar.

To the back of the photograph, Jinx had attached a Post-it note. Upon it she had written in small capital letters, cramped and shaky from having to use her wrong hand, 'Mouse and picture belonging to Haruto Hinode, who was a guard at Sime Road camp in Singapore, 1945. He was kind when kindness was in short supply, and he loved his daughter very much indeed. Please let her know.'

'I need to talk to that woman,' said Hikari.

Taking images from CCTV, Tommaso soon circulated Jinx's picture. It was high season, and heaven knows his team had more than enough to do, keeping up with the pickpockets who followed the tourists around Florence as remoras follow whale sharks. But maybe, just maybe, someone would spot the elderly English woman in a wheelchair and her young companion. Maybe Hikari would get her wish.

Outside the Hotel Fiesole, while every passenger on the Team Merevale coach looked on, Jinx explained the situation to the kind *carabinieri*. Though they offered to take Jinx back to Hikari's shop in their squad car, she refused.

'I would be holding up all these good people,' she said.

'We'll wait,' Glenn promised her. 'This sounds important.'

But Jinx was insistent. 'I don't wish to keep anybody hanging around. Please tell Hikari that I will telephone her and tell her all she wants to know then. Glenn, I do not want this broadcast to the others on the coach.'

There would be no emotional meeting. There would be no phone call, either; Jinx already knew that much. She had done what she came to Florence to do. The porcelain mouse and the photograph were where they belonged – in the hands of Haruto's great-granddaughter. That was enough. Jinx had done the right thing by Haruto. She did not want to say anything more. She did not want to have to talk about redemption.

The fact was, sometimes Jinx felt as though she had put those years in camp behind her, but sometimes she did not. The road to forgiveness was steep and rocky, and every step forward might be followed by a long slip backwards towards anger. It was best that Hikari didn't know that.

A burst of rapid Italian from one of the police officer's radios pulled their attention away from trying to persuade Jinx otherwise. While they responded to news of an incident in a nearby wine shop, Jinx had Glenn and Thea help her onto the coach.

Up and down the coach, Jinx's neighbours whispered.

'What was going on out there? Why did the police want to speak to her?'

Sitting down beside Jinx, Thea took her hand and squeezed it.

'Gun the engines,' Jinx told Ivor the driver. '*If the police can get a car on that bridge before we've got across it, we're done for.*'

'*But it's a gamble we've got to take.*' Ivor replied.

The Colonel slapped his thighs and whistled in delight.

'*The Italian Job! You were only supposed to blow the bloody doors off!*' he shouted at the top of his voice.

Chapter Forty-Three

South Kensington, January 2024

In a large, white-painted house in South Kensington, the Williamson sisters and their long-suffering great-nephew Archie were enjoying a lazy sort of Saturday. As a chicken roasted in the oven, Penny Williamson (a hundred years and one day old) sipped a Martini (and complained, as usual, about the ratio of gin to vermouth), while Archie read aloud the most interesting stories in that day's newspapers.

Penny was fascinated by the ongoing travails of a newsreader who had found himself in hot water after he sent a naked video of himself singing 'Handbags and Gladrags' to an Instagram scammer purporting to be Sir Rod Stewart.

'Scams are getting very sophisticated these days,' said Archie, leading Penny to snort.

'Or people are getting very stupid. He sent a naked video to someone on the internet just because they asked him?'

'He did think he was sending the clip to Sir Rod, Auntie Penny. Apparently, they'd previously met at a Children in Need thing, so it wasn't without the realms of possibility that he would be in touch.'

'And if Rod Stewart asked you for a video of you singing in the buff?'

Archie wasn't sure where the conversation was going. 'Well ...'

Penny tutted. 'Never send anyone a video of yourself in the noddy, Archie. Even if you think you do know them. Have Josephine and I taught you nothing over the years?'

'I ...' Archie could find no comeback to that.

'Honestly, collecting *kompromat* used to require a degree of skill,' Penny complained.

'Yes,' said Josephine (101 and a half), waking briefly from a nap. '*Kompromat*. I remember. Oh we had some fun in the old days, me and the Third Sea Lord.'

Before she could elaborate on exactly what sort of fun they'd had, Josephine fell back into a doze. This was happening more and more often, to Archie's enormous frustration. Every time he thought one of his great-aunts might be about to reveal some important secret about their wartime careers at last, she fell asleep.

'Any more scandal in the news today?' Penny asked hopefully.

'What did Auntie Josephine do with the Third Sea Lord?' Archie wanted to know. There must be some real scandal there.

Josephine opened one eye. 'I could tell you, but then I'd have to kill you.'

'That's my line,' said Penny, full of little-sister indignation. 'I'm the trained killer in the family.'

'Yes, Auntie Penny,' said Archie. 'And you said you'd tell me all about that.'

Penny deftly changed the subject. 'What's happening with that politician who was rushed to hospital after falling onto a hairbrush while not wearing any pants?'

'That story has gone quiet,' said Archie. 'Thankfully.'

Archie set down the *Daily Mail* and picked up *The Times*, hoping to find something more edifying to read aloud. One of the top stories in *The Times* that day was about the link between dementia and loss of inhibitions, which made people with the condition increasingly amused by the sort of ribaldry and coarseness that wouldn't have interested them before. It definitely seemed to be the case that Penny was getting ruder as she got older. Though perhaps it was just that Archie, now in his mid-forties, was suddenly becoming more staid.

'You think I was rude, Archie? What's the point of being a hundred years old if you can't upset a few people?' Penny had said just the other day.

Archie did not read the dementia report out loud. He never drew Penny or Josephine's attention to that sort of thing. He didn't want to read out anything about the latest horrors from far-flung wars either, though any talk of war was usually a good way to get Penny reminiscing about her time in the FANY. The official story of her time in the FANY, that is …

'Pass me the money pages,' said Penny.

Archie did as he was told. With Josephine snoozing and Penny absorbed in share prices, it seemed like a good moment to check on the chicken. While Archie was in the kitchen, a bundle of post came through the letterbox. Archie filleted the bundle as he stood in the hall, putting the junk mail straight into a pile for recycling. There were just two interesting envelopes left. Archie picked up the sisters' dagger-shaped letter-opener and carried the two remaining letters into the sitting room.

'Any excitements?' Penny asked.

Both envelopes were addressed to her. The first contained a birthday card. King Charles III and Queen Camilla wished their loyal subject a very happy hundredth birthday.

'A bit late,' Penny observed. 'Old Liz would have made sure her card got here on time.'

'There has been a postal strike,' said Archie.

'And? A footman could have got here from the palace in twenty minutes by bike.'

'Well, isn't it nice to have the card now?'

'Have what?' Josephine had woken herself with a snore. 'What excitements do you have for us today, Archie?'

'A card from the King, Auntie Josephine. For Auntie Penny. For her hundredth birthday.'

'Penny isn't a hundred,' said Josephine. 'And what's that old woman doing in my house?' She pointed at her sister.

'Huh! Old! I'll always be younger than you, you crone.'

The sound of Penny's voice seemed to convince Josephine that the 'wrinkled old bag' was in fact her younger sibling.

'Well, you've not aged well,' Josephine chortled.

'I've a mind to ban you from my birthday party,' Penny told her.

'Auntie Penny,' Archie intervened. 'Auntie Josephine can't help it if she gets a little forgetful. Why don't you open your other letter? It might be someone RSVPing to your invitation. Everyone is very excited about the party next week.'

'Are they? Judy Menkes isn't coming,' Penny tutted. 'I suppose she thinks she's got somewhere better to go.'

'Well, you see, Judy Menkes has been dead since 2013,' Archie said for the eighth time. 'Her daughter did send her best wishes, though.'

Penny picked up the dagger-shaped letter-opener again and, with only a little difficulty, slit open the smart cream envelope. Inside was a sheet of writing paper, wrapped around a card. Archie watched with interest as Penny unfolded the paper, on which was written a brief note.

'Oh, I can't read this,' she complained. 'What does it say?'

Archie took over. The writing *was* appalling.

'I think it says, "Happy 100th Birthday, you old ..." Oh, my goodness. Some people.'

'Archie, what does it say?'

'It says "Happy 100th Birthday, you old cow. Was in Florence over the summer. I thought you might like to have this." Auntie Penny, who on earth would call you a cow?'

'Half the First Aid Nursing Yeomanry,' said Josephine, who was always awake for an insult.

'And what does the card say?' Penny wanted to know.

Archie turned the filthy thing over and held it by its edges. His eyes widened. 'Well, I definitely can't read that message out to you, Auntie Penny. It's disgusting!'

'Give it back here, then. And find me my magnifying glass.'

As she read the words she had written herself back in 1966, Penny laughed out loud.

'Archie, is there an address on the back of that envelope?'

Chapter Forty-Four

The Cotswolds, January 2024

On Friday morning, Glenn took his roll call as usual.

'I won't call it tenko any more,' he'd told Jinx, having heard the story of her war years, but Jinx told him, 'You can call it what you like, Glenn. Sticks and stones.'

When she saw that Glenn was walking up the path accompanied by the Colonel, Jinx knew she would not be able to get away with her usual Morse flash of the blinds.

Checking her hair in the hallway mirror, she made her way carefully to the door. It took some effort to open it with the mended fracture in her clavicle still prone to complaining.

'You've got another stiffie!' the Colonel announced with unnecessary glee.

'I do wish you'd stop saying that,' Glenn hissed.

'Jennifer knows what I mean.'

Jinx merely raised an eyebrow. She took possession of her mail. Three bills and a white envelope, which looked much the same as the one before. Her name and address were typed on the front. There was nothing identifying the sender on the back.

'I imagine it's the old people's home again, inviting me for a glass of substandard fizz and a sales pitch.'

'The fizz is not bad,' said the Colonel. 'Though alas they've stopped inviting me, now they know I'm only there for the canapés. You'll never catch me in a home. Never again ...' he added so quietly that Jinx and Glenn almost missed it. They both gave the Colonel a sympathetic nod. Jinx had come to know the Colonel's childhood story. Glenn and Thea had bought him a subscription to one of those DNA sites for Christmas in the hope that he might find some family there.

'Do you need some help with that stiffie?' the Colonel asked Jinx now.

'Yes, please. Then you can throw it away for me, too.'

The Colonel pulled out his Swiss Army knife and deftly slit open the envelope. He pulled the card inside halfway out, then held it towards Jinx so that she could finish the job.

It was not an invitation to a sales pitch by Merevale's premier retirement complex.

In elegant dark blue print, on rigid thick cream card, was written, 'You are invited to celebrate the 100th birthday of Penny Williamson at the Royal Automobile Club, Epsom, on Sunday 27th January.'

Though the envelope had been correctly addressed to Mrs Sullivan, the sender had scribbled 'Jinx' in the top left-hand corner of the card. And on the back, in the same handwriting was the phrase, 'The wench is not quite dead.'

Jinx's eyes might have misted over as she stared at the writing – familiar, if quite a bit shakier than she remembered. This card, those few words, represented all at once an invitation, a rapprochement and a dare. *Not quite dead.* Still able to write and talk and, at one hundred, with not much time left to worry about the consequences. An RSVP was requested.

Oh, Jinx would RSVP all right.

Chapter Forty-Five

The South of France, 1966

When the night train stopped in a siding, Jinx clambered out and picked her way across the tracks. She was too old to be jumping from moving trains these days. As dawn broke, she found her way to the nearest farmhouse and spun a yarn about having had an argument with her husband, who'd pushed her out of the car. The young farmer and his wife listened agog and agreed to take Jinx – who had introduced herself in impeccable French, and with a hint of pleasure, as Bruna – as far as the next big town in their van as soon as she'd had some breakfast and taken a moment or two to tidy herself up.

The farmer asked if 'Bruna' wanted him to remind her husband of his duties, but 'Bruna' responded that she'd been forced into the marriage and was grateful to have a reason to ask for a divorce. The farmer's wife crossed herself at the word, but agreed it was probably for the best.

By the time she got to Lyon, Jinx had cast off her French accent and was thoroughly Anglaise again. The newspapers all carried reports of the robbery, but Interpol weren't looking for an English woman. Whatever, the diamonds were too hot and she needed to be rid of them. She was going to have to meet

Connor. Connor O'Connell, small-time horse trainer, big-time crook, and Penny Williamson's new husband.

Connor was the last person Jinx had expected to see in Rome a week earlier, but there he was, in the bar of the Hotel Britannia, when Jinx came back from liberating a fistful of gems from a shop on the Via del Corso.

'Well, if it isn't little Miss Jinx.'

There was no love lost between Jinx and Connor O'Connell. Jinx thought Penny was too good for him, but since Penny was no longer speaking to Jinx, she couldn't tell her.

'What are you doing here?' Jinx asked.

'I'm on honeymoon.'

Jinx scanned the bar for his bride.

'Don't worry. Penny's not here. We're staying at the Hassler. Couldn't bring my new wife to a fleapit like this.'

'Then why are you here?'

Jinx guessed that Connor must be meeting one of their 'mutual friends' in the Mafia.

'How's business?' he asked her. He knew, of course, how Jinx and Penny made their money. When Penny and Frank fell out, after he revealed that it was he who had put the kibosh on Penny going into France with F Section, she'd entrusted Connor with shifting the jewellery they stole. Jinx had never liked the man. She'd stayed loyal to Frank, ending her friendship with Penny in the process. Though she had hoped that Penny would come to her senses. Of course she had hoped for that. Even if she had enjoyed having Frank to herself in the meantime.

'Business is fine,' Jinx assured Connor.

'Penny's shopping this afternoon. Why don't we have a drink?' he suggested. 'You know I've always admired you, Jinx. You're tough. But then I guess you've had to be, after everything you went through in Singapore.'

298

Jinx hated that Connor knew anything so personal about her, but she tried not to let it show.

Connor told Jinx about the itinerary he and Penny had planned for their honeymoon. They were going to Genoa next morning, then on into the south of France. He told her a lot more besides, obviously assuming that Penny and her former protégée would never be reconciled. Connor was far from the doting new husband.

'We could work together, you and I,' he suggested. 'I might be looking for a new partner shortly.'

With a pocket full of hot rocks and Interpol on the case, Jinx found herself looking Connor up in Antibes. She went to the hotel, wearing a brown wig over her blonde hair, and watched from the corner of the dining room while Penny and Connor had lunch. She waited in the lounge until Penny left the hotel alone an hour later. She already knew which room they were staying in. Connor had told her he was booking the 'Scott Fitzgerald Suite'.

Jinx knocked at the door. There was no answer. Perhaps Connor was on the balcony. But when she opened the door, she saw that the curtains were closed and there was a lump in the bed. Dirty bastard. Was he expecting her to join him? She flicked on the light.

Jinx knew at once that Connor was dead. His expression was far from peaceful. Must have had a heart attack, Jinx concluded. Should she close his eyes for him? Let room service know that the bed in the Scott Fitzgerald suite would require a new set of sheets? No. Not her business. Best just to disappear.

She felt not a flicker of sadness. She only hoped Penny had taken out life insurance on the bastard, just as Connor had taken out a huge insurance policy on her. Then Jinx noticed that there was an emerald ring on the bedside table. Jinx picked it up and slipped it into her pocket.

In the town half an hour later, Jinx dipped into the coolness of a church. The priest was in the confessional, and Jinx suddenly felt moved to do something she'd never expected to do. She stepped inside the box and drew the curtain across. On the other side of the screen, the priest shifted in his seat. Did he speak first, or should she?

'Forgive me, Father, for I have sinned,' she said in perfect French.

Was that right? She'd soon find out if she had made a faux pas. She hadn't. The priest asked her to go on.

'Where to start? Do you have all day?'

She laughed at her own joke. The priest didn't. His silence made her realise that this was a stupid thing to do. To think about saying anything about the way she lived to a stranger. She thought that the confessional box was like the diplomatic mail. You could say anything in privilege. But she didn't know for sure.

'Go on,' the priest prompted.

'I've betrayed a friend,' Jinx said. 'Someone who cared for me deeply and did her best to smooth my way through the world. I made the wrong choice and we've fallen out, and I miss her more than I can say.'

The priest prescribed the saying of some prayers that Jinx didn't know and sent her away, feeling rather silly. On her way out of the church, she dropped the ring she had taken from the bedside in Penny and Connor's room into the poor box.

Jinx stepped into the sunlight, feeling very much lighter for having disposed of the gem. Standing on the steps, she popped her sunglasses back on. As she did so, she caught sight of a familiar figure sitting at a table outside a café across the square.

Penny. It had to be. She seemed deep in thought, as she looked into her glass of cloudy Pernod and water.

Before Penny could look up and see her, Jinx slid down an alleyway. Penny need never know she had been there.

However, just a couple of days later, the two women did meet again at that Riviera hotel. Jinx had called Frank, looking forward to hearing his reassuring voice on the phone, and received news that left her speechless. Frank was dead; killed in a shoot-out in the East End while on duty. Frank had always said that he was far more likely to be killed in uniform than out.

'Will you let Penny know?' his colleague asked.

Jinx called Josephine to ask for Penny's whereabouts. She could not reveal that she already knew exactly where Penny was staying. That same day, Josephine had flown to the South of France to look after her sister in the aftermath of Connor's death. Jinx met her in the hotel lobby.

'She seems to be taking things rather well, considering,' said Josephine. 'But then she always had a good poker face. Who knows how she's feeling inside. She must have loved the man.'

Connor? Jinx doubted it. Indeed, Penny was dry-eyed when Jinx walked into her room.

'You,' Penny spat. 'What are you doing here?'

'I've got news. You need to sit down,' Jinx said.

Penny sat on the silk-covered armchair.

The moment Frank's name escaped Jinx's lips, Penny's face went absolutely white.

Jinx went to Frank's funeral because Penny couldn't. She stayed at the back of the church, intending to make it out at the end of the service without being noticed, but as Frank's family filed from the pews, his wife caught sight of her and when Jinx left the church, Frank's son was waiting.

'Mum wants to talk to you,' he said. 'We know who you are. You're her sidekick, aren't you? Penny's. We've got some things for her. You'll have to come to the house.'

At the house, Christina handed over three things. The old silver-plated matchbox, which Jinx knew very well, a ring box and a letter.

'You won't want to stay for a drink,' Christina said. It was an instruction, not an invitation.

'Of course not,' said Jinx. 'I'm sorry. Frank was a good man.'

Christina merely sighed.

Out of respect to Christina and Frank's children, Jinx left right away. She did not open the ring box until she was back in her own flat.

The box contained a diamond solitaire – far smaller than the one Jinx had lifted from that shop on the Via del Corso. The letter was addressed to Penny, of course. Jinx almost opened it before her conscience got the better of her.

But Penny never found out what Frank had written in his last message to her either, because she didn't ever receive it.

Replaying the moment when she met Frank's wife, Jinx had found herself growing angry. It seemed that everybody had a claim on Frank except Jinx. His wife, Penny, his colleagues ... They were all allowed to mourn. But nobody acknowledged what he had meant to Jinx or what she was sure she had meant to him. When Jinx next saw Penny – at a meeting which took a very long time to arrange – she handed over only the silver matchbox, engraved with the second verse from 'Invictus'. *Bloody, but unbowed.* She kept the ring for herself.

Penny took the matchbox and crumpled to the floor as she held it to her heart. Jinx could not have begun to understand the significance of the thing. She didn't know its provenance, or about the moment when Penny first saw it, on a clear, starlit night in the Highlands in 1943. When Penny was in training to be an SOE agent for F Section, codename Bruna, and Frank was the man assigned to show the young cadets how to kill a man with their bare hands. With a matchbox, just like this one.

Penny's grief was frightening. Jinx would never have believed that the disciplined, endlessly cheery woman she thought she knew could have contained such a pathetic creature as the one before her now. Penny rolled into a foetal position and rocked upon the carpet. She brought the matchbox to her mouth and kissed it, crying Frank's name over and over.

For a moment, Jinx felt a tug deep within her, urging her to wrap her arms around Penny and hold her as she cried, to let her know that there was more, to tell her about the ring and the letter. To let her know that she, Jinx, was grieving Frank, too. They could grieve him together. They could help each other through. But that feeling was soon overcome. Instead, Jinx told her, 'I've got to catch a train. I'm sorry. I know Frank meant a great deal to you.'

Penny, still sitting on the floor with her long legs akimbo, looked up at Jinx as though she didn't know her. As though they had never lived together and laughed together and loved each other like sisters. As though they had never been the best of friends.

'Goodbye,' Jinx said. Penny didn't respond.

Jinx walked as far as the door of the flat, but ran down the stairs and was almost in tears by the time she reached the street.

'I do not cry,' she reminded herself. And so she didn't. Just as she had not cried when she heard that her father died in Changi.

And so the ring remained in Jinx's possession – the love letter that accompanied it unread – in the wooden love box from India, for years and years and years.

Though Penny had once accused her protégée of being

'absolutely amoral', that ring could make her blush with guilt. In the short list of scenes from her life that could pierce Jinx's heart and make her want to die of shame, the moment she decided to give Penny only the matchbox was near the top. Penny's face when she held that matchbox. She had been so happy to have it. A scrappy silver-plated piece of the man with the golden heart.

Without Penny and without Frank, Jinx's career was much less interesting than it had been. She realised that she'd been lucky, protected by working with those two. There was no honour among thieves. Jinx got ripped off a few times. Her flat was turned over. Warnings were delivered in dark alleyways. She spent a short spell in prison for something she hadn't done. As she aged, going unnoticed was no longer a matter of skill. She didn't turn heads. When a young man looked her way on the Tube, it was to check whether he should be giving up his seat for her. She retreated from the elite criminal world she had been moving in and chose softer targets, looking for bounty that she could more easily shift without middlemen.

Her flat in London soon became too expensive to maintain. She needed to move somewhere cheaper. Then Eddy got his diagnosis. Skin cancer. The terrible sunburn he'd picked up during those endless tenkos at Sime Road had left behind scars at a cellular level. By the time the doctors realised what was going on, the cancer had metastasised and made its way to Eddy's organs, already compromised by childhood malnutrition.

'I'm coming to look after you,' Jinx told him. She was the only family he had, since Norma had died in '72.

Jinx nursed Eddy until the end.

'You always looked after me,' he said. 'You're my best friend.'

Which made Jinx want to cry for all the years she had not been there, the years when she had left him behind while she travelled the world with Penny. Only she didn't cry because that would not be fair.

Night after night, she and Eddy sat side by side on his sickbed and watched television until the test card came on. Then Eddy would ask Jinx to tell him about the 'olden days'.

'About camp?'

'No. Not about camp. Before then. About the time you saw a tiger.'

'I was in the garden, playing with my doll in a pram. I saw something move in the trees.'

'The tiger,' Eddy breathed in satisfaction. *'Harimau.'*

He used the Malay word.

'Am I telling this story or are you?'

She pulled Eddy closer, wrapping her arm around him as she did when he was tiny. He was tiny again now. Thin as a lizard. Delicate as a bird. His hollow chest fluttered and fell still.

And that was the moment when Jinx realised she was truly alone in the world. Her parents gone. Frank gone. Penny might as well be dead. And now Eddy had left her, too. No one would ever call her Jinx again.

Chapter Forty-Six

Epsom, January 2024

Glenn and Thea were delighted to be asked to be Jinx's 'plus two' for Penny Williamson's hundreth birthday party.

'We'll take your wheelchair,' said Glenn. Just the previous month, Jinx had admitted that she needed one for longer forays from her bungalow now. All the same, she said, 'I don't think so.'

If Jinx was going to this particular party, then she was going to walk into the room.

They arrived at the country club half an hour after the time stipulated on the invitation, and there was the birthday girl in the club's grand dining room, already surrounded by admirers. A small queue had formed of people who were determined to speak to her, to take a selfie they would post on social media and caption in gushing (and slightly patronising) terms.

A tall man in his forties seemed to be acting as a sort of bouncer, cleverly gathering names so that he could give Penny a clue as to the identity of the person standing in front of her. He stuck out his hand and gave Jinx's a hearty shake. 'Hello, hello. I'm Penny's great-nephew Archie Williamson. And you are?'

'Jennifer Sullivan,' Jinx said. 'And these are my friends Glenn and Thea Turner.'

'Ah, yes. Welcome. Welcome to you all. And you know my Auntie Penny through ...?'

'We're very old friends.'

'The FANY?'

'Not *that* old,' said Jinx. 'Your great-aunt and I met *after* the war ... We worked together in the fifties and sixties.'

'Ah, you were a charity worker, too?'

'Something like that,' said Jinx.

Archie looked towards his great-aunt Penny. 'The queue to pay homage seems to have died down a bit. Let me take you right over, Mrs Sullivan. But before I do, I should warn you that she might not recognise you. She's a little forgetful these days.'

Jinx nodded. 'I understand. When you get to a hundred years old, I'm sure there are plenty of things one wishes to forget.'

'Indeed!' Archie chuckled. 'Indeed. I'm sure there are!'

Penny was sitting in a wheelchair, but as she saw Jinx approach, she started to lever herself upright, causing Archie to flutter about her in a panic.

'There's no need to stand,' said Jinx. Glenn had already been dispatched to fetch a chair, so that Jinx could sit down next to Penny and be on a level. Penny sank back down onto her cushions.

'Auntie Penny,' Archie said in what Jinx's mother would have called an 'outdoor voice'. 'Auntie Penny, this is Mrs Sullivan. Jennifer Sullivan, with her friends Glenn and Thea Turner. She says you worked together after the war. When you were a social worker, Auntie Penny. When you were an almoner. That's right, isn't it, Mrs Sullivan?'

'That's a perfectly good introduction,' said Jinx.

Glenn returned and placed an upright wooden chair next to Penny's wheelchair. Both he and Archie raced to help Jinx onto it.

'Thank you. I can manage. Could you lovely young people get me and the birthday girl a drink? Thea, help your father. Archie, isn't it? I'm sure there must be other guests requiring your attention.'

Glenn and Thea seemed to understand they were being dismissed, and headed for the bar.

Archie hovered. 'If you're certain. But if there's anything you need, just shout.'

'We'll be fine,' Jinx reassured him.

Archie left, not looking reassured at all.

As soon as he was out of earshot, Jinx leaned forward and whispered, 'Hello, wench.'

'Jinx,' said Penny. 'I knew you'd come.'

The party faded into the background as the two women sat face to face for the first time in nearly six decades. Penny's face may have betrayed every one of her hundred years, but the eyes that twinkled out were still the eyes that Jinx remembered. Keen and interested, always crinkled up in a smile.

'And now you're Jennifer Sullivan,' Penny said. 'Did you get married?'

'Did I hell.'

'Good choice. But the young man and girl you brought with you? Relations?'

'Friends, I suppose.'

'I didn't think you had any friends.'

'Neither did I. You've got a few, though. Big party.'

'They're mostly World War 2 podcasters. All the interesting people are dead.' She paused. 'Except for you, Jinx. Gosh, we have a lot to catch up on.'

308

'I've brought something for you,' Jinx said.

'A gift? You really shouldn't have.'

'Oh, but I should. You see, Penny, it's not so much a gift as the return of something I should never have borrowed.'

Jinx handed over the small gift bag that Thea had picked up for her at the village shop. It was stuffed with tissue. Penny went to pull the tissue out, but Jinx stopped her. 'If I were you, I would open this later. When you're alone.'

'Oh, it's that sort of gift, is it?'

'Perhaps.'

Penny had Jinx set the unopened gift bag down with all the others on the table to her left. It seemed that very few people had taken any notice of the diktat on the invitation, which very clearly stated, 'No presents.'

'Archie will have to go to the charity shop on Monday,' Penny complained.

'Don't let him take my gift there.'

'It must be good ...'

'I think you'll be glad to have it ... So, you're a hundred now. Bloody hell.'

'I know. It's rather embarrassing to have got so ancient.'

'And Josephine?'

'Still hanging on. She's asleep over there by the cake. Becoming quite a liability in her old age. The other day she almost told Archie about the Third Sea Lord.'

'Oh dear.'

'I told Archie she's mixing life up with the novels we read as children.'

'Very clever.'

'You know me. He bought it. Men like to think we're simple creatures.'

'Much to our advantage.'

'You made it to Florence, I see. Thank you for the postcard.'

'I had to get there on a coach trip, would you believe?'

'Good Lord,' said Penny. '*Quelle horreur!*'

'I had a nice time.'

'No, you didn't. And why did it take you so long to work it out anyway? *The wench is dead.* It was bleeding obvious.'

'Was it? When did you work it out?'

'1965. I was snowed in at Josephine's house. Nothing to read in that guest room but bloody poetry.'

'I had to be told by a sixteen-year-old girl.'

'The one with you today? Your apprentice?'

'Not my apprentice. I think ours is a dying profession, Penny. There won't be any more like me and you.'

They were interrupted by another party guest, who wanted to pay his respects to the birthday girl. Penny shooed him away quite rudely. 'Not now, dear.'

'He'll excuse me because of my age,' she told Jinx. 'No one thinks I know what I'm saying any more.'

'I do.'

'Of course.'

Penny reached to take Jinx's right hand. Her fingers were dry and cool. Jinx found herself having to blink quite hard as she saw their hands intertwined. Old hands. Both of them. Where had the time gone?

'I have thought about you a great deal over the years, Jinx. And wondered how it came to be that you and I became estranged. Well, I know why we fell out, of course, but what I never understood was why it stuck.'

Jinx shrugged. 'I don't know either.'

'Why didn't you ever call me? Why didn't I ever call you?'

'Because we're two proud old birds?' suggested Jinx.

'Two stupid old birds,' said Penny. 'But now I have tracked you down, I will not let you go again so easily. You and I have a great deal to talk about. Oh, we had some fun.'

'We did. And you taught me a great deal. And not just how to lift a diamond solitaire.'

'Now you admit it.'

'What was in the tin box, Penny? In Florence.'

'Bloody dog bones.'

'So I saw.'

'And perhaps a little Renaissance thingamajig or two.'

'Which paid for the house in South Kensington?'

'I did use some of the money to build a school.'

Jinx snorted at that.

'I'm sorry you only got to see the bones,' Penny told her.

'The hours I spent trying to unravel that code.'

'Which wasn't a code at all.' Penny sighed.

'We should have worked it out together.'

'I wanted that more than anything. I have missed you so much.'

While the two women had been talking, a band had been setting up on the stage at the other end of the room. The band comprised a keyboard player, a saxophonist and two female singers with their hair in victory rolls. Archie had joined them on the stage, taking the microphone to address the party.

'Ladies and gentlemen,' he began. 'I want to thank you all for being here today to celebrate the most wonderful centenarian in town – apart from her sister – my fabulous Great-Auntie Penny!'

There was a round of applause and some whistling.

'I hope you've all had a chance to fill your plates at the delicious buffet. In a few minutes' time, we'll be bringing out the birthday cake. But while the catering staff circulate with champagne for the toast, we're going to have a brief musical interlude. Without further ado, let me introduce the Swinging Singers, who will be entertaining us for the rest of the afternoon with songs from the 1940s. Take it away!'

'Did you ever really like "Cliffs of Dover"?' Jinx asked her old mentor as the Swinging Singers hit the first notes.

'Hell, no,' said Penny. 'But I haven't the heart to tell Archie I'd rather have had a Stones tribute band. Did I tell you about the night Mick Jagger asked me to sleep with him?'

'Several times,' said Jinx.

'It was before he was famous, of course. Oh, no. Archie's coming to get me. I think I've got to make a speech. We'll see each other again, won't we, Jinx? Now that we've found each other.'

'Perhaps not,' Jinx told her. 'I don't have much time. Weeks, possibly.'

'I see.' Penny nodded. She didn't need to press for details.

'In any case, you might not ever want to see me again when you find out what's in that bag.'

'I can't imagine anything that would make me not want to see you again, my dear, dear friend.'

'Oh, you might be surprised.'

Jinx heard her voice getting high as her chest tightened. Deep inside, another voice piped up, 'I do not cry.'

On stage, the singer was announcing the next song.

'I think you'll all know this one ...'

'It's going to be "We'll Meet Again",' said Jinx. 'I'm off.'

'Will we meet again? We had some good times, didn't we?'

'We had a whirl,' Jinx agreed.

'I loved you, Jinx.'

'I loved you, too, Penny. It was *toujours gai*, wasn't it?'

'Absolutely. It was *toujours gai*.'

Jinx brought Penny's tiny, cool hand to her mouth and kissed it. Then she beat a retreat. As fast as any 89-year-old with limited mobility could.

Chapter Forty-Seven

London, that Sunday evening

Penny's memory was not what it used to be. Though Archie was endlessly kind about it, Penny knew it was getting much worse. While she knew that Jinx had been at the party, she forgot all about the gift Jinx had brought with her until much later that night, when her new carer Wilma was helping her to get ready for bed.

Once she was tucked up under the duvet, Penny asked Wilma to leave the light on.

'I may read for a little while,' she said.

'Not for too long!' Wilma warned her. 'I'll come back upstairs in half an hour. I'm sure I'll find you asleep.'

'You probably will, dear.'

Penny made a show of picking up the paperback that had been on her bedside table for months. Wilma left, closing the door behind her with a careful, quiet click.

Penny was straight out of bed. Wilma had arranged Penny's birthday gifts on the dressing table. There was Jinx's package and the letter that came with it.

But it wasn't Jinx's handwriting on the envelope.

It was Frank's.

Penny. My only love.

For how much longer are you going to refuse to take my calls and leave my letters unanswered? As I said in the last ten letters I sent you, I am sorry. I understand why you are so angry with me. I have no excuse other than I love you and I wanted to keep you all for myself. I didn't want you to die. I see now that I was wrong, that I stood in the way of your determination to make a difference in the war. You're right. You would have made a wonderful agent.

It's not just your SOE career that I stopped in its tracks, though, is it? By allowing myself to get involved with you again, I know I've held you back in other ways. I've kept you from having the sort of life you deserved. You should have had a husband and children. But don't marry Connor, my love. I don't know how that bastard got anywhere near you, but he doesn't deserve you. I know I don't deserve you either, but I can guarantee you that I love you far more ardently than he ever could.

I've told my wife that I want a divorce. She knows about you and she knows that I am determined to spend the rest of my life with you, if you will have me. If I don't hear anything from you in response to this letter, you will never hear from me again, but if you can forgive me, you know where to find me, anytime, night or day, for the rest of my life.

Your Frank.

PS. Of course I bought the ring. I didn't steal it. If you'll have me, then perhaps we can go straight together.

Penny opened the ring box. Inside was a small gold band, set with a solitaire that wasn't much bigger than a peppercorn. The diamond was not a good one. You didn't need to pick up a magnifying glass to see that. The colour was muddy. It would be full of inclusions. The cut was imperfect, too. But that was the point. Penny could imagine Frank choosing it and rehearsing the story he would tell when he and she were together and she let him slip it on to her finger.

'It's like us,' he would have said. 'Complicated and imperfect, but enduring. It's been forged in fire and it will last forever, like the love I have for you.'

Yes, that's what he would have told her, but he never got the chance to. And Penny had spent almost sixty years not knowing, thanks to Jinx.

Bloody Jinx.

Penny wondered if they really had met for the very last time. She suspected that was the case. Jinx had not lingered long enough at the party to see Penny blow out her candles. More than that, Penny had always known that when Jinx decided to make amends, it would be only because she had entirely run out of road; when it was a question of 'now or never'. What had she said? 'I don't have much time.' Penny instinctively knew what she had meant. Jinx was dying. Hell, none of them had much time now.

Penny slipped on the ring, then she put Frank's letter away in her jewellery box, along with a photograph of the three of them – Jinx, Frank and Penny – in London in 1964, when they were still the three musketeers. Chosen family. When the whole world was their playground. When it seemed like the fun would never end.

'Goodnight, Frank,' Penny said, kissing the picture. 'Goodnight, Jinx, my lucky charm.'

315

Chapter Forty-Eight

Merevale, 2024

If Glenn and Thea were disappointed to have to leave the hundredth birthday party so soon after arriving – 'There were celebrities! I saw Dan Snow.' – they tried hard not to show it. You did not argue with an eighty-something when she said she wanted to go home.

Upon seeing that they were leaving, Archie Williamson had cantered after them and insisted they take a goodie bag, which included another copy of Penny's autobiography, written with her sister. This one was signed by both.

Archie also would not let them go until he had made sure they took with them a box of sandwiches and three slices of hundredth birthday cake.

At home in Jinx's bungalow, Glenn decanted the sandwiches onto Jinx's best china and laid out a little tea in her sparsely decorated sitting room.

They both wanted to know more about Penny. 'Remarkably sharp for her age,' Glenn observed. 'How did you meet her again?'

Jinx might have repeated the same old lie. Instead, she said, 'It was when I was a teenager. She was the almoner – that's a sort of social worker – assigned to our family. She was supposed to find us a better place to live. That sort of thing. But she took me under her wing and taught me how to be a jewel thief.'

How Glenn laughed at that. 'A jewel thief!'

'Yes. She was a secret agent, you see, during the war, and she knew how to get away with anything.'

'A jewel thief and a secret agent? You do tell a good story, Mrs Sullivan.'

Jinx smiled. 'I suppose I do.'

'When you have your hundredth birthday, we'll have to have a party,' Glenn said.

'I'm only eighty-nine,' Jinx reminded him.

'Plenty of time to plan in that case. Though why wait? We should celebrate your ninetieth birthday. That band was good. But then we've got Marilyn. She'd probably be offended if we booked the Swinging Singers instead.'

'If you book the Swinging Singers for anything, it had better be my funeral.'

'Aw, Mrs Sullivan. That's a bit bleak,' said Thea.

'As it happens, I would like to talk about my funeral plans. In short, I don't want to have one. They're expensive, and I can't bear the thought of Val and Cynthia turning up in black. They'd be delighted. Black is very slimming.'

'But does it go with their seasonal skin tones?' Thea joked.

'Let's not talk about funerals,' said Glenn.

'Unfortunately, I need to. Glenn, do you remember that letter from the hospital, that you delivered on the day of the first stiffie?'

Thea covered her ears. 'Stop using that term!'

'The first invitation, then. It wasn't about an appointment. It was confirmation that I had refused treatment for skin cancer, which has metastasised and spread to some of my organs.'

'You can't just refuse to have treatment!'

'I can and I have. I've lived a good life. Well, a long one. And I've had some fun.'

'What treatment have you refused?' Glenn asked.

Jinx glanced at Thea, who already knew because they'd talked about it before. Thea gave Jinx a small nod.

'All of it,' Jinx said. 'Chemotherapy, radiotherapy, having bits cut out or off ...'

'But how ...?'

'How long? Is that what you want to ask? I don't know. A few months or so. I don't feel terribly unwell at the moment, but the doctor assures me I will in due course.'

Glenn, for once, couldn't seem to find the words.

Thea took over. 'We'll look after you, Mrs Sullivan,' she said. 'When you need looking after. Whatever you need help with, we'll be here.'

'Well, I will need you to take me into town on Tuesday morning. I have an appointment with my lawyer.'

Jinx had already been in touch with the offices of Duke and Harris, to let them know that she wished to change her will. She had sent over the amendments by email, and a draft had been sent for her approval the following day. All that was required of her now was a witnessed signature and, upon her death, the bulk of her estate would go to Glenn and Thea, with a little left over for the dogs' home, previously the sole beneficiary. Jinx made no stipulations about how the money should be spent, except to say that, if Glenn and Thea were minded to make a trip around the world, she would be very grateful if they could stop off in Singapore and take some flowers to Changi in memory of her father.

They ate Penny's hundreth birthday cake – a bit dry, they all agreed – and moved on from tea to something stronger.

318

At one point, Thea got up and fetched the photographs down from the mantelpiece. She asked Jinx to tell her about the people therein.

'Mum and Dad. Norma and Maurice. The baby is my brother, Eddy. He was about four months old.'

'And the animals?'

'That's Mr Snappy, my pet crocodile, in the bucket. The one I told you about. You can just see the tip of his snout.'

'You weren't joking. You really had a pet croc.'

'Yes. And a tiger used to come into our garden. I saw him once.'

'You saw a tiger?' Glenn was astonished. 'Weren't you scared?'

'I did hold my breath. I think he thought I was too small to be worth bothering with.'

Thea put the photographs back in their spot above the fire-place. She turned and asked, thoughtfully, 'Mrs Sullivan, can I call you Grandma?'

'Certainly not. But you can both call me Jinx.'

Chapter Forty-Nine

Glenn and Thea didn't leave until it was almost bedtime. Alone in the house, Jinx logged into Facebook and checked her messages. There were several for her alter ego, Jenice – the pretty young thing she had created with photographs lifted from an aspiring lingerie model's page. Three of her hopeful marks had agreed to send money to pay for her flight over to the States to visit them. Jinx crafted a response that would work for them all.

My dear, I regret I will not be able to visit you in the States after all. Neither do I want you to visit me in Amsterdam. The thing is, I'm not actually in Amsterdam. Neither am I a 21-year-old medical student paying her way through university by modelling lingerie. I am an 89- year-old former jewel thief from England. I wear surgical stockings, not a peephole bra. Had you fooled, eh?

I suggest you delete your Facebook profile, turn off your laptop or your phone, and take the wife who 'doesn't understand you' out to dinner. Hopefully, if you can tear your eyes away from the screen for long enough, you'll see what a lucky man you were to have married her. Hopefully, she will look at you – paying her attention for once – and feel like she got lucky too. I have returned the money you sent me, so that you can take her to the kind of restaurant she deserves. I would strongly advise you to do as I suggest. I do retain a large number of photographs that could be enormously helpful to her should she decide to seek a divorce.

Wishing you the very best with your future endeavours. Jenice.

Jinx didn't wait for their answers before she deleted her own Facebook account.

Then she closed her laptop, feeling a degree of relief that she need never open it again.

Something had shifted, Jinx realised as she tried to fall asleep. It was as though she had been lying on her back in mud, with a large stone on her chest, for the past eighty years. The feeling of being crushed had become her normal. But now the stone was gone, and she could sit up and look around her and see things from a very different perspective. Able at last to take a deep breath, she could see the world as it really was. It wasn't half so bad as she thought.

Jinx had been alone for a very long time. Sure, there had always been people around, but they had never come close to being allowed to really know her. After the losses became too much – her father, her mother, Eddy, Penny and then Frank – it had seemed so much easier not to hold anyone close again, to avoid the inevitable pain of having to let them go. Most of the people she'd encountered seemed to understand and soon gave up trying to change her mind. Why was it different with Glenn and Thea? They were relentlessly kind. Perhaps that was it. No one can resist kindness forever.

*

Jinx did not think she ever dreamt any more, but that night she did. She dreamt that she was back in Malaya, in the house with the veranda where they were living when Eddy was born. Where they had all been so very happy. Before the war came to Singapore.

Jinx saw herself in the kitchen. Her mother at the stove. Her father, sitting at the kitchen table with baby Eddy on his lap. Going to the kitchen door, Jinx saw her tiger in the garden. Its brown eyes held hers for a moment before it turned to walk away. Putting on her *terompah*, Jinx followed him deep into the forest.

'You're nearly home again,' he told her. 'Nearly there.'

Chapter Fifty

Merevale, February 2024

The postman always rang twice on a Friday. And this Friday was no different to any other. But when Glenn rang Jinx's doorbell this time, there was no answer. Not even in code. Neither did he get any response when he tapped on the kitchen window. He peered through the half-open blinds, hoping to see her sitting in front of her laptop with her headphones on, but she wasn't there. He went round the back of the house. Jinx's bedroom curtains were still drawn against the light, though it was almost lunchtime.

As he went from window to window, trying but failing to catch a reassuring glimpse of his friend, Glenn felt his anxiety rising. Was there a way to get into the house? He checked all the usual places an old lady might hide a spare key, but found none. He knew none of the neighbours could help him. He was the only person who had been given a key to Jinx's home, but he had left it hanging on a hook in the kitchen at his own house. Of all the days. She could be lying there on the floor, too weak to cry out, and he was stuck outside, unable to get in.

Glenn didn't have time to go back to his place. He would have to phone the police and ask for an ambulance, too, and then go across the close to the Colonel and borrow some tools to try to get the door off the hinges.

But was it worth it? Glenn sank down onto the step. He knew what the police would find when they broke in. He knew. He could already feel it, that heaviness creeping into his heart. Jennifer 'Jinx' Sullivan was gone.

'Happens to all of us, Glenn,' she'd told him when they last spoke. 'I've been around for very much longer than I expected to be, and I've had the chance to set a few things right. I'm happy with that.'

The ambulance and the police car arrived at the same time. The Colonel joined Glenn in the front garden. He took off his winter hat as a mark of respect, bald patch be damned. Curtains were soon twitching and, though it was cold outside, within minutes most of the ladies on the close were there with them, ready to form a guard of honour when Jinx was brought out of the house.

'We had our differences,' Val was saying. 'But I'll miss the old girl.'

'Me too,' said Pat. 'She may have been brusque, but underneath she was always very kind.'

'Does anyone know who she'll have left her house to? If she died intestate, it will be a quick sale, won't it?'

'Not the time, Cynthia,' the Colonel said. 'Not the time.'

Glenn could hear Jinx's voice in his head so clearly. It was just as she'd once said: 'When you know someone really well, death isn't the end. You can still have a conversation with them because you know exactly what they'd say.'

He thought that in this instance Jinx would say, 'Eff off, Cynth.'

'I'll always keep her here,' said Glenn, bringing his fist to the left side of his chest and tapping his heart.

The police officers were ready to break into the house. Glenn gave the nod. Then he turned to the Colonel.

'If she isn't dead, she's going to be furious when she sees her door.'

Alas, Glenn's instinct had been right. Jinx had died in her sleep. Glenn and Thea declined to see her that day, but Marilyn and Evan, who did their utmost for Jinx at the funeral home, said that she truly looked peaceful and happy.

She had been ready to go, Glenn and Thea decided later on. On Jinx's kitchen table, they had found a small pile of correspondence, waiting to be posted. Glenn furnished the envelopes with stamps, except for the one that was addressed to Thea. Thea collected that from Jinx's kitchen table herself. Along with a small seedling in a terracotta pot, which Jinx's letter explained had been grown from an olive she'd plucked from the olive tree in the garden of the Hotel Regina on the last day of the Tuscan Splendour tour.

'*I didn't expect it to grow,*' Jinx wrote,

But sometimes the most unpromising beginnings belie the potential for astonishing growth and joy. Rather like our friendship, dear Thea. I know you will look after this little seedling. And I hope that whenever you look at it, you'll remember our time together in Italy and remind yourself that the best way to honour the ones we have lost is to take them with us in our hearts as we embark on all the adventures they would have wanted for us. I hope you'll think of me when you drink your first Martini! Live every moment of your life, dear heart. With all my love, your friend Jinx.

Acknowledgements

July 2024

Dear Reader,

Thank you for reading *Bad Influence*. I hope you've enjoyed the time you've spent with Jinx, Thea, Penny and friends.

Though a book ordinarily has only one name on the cover, no writer truly works alone. I consider myself extraordinarily fortunate to be represented by United Agents. Jim, Amber, Amy, Alex, Lily and Jennifer, thank you very much indeed.

My editor, Sam Eades, and the team at Orion, have been such a pleasure to work with. Special thanks to Frankie Banks, for all those 'Frankie Fridays' filled with good news about *The Excitements* (my first book as CJ Wray). Over in the US, thanks are due to Rachel Kahan and Mary Interdonati for all wonderful news and reviews from that side of the pond.

My first reader for *Bad Influence* was Marguerite Finnigan. Thank you, Marguerite, for your kind and helpful feedback on that early draft. Thanks also to my Peter Jones crew, Victoria Routledge and Alexandra Potter. Your friendship is truly precious.

The Excitements had some wonderful cheerleaders, whose encouragement spurred me on to make *Bad Influence* a worthy follow-up. Thank you, S.J. Bennett, Faith Bleasdale, Carole Bourne Taylor, Amanda Brookfield, Matt Cain, Jenny Colgan, Kate Eberlen, Mike Gayle, Holly Hepburn, Wendy Holden, Helen Lederer, Annie Lyons, Jill Mansell, Alex Marwood, Freya North, John Sutherland, Patsy To, Fiona Walker, Olivia Williamson and Jane 'from school' Wright, for your enthusiasm and support.

I owe a huge debt of gratitude to Olga Henderson, whose experiences as a child prisoner of war in Singapore between 1942 and 1945 inspired Jinx's backstory. Thank you, Olga, for opening my eyes to a part of history that should be more widely known, resulting as it did in the deaths of so many innocents on both sides. I hope I have managed to portray the conditions at Changi and Sime Road accurately and without sensation. Any mistakes are my own.

Simon Robinson. Thank you, my most excellent friend, for all the 'excitements' in 2024. Our Normandy adventure will go down as one of the highlights of my life. This book would not have happened without you.

Finally, Mark. Thank you, as always, for everything. And the tea.

Chris 'CJ' Wray

Credits

CJ Wray and Orion Fiction would like to thank everyone at Orion who worked on the publication of *Bad Influence*.

Editor
Sam Eades

Copy-editor
Francine Brody

Editorial Management
Anshuman Yadav
Jane Hughes
Charlie Panayiotou
Lucy Bilton
Patrice Nelson

Audio
Paul Stark
Louise Richardson
Georgina Cutler

Proofreader
Steve O'Gorman

Contracts
Dan Herron
Ellie Bowker
Oliver Chacón

Design
Rachael Lancaster
Nick Shah
Deborah Francois
Helen Ewing

Finance
Nick Gibson
Jasdip Nandra
Sue Baker
Tom Costello

Inventory
Jo Jacobs
Dan Stevens

Production
Ruth Sharvell
Katie Horrocks

Marketing
Javerya Iqbal

Publicity
Sarah Lundy

Sales
Catherine Worsley
Dave Murphy

Victoria Laws
Esther Waters
Group Sales teams across
    Digital, Field, International
    and Non-Trade

Operations
Group Sales Operations team

Rights
Rebecca Folland
Tara Hiatt
Ben Fowler
Alice Cottrell
Ruth Blakemore
Marie Henckel